PRETTY PLEASE

Still holding Maggie in his arms, Dominick drew his lips away from hers and softly said, "Don't be afraid. I'll leave your virtue intact. I could never make love to a woman who believes me a fiend."

"Don't, Dominick . . ." she gasped.

"Don't what, Maggie? Don't kiss you? Don't touch you here and . . . here?" He ran his hands down her lovely warm body in a slow, tantalizing, rubbing motion that was meant to torment. His pleasure increased when she began to writhe beneath him.

Her body on fire, Maggie wanted desperately to touch him back. But he wouldn't let her. Every time she freed her hand and reached for him, he grabbed her wrist.

At last she could hardly stand it. She was consumed with desire. Wanting him became a burning need. "Please, Dominick . . . please don't do this to me. . . ."

Smiling, he moved his hands down to her thighs. . . .

THE KISSING BANDIT

by

Margaret Brownley

A TOPAZ BOOK

TOPAZ
Published by the Penguin Group
Penguin Books USA Inc., 375 Hudson Street,
New York, New York 10014, U.S.A.
Penguin Books Ltd, 27 Wrights Lane,
London W8 5TZ, England
Penguin Books Australia Ltd, Ringwood,
Victoria, Australia
Penguin Books Canada Ltd, 10 Alcorn Avenue,
Toronto, Ontario, Canada M4V 3B2
Penguin Books (N.Z.) Ltd, 182–190 Wairau Road,
Auckland 10, New Zealand

Penguin Books Ltd, Registered Offices:
Harmondsworth, Middlesex, England

First published by Topaz, an imprint of New American Library,
a division of Penguin Books USA Inc.

First Printing, July, 1993
10 9 8 7 6 5 4 3 2 1

 Topaz is a trademark of New American Library,
a division of Penguin Books USA Inc.

Printed in the United States of America

To Darin Keith
For All the Right Reasons

Chapter 1

1876

The wine-red stagecoach shimmied and swayed along the narrow dirt road, which had been dangerously rutted by recent heavy rains. At times, the road nearly disappeared beneath a mound of fallen rock or an uprooted tree, forcing the stage to swerve and testing its leather-thonged springs to the utmost.

The fleshy driver met the least hesitation on the part of the high-strung horses with a loud, cracking whip and a string of colorful words that were absorbed with great interest by five-year-old Jamie Turner, who sat on the rock-hard horsehair seat inside the stage, next to his mother and his little sister, Laurie-Anne.

"What's 'damned mudder-lovin' britches' mean?" Jamie asked after one particularly crude tirade.

His mother moaned softly, her cry barely audible above the rattle of wheels. Despite her horror at hearing such words come from her young son's mouth, she was far too indisposed to scold him.

Jamie repeated the question, and Maggie Turner tried her best to hush him, but her gentle admonition turned into a high-pitched cry as the stage veered in one direction and then lurched in another, tossing her small, delicate frame back and forth like a cork in a stormy sea. It was a wonder that her flesh had not been shaken off her bones, she thought feverishly.

As she lifted her hands weakly to her brow, her fingers became entangled in feathers and net. The hat that had been designed to make a favorable impression upon her arrival in Santa Barbara had shifted from the back of her head to the front and at one point had fallen directly over her eyes.

She wanted to die. Nonetheless, she forced herself to sit up straight with as much decorum as was possible under the circumstances, as much for her two young children, who sat wide-eyed and fretful on either side of her, as for the three men who occupied the seat directly across from her.

One of them, a prisoner, seemed to take great pleasure in further tormenting her by watching her with dark, shining eyes, as if he were privy to some mirthful jest at her expense. The prisoner's swarthy hands were held together by steel cuffs. Far more disturbing was the chain that snaked from his booted foot to a heavy black ball.

Once or twice the stage jolted up and down so violently that Maggie feared the heavy steel ball would break through the wooden planks of the floor.

She had a strange feeling that the prisoner did not miss a single detail of her disheveled dress, damp now from the heat and covered in the dust and grime that had filtered through the leather curtains and settled upon the travelers like fine, sifted flour.

Mile after torturous mile, the dark eyes regarded her with calculated cynicism. Weary of the man's ill-mannered watchfulness, she inhaled deeply and licked her lower lip. She sensed a change in his expression and realized, to her embarrassment, that his gaze had shifted to her lips.

Maggie was sorely tempted to lean forward and ask the prisoner just what he thought he was staring at. She was tempted, but speaking to a prisoner was, of course, unthinkable.

Equally contemptible was the short, red-faced man who sat next to the prisoner. Supposedly he was the guard, though he appeared much more interested in sleeping than in watching his charge. The man had absolutely no manners, and despite Rule Five of The Ten Rules for Passengers clearly posted overhead—declaring snoring a disgusting habit—he bellowed like a raging bull the entire time he slept.

Beside the guard was the only respectable man on the stage. Maggie guessed him to be in his late thirties. Dressed in a fine worsted suit and a shiny silk vest, he had the blondest hair she'd ever seen on a man, with full, sweeping sideburns and finely arched eyebrows. Not only was he well dressed but he was obviously quite educated, his nose buried in the pages of Shakespeare's sonnets.

As much as she respected the man's taste in reading, it irritated her that she was on the verge of death and the only one of the three men who seemed to notice was the prisoner.

She forced herself to remain staunchly in an upright position, despite the wave of dizziness that suddenly assailed her. Bile rose to her throat, but not wanting to open her mouth in the presence of the prisoner, she forced herself to breathe through her nose.

She was *not* going to be sick, she told herself with grim determination, reminding herself of the strength and tenacity that had surfaced after the death of her husband a year earlier. She would not, she told herself, make a fool of herself, particularly not in front of a prisoner.

Between Santa Maria and Ballard, Maggie Turner made a fool of herself.

With a frantic leap forward, she grabbed hold of the window frame and thrust her head through the open window, tears running down her face. Rolling green hills blurred by as she leaned out the window and heaved. The wind whipped her feather unmercifully. Clouds of fine dust billowed up and threatened to smother her. Never in her entire life had she endured such misery!

While she heaved, her body was thrown from one side of the window frame to the other. Her hat cushioned the blows to her head; the plume that had arrived by boat from Paris drooped down and swayed back and forth.

Behind her she could hear a male's voice ring out. "Driver, stop this stage at once." This order was followed by a deliberate thumping that sounded like fists pounding on the roof.

With a powerful lurch, the stage ground to a halt, throwing Maggie backward into the carriage, where she landed, sprawling like a drunk across the floor at the feet of the three astonished men.

"Good heavens, Miss, are you all right?" This was from the blond man, who had managed to pull his attention away from Shakespeare. Maggie recognized his voice as the one that had ordered the stage to stop.

"I'm quite all right," Maggie said, struggling with her skirt, which had ridden up to reveal linen pantaloons edged in lace and ribbon and her black calf boots. To their credit, the guard and the gentlemen glanced away discreetly. Much to her mortification, however, the prisoner eyed her lace-trimmed pantaloons boldly.

"Now what?" the driver barked, ripping open the door. Thrusting his beefy red face inside the stage, he glared accusingly at Maggie, who was still on the floor. "This here's the third unscheduled stop since I picked you up! Keep this up and you're gonna get us killed."

Maggie straightened her hat, but there was no hope of ever fixing the plume; it bobbed up and down in front of her face as she pulled herself up and glared back at the driver. "If we get killed it won't be because we stopped!" she retorted. "It'll be because of your maniacal driving!"

"While we're sittin' like ducks on a pond, ever' robber in the area has a crack at us," the driver bellowed back.

Maggie refused to be intimidated. "I would rather

take my chances with a robber than go flying over the side of a mountain!"

Muttering a curse, the driver slammed the door shut. Maggie struggled to her feet and returned to her seat, trying to ignore the curious gazes of the three men opposite her.

"Are we really going to see a robber, Mama?" Jamie asked, his blue eyes wide with interest.

With a loud "Gid-up, you damned bastards" from above, the stagecoach took off like a bolt of lightning.

"We'll see heaven's gates before we see a robber," Maggie muttered. She ran a hand through her son's fine blond hair. "Go to sleep, Jamie."

The stage continued its dangerous swagger around hairpin curves and along a road so narrow that tree branches scraped either side of the coach and pieces of twigs and leaves flew through the windows like swarming locusts.

Much to Maggie's relief, the road finally straightened at the bottom of a valley, offering a much-needed respite.

Her young son stirred. "I want to go home," he complained.

Maggie felt a pang. She pulled him closer to her and stroked the head of her daughter, who was curled up in a corner of the seat, sound asleep. A lifetime ago, home had been the little clapboard house in San Francisco that she'd shared with her husband, Luke. But the San Francisco fogs had been more than her husband's weak lungs could bear. After his death, she had done her best to maintain the shoemaking business he had opened shortly after they were married.

When his health began to fail, she had insisted that he teach her the business. Though he was reluctant at first, he taught her how to tan leather and design men's boots and women's fashionable footwear. Impressed by her deft hand and eye for good design, he quickly became enthusiastic about her progress. Before long, she was able to work as fast, if not faster, than he could, and soon she began combining leather and fabric in a way that was not only fashionable but functional. After his death, she continued to fill orders. A few customers objected to wearing footgear designed by a woman, but enough stayed to allow her to support herself and her two children in relative comfort.

She would have gladly remained in San Francisco, raising her children and building her business, had her son's already precarious health not taken a turn for the worse. In the months following his father's death, Jamie could hardly leave his bed. The least bit of exertion brought on a fit of coughing that left him gasping for breath and turned his lips an alarming blue.

Terrified that she would lose Jamie to the same lung condition that had claimed Luke's life, she felt she had to seek a more suitable climate. After she read an advertisement that named Santa Barbara as a town blessed with certain health properties, she decided to sell her house and business and move there. Neither brought the price she had hoped for, and by the time she paid the fare to Santa Barbara and sent a bank draft to the boardinghouse where she and the children would be staying, there was precious little money left to tide them over until she established her shoemaker shop. In the meantime, she could only pray that no untoward expenses would arise.

Next to her, Jamie grew more restless and irritable by the mile.

"Hush, Jamie. Go to sleep."

But the boy couldn't seem to settle down enough to sleep. He wiggled and complained that the dust was making him cough.

Maggie sympathized. "I know, dear heart. It's making me cough, too. It might help if you lie still."

But Jamie didn't lie down. Instead, he threw off his porkpie hat and, between bouts of coughing, bounced up and down until he quite drove his poor mother to distraction. Despite his weak constitution, he'd always been a restless one, his bright, curious mind never seeming to stop, his arms and legs in constant motion.

Maggie finally persuaded Jamie to lay his head on her lap. She let her own heavy lids drift downward, but only for a moment, for she felt the prisoner's gaze boring into her. Opening her eyes wide, she looked straight at the man.

It was the first time she had allowed herself actually to meet his gaze head on, but if he insisted upon staring at her, she decided she'd give him a dose of his own medicine.

She was surprised to find that he looked less menacing than she had at first supposed. A closer scrutiny of his features revealed an unexpected upward turn at the corner of his mouth. His skin was bronzed dark by the sun, and one could only assume that the fine lines at his brow had been etched by the wind. His hair was as dark as a raven's wing, his sideburns hugging either side of his rugged square face.

He was dressed in black trousers and black shirt—the perfect attire, she decided, for a prisoner. But if the black represented his dark side, the bright-red sash tied at his waist restated the boldness in his eyes. Nervously, she double-checked the handcuffs and glanced down to be sure that he was still chained to the ball.

Clothing aside, he didn't look like a criminal. Not that she'd ever seen one before, but she had a preconceived idea of how certain people should look and it jolted her that the man sitting in front of her did not meet her expectations. If his boldness had aggravated her before, this latest affront had her positively gritting her teeth in irritation.

A movement at her feet commanded her attention. Shifting her gaze downward, she discovered to her horror that her young son was on the floor of the stage, playing with the prisoner's ball.

"No, Jamie!" she gasped. "Come back here at once!"

Surprised by his mother's outburst, Jamie did as she

bid him. But his round eyes continued to look long-ingly at the ball. "Why does that man have a ball on his leg?" Jamie asked.

"Hush, now, Jamie. It's not polite to ask questions in company."

"Would you tell me later when we get to Sana Baba?"

She glanced at the prisoner's face. "Yes, later. Now be a good boy and go to sleep."

The blond gentleman momentarily abandoned Shakespeare and leaned toward Jamie, a smile on his handsome face. "Here, young man, have a sweet," he said kindly. He held a paper sack toward Jamie. Jamie glanced at his mother, and when she gave her ap-proval with a slight nod, he jammed his hand into the bag and pulled out a chocolate ball.

"They are called bonbons," the stranger explained. "All the way from France."

Maggie smiled gratefully at the stranger. "Say 'thank-you' to the kind man," she admonished her son.

"Thank you," Jamie said, sinking his teeth into the delicacy.

"W. K. Stevens," the bonbon man said, turning his attention to Maggie.

Maggie smiled. "Mr. Stevens. I'm Maggie Turner."

"Where are you heading?" Mr. Stevens asked.

"Santa Barbara. My husband . . . died a year ago."

"I'm sorry." He glanced at the two children.

"And you, Mr. Stevens?" Maggie ventured. "Are you going to Santa Barbara?"

"I'm afraid not. I'm a rancher looking to buy prop-erty near here. I'll be getting off at the next stop."

"Oh." Maggie glanced at the prisoner, who re-garded her with eyes so dark they could have been black. She was tempted to ask him if by some stroke of luck he would be getting off as well. She quelled the temptation. As far as she knew, Santa Barbara had the only courthouse in the area.

It appeared that, like it or not, she would be stuck with the bold-eyed prisoner for the remainder of the trip. With an exasperated sigh, she clamped her mouth tightly shut.

The prisoner smiled inwardly at the stern young face with its upturned nose, wide blue eyes, and firm, straight mouth. She was a sight for sore eyes, all right, he thought. Amused at the irony of finding himself in the company of such a beguiling creature while being incarcerated in ball and chain, he shamelessly took in the slender figure dressed in a sunshine-yellow traveling suit.

Despite the heat of the day, she wore a matching cape around her shoulders. A ruffle trimmed in black braid edged both her cape and her skirt. Sunshine and ruffles. He wondered idly if the yellow meant she had a sunny nature when she was not fighting motion sickness. He also wondered if the ruffles indicated that despite her rigid countenance she also had a soft, feminine side. Judging by her ramrod demeanor, he doubted it.

Lifting his gaze, he stared at the perky hat that was tilted forward on her fine, pale forehead. The hat dipped at the brim and was decorated with a black feather that was now bent in two. She wore her honey-colored hair in a tight bun at the back of her head, and he wondered if it was ever allowed to fall loosely to her shoulders. A sight for sore eyes indeed, he thought, suspecting that she probably looked the worst at this moment that she'd ever looked in her entire life. Her lovely, smooth skin, which had been the color of rich cream when he'd boarded the stage a few hours before, now held a decidedly green cast.

Earlier, her cheeks had been all blushing and rosy, but the color had long since faded, and her eyes had lost some of their sparkle, although she still managed to shoot daggers in his direction on occasion. The fool woman didn't have the sense to lie down or to try to get some sleep. Instead, she sat tall and straight like a fussy old schoolteacher, her shoulders pinned back against the leather seat, her feet perfectly flat on the floor.

He shifted his stiff body. The steel cuffs were cutting into his wrists, and the chain at his foot bit into his ankle. It would be interesting to see who would better survive the trip, he thought grimly, himself or Miss Prim and Proper. If he were a gambling man, he might well bet on the lady.

Chapter 2

The coach lurched dangerously, and Maggie's heart rose up to her throat. The driver's voice thundered overhead. "You damned no-good beasts. Git it up! Before I beat the hell . . ."

Mortified, Maggie glanced at her son, who had quieted at the sound of the driver's voice and was taking in every word with grave interest. The driver continued to bellow, his language growing more colorful with each passing mile.

"What does 'damned mudder-lovin' . . .' "

"Shhh, Jamie. Civilized people don't use those words."

The guard snorted in his sleep, the dark, disturbing prisoner shifted in his seat, the stranger with the sweets returned to his book, Laurie-Anne slept, and Jamie sat in absolute rapture, listening to every word the driver uttered. Maggie didn't have the energy to distract him; she was too busy fighting another wave of nausea.

The stage jolted and shuddered to a stop.

"Ballard!" the driver yelled. The door flew open. He pulled a pocket watch from his vest and glanced at it. "Twelve minutes late," he said peevishly, casting an accusing eye in Maggie's direction.

Maggie and her two children were the first to disembark, followed by the prisoner, who cradled the steel ball in his hands. The guard was close behind him, leveling a gun at his back. Maggie couldn't imagine why the guard thought it necessary to hold a gun on

a shackled prisoner, but it did seem to suggest the
man might be more dangerous than she had supposed.
She shuddered at the implication. A murderer. He
had to be a murderer.

"I guess this is farewell," the blond stranger said,
donning his straw cut-down hat and tucking his leather-bound book beneath his arm.

"Thank you for the bonbons," Maggie called after
him. His presence had been comforting, despite his
preoccupation. She dreaded thinking of her and the
children alone in the stage with the prisoner and his
rude, inattentive guard.

"Come along," she said to Jamie, leading him and
a sleepy-eyed Laurie-Anne to the one-story adobe
house that served as a stage stop.

Inside, long wooden tables were set with heavy sil-
verware and plain crockery dishes for the guests. The
proprietor was a ruddy-complexioned man with a jo-
vial voice and rotund body, who laughed easily. His
wife was more reserved, but she chatted openly as
she showed Maggie to a small anteroom containing a
washbasin and a beveled looking glass.

"After you clean up, you'll feel the world better,"
she said. "It's a terrible thing having to travel alone
with two children." She patted Laurie-Anne on the
head and smiled at Jamie, who was splashing his hands
in the water. "But you don't have to worry about
robbers. That old driver, Crabshaw, is a force to be
reckoned with on the road. Word is that road agents
see him coming and head for the hills."

Maggie shivered. She knew the woman was trying
to be kind, but whipping around those mountains with
the man named Crabshaw at the reins wasn't her idea
of being safe. She thanked the woman and bolted the
door after her. Grateful for the basin of warm, soapy
water, she washed the road dust off the hands and
faces of both children and then attended to her own
appearance.

She brushed the dust off her yellow traveling suit,

straightened her bustle, and checked the little pouch that had been sewed beneath her dress to hold what precious money was left over from the sale of her house and shop.

"Are we in Sana Baba?" Jamie asked.

"Not yet, Jamie. Soon."

"I wanna go home," Laurie-Anne whined.

"Santa Barbara is going to be our new home." Maggie removed her hat altogether, tidied her bun, and fluffed out the curls on her forehead.

She made an attempt to restore her hat, but it was soon apparent that the tapering felt brim and the black-jetted quill were beyond repair. Leaving the hat on the marbled top of the dry sink, she hustled both children into the dining room, where platters of roast pork, sweet potatoes, and garden-fresh peas, along with pitchers of freshly squeezed lemonade, awaited the passengers.

"What's the man doing with the horses, Mama?" Jamie asked, climbing on a straight-back chair next to his sister and watching the driver through the wavy glass panes of the window.

"He's adding two more horses to help us over the mountain that's ahead." Despite the friendly assurances of the proprietor's wife, Maggie shuddered. Tales of the infamous San Marcos Pass had traveled as far as San Francisco. She remembered one of her husband's customers talking about being robbed at gunpoint along the notorious pass. She was beginning to think she'd made a mistake in not spending the extra money to book passage on a liner. But at the time she'd made her decision she had suspected that the tales of road agents were more fictional than real, and traveling by land was far more economical. Since she had no way to know how long it would take her to establish her business in Santa Barbara, she would have to watch her money with the greatest of care. Still, she wished now that she had not been so frugal.

"Turn around, Jamie," she said, forcing herself not

to think of the dangers that might lie ahead. She ignored the prisoner and his guard, who sat at the far end of the table, and filled her children's plates with food, cutting Laurie-Anne's meat into bite-size pieces.

"Eat up now, or you'll be hungry," she said. Inadvertently her attention wandered toward the prisoner, who nodded his head in acknowledgment. She looked away quickly and reached for a pitcher of lemonade. When at last the guard snapped the handcuffs back on his prisoner and led him outside, she felt profound relief.

Laurie-Anne dawdled over her food, and Jamie found watching the horses through the window more interesting than anything on his plate, but Maggie finally managed to get the children to eat a little, though she barely touched her own meal.

Feeling slightly more civilized now that her stomach had settled down and her head had cleared, Maggie paid the friendly proprietor and his wife and hustled Jamie and Laurie-Anne outside, where the driver stood, whip in hand, glaring at them.

The prisoner and guard were already seated inside. Jamie ran ahead, clambered up the step, and disappeared into the stagecoach's interior. Maggie lifted Laurie-Anne and set her inside the door.

Before climbing aboard herself, Maggie stepped back and looked up at the driver, who had taken his place upon the driver's seat, the soles of his dusty boots braced against the footboard. "Excuse me, sir," she said boldly, shading her eyes against the sun. "I would greatly appreciate it if you would consider the delicate sensibilities of small children when you speak. I find your language quite vulgar."

The driver spit out a brown stream of tobacco juice and wiped his whiskered chin with the back of his hand. "Sorry, ma'am, but these damned beasts don't know gentle language. Cussin' is the only language they knows."

"Well, it seems to me, sir, that you might have a bit of consideration for your passengers."

"I do have consid'ration for muh passengers," the driver argued, taking the reins in hand. "If I don't cuss, we ain't going nowhere. That's why I cuss. If that ain't consid'ration, I don't know what is."

Realizing the futility of arguing with such logic, Maggie huffily lifted her skirt and climbed into the stage, slamming the door shut behind her. Taking her place between Laurie-Anne and Jamie, she folded her hands together on her lap. She glanced at the two men across from her, only to find the prisoner, as usual, watching her every move.

"Must you stare at me?" she demanded, her frustration with the driver fueling her boldness.

The prisoner looked unperturbed. "Would you deny me this one pleasure," he asked, "knowing the bleak future that lies ahead of me?" He held up his shackled hands.

Blushing, Maggie glanced away, surprised at the gentle lilt of the stranger's voice, the almost lazy drawl that gave each word a sensuous twist. He sounded less like a prisoner than he looked. His dark good looks suggested the possibility that he was foreign-born, either Italian or Spanish, and his clothes seemed to confirm it. But there was no sign of an accent. He spoke like a true American, yet acted twice as bold as any Frenchman she'd ever met.

She glanced helplessly at the guard, who gave a careless shrug and pulled his stained rawhide hat down over his eyes. She decided to ignore the two men. She hugged her young daughter and smiled at Jamie, who was busily trying to capture a fluttering moth in his hand.

She straightened the folds of her gown and concentrated on the scenery. But as the stage lumbered ever closer to the infamous San Marcos Pass, her heart began to beat more quickly. She sat perfectly still, her ears straining to capture the least suspicious sound.

But all she could hear was the rumble of wheels and the driver's curses, punctuated by the loud, snapping crack of his whip.

Pulling her gaze away from the window, she accidentally let it drift toward the prisoner, who acknowledged her with an arch of a dark brow.

She glanced up at the rules posted on the roof. Surely there had to be a rule against staring. If so, she was quite within her rights to stop the stage and order the driver to reprimand the offender. But there was no rule that applied, and she was left with no choice but to endure the prisoner's disturbing eyes.

The road inclined sharply, and it was all Maggie could do to keep from slipping off her seat. The stage slowed and then stopped altogether, and Maggie's heart nearly stopped with it. Anxiously, she peered out the window, positive that masked robbers surrounded them. But it was the driver who flung the door open, his pudgy face red from the heat.

"You're going to have to get out and walk to the summit," he ordered.

"We can't get out here," Maggie protested. "It's too dangerous. The Kissing Bandit . . ." She'd heard that the notorious bandit stole more money from Wells, Fargo than any other man alive. If that weren't bad enough, there'd been frightening tales of how he shamelessly kissed the women passengers he robbed. She had discounted such farfetched stories, thinking them nothing more than figments of her customers' imagination. Now she was willing to believe anything.

The driver snorted, pushed his dusty rawhide hat back, and wiped his face on the sleeve of his shirt. "Shall we tell the little lady the good news?" he asked, glancing toward the guard and his prisoner.

Maggie frowned. "What are you talking about? What good news?"

"Why this man right here," Crabshaw pointed to the man in black, "this is the Kissing Bandit." The driver grinned, but there was no mirth in the yellow-toothed smile.

The guard concurred, speaking for the first time. "I promise you, his stage-robbin' days are over. And as soon as we git to Santa Barbara, the rest of his days will be over. I guarantee it."

Maggie swallowed hard. The Kissing Bandit? In the stage with her? Breathing the same air as her children? Shocked, she scrambled quickly out of the stage and hurriedly lifted Jamie and his sister to the ground. Not only did she intend to walk up to the summit, she vowed to walk the rest of the way to Santa Barbara, no matter how long it took her!

Despite her better judgment, her curiosity overcame her, and she stood watching, fascinated, as the bandit and the guard followed her out of the stage. Despite being weighted down by the heavy ball, the dark prisoner stood far taller than the guard. As if he sensed her eyes on him, he lifted his head and looked straight at her, his full and surprisingly sensuous mouth curving in a smile. To her mortification, she found herself wondering what it would be like to be kissed by the likes of him. She narrowed her eyes and glared at him, as she repressed her thoughts.

She was horrified when he puckered his lips and threw her a kiss. Maggie quickly lowered her gaze and busied herself tying the ribbons of Laurie-Anne's bonnet, furious at finding herself the victim of such a blatant transgression.

She had the strangest feeling that the man could read her thoughts. It shocked her to think she was so transparent to him. For as hard as she tried to think and do that which was proper, she had to admit there were times when her thoughts ran rampant. But never had her thoughts been so audacious as during the last few hours in this dreadful man's company!

She waited until the prisoner and the guard had walked past her before she started along the dirt road. Although she kept her eyes fixed squarely on the

broad shoulders of the taller man, she scrupulously
guarded her thoughts, just in case he did, indeed, pos-
sess an amazing ability to read her mind.

By the time they reached the summit, Maggie was
forced to reconsider the wisdom of walking the rest
of the way to Santa Barbara. For one thing, it was
unseasonably hot, not to mention dusty. For another,
Laurie-Anne was having one of her crying spells and
refused to walk of her own accord, so Maggie had to
carry her. To make matters worse, Jamie had dashed
ahead, disappearing over the rise of the road.

She called to him, but he failed to respond.
Alarmed, Maggie set Laurie-Anne down and hurried
past the prisoner. "Jamie!" she called anxiously.
"Come back here at once."

A spasm of coughs coming from the side of the road
led her to Jamie, who was bent over behind a tree,
gasping for breath. She rubbed his back until he recovered, but she didn't have the heart to scold him. It
was only normal for a child his age to want to run
and jump, especially after being confined for so many
hours.

With her help, he soon recovered and wandered off
in another direction. Despite her warning not to run,
in a moment he was off, chasing a squirrel into a thick
growth of bushes at the side of the road.

Feeling sticky and damp from the heat, Maggie carried Laurie-Anne toward the stagecoach, which now
was parked in the shade of a sprawling sycamore.

She breathed a sigh of relief when she spotted Jamie
sitting next to the driver.

"Can I stay up here, Mama, please?" Jamie called
between coughs.

"Absolutely not," Maggie said. "Hurry now,
inside."

She waited for both children, then turned and almost bumped into the prisoner. He regarded her with
a sardonic expression that nonetheless made her heart
skip a beat.

"After you," he purred softly.

She lifted the hem of her skirt and used the door frame to pull herself up into the stage. She settled on the seat next to Jamie and lifted Laurie-Anne onto her lap.

The next half hour passed without incident. Much to Maggie's relief, both children fell asleep. The guard resumed his snoring, and the bandit continued to watch her with dark, lustful eyes. He looked like a falcon, she thought, the way he watched her as if she were prey to be pounced on and devoured. The thought made her shudder and did nothing to calm her raw insides. Only a stern reminder to herself that he was soundly shackled and could do her no physical harm allowed her to relax enough to concentrate on the scenery.

The scenery began to blur as the stage picked up speed and then flew down the mountainside so fast that Maggie froze in terror. To her mind, the only possible explanation for such speed was that the driver was purposely trying to kill them.

"On the floor!" the bandit cried out suddenly. "Quick!"

Maggie stared at him. "I beg your par—"

"The floor, dammit!"

Instinctively, she pushed Laurie-Anne down to the floor and quickly grabbed Jamie off the seat, almost losing her balance as she did so. Before she could get down herself, the stage lurched dangerously, throwing her against the door, then pitching her in the opposite direction. Her hands thrust out in front of her as she sprawled on top of the two small bodies that were huddled between the seats.

The stage whipped back and forth, up and down, tossing the passengers about like dice in a gambler's fist. Then the world began to spin.

Chapter 3

Maggie's eyes flickered against the blinding white light. Squeezing her lids tight, she moaned softly, unable to identify the source of the pain that seemed to radiate from every part of her body. She peered cautiously through the heavy fringe of her eyelashes and tried to make sense out of the confusion.

Sky.

All she could see was clear blue sky framed by the pointed peaks of the surrounding mountains.

Slowly she sat up, flinching against the pain, which she managed to isolate in her right shoulder. Eyes wide with alarm, she quickly focused on a moving shadow and felt a profound relief when her vision cleared and the shadow turned out to be Jamie.

"Stay still," a man's voice called sharply from nearby. "You have a bump on your head."

Dazed, she touched her forehead and winced. The man's voice sounded familiar, but she couldn't put a name to it. Moving gingerly, her hand brushed against a wooden wheel that lay next to her. Further away, she spotted a splintered piece of wood with the name "Wells, Fargo" written across it. Her mouth grew dry at the sight of a man's boot half buried in the dirt. Then the whole terrible nightmarish experience began to come back.

"Come on, Jamie, that's a good boy. Check all the pockets. There's got to be another key in there somewhere!"

The voice was sharper this time, demanding and

threatening at the same time. Alarm surmounted her discomfort and helped clear her head.

Jamie was standing on the other side of the man's boot. Recognizing the trousers as the ones worn by the guard, a gut-wrenching fear welled up inside of her. Some inner sense told her the man was dead.

"Jamie, get away from there, this instant, do you hear your mama?" No sooner were the words out of her mouth than she was chilled by another thought. "Laurie. Laurie-Anne. Where are you?"

"She's all right," the prisoner said. He moved into her line of vision. "Laurie-Anne has a bump on her head, but otherwise she's fine. She's resting."

The bandit stood over her, looking taller and more menacing than before. Cradling the ball in his hands, he held it in such a way that she couldn't help but feel she was being held hostage. One wrong move on her part and that ball would make a fierce weapon. A shudder went through her, and she watched helplessly while his eyes swept down the length of her.

She measured him cautiously, with her heart pounding, as she forced herself to her feet. Aching muscles protested her every move, and she cried out in pain.

"Are you all right?"

The note of concern in the bandit's voice surprised her. She nodded in response and held her breath. For a brief moment the earth began to spin and she swayed slightly.

The bandit was watching her intently. When it appeared that she wasn't going to topple over, he turned his attention back to Jamie. "Hurry, Jamie, check the other pocket. There's got to be another key. Keep looking. That's a good boy."

Battling the wave of dizziness that assailed her, Maggie glanced at her son. "Key?"

"The key in the guard's pocket." Jamie held it up proudly. "There's only one key. I can't find the other one." Jamie gave the bandit a worried frown. "Are you still going to buy me a treat in Sana Baba?"

"Are you sure there's no other key?"

Jamie nodded.

"I would say a deal is a deal, wouldn't you? Bring the one you found over here."

"I'll take the key, Jamie," Maggie said firmly, grabbing a tree trunk to keep from falling. "Jamie!"

Surprised by his mother's sharp voice, Jamie walked over to her and handed her the key. She tried to speak but couldn't. Her mouth was too dry. Nodding approvingly at her son, she promptly dropped the key into the bosom of her dress.

The outlaw stood watching her. "I want the key," he said curtly.

She lifted her chin. He wasn't going to intimidate her.

His eyes raked her over in cool appraisal. "I can't help you unless you give me the key."

Maggie glared at the man. "Do you think I would trust you to help me?"

"It seems to me that you don't have a whole lot of choice in the matter. The driver is dead. The guard is dead. The stage is broken into a thousand pieces. It'll be dark soon. Your little girl possibly has a mild concussion. I'm the best chance you have of getting to Santa Barbara safely."

At the mention of Laurie-Anne, Maggie glanced around anxiously. "Where's my daughter?" she stammered. She wasn't making any decisions until she verified Laurie-Anne's condition with her own two eyes.

"She's over there by that tree. I told you, she's fine."

Maggie hobbled over to her young daughter's side, ignoring the soreness that spread upward from her own legs. "Oh, my poor sweet baby." She was surprised to find Laurie-Anne wrapped securely in a buffalo blanket. Obviously the prisoner wasn't as helpless as she supposed. It was a worrisome thought, tempered slightly by the fact that he'd shown concern for her daughter. Concern hardly seemed like a trait of an outlaw. Still . . .

Maggie comforted Laurie-Anne in a soothing voice as she examined the red mark on her daughter's forehead.

"I want to go home," Laurie-Anne cried.

"I know, little one. I know."

A nearby thud sent rocks and dirt sliding down the hillside. The prisoner had dropped the steel ball onto the ground directly behind her. "Are you going to help me or not?" His voice was hard, his eyes cold. He looked and sounded exactly as she would expect an outlaw to look and sound, only more so.

A shiver passed through Maggie. She patted Laurie-Anne and stood up. "Help you do what?" she asked, in as steady a voice as she could muster. The last thing she wanted was for him to know how frightened she was. "Escape? So that you can continue to terrorize people?"

"Are you foolish enough to think you can make it to Santa Barbara by yourself?"

Maggie studied him with the same concentrated attention he bestowed on her. They stood weighing each other like two enemies about to embark on a battle to the end.

"Do you think I'm foolish enough to think you would help me?"

"You have my word."

"Ha!" she said with contempt. "The word of an outlaw."

His face darkened. "What choice do you have?"

Taken aback by the question, Maggie hesitated. "I . . . I have choices," she said stubbornly.

"Name one."

"I am under no obligation to disclose my choices!" she retorted. Indeed, her options did seem woefully limited, but she didn't need him to point that out.

"Very well. But you could at least tell me why you refuse to set me free."

She stared at him in disbelief. "You are a bandit."

"That I am."

Startled that he would so willingly admit it, she continued, "You have been known to afflict certain unwanted attentions upon women."

"I've never inflicted unwanted attentions upon anyone."

"There must be a reason you're called the Kissing Bandit."

"Rest assured that I've never kissed a woman who didn't want me to kiss her," he insisted. "Besides," he added, letting his eyes linger on Maggie's lips, "robbing someone isn't the only criterion for kissing. There are others."

Blushing, Maggie took an unsteady step backward. She was not going to let him trap her into pursuing this ridiculous conversation.

She peered down the mountainside, suddenly realizing how lucky they were that a thick growth of trees had prevented the stage from tumbling any further down. Parts of the stagecoach and their belongings were scattered all around them. She looked upward but was unable to see the road. "How far are we from Santa Barbara?"

"A couple of hours," the bandit said. "Unfortunately, the horses broke free. They could be miles from here by now."

"We'll have to walk," Maggie said.

"How far do you think I'm going to walk carrying a fifty-pound weight?" he growled.

Maggie enjoyed tormenting the man, although under normal circumstances she would have been shocked to discover such a dark side to her personality. But in this case she felt thoroughly justified—after all, he had tormented her by staring at her for hours on end, knowing full well that she was ill enough to want to crawl into a hole. Ah, yes, he'd earned everything she intended to dish out. "You'll just have to stay, won't you? And wait for the next stage." She waited for a show of temper, but he surprised her by stepping backward and casually shrugging his shoulders.

"I guess I could do that." He sat down next to a tree, stretched out his long legs, and dropped the ball between them. With a contented sigh, he leaned his head against the tree trunk. "Of course, that means you'll have to continue along the San Marcos Pass without benefit of a male protector."

She laughed at this. The man was simply not to be believed! "A protector? You? You're the one who made the pass so notorious."

"Obviously you're a stranger in these parts. The Kissing Bandit is only one of many bandits to call the pass home."

Maggie's throat grew dry. "There're more?"

"Absolutely," the robber assured her, smiling as her stubborn chin lowered a mite. "Some of them don't stop with only a kiss." He closed his eyes and waited.

Maggie shuddered, but refused to allow herself to dwell on the further improprieties an outlaw could inflict upon a woman.

"Then, of course, there's the bear factor . . ."

Maggie froze. "What bear factor?"

He lifted one lid. "Surely you know that this is bear territory. Grizzly bears, that is. But they won't bother you if you stay downwind."

Fear crept into Maggie's mind. She looked around, measuring their distance from any bush or boulder large enough to hide a bear. "How do you know whether or not you're downwind?"

The bandit shrugged. "You don't. Unless, of course, you see the bear coming toward you. Then you can pretty well assume you weren't downwind."

Maggie checked Jamie's whereabouts and turned back to the bandit. It was then that she noted a suspicious softening at the corner of his mouth. "You like to frighten me, don't you?" she stormed. "You want to see me worry. I wouldn't even be thinking about bears if you hadn't told me about them. And as for robbers . . ."

"Do feel free to continue," he encouraged.

"Never mind!" she bristled.

"I think it's important that you be prepared for all the possible dangers out there," he said reasonably.

"I don't think you care one way or the other whether or not I'm prepared for the dangers." Maggie felt close to tears, but she would rather die than let him know that. "You just want to scare me in hopes that I will foolishly set you free."

"Why, Mrs. Turner, you misjudge me completely. My sole concern is for your safety."

"Humph," Maggie muttered, inching her way down the mountain. She scanned the debris for her belongings.

"Be sure to watch out for snakes," he called after her.

Her foot slipped. Regaining her balance, she looked nervously back at him.

He lifted his shoulders in a casual shrug. "I just thought you ought to know that there are rattlers around here. Nasty fellows, rattlers. Like to sink their fangs all the way to a person's bone." He grimaced. "Terrible creatures."

Maggie gritted her teeth and worked her way downhill, but her eyes were glued to the ground and her ears were primed to pick up the softest sound. And while she watched and listened, her heart was pumping so fast in her chest that she was afraid that it would jump out. To make matters worse, the long shadows told her that it would soon be dark.

The slope gave way to a straight drop. A gurgling stream rushed by directly below them. Maggie gazed longingly at the water, licking her parched lips. What she would give to be able to soak her aching body in that cool, clear water.

She turned back to check on Laurie-Anne, who lay huddled motionless beneath the blanket. Nearby, the bandit sat against the tree trunk looking absurdly self-assured for a man shackled to a ball and chain.

"How long did you say it would take us to reach Santa Barbara?" she called.

He lifted one eyelid. "By 'us,' do you mean you and me?"

"Yes, I mean you and me!" she said through clenched teeth.

"Well, considering that you have two young ones and I have a very heavy ball to contend with, I'd say a day or so. Maybe two. We have a better chance of getting help the closer we are."

"I want to go home," Laurie-Anne whined.

Maggie knelt at her daughter's side. "I know, dear heart. Just keep still. Mama's trying to think." She looked over at her son, who was busily examining the broken pieces of the stagecoach. "Come over here, Jamie. I don't want you wandering away."

Since the outlaw's eyes were closed, she could study him at her leisure. She had never seen a man with such dark brows and lashes or such a noble nose. In some ways he looked like a Greek god, chiseled out of not marble or stone but gleaming bronze. He didn't look dangerous. Still . . .

Suddenly she saw that he was gazing at her through tiny slits of his eyes. "If you're finished admiring me, I suggest we get started. We only have an hour or two of light left."

Maggie blushed. "I was not admiring you!" she sniffed. What a contemptible, egotistical man.

He opened his eyes fully and grinned. "Are you going to give me that key or are you going to force me to haul this ball all the way to Santa Barbara?"

"I most certainly will not give you the key," she declared haughtily. She stood and straightened her skirts and cape.

"Very well. But don't expect me to come to your rescue should we meet up with outlaws."

"I wouldn't think of it, Mr. . . . ." She stopped.

He bowed his head. "Dominick Sanders, at your service."

"Mr. Sanders."

"So shall we get started, Mrs. Turner?"

She glanced at him sharply, realizing it wasn't the first time he had referred to her as such. "How do you know my name?"

"You introduced yourself to one of the other passengers. Don't you remember?"

"I remember." She wished with all her heart that the blond man was here now. He'd know what to do. "Jamie, come over here this moment," she said more sharply than she meant.

Jamie ran over to his mother's side. "Is that man dead?" he asked, pointing to the body of the guard.

"Yes, dear," Maggie said softly. From where she stood, she had a better view of the guard than she had earlier, and it was with surprise that she noticed the upper part of his body and his head had been covered with a piece of the stagecoach's leather curtain. Covering the face of the dead was done, generally, out of respect, and it surprised her that a prisoner would show such consideration toward a man who was taking him to jail, possibly even to his own hanging.

She wondered if the bandit had bothered covering the driver, but of course she had no intention of walking over to the body to find out.

Shuddering, she pulled Jamie away. "I can't leave without my valise. You know, the one your Aunt Kathleen gave me for Christmas."

"I saw it over there," Jamie said, pointing toward the overturned frame of the stagecoach.

Dominick frowned. "We can't load ourselves down with possessions."

"I'm not leaving without my valise," she said stubbornly. It had taken her months to save for the Blake sewing machine that allowed her to stitch up to a dozen pairs of shoes an hour. But a man who made his living robbing people could hardly be expected to understand what it was like to skimp and sacrifice as she had done to acquire the machine.

Making as wide a circle as possible around the body of the guard, she carefully worked her way down the mountainside to where Jamie had pointed. The valise lay several feet from the overturned stage, and a cursory look inside revealed that her precious sewing machine had not been damaged. She took the handle and lugged the tapestry bag back to where Jamie and Laurie-Anne waited for her.

Dominick stood watching her. "You fool woman, you're not going to carry that damned thing with you!"

Maggie glanced at him curiously. Just who did he think he was to give her orders? "If I leave it here, it'll be stolen by your bandit friends," she replied. "And I can't afford that."

Dominick narrowed his eyes. "What have you got in there? Gold?"

"What I have is better than gold. But, of course, you wouldn't understand that."

He regarded her thoughtfully. "You'd be surprised what I understand. Right now gold would be of no value to me. What I need are keys. Jamie could find only one key in the guard's pockets. There should have been two. One for the handcuffs and one for the ball and chain around my ankle. I think it would be a good idea for you to check for yourself and see if you can find the other one."

She gave him a determined look. "I have no intention of going through the pockets of a dead man, and certainly not for a key that you're not going to need." She leaned over and brushed dusty strands of hair from Laurie-Anne's forehead, tucking them beneath the brim of her bonnet. "Do you think you can walk?" she asked.

Laurie-Anne nodded and Maggie helped her to her feet. "Keep the blanket around your shoulders, that's a good girl." She turned, her eyes colliding with the outlaw's. "Mr. Sanders, I think it would be best if you go first."

"Why? So you can keep your eye on me?"

"So I'll know whether or not we're walking downwind," she said sweetly.

"You disappoint me, Mrs. Turner. I thought you were going to take me with you out of concern for my welfare. Now it turns out you only want to use me as bear bait."

The prisoner struggled to his feet, picked up his ball, and started up the side of the mountain toward the road with surprising ease. Maggie took Laurie-Anne's hand, grabbed the handle of the valise, and started after him, turning to be certain that Jamie was following close at hand.

Jamie ran ahead and disappeared over the top of the incline along with the prisoner. "Jamie!" Maggie called as she struggled up the slope. Never would she have imagined that the sewing machine could be so heavy. She hadn't even gotten up to the road when her bruised shoulder began to ache. To make matters worse, her feet kept slipping, sending dirt and rocks down the mountainside.

Tears of discouragement stung her eyes, and she set the valise down. Laurie-Anne balked and sat down, crying. Maggie straightened up and visually measured the distance to the top. It took two trips, but she managed to haul both child and valise up the slope.

"See if you can walk by yourself for a little while," Maggie pleaded. Her head was throbbing, and the deserted dirt road held no sign of Jamie. "Jamie, where are you?" she called irritably.

"I'm over here, Mama," Jamie responded.

Maggie peered through a clump of trees and was able to make out her son's shining blond hair. He was sitting on a fallen log next to the outlaw.

"Come on, Laurie-Anne, be a good girl for Mama." Still entreating her daughter to follow, Maggie made her way over to where Jamie and the outlaw were sitting.

She could hear Jamie's high-pitched voice telling Mr. Sanders the entire story of their lives. "My papa died, and my mama is going to Sana Baba to make shoes."

"I really don't think Mr. Sanders is interested in why we're going to Santa Barbara," she scolded lightly. She set the valise down by her side and rubbed her aching shoulder. "And Jamie, would you please stop playing with that ball? It's not a toy."

"But you never told me why Mr. Sanders has a ball on his leg."

Maggie met the man's dark eyes. "Mr. Sanders is an outlaw."

Jamie's eyes shone with interest. "What's an outlaw?"

"He's a person who robs people," Dominick said, before Maggie could answer. "He takes things that don't belong to him."

"Laurie-Anne took my slingshot. Does that mean she's an outlaw."

"Certainly not!" Maggie exclaimed. "The very idea . . ."

"Why can't she be an outlaw?" Jamie asked. "If she took something?"

"She's too young to be an outlaw," Dominick explained smoothly. He gave Maggie a beguiling smile, then added irrelevantly, "She's also too pretty. Shall we get started?"

He turned to Jamie. "Where's your walking stick?" he asked.

Jamie reached over and picked up a sturdy limb. "Right here."

Dominick nodded. "That's a good boy." He paused for a moment. "Such a dull word for such a splendid young fellow. When I was your age, my father always called me *mutikua,* which he thought sounded far more important than the word 'boy.'"

Jamie's eyes lit up. "You can call me a *mootiokooa* if you like."

Dominick threw back his head and laughed, the merry sound reaching the treetops.

Maggie could no longer hide her curiosity. "Are you Spanish?" she asked; then, because of the boldness in his eyes, she added, "Or French?"

"I'm American," he replied, with an amused expression. "But my parents were Basque."

"Basque?"

"That means that they were both Spanish and French and yet neither." He grinned. "They came from a little village in the Pyrenees, the mountains that lie between France and Spain. The Basque people have their own language, their own way of doing things. My father came over here when he was seventeen. Several years later, he sent for my mother."

"Why did your father come here?" she asked. She hated admitting even to herself that she was fascinated by the man.

"That's easy to explain. In my country we have a tradition. The oldest son goes to the church. The second son follows his father's work, and the third son goes to America, land of opportunity." He grinned. "Would you like to guess which son my father was?"

"The son who went to the church?" she asked mockingly. He laughed heartily at this, so heartily in fact, that even Laurie-Anne laughed. And Jamie, who had been investigating a hole in the ground, ran over to join the fun.

"What would your parents think if they knew you were nothing but a common thief?" Maggie asked.

"I may be many things, but I'm not common." He gave her a piercing look, then suddenly stood up. "We'd better get going. It'll be dark soon."

Shuddering at the thought, Maggie took her valise firmly in one hand and, after insisting that Jamie hold hands with his sister, marched forward.

"Stay downwind," Dominick called after her, "and watch out for snakes."

Maggie ignored him and plowed ahead, but she could hear him muttering something that sounded suspiciously like "Damned stubborn woman."

She smiled to herself. "Well, at least you have that right," she said under her breath.

They trudged on in silence for twenty minutes or more before either of them spoke.

"My arms feel like they're about to fall off from carrying this weight," he called to her. "Have you absolutely no mercy? Has your heart turned to coal?"

Trying her best to ignore the prisoner, Maggie stomped along the dirt road. But there was no ignoring him. She could feel his eyes on her back, burning through her like branding irons. At her side Laurie-Anne whimpered, and Jamie complained about having to hold his sister's hand.

"Can I walk with the outlaw?" he asked.

"Absolutely not!" Maggie said.

"Watch out for that rock ahead!" Mr. Sanders called after her. "It's called Outlaw Rock."

Maggie faltered to a stop. Releasing Laurie-Anne's hand, she dropped the valise in front of her and spun around.

Dominick paid no attention to her. He hobbled around in a circle around his ball, his head down. "It looks like there was a fairly recent robbery here," he called out. "You can see hoofprints surrounding the wagon wheel tracks. Probably within the last day or so."

Maggie cringed. Then what he said was true. There really were other robbers. She squeezed Laurie-Anne's hand tightly in her own. With wide eyes, she searched the shifting shadows on either side of her. Suddenly every sound or movement, from a flitting bee to a snapping twig, suggested impending doom. If the outlaw was right about the robbers, he could just as easily be right about the presence of bears and snakes.

Dominick picked up his ball and ambled toward her. "Are you sure you don't want to give me the key? I still won't be entirely free, but if it's the key for the ball and chain, we can make better time."

"Surely you can't be serious?" she replied scornfully. "Do you think I would take a chance on your murdering me and my children?"

He managed to give her an offended look. "That you would think me capable of such a dastardly deed wounds me deeply."

"I doubt that very much, Mr. Sanders. I think the only thing that wounds you is that you can't win me over with your charm."

He gave her a wicked smile. "So you admit I'm charming, do you?"

Maggie glanced at him askance. "I admit no such thing. You're an outlaw, a scourge to society. A no-good rogue." It peeved her that she had so few words at her disposal to describe him. "You should be ashamed."

"Would it make you feel any better if I told you I *am* ashamed? From here on in, I'm turning over a new leaf!"

"Really, Mr. Sanders? Does that mean you're going from robbing stagecoaches to robbing trains?"

He laughed and broke into song:

The bandit grins like it's a joke.
He stops the stage and lifts your poke.
You want to scrap, but sakes alive.
That bad man totes a forty-five.

Clamping her mouth shut in disapproval, Maggie turned, picked up her valise, grabbed Laurie-Anne by the hand, and marched on ahead. If he insisted on making light of his criminal acts, she had no intention of being subjected to it.

Despite her resolve, Maggie soon found herself holding back to keep Mr. Sanders's reassuring voice (but not the offensive words) within hearing range. The sunlight was fading rapidly, and the long shadows from the trees crisscrossed the winding dirt road.

A deer leaped across the way, scaring her practically to death. With her heart pounding, she stopped and dropped the valise to rest her shoulder. Laurie-Anne looked as if she was about to cry. Maggie smiled at her reassuringly. "It was just a deer."

"The bandit grins like it's a joke . . ."

"I'm tired, Mama," Laurie-Anne complained.

"You want to scrap, but sakes alive," Jamie's voice rang out. *"That bad man totes a forty-five."* Maggie glanced back just as her son leveled his walking stick and swung it all around, making bang-bang sounds.

Maggie nearly fainted. "Jamie! Come here at once!"

Confused by the anger in his mother's voice, Jamie dropped his stick and ran toward her.

"Don't you ever let me hear you sing that terrible song again," she scolded. "Do you understand?"

Jamie hung his head and poked out his lower lip.

Mr. Sanders shuffled toward them and sank down on the ground, dropping the ball between his feet. Maggie glared at him. "I would appreciate it if you would not teach my son such unsavory songs, Mr. Sanders. In fact, I would rather that you not talk to my son at all."

"Would you rather let him roam free and get into all sorts of mischief?"

"I would rather that you let me worry about my son!" she stormed.

It was at this moment that Maggie noticed Jamie had disappeared again. "Now where is he?" she looked around anxiously. Not only could she not see him but she could no longer hear his intermittent coughing. "Jamie! Answer me this minute!"

When there was no response, panic rose up inside her. She turned to the outlaw, surprised to find him already on his feet and moving more quickly than she had ever seen him move before.

Her gaze followed the granite walls of a towering ridge off to the left side of the road and lingered on an outcropping of rocks high over her head. Jamie was a climber. She narrowed her eyes as she tried to pick out her son, but her thoughts were interrupted by the bandit's voice, coming from the right.

"Over here!"

Something about the purposeful way he moved and took command made her pick Laurie-Anne up and dash after him. She ran blindly through clumps of bushes and undergrowth until she broke loose and almost fell headfirst into a clearing.

She set Laurie-Anne down and recovered her balance. That was when she saw the bandit at the edge of a very steep and very dangerous cliff.

Chapter 4

Indescribable horror filled her thoughts in the few seconds it took to race to Mr. Sanders's side. She nearly fainted in relief at the sight of Jamie lying some twelve feet below them on a rocky ledge that jutted out from the side of the granite drop. But her relief was short-lived; the ledge couldn't have been more than five feet wide.

"Careful," the outlaw cautioned, pointing to where the ground had given way beneath Jamie's feet. "You may not be as lucky as your son."

"Are you hurt, Jamie?" Maggie cried out, holding back tears.

Jamie rubbed his leg. "I skinned my leg."

Maggie implored Mr. Sanders, "We've got to do something."

"We will. As soon as you give me the key."

Maggie's eyes widened. "What?"

"The key, dammit! Unless you plan to climb down that mountain and save your son yourself, you'd better help set me free."

"How do I know that you won't take off and leave us here?" Maggie asked through quivering lips.

"You don't!"

She looked down at Jamie, whose short, panting breaths were punctuated with dry, hacking coughs, and her heart squeezed with fear. The last time he had suffered such an attack, he'd stopped breathing and turned blue, and it was only by shaking him that she got him to breathe again.

"Hold on, Jamie." To the outlaw she said, "All right, I'll help you." She turned her back to him and reached inside her bodice.

"You're going to have to help me get out of both the handcuffs and the ball," he said. "That is, if you want me to rescue the boy."

She spun around, eyes flashing. "You know I do," she raged, hating the arrogance on his handsome face. "But if you leave us, so help me you'll live to rue the day."

"Why, Mrs. Turner, that sounds like a threat."

"I don't make threats, Mr. Sanders, I make promises."

He grinned and held his shackled hands out in front of him. "You're my kind of woman, Mrs. Turner."

She glared at him icily. "I could never be your kind of woman, Mr. Sanders!"

"I would love to discuss the matter in more detail, but it seems like neither the time nor the place. Shall we see which lock the key fits?"

Hoping he didn't notice how much she was shaking, she inserted the key into the tiny rusty lock of the handcuffs. No sooner had she turned the key than a soft click signaled success, and the cuffs fell to the ground.

Cautioning Laurie-Anne to stay by her side, she peered again over the side of the cliff and swallowed hard. Jamie sat huddled, his knees drawn up to his chest. Despite his five years, he looked small and helpless on the ledge, his eyes full of fear as he looked up at her. He coughed and gasped for air.

"Take a deep breath, Jamie." She demonstrated. "Come on, Jamie. Breathe!"

She turned back to Dominick, who was rubbing the black and blue marks that circled his wrists.

"What's wrong with his breathing?" he asked.

"He has a lung weakness. His father died of the same condition." She briefly met his eyes and then quickly turned back to her son.

Jamie was growing restless. "I'm scared, Mama."

"I know, dear. But Mama's here, and Mr. Sanders is going to save you. Now be a good boy and don't move around so." Jamie's father used to say that telling Jamie to keep still was like trying to stop a runaway bull with one hand.

"Can't you hurry?" she urged.

"I am hurrying," Dominick growled. He grabbed a rock the size of a fist. Settling himself on the ground, he pulled the chain taut around his ankle and began pounding the links with the rock. Each resounding blow was met with a shower of blue sparks.

"You can't!" she gasped.

"If you think I'm climbing down that mountain attached to a fifty-pound ball you'd better think again."

Maggie wrung her hands. He was right, of course. To save Jamie, he had to be free. But if he were free, he might just as well run off and leave them stranded. Still, he was the only hope she had. "That isn't going to work," Maggie said impatiently, tapping the toe of her boot.

"I asked you to check the guard's pocket," he growled.

"Shall I go back?"

He thought for a moment. "It's too far away. Besides, it'll soon be dark and you won't be able to find your way back. In any case, Jamie checked the pockets pretty thoroughly. The key probably broke free from the ring and fell out of the guard's pocket sometime during the crash. Our best chance is to try and break the chain." He looked up. "Unless, of course, you have a better idea."

She was tempted to suggest an idea or two having to do with his demise, but thought better of it. Like it or not, she needed him.

Laurie-Anne began to cry, and Maggie braced herself against the panic that threatened to overcome her good judgment. She needed to remain strong for the children's sake. "Hush, hush, little one." She checked her daughter's forehead. The bump over her left eye was slightly blue, but the swelling had gone down and it appeared less sensitive to the touch.

Cradling Laurie-Anne in her arms, Maggie looked down at her son and forced confidence into her voice to hide her fear. "Jamie, it won't be long. I promise you. Just hold on."

The dull sound of rock striking metal made her already throbbing head pound that much more. "How much longer?"

"I don't know!" Dominick replied. "One of these links appears weak, but it's going to take time." The outlaw looked at her, his hand pausing between blows. "I don't know how strong that ledge is. It could be sandstone. Try to keep him from moving around too much."

Turning back, she watched her son worriedly. "Jamie, you must keep still."

"There's a lizard down here, Mama."

"Leave it alone, Jamie."

For the next hour or so, Maggie tried everything she could think of to distract Jamie. She played his favorite guessing games and told him stories. His breathing returned to normal and his cough subsided, but he was beginning to grow bored and restless again.

"I'm tired," he complained.

It was dark enough to see sparks fly each time Dominick hit the chain with the rock. "I don't think I can keep him still much longer."

He stopped banging and hobbled closer to the edge of the cliff. "Come on, *mutikua*," he called. "Let's sing." He lifted his voice in song. *"The bandit grins like it's a joke. He stops the stage and lifts your poke . . ."*

A young voice drifted up from below. *"You want to scrap, but sakes alive."* Jamie coughed and then continued, *"The bad man totes a forty-five!"*

At the sound of Jamie's voice, Maggie eyes burned with tears. First the stagecoach had run off the road.

Now Jamie was only a few feet away from death. How much more could she possibly endure?

"Are you going to save me, Mr. Outlaw?"

"You bet I'm going to save you," Dominick called back. "How many times do you think you can sing that song?"

"A hundred!" Jamie boasted, with typical five-year-old confidence.

"It's a deal. You sing it a hundred times and I'll save you," Dominick called back. He flashed Maggie a mocking smile. "Unless, of course, your mother objects?"

Not wanting to argue with him, Maggie held her tongue and was relieved when he picked up the rock and started pounding again.

Shivering, Maggie now noticed that the shadows were moving in with the stealth of an ambushing army. It was getting darker and colder by the minute. Overhead, stars were beginning to twinkle.

The only thing that kept Maggie's hopes alive was Jamie's voice drifting up from the ledge below. His breathing was still labored, but not even his dry, hacking cough prevented him from doing the job Dominick had given him to do.

"That's three," Jamie called earnestly, upon finishing another refrain. Without hesitation, he immediately began again. *"The bandit grins . . ."*

Despite the earsplitting sound of rock against metal, Laurie-Anne fell asleep in her mother's arms. Maggie gently laid her in a pile of pine needles and covered her with the buffalo blanket.

She then moved as close to the edge as she dared. It was too dark to see down the mountainside, but she could still hear Jamie's thin voice singing. "That's a good boy, Jamie," Maggie called to him.

"Mama, I'm scared. It's dark down here."

"I know. It's dark up here, too. But Mr. Sanders is going to save you. Come now, sing." Despite her better judgment, Maggie lifted her own voice in song.

"The bandit grins like it's a joke . . ." Behind her came the warm, rumbling sound of a soft chuckle, which she chose to ignore.

It seemed that hours passed, although it could have been mere minutes. The pounding sound of rock against metal continued, punctuated by the outlaw's curses. At one point, Laurie-Anne cried out and Maggie rushed to comfort her. But for the most part, Maggie stayed riveted to the edge of the cliff, trying to keep Jamie occupied.

The night air turned decidedly colder when a slight breeze blew in off the distant ocean and rustled the trees that towered over them. Fear gripped Maggie's heart: Fear for her son, who lay a few feet from death. Fear of the possible dangers that lurked all around them. Fear of the dark and handsome outlaw—a man she had no choice but to trust.

It was taking so long that Maggie wanted to scream.

"Did I sing it a hundred times yet?" Jamie called out. He coughed and gasped for air.

"Not yet," Dominick called. "Keep singing."

Jamie began singing again, but his words soon slurred, and silence followed.

Maggie called to him. "Jamie, wake up. Don't go to sleep."

"It's no use," Dominick said at her side. "Poor little fellow is probably exhausted. Let's just hope he's sleeping too deeply to move around much."

It was too dark for Maggie to see Dominick's face, but she could feel his eyes on her. "Keep going!" she cried, with renewed urgency in her voice. "You can't stop now."

"I don't have much choice," he answered. "I can't see what I'm doing. As soon as it's light, we'll figure out another way. Maybe you can go for help, while I stay here with Jamie and Laurie-Anne."

"No! It might be too late. Jamie might . . ." Tears sprang to her eyes. "You can't give up now."

"I'm not giving up, dammit! I'm simply saying that I can't break through the chain."

"Then I'll break it!" She bent over and felt around for the rock. Crawling on hands and knees, she located his chain and pounded it with every bit of strength she had.

Dominick grabbed her by the shoulders and pulled her to her feet. "Calm down," he murmured into her ear. "This is no time to lose control. We must think of another plan." He held her close to him, and for a moment Maggie relaxed against the massive span of his chest, his arms around her waist. It felt so warm next to him, so safe.

Then, astonished at herself for forgetting even for a moment that he was a dangerous man, she pulled away.

Edging toward the brink again, she called Jamie's name, praying he would answer her. And when he didn't, she hoped he would cough so that she would know he was still on the ledge.

Behind her, Dominick shouted aloud. "You're a genius, an absolute genius!"

Turning, she tried to pick him out of the darkness, but she could see nothing but a pitch-black void. Had he gone mad? "What are you talking about?"

"You broke the chain."

She couldn't believe her ears. "You mean . . . ?"

"I'm free." Suddenly she felt his closeness. She was in his arms once again, and the frightening darkness was replaced by his warm, demanding lips on hers. But the reprieve was only momentary, for he released her as abruptly as he had grabbed her.

Fighting for composure, Maggie tightened her fists by her side. "Mr. Sanders!" she exclaimed, backing away. Her foot slipped and as she struggled to regain her balance, she screamed. The outlaw caught her in the nick of time and pulled her to safety.

"How dare you!" she exclaimed.

"I'm sorry," he said lightly. "I thought you would want me to save you from going over."

Confused, her mind teetered back and forth. "I was referring to your kiss."

"My sincere apologies. I thought you were referring to my saving your life."

Maggie's face burned. "Well, of course I'm grateful." What an impossible man! "But you had no right to kiss me."

"I told you there were other reasons to kiss a woman besides robbing her. What better way to show my gratitude to you for freeing me from that tiresome piece of iron?"

"A simple 'thank-you' would have been sufficient!" she stormed, backing into a tree. With an exasperated sigh, she walked forward again, her arms extended in front of her as she made her way in the dark. Somewhere nearby was the tree where Laurie-Anne slept. She wanted to be sure the little girl was safe before working her way over to the cliff and Jamie. She wanted to put as much distance as possible between herself and this disturbing man.

To her surprise, she bumped into warm, bare skin.

"Watch it!" he said softly. "I don't have any clothes on, and you might not be able to control yourself near me."

Maggie froze, her arms rigidly at her side. "Why . . . why don't you have clothes on?" she stammered.

"I'm using them to make a rope to get to Jamie. I need at least twenty feet. Give me your cape and take off your skirt."

Her mouth was perfectly dry. "My . . . my skirt?"

"Why, Mrs. Turner, you're not thinking what I think you're thinking, are you? A lady like you?"

Maggie's cheeks grew warm. "The only thing I'm thinking about is saving my son!" she retorted.

"Are you sure you're not thinking what I think you're thinking? I wouldn't blame you if you were, me standing here naked and all."

Maggie's heart beat wildly. By naked, did he mean naked from the waist up only? Or was he naked all over? And what possible difference could it make as long as they saved Jamie?

"I have no idea what you're talking about!" she said, tugging at her waist, her fingers fumbling with the hooks and eyes. She stepped out of her skirt. "Where are you? I can't see you."

"Is that a complaint, Mrs. Turner?" She heard a movement and sensed that he was close. Again, she wondered about his dress, and her wayward thoughts sent the blood rushing to her head. "Or are you simply stating a desire?" He took the skirt from her, and she heard the fabric ripping.

"Neither!" she mumbled. She waited for what seemed like an eternity. "What's taking so long?"

"Patience, my love." A moment later he added, "I tied one end of the rope to this tree, but I'm going to need you to pull on it when I give the word." He shoved a piece of the fabric rope into her hand. "After you pull Jamie to safety, throw the end of the rope back down to me."

"Is that all I can do?" she asked.

"You can prepare to show your gratitude after I rescue your son."

Maggie held her breath. She couldn't see him, but she could tell by the sound of falling rocks that he had lowered himself over the edge.

Frozen in place, she strained her ears, but the only sounds that stirred the night air were the water rushing along in the stream far below them and the rustle of wind in the trees overhead. There was not one sound from Jamie.

With her heart pounding, she tightened her hands around the fabric rope and prayed.

"All right," Dominick called at last. "Pull it up!"

Maggie tightened her hold on the makeshift rope and pulled.

"Pull!" Dominick shouted.

"I am pulling," she cried. Gritting her teeth, she heaved, and the fabric cut into her hand. Finally she felt something brush against her foot.

"Jamie! Is that you?"

"Mama?"

With a cry of relief, she bent down, grabbed his hand, and pulled him to safety.

"That was scary," Jamie said, clinging to her.

"I know, dear heart," she whispered, hugging him close. "I know." She could feel his little heart beating against her chest.

Dominick's impatient voice rose from the ledge. "Toss the rope down to me." After a moment, he called again, "Hurry, dammit! I have no clothes on and it's cold down here."

Brushing away tears of relief, Maggie undid the knot underneath Jamie's armpits and checked to be sure that the other end was still tied securely to the tree. Then she threw the free end down to the bandit. "I wouldn't want you to catch a cold."

She picked Jamie up and walked blindly through the darkness over to where his sister slept. When he was settled down on the bed of pine needles, she whispered, "Stay here. I'll be back in a little while." She covered both children with the blanket and felt her way back toward the top of the cliff.

Careful not to venture too close to the edge, she held on to a tree trunk and called, "Mr. Sanders?"

From behind her came his soft baritone voice. "Yes."

Hand on her heart, she whirled around. "Did you have to sneak up on me like that?"

"You're the one who called my name," he said pointedly.

"I thought you were still on the ledge," she argued.

"I came back to help you up."

"You disappoint me, Mrs. Turner. I'd rather hoped you came back to reward me for rescuing your son."

A hot flush swept over her. "You . . . you have my hearty gratitude."

"I find gratitude to be more tiring than satisfying," the bandit replied.

"That doesn't surprise me in the least," she shot back, shivering suddenly. Then, because she really was grateful to him, she added, "I'm very much obliged to you, Mr. Sanders."

There was a moment's silence before he responded. "It was my pleasure." For once he spoke without the usual mockery, as if the sincerity of her gratitude demanded a truce.

"Now, if you'll excuse me," she said, "I wish to join my children." With nothing more than a narrow strip of starlit sky overhead to show the way, she headed back to Jamie and Laurie-Anne.

"Mrs. Turner."

She froze in her tracks. "Mr. Sanders?"

"Would you care to have your skirt back?"

Chapter 5

Dominick woke at dawn. Stretching his arms over his head, he opened his eyes and tried to put a name to the strange humming sound that disturbed the early-morning stillness.

He sat up to work the kinks out of his back and saw that a few feet away, Jamie and Laurie-Anne were huddled together on the ground beneath the buffalo blanket. Jamie's breathing sounded rather like a ranting bull, but his color looked normal and he was no longer coughing.

The sun was just beginning to climb over the mountain peaks, sending shafts of golden light through the softly swaying treetops.

Dominick took in the surroundings with narrowed eyes, his every sense alert.

There was no sign of Maggie Turner.

Swearing under his breath, he jumped to his feet and set out in search of the humming sound.

It didn't take long to find her. She sat daintily on a log, as prim and proper as a guest at a tea party. A remarkable accomplishment, he thought, considering that from the waist down she was dressed only in pantaloons. Her face was set in the same determined expression that had become all too familiar to him in the short time he'd known her.

She was busily feeding the fabric of her yellow skirt through a machine that sat on a large flat rock in front of her. This was the source of the humming sound he'd heard. His guess was that it was a sewing machine, though he'd never seen one shaped quite like this one.

"What the hell!"

Maggie lifted her foot from the iron treadle. "Do you have a problem, Mr. Sanders?" she asked, impatiently brushing back a strand of hair that had escaped from its bun.

"Is that what you had in that damned valise you insisted on dragging with you? A sewing machine so that you could repair damage done to your clothing?" He was incredulous. If she was so almighty practical, she could have thought to bring along something more useful, like a shotgun.

"This is no ordinary sewing machine," she explained. "It sews shoes. It's designed for leather, not fabric, but I think the stitches will hold until I get to Santa Barbara." She shook the skirt out and examined a seam.

"Why would you cart along a heavy machine like that?" he asked.

"I need this for my business."

He remembered Jamie's telling him something about his mother making shoes, but he'd not thought about her doing it professionally. "You're a shoemaker?"

"I am." She glanced up at him. "Don't look so surprised, Mr. Sanders. I can assure you I'm a very good shoemaker."

He considered this for a moment. "It hardly seems like an appropriate occupation for a woman."

"Appropriate, Mr. Sanders?" she sputtered in astonishment. "Would you rather that I rob stages?"

He pondered this, then shook his head. "No. That's a rough job for a woman. You're probably better off making shoes."

She couldn't believe it. He actually thought she was asking his opinion on the matter! She cleared her voice and glanced at his shabby black boots. "You might invest in a decent pair yourself. I guarantee you'll never find boots kinder to your feet than the

ones I make." What she wanted to do was cram his
feet into a boot two sizes too small.

He regarded her with dark, penetrating eyes. "Is
that right, Mrs. Turner? Maybe I'll take you up on
that offer." Then he looked up at the clear blue sky.
"It looks like it's going to be another hot day. I think
we should get the children up so we can get started.
With a little luck, maybe we can hitch a ride and reach
Santa Barbara by this afternoon."

"Very well, Mr. Sanders."

He turned and ducked out of sight. Maggie waited
to make certain he was not coming back before she
stood and worked her skirt over her head and down
her body. The skirt was wrinkled and covered in dust,
but at least it allowed her a measure of modesty. She
repacked her sewing machine carefully in her valise
and hurried to wake Jamie and Laurie-Anne.

"I'm hungry," Laurie-Anne said, rubbing her eyes.

"I know," Maggie said. "As soon as we get to Santa
Barbara, we'll eat."

"Jamie?" She looked around, her heart pounding
wildly. "Jamie, where are you?"

"I'm here, Mama."

Jamie and Dominick emerged from behind a clump
of bushes. "Look what we found," Jamie said. With
a lopsided grin, he held out hands filled with juicy
blackberries.

"That's wonderful," Maggie said. "Share some with
your sister."

Dominick walked toward Maggie. "Would you like
some?"

"Thank you," she murmured, finding herself blushing beneath his steady gaze. He emptied his berries
into her hand and watched as she pushed them one by
one into her mouth and savored the lovely sweetness.
"They're delicious."

He nodded. "I think we'd better get going," he
said. He reached into his pocket, drew out a flat,
round woolen cap, and put it on his head.

She glanced at him, unable to quell her curiosity. "I must say, Mr. Sanders, I was mighty surprised to see you this morning." Surprise did not begin to describe how she had felt upon awakening and finding him asleep practically on top of her and the children. The man had no sense of propriety. Not that she minded, of course. As strange at it seemed given his unlawful behavior, it did give her a sense of security knowing he had been so close. Still, he could have allowed more space between them. "I fully expected you to sneak off during the night."

"What kind of a man do you take me for? Certainly you don't think I would leave a woman alone in the mountains with two small children. Not that I think you can't take care of yourself, mind you. I shudder to think of the trouble you would be likely to inflict upon anyone unfortunate enough to try anything."

Thinking he was mocking her, Maggie gave him a sharp look and was surprised to find him quite serious.

"Besides, did you really think you'd get rid of me that easily?"

"Aren't you afraid of being caught?"

"No one knows who I am but you," he said. "Do you plan to turn me in?"

"You're an outlaw. It's my duty to turn you in."

"But think how rotten you'll feel afterward."

"Rotten?"

"I saved your son. Turning me in is hardly what I call adequate reward for such a magnificent deed." He grinned. "You appear to be a woman of good conscience. As such, it seems to me you have no choice but to keep my identity hidden."

"Mr. Sanders," she began evenly, "the law is quite clear as to what my responsibilities are." She surveyed him out of the corner of her eye. Something in the way he was contemplating her made her wish she had a hairbrush and a looking glass. But she despised the womanly part of her that longed to look attractive in his presence and forced the thought out of her mind.

He was an outlaw; what he thought of her appearance was of no consequence.

"Since you're so concerned about my conscience, I'll put in a good word to the judge on your behalf."

He bowed. "Your generosity overwhelms me." He picked up her valise and without another word started along a narrow dirt trail with Jamie by his side.

"Come along, Laurie-Anne," Maggie said, watching him. It wasn't until Laurie-Anne tugged at her skirts that she realized how long she had stood staring at the man. Sighing, she took her daughter by the hand and trudged after him.

The winding road narrowed further and led them through fields of colorful wildflowers. The air was filled with the sweet fragrance of lupines and wild irises and more golden poppies than Maggie had ever seen in her entire life. As they came to a rise, she could see beyond the ragged ridges and the carpets of flowers all the way to the Pacific Ocean. The fields of blue and gold combined with the glistening ocean and deep azure sky to lift her spirits. The sore muscles and bruises caused by the accident and the night spent on the cold, damp ground were soon forgotten.

Even Jamie, who had not left Dominick's side for a moment, seemed more comfortable in this environment. He'd hardly coughed all morning, not since he first woke up. Any lingering doubts as to whether she'd made the right decision in moving to Santa Barbara evaporated, and she felt surprisingly carefree as she hastened to catch up to Jamie and the outlaw.

They walked for a good portion of the morning and stopped only when Laurie-Anne complained that her legs hurt. While they rested, they watched a flock of sheep grazing on a steep, velvet-green hill.

"Look, Mama," Laurie-Anne said excitedly. She pointed to a bird that stood on the back of a heavily fleeced sheep, searching for seeds in the animal's thick wool.

"Why is that bird standing on the sheep?" Jamie asked.

Without hesitation, Dominick quipped, "He wants to keep his feet warm."

Maggie couldn't help but laugh. The man definitely had a sense of humor.

Dominick grew suddenly alert and turned his attention to the sound of a bleating sheep. He narrowed his eyes and scanned the scattered herd until he had identified the sheep that was making the racket. "Wait here," he said. In an instant his long, powerful legs had carried him easily over the hilly terrain, out of sight.

Jamie looked worried. "Where did the outlaw go?"

Maggie gave her son a reassuring pat on the back. "I don't know. And it's not polite to call someone an outlaw. His name is Mr. Sanders."

"Will Mr. Sanders come back?"

"Of course he will," she replied, her eyes riveted to the spot where he'd disappeared. A short time later his tall, lean body came back into view. "See? I told you."

Jamie and Laurie-Anne ran across the field to meet him. Their racing feet a blur, they skimmed easily through the wild grass that grew in bright-green clumps and dashed to the top of a clover-covered hill. Smiling at their enthusiasm, Maggie couldn't resist lifting the hem of her skirt and running after them.

Dominick was carrying a baby lamb in his arms that couldn't have been more than a few days old. He set the spindly-legged lamb down on a patch of green grass and murmured words of encouragement as the small animal bleated. "It's all right, little fellow. Don't be scared."

The little lamb's loud cries turned to soft bleats when its mother called back. With a flick of its stubby tail, the baby ran on wobbly legs to join her. Dominick, Maggie, and the children watched the ewe nuzzle her youngster, then guide the little lamb back to the flock with a gentle nudge.

"How did you know that lamb was lost?" Maggie asked.

Dominick shrugged lightly. "It was easy. The bleat of a ewe looking for her lost lamb is different from any other bleat."

"But you found the lamb so quickly." The area was filled with deep ravines and narrow crevices cut into the hard rock ground. "I wouldn't have known where to begin looking."

"When looking for a lost sheep, you always head downhill. In this case, the little fellow had fallen into a gully at the bottom of the hill, and wasn't yet strong enough to get himself out. Sort of like Jamie." He realized that time was fleeting. The sun was nearly overhead, and it was growing hotter by the minute. "Shall we continue along our way?"

She nodded. She surely didn't know what to think of an outlaw who not only rescued small children and animals but seemed to speak the special language of both.

They had barely resumed their journey when they noticed that a distant cloud of dust was moving along their path in a southerly direction. Presently, a horse-drawn wagon appeared. Dominick and Jamie raced ahead, waving their hands over their head, and shouting until at last the driver halted his wagon and waved back.

"Look over there!" Maggie said eagerly, pointing for her daughter's benefit. "We have a ride. Come along, now. You can walk just a little further." With Laurie-Anne in one hand and her valise in the other, she hurried to join the others, relieved that their ordeal was finally over.

The driver of the wagon held the reins and pushed back his cowhide hat. His leathery face was creased like an old prune and had been browned by the sun until it was nearly as dark as one.

Dominick introduced himself to the driver, who said his name was George Pickings. Shaking his hand, Dominick explained their plight. "Believe me, Mr. Pickings, you're a sight for sore eyes. My family and I were the unfortunate victims of a stagecoach accident."

"That must be the one that never showed up yesterday. Rumor has it that it was held up and everyone left for dead. When I was in town this morning, the sheriff was busy rounding up volunteers to go with him and have a look."

"The stage flew off the mountainside," Dominick explained. "My wife and I have had a long night."

Next to him, Maggie gasped, protesting no doubt to his referring to her as his wife. He gave her a visual warning, then turned back to the driver. "Do you suppose you can take us into town?"

"Mighty glad to," the man agreed. "Better yet, I'll take you to the house." He nodded. "Just down the hill a ways. The wife can fix you something to eat."

"We can sure use that." Dominick lifted Laurie-Anne into the back of the wagon. He then turned to Maggie, who was glaring at him like a bear with a bad case of hives. She looked so indignant, it was all he could do to keep from laughing.

"How dare you tell that man that I'm your wife?" she stormed, keeping her voice remarkably low considering the degree of rage that was evident on her face.

"I was only thinking of your reputation," he whispered back. "How do you suppose it looks for a woman to spend the night in the wilderness with a man she hardly knows?"

With a glance toward Mr. Pickings, who was watching them, Maggie allowed Dominick to help her into the wagon. As soon as the driver had turned his back and picked up the reins, though, she pried her arm from his grasp and continued her tirade. "I doubt very much that you care a fig for my reputation. Just you wait, Mr. Sanders. Just you wait until I see the sheriff. He'll put you behind bars where you belong!"

"What a pity you feel that way, *Mrs.* Sanders. I was beginning to think that you and I would make an interesting team." She looked so appalled that he just had to add, "Robbing stages is much more profitable than making shoes, and you wouldn't have to deal with foul-smelling feet."

Arms folded across her chest, she glared at him. "Sit down, Jamie," she said. To Dominick she declared, "On second thought, forget what I said about putting in a good word for you. I fully intend to tell the judge that you propositioned me!"

He allowed an evil smile to spread across his face and took great delight in watching her cheeks turn a bright, but no less fetching, red.

"I was talking about your offer to make me an accomplice in robbing stages," she added hastily.

His grin widened. "I *know* what you were referring to." Watching her blush spread, he added, "If I'd honestly thought you were going to turn me in, I wouldn't have been such a gentleman last night." His eyes drifted down the length of her. "A pity, isn't it? Now neither one of us will ever know what we missed."

"I'll tell you what's a pity . . ." she began, but before she could finish, the driver called out to them.

Disappointed that he was denied the pleasure of hearing her retort, Dominick turned his head in the direction the driver was pointing.

"See that farmhouse over there? That's where we're heading."

"Does that mean we can eat?" Jamie asked.

Maggie avoided meeting Dominick's eyes. "Yes!" she snapped.

"I'm firsty," Laurie-Anne said.

"Look over there," Dominick said. "See that cow? I bet you can have some of her warm, sweet milk."

The wagon stopped in front of an adobe brick

house, with a red-tiled roof and green shutters. A woman came out of the house waving.

"That's Mrs. Pickings," the driver explained. The woman walked over to the wagon, tying a bonnet onto her head.

In quick order, Mr. Pickings explained the plight of his passengers to his wife, who clucked her tongue and leaned over the side of the wagon to give Maggie a sympathetic pat on her arm.

"You poor, poor thing," she said. She was an enormous woman with a wide, friendly face, and her skirts made a perfect circle around her ample body. "What a dreadful experience you had. Simply dreadful. But it was bound to happen sooner or later. I told my husband only last week—didn't I, George?—that if the good Lord meant for us to travel along those mountain roads, he would have made mountains flat."

Dominick jumped over the side of the wagon. "My wife and children are in need of lodgings and food," he explained. "Is there a place in town where we can stay?"

"Actually, we have lodgings," Maggie said, glaring at Dominick. "Mr. Kinsberg from the Bank of California sent a draft to a Mrs. French. Perhaps you've heard of her? I understand she owns one of the most respectable boardinghouses in town."

"Oh, dear!" Mrs. Pickings exclaimed. "This is dreadful. Mrs. French, you say? I guess you haven't heard."

"Heard what?" Maggie asked.

"Mrs. French's boardinghouse burned down, didn't it, George? Barely three weeks ago."

A look of dismay crossed Maggie's face. "Are . . . are you sure?"

"Quite sure. Burned clear down to the ground, didn't it, George? Poor Mrs. French was so distraught, she left town on the very next stage and no one has heard a word from her since."

"But this is most distressing news," Maggie exclaimed. "Where in the world will we stay?"

"Don't worry, my dear," Dominick said. "I'm sure there are other respectable places in town."

"I'm not so certain," Mrs. Picking said, watching Jamie, who was busily climbing over the side. "There's the Occidental Hotel, of course, but it has a billiards hall and a saloon." She frowned in disapproval. "Definitely not a good place for children. It can be terribly rowdy at times, can't it, George? Then there's the Lincoln House. Much more refined, but expensive." She listed the various hotels and boardinghouses in Santa Barbara, none of which met her approval. "You were absolutely correct to choose Mrs. French's boardinghouse. It was the best to be had."

"Now what will I do?" Maggie lamented. "I don't suppose Mrs. French left a forwarding address. She owes me three months' rent."

"Oh, dear. I'm sure it never occurred to her. I can't tell you how upset she was. She couldn't leave here soon enough. But meanwhile, we simply must find you another place to stay." Suddenly her face lit up. "I have a better idea. My sister lives only two blocks away from State Street, doesn't she, George? She's getting ready to travel to Los Angeles to care for our father, who has been taken ill. I don't know how long she'll be gone, but I'm sure she would be relieved to have someone take care of her house and garden in her absence, wouldn't she, George?"

Although George seemed oblivious to his wife's prattle, he always managed to nod at the appropriate times.

"That's most generous of you," Dominick said.

"We couldn't impose," Maggie said, realizing the complications that had arisen. They had not yet arrived in town, and already two people thought she and Dominick were married. And, unless her suspicions were wrong, anyone as loose-tongued as Mrs.

Pickings was bound to have the word spread throughout town, if not the entire county, by nightfall.

"It's no imposition," Mrs. Pickings declared, nodding her head in a way that suggested the matter was settled. "Connie Mae will charge you less than anyone else in town, won't she, George? The problem is, her house is adobe with a red-tiled roof. A real treasure, if you ask me. But the folks in town don't see it that way. They're tearing down anything even remotely Spanish and putting up the most dreadful wooden houses. Barbaric. Aren't they, George? Not to mention a fire hazard."

George grunted and reached in his pocket for his pipe.

"When will your sister's house be available?" Dominick asked.

"I don't see any reason why she couldn't leave today. There's a stage for Los Angeles this afternoon." For once she didn't stop to ask George to confirm her statement. "I'll take you there now, if you like."

Maggie tried to think what to do. The only way she could afford to pay for lodgings was by using the money she had set aside for starting her business. The unexpected expense of paying twice for a place to stay was going to impose a severe hardship on her and the children and have a direct bearing on their future.

"That would be most considerate of you," Dominick said with a bow. "Don't you agree, Mrs. Sanders?"

Maggie gave him a dark look. "I really think we should consider the offer more carefully," she said through clenched teeth.

Dominick narrowed his eyes in warning before turning back to Mrs. Pickings. "What my wife is trying to say is that we have not eaten since yesterday."

"Oh, dear, how thoughtless of me." The woman fluttered her hands frantically. "Come, come along, all of you. Inside. I have bread in the oven, and some homemade cheese. And I just baked two of my famous berry pies, didn't I, George?"

The woman kept up a nonstop discourse on anything and everything as she herded both children into the house, with George in tow behind her.

Before following them, Maggie turned to Dominick, her hands on her hips. "You're going to have to tell them that we're not married."

"What? And ruin your reputation?"

"You don't think that pretending I'm married to an outlaw won't ruin my reputation?"

"It's a perfect arrangement," Dominick said. "We both need a place to live. What could be better?"

"Anything would be better than our living under the same roof."

"So what do you plan to do? Turn me in? Watch me being hung by the neck? Jamie will love you for that."

"Mr. Sanders . . . I . . . listen . . . if you go, leave now, I'll not tell anyone your real identity."

"That's a most generous offer. I wish I could take you up on it. If for no other reason than to see how you manage to explain to the Pickingses how it is that your husband disappeared." A broad grin crossed his face. "I have the feeling that a missing husband would not escape Mrs. Pickings's notice."

Maggie stuck her chin out defiantly and met his gaze head on. "I'll tell them you went back to San Francisco. That we got a divorce."

"A divorce? You'd ruin your reputation just like that?"

"And just exactly what do you suppose my reputation will be like when the truth comes out?"

"The truth doesn't have to come out. We can always bribe a traveling preacher to make us man and wife."

Maggie couldn't believe her ears. Was there no end to the dastardly deeds he was capable of perpetrating?

And to think she had spent the night in his company. "I would never marry an outlaw!"

He shrugged. "I seem to recall that you said practically the same thing about freeing me from those tiresome confines." His arched eyebrows gave him a fiendish look. "You remember, the handcuffs and the ball?"

"It's a pity that you're not still in them!"

"Now, now, Mrs. Turner. The truth of the matter is, you need me more than I need you."

"I need you, Mr. Sanders, like I need a rattlesnake bite."

"I wouldn't be so sure about that. You can't afford to pay for your lodgings and I can."

It galled her that he had so accurately assessed her circumstances. "As soon as I locate Mrs. French, I shall have no problem covering my own expenses, thank you very much."

"Ah, yes, Mrs. French. The poor dear woman who lost everything she owned in an unfortunate fire. I'm sure she will be most eager to refund your money."

Seething, Maggie stubbornly folded her arms across her chest. "It will be a cold day in hell before I accept charity from an outlaw!"

Mrs. Pickings stuck her head out the door. "Are you coming, Mr. and Mrs. Sanders?"

Dominick grinned at Maggie and held out his arm. "Let's not keep our hostess waiting."

In no time at all, Mrs. Pickings had led them to a cozy kitchen filled with the fragrance of freshly baked bread and seated them at a table set with gold-stippled porcelain ware.

Platters filled with sliced smoked meat, cheese, and fruit were arranged around loaves of freshly baked bread and newly churned butter. The woman's efficiency was in no way impaired by her constant chatter.

She plied them with food and drink and enough gossip to scandalize the citizens of Babel.

"Is it any wonder that the man can't tell the difference between a harbor and a bay when he thinks nothing of bedding down any woman he can get his hands on, regardless of her marital state?" she asked, after detailing the unbelievable exploits of a man named Willie Parker.

Maggie reached over and cut Laurie-Anne's meat. "I don't understand what the harbor has to do with anything."

"Why it has everything to do with it. The reason we don't have a train station is that the man who's so busy chasing skirts says we don't have a harbor. Isn't that right, George?"

"Hmmmmm."

"Says Santa Barbara's not landlocked and therefore not safe enough for a harbor." Mrs. Pickings clucked like a hen with an egg to lay. "If that's not the most ridiculous thing I've ever heard. There's hardly a day goes by that a ship can't go in and out of our bay. That's not true of San Francisco. They might have a harbor, but there's many a day that a ship had best not sail into the Golden Gate. And without a proper harbor, the train will never come to Santa Barbara."

"I can understand how the area would benefit from a train terminal," Dominick agreed.

"Indeed we would. Why some of the best fruit in the state is grown right here in Santa Barbara. But we don't have sufficient means by which to transport it." Mrs. Pickings leaned over and patted Maggie on the arm. "It would also prevent the kind of thing that happened to your little family. The train would put the stagecoaches out of business—none too soon if you ask me."

She then proceeded to recount every mishap, large or small, that had occurred on the San Marcos Pass in recent years. "Ever since Fremont sneaked his men over the pass to capture Santa Barbara from Mexico, it's been one thing after another," she complained, as if the lieutenant colonel and his battalion were to blame for everything that followed their heroic deed. "Accidents. Robberies. Landslides." She snorted. "Mark my words, when they build a railroad through here, it will put an end to the Kissing Bandit!"

Maggie glanced across the table at Dominick, who gave her a warning look. "You don't think the bandit will take up robbing trains?" he asked.

Mrs. Pickings appeared to be stumped by the question. "Oh, dear, I never thought of that. It just proves my original contention that the sheriff needs to earn his keep and capture the man. No one will be safe until that bandit is hanging from a tree, isn't that right, George?"

"Hmmmmm."

Chapter 6

After lunch, the Pickingses drove them by horse and buggy along a surprisingly well-maintained packed-dirt road, past beautiful golden fields of wheat, past scented citrus groves and abundant walnut orchards, toward the quaint, peaceful town of Santa Barbara.

Mrs. Pickings abandoned local gossip in favor of pointing out various landmarks. "Over there to the north is the mission," she explained, nodding toward an old Spanish building with a gleaming red-tiled roof that was outlined against a background of rolling green hills. The colorful flower gardens and vegetable plots surrounded the mission like a lovely patchwork quilt spread out in the sun to dry.

A Franciscan father dressed in a long brown robe girded at the waist stood by a grove of dark-leafed olive trees, his prayer book in hand. Mrs. Pickings waved as they passed, and he nodded his shaven head in return.

Leaving the Santa Ynez Mountains behind, they followed the wide dirt road from the mission to the heart of the village.

Santa Barbara, or El Pueblo Viejo, as it had been called in earlier times, occupied the center of a narrow valley that was sheltered by the mountains and the sea. Every street was lined with tall, graceful eucalyptus or pungent-smelling pepper trees that had been imported from Peru early in the century. Mrs. Pickings explained that the palm trees had first been introduced to the area by the Spanish friars who had traveled to Santa Barbara to work at the mission.

Beyond a barrier of gently rising dunes covered in rank grass, the sparkling blue bay was dotted with fishing boats and Chinese junks. In the distance, the Santa Barbara Islands floated in the mist like anchored ships waiting to be unloaded.

Broad avenues so unlike the narrow streets of San Francisco earned Maggie's approval, as did the little cottages and flowering wisteria vines that trailed up the stucco walls and formed purple archways between neighbors.

As strange as it seemed, Maggie felt as if she'd come home. "I never thought it would be so beautiful."

"It could be," Mrs. Picking said, casting a scornful eye at a small square adobe thatched with reeds, with neither a door nor windowpanes to protect the inhabitants from the elements. "You can say what you want about the Spanish. But at least they learned to enclose their yards." She wrinkled her nose in disapproval as they drove past the section known as Chinatown. Bold Chinese characters painted on wooden signs identified the many little shops that lined both sides of the streets. Displays of dried herbs and exotic curios filled the windows.

"If only the Chinese would learn to do likewise, we would all benefit, wouldn't we, George?"

"Hmmmmm."

Craning her neck to get a better look at the yard of a Chinese family, Maggie was amazed at how many people, mostly children, she could count. Equally amazing was the number of barnyard animals that were crammed into every available space.

"This is Spanishtown," Mrs. Pickings explained as they reached Mission Street.

Although she sympathized with the Chinese families in the area they had just left, Maggie looked at the narrow little side streets of Spanishtown and had to agree that the tile-roofed haciendas with their enclosed courtyards and flower-covered walls were a delight to the eye.

Mrs. Pickings pointed to an enormous building that took up an entire block. "That's the Arlington Hotel."

High Gothic arches allowed the passersby only a glimpse of the lush green velvety lawns and exotic plants that grew inside the walls.

"The streets appear to run diagonally," Dominick said, checking the sun's position. "Neither north nor south, not even east or west. Isn't that confusing?"

"Not if you remember that everything north of State Street is east and everything south of it is west," Mrs. Pickings said matter-of-factly.

Maggie was still trying to comprehend this puzzling geographical oddity when George turned down one of the streets off State, shot up another, and cut a quick left. He then pulled the wagon to a halt in front of a small adobe house that was half hidden by the sprawling branches of an enormous oak tree. Flowering vines climbed up one sparkling white wall, dropping bright-red petals into a gently flowing water fountain in the center of a tiny brick courtyard.

The door flew open, and a woman who looked almost exactly like Mrs. Pickings bustled out amid swaying skirts and flying apron strings.

Mrs. Pickings quickly introduced her sister as Connie Mae Simpson, and explained the situation to her. "I was telling George what a perfect solution this is. You can go to Los Angeles and take care of Papa, and you won't have to worry about someone tearing down the house in your absence."

Mrs. Pickings pointed out an empty field across the way. "That's where the Crummers' old place used to be. And a beautiful place it was. Word is that it was built for a Spanish nobleman. The Crummers went out of town, and when they came back they found their house completely destroyed by vandals."

Maggie's eyes widened. "But who . . . ?"

"Like I explained earlier, there's a group of radicals

who want to get rid of the Spanish influence. Their idea of progress is to put up those dreadful wooden shacks. If you ask me, it makes Santa Barbara look like some frontier town. It's a crying shame. Why," she continued with barely a pause for breath, "they even want to get rid of the Spanish street names. Isn't that right, George? Want to name the streets A, B, and C. It's bad enough that we already have a First, Second, and Third, just like any other town. Why don't they just be done with it and change the name of Santa Barbara to Jonestown?"

"It's a shame," Maggie agreed. She put an arm around Laurie-Anne and looked around for Jamie. There he was, hanging over the fountain, with his feet dangling in the air. She let out a gasp.

But before she had a chance to react, Dominick had grabbed Jamie by the legs and pulled him to safety with a firm but gentle scolding.

Irked that Dominick had seemingly slipped into a paternal role so readily, Maggie tried to concentrate on what Mrs. Pickings was saying. But it wasn't easy. Not with Dominick acting as though he had a right to discipline her children. First Jamie and now Laurie-Anne. He pulled the little girl away from the roses and lifted her into his arms. Maggie watched as he whispered something in Laurie-Anne's ear that made her giggle. What nerve the man had!

While she stood there, hating the way he seemed to be taking over her life, she nodded in agreement with something Mrs. Pickings had said. "We're not going to have trouble, are we?" she asked. "With these radicals?"

"Now, don't you worry about a thing," Mrs. Pickings assured her. The woman stooped to pull a weed from the otherwise perfectly maintained rose garden, then straightened and brushed off her hands. "As long as there's a family living inside, no one is going to bother the place. They only take it upon themselves to tear down buildings that appear deserted. Isn't that right, George?"

George grunted and puffed on his pipe.

"Come along, now," Mrs. Pickings said. "Connie Mae will show you around. Won't you, Connie Mae?"

Connie Mae, taking her cue from George, nodded and led the way through the carved mahogany door into a tiled entryway. They followed the narrow hall to a parlor filled with enough furniture and knick-knacks for a room four times its size.

Maggie's senses began to spin from the sheer visual impact. She quickly yanked Laurie-Anne's hand away from the fragile, hand-painted globe of a gaslight and threw Jamie a warning look. But Dominick already had him firmly in tow.

Although Mrs. Pickings did her utmost to prompt her sister to point out the special features of the house, Connie Mae seemed reluctant to say much. After several unsuccessful attempts to get her sister to cooperate, Mrs. Pickings assumed the role of hostess herself, with her usual aplomb. "As you can see, my sister is an incurable collector."

As she dutifully admired a walnut table filled to capacity with delicate china figurines, Maggie had to agree. Connie Mae certainly seemed to think that in matters of decor, more was better. Every chair, every cushion, and every doily was tufted, ruffled, tasseled, or otherwise trimmed.

Despite the clutter, though, the room had a certain charm. Fringed window shades were half drawn behind spotless white lace curtains, allowing a view of the appealing tree-lined street. Heavy brocade draperies hugged the window frames and puddled onto the polished hardwood floors. Flocked floral wallpaper, rising from the eight-inch baseboard to the ceiling, provided the perfect background for the red-velvet divan and the two matching overstuffed chairs that were pulled close to a cast-iron wood stove. A fine spinet piano was positioned so that the light from the window fell across the dog-eared sheet music.

Maggie expressed surprise that there was no fireplace.

"The Spanish didn't have fireplaces in their homes," Mrs. Pickings explained. "Don't ask me why. But you needn't worry; the stove is most efficient, isn't it, George? The woodpile's at the side of the house and every Tuesday and Thursday the woodman comes by selling almond wood." She closed her eyes and inhaled deeply. "Believe me, after burning almond wood, you'll never settle for anything less."

The house had two bedrooms, a small but adequate kitchen with a well-stocked pantry, and a necessity room. Each room was packed with furniture, and every imaginable space was filled with knickknacks.

Even the walls of the hallway had been used to full advantage. Oil paintings in elaborate frames vied with ornate mirrors. Squeezed in between were bracketed shelves replete with more trinkets than Maggie had ever seen in one place.

Outside in the back yard grew an abundant vegetable garden that included tomatoes, snap beans, peas, onions, and parsley. Bushes bursting with ripe, juicy blackberries bordered the garden. On the other side of a narrow alley along the length of the property stood a grove of citrus trees. The overburdened branches hung low with lemons and oranges whose lovely fresh fragrance filled the afternoon air.

Laurie-Anne tripped over one of the many clay pots that dotted the yard. This particular one was planted with bright-red geraniums. Dominick picked Laurie-Anne up off the ground and lifted her to his shoulders. She was so intrigued with her high perch that she quite forgot she'd skinned her knee.

"I'm taller than you, Jamie!" she called out merrily.

Jamie made a face and hopped along the stepping-stones toward a swing that hung from the gnarled branches of a sprawling oak.

Maggie set the clay pot upright. "I've never seen so

many geraniums as here in Santa Barbara," she told
Mrs. Pickings. In San Francisco geraniums were considered a nuisance and no self-respecting gardener
would tolerate them.

She followed Mrs. Pickings along a narrow dirt path
leading to a spacious carriage room that was completely empty. Given Connie Mae's obsessive need to
use every possible inch of space, Maggie thought it
odd that she would leave the carriage room bare.

The tour complete, Mrs. Pickings showed them
back to the parlor.

Dominick continued to carry Laurie-Anne, freeing
Maggie to keep a watchful eye on Jamie. She dreaded
the thought of staying in a house that was literally
wall to wall with breakables, so she tried to think of
a way to turn down the offer without offending the
two sisters. "It's very kind of you to let us stay, but
we simply couldn't accept your offer."

"Don't be ridiculous," Mrs. Pickings exclaimed.
"You're doing us the favor."

"But . . ."

"What my wife is trying to say," Dominick interjected, "is that we gratefully accept your most generous offer, and we will do everything in our power to
make certain that your house is safe and sound when
you return."

Glaring at him, Maggie politely but firmly protested—to no avail. It was obvious that Mrs. Pickings
considered her objections nothing more than good
manners.

"How sweet of you to be concerned about Connie
Mae's belongings. But if you ask me, should the children accidentally break something, they would be
doing her a favor."

"But ... ."

"Where she gets all this stuff, I have no idea. She's
always had too many things, hasn't she, George?"

George grunted and Maggie, who was feeling sorry

for Connie Mae, decided not to pursue the matter any
further.

"Now don't you worry about a thing." Taking Maggie's silence as compliance, Mrs. Pickings clapped her
hands together in approval. "Then it's settled."

Dominick insisted on paying Connie Mae for three
months in advance. "I doubt we'll be staying that
long, but you never know."

A sick feeling washed over Maggie as she watched
Connie Mae tuck the money into a little purse. She
hated feeling indebted to anyone, but the mere
thought of being obligated in any way to Dominick
Sanders was intolerable!

"Three months will be fine," Connie Mae gushed.
"I'm sure my father will be fully recovered by then."

Mrs. Pickings glanced worriedly at the grandfather
clock that stood in a corner. "If you're going to make
the afternoon stage, I do believe you'd better hurry.
I'll help you pack. George, why don't you go and
purchase her ticket so they know to save room?"

George grunted and headed out the door.

Mrs. Pickings hustled her sister toward one of the
rooms at the end of the hall. "Make yourselves at
home," she called over her shoulder. "It won't take
us long, will it, Connie Mae?"

Maggie pulled Laurie-Anne's hand away from a
lovely cut-glass vase. "Jamie, be a good boy and take
Laurie-Anne out back. I'm sure she'd love for you to
push her on the swing." She narrowed her eyes at
Dominick, who was flipping through a leather-bound
book. "I wish to speak to Mr. Sanders."

At mention of his name, he replaced the book and
lifted a questioning eyebrow as if he couldn't imagine
what she might want to talk about. His feigned innocence was galling.

Trying to contain her irritation, she gently pushed
Jamie and Laurie-Anne toward the kitchen door.
"Hurry up, now! Run along!"

Surprised by his mother's clipped voice, Jamie took

his sister by the hand. "Come on, Laurie-Anne. The last one outside is an ugly green frog."

"I don't want to be a frog," Laurie-Anne protested, running after her brother.

"Don't push her too high," Maggie called after them. No sooner had the back door slammed shut than she marched back into the parlor and confronted Dominick directly, her eyes blazing.

"Mr. Sanders!" she stormed. "We have been in town for only a few hours, and already three people think that we're married!"

"Four," Dominick replied, unperturbed. "And you'd better lower your voice."

"Four?" she gasped in uncertainty.

"If you look out the window, you'll see that Mrs. Pickings is at this very moment telling the news to one of the neighbors."

Maggie hurried to the window, nearly knocking over a Waterford vase in the process, and peered through the lace curtains. Much to her dismay, Mrs. Pickings was standing in front of the house in deep conversation with another woman. It wasn't hard to guess what the two women were talking about.

Maggie turned around and met Dominick's dancing eyes. The fact that he was enjoying himself made her so furious she could hardly maintain her composure, let alone a thought.

Jamie and Laurie-Anne ran inside the house to tell her about a kitten they'd discovered in the back yard.

"Can we keep it, Mama?"

"I don't know, Jamie. It might belong to someone. We'll see. Now run along. Mr. Sanders and I have not finished our talk."

The children ran noisily out, and the back door slammed shut again, which caused a collection of dishes on a wall shelf to rattle. The next instant Connie Mae returned, dragging a valise behind her and complaining about her sister's desertion. "What do you suppose is so important that she must devote her time to the neighbors rather than helping her very own sister pack?"

"I can't imagine." Dominick winked for Maggie's benefit, then went to help the struggling woman. "Let me get that for you."

"Thank you. My, my, how strong you are." Her hand fluttered to the ruffled bodice of her dress. "This is all so unexpected. I had no idea it would be possible for me to go to our dear father so quickly. No idea at all. Why, it was only the day before yesterday that his letter arrived and we learned of his latest health problem. It's so hard to think on such short notice. I know I'll forget something important. I just know it."

"Don't worry," Maggie said. "We'll . . . ah . . . I'll take care of everything in your absence."

"Yes, yes, of course. I knew as soon as I set eyes on you that you could be trusted." She glanced up at Dominick. "And I'll have you know that I am an impeccable judge of character."

"I'm sure you are," Maggie said evenly, but she refused to meet Dominick's eyes. Oh, how the man was enjoying every moment of this. Well, just wait . . .

"There's plenty of food in the pantry," Connie Mae rambled on. "I made plum jelly, and there's smoked ham and cheese."

"Hurry now, Connie Mae," Mrs. Pickings urged, as she came into the parlor with quick, determined steps. "George is here and it will soon be low tide." She explained for Maggie's benefit: "The stage to Los Angeles follows the beach to Carpinteria. The last time Connie Mae took the stage, it got stuck in high tide."

"It didn't get stuck," Connie Mae argued. "It turned over."

"How awful," Maggie said.

"Yes, it was awful," Connie Mae agreed. "I nearly drowned. As it was, everything I took with me was absolutely ruined."

"That's terrible."

Mrs. Pickings dismissed her sister's misfortune with a wave of her hand. "It's your own fault, Connie Mae, for not taking the steamer."

"You know how the ocean affects me."

"Well, then, come along. If we don't hurry, you'll make the stage late, and you'll end up sitting in the surf again!"

Mrs. Pickings led the way outside, and Maggie and Connie Mae followed. Dominick came last, with Connie Mae's valise. After a flurry of last-minute instructions and farewells, Connie Mae and the Pickingses drove off, disappearing in a cloud of dust amid the rumbling of the wagon wheels.

Maggie stood in front of the fountain and waved politely, but as soon as the wagon had driven far enough to be out of earshot she turned on Dominick. "You cannot stay in this house!"

Dominick took her firmly by the arm and walked her into the house. "Keep your voice down, my dear. We don't want the neighbors to talk."

"I don't care if the neighbors talk," Maggie spit out.

"Yes, you do." He closed the door behind them and released her. "What they say about you reflects on Jamie and Laurie-Anne. Remember? You said so yourself."

"And you don't think the fact that we're living in sin will reflect on them?" she stormed.

"Living in sin?" A wicked grin spread across his face. "Why, that's an excellent idea. I was only suggesting that we live under the same roof. But now that I think about it, I do believe your idea has much more merit."

"What I meant," she chewed out, her cheeks ablaze—the very thought!—"is that people will *think* we're living in sin."

Dominick followed her to the parlor and sat on the divan. With deliberate movements, he put his booted feet up on a needlepoint footstool, crossing them at the ankles. He looked relaxed and perfectly at home.

And despite the two-day stubble on his chin, he was handsome in a devilish sort of way. Maggie was incensed that he had suffered through the same ordeal as she had, yet looked none the worse for wear, while she felt thoroughly bedraggled and exhausted.

"No one will think we're living in sin," he said reasonably. "I would say that about now Mrs. Pickings has managed to inform half the population about our holy alliance. By nightfall at the latest, the rest of the town will know about us."

He looked so almighty sure of himself, it was all she could do to keep from picking up one of Connie Mae's glass vases and throwing it at him. Shocked at how close she was to committing such a violation of good manners, she gritted her teeth and clenched her fists, determined to maintain her composure if it killed her. It would never do to let him goad her into some brash reaction. She simply refused to lower herself to his level.

He gave a careless shrug. "Why not sit down and relax? No one will ever suspect that we're anything but a loving and devoted couple."

"Oh, yes, they will!" she snapped. "For I intend to tell the sheriff who you are." She folded her arms across her chest and gave him a self-righteous smile. "Once you're behind bars where you belong, everyone will know how you forced me to lie for you."

Dominick leaned back and stretched his long body to its full length. Watching her like a wolf watches a lamb, he folded his hands behind his head. "Is this the appreciation I get for saving your son?"

He sounded genuinely offended, and she momentarily lowered her guard. "One good deed does not make up for your past transgressions."

"But you do owe me a certain amount of consideration." His expression challenged her to disagree. "Come on, Mrs. Turner—even you can't deny that."

Maggie felt a surge of guilt. She considered herself a fair-minded person who never failed to repay a kindness or service. But that was before she had met the likes of Dominick Sanders. The thought that she owed him anything was disconcerting. On the other hand, she could hardly deny that he did save Jamie. Nor could she deny that had he not paid for their lodgings, she would have been in a fine pickle indeed!

"I'll willing to consider a compromise," she offered. "You leave this house at once and I won't tell the sheriff. As for the money you paid Connie Mae, I can assure you I shall pay back every cent. What do you say? Do we have a deal?"

Dominick took his own sweet time to mull over the offer. Tapping her foot impatiently, she waited. Finally he sat forward, hands clasped between his knees. "I'll leave in the morning."

"Not good enough."

He jumped to his feet. "I said I'll leave tomorrow!"

"No!"

They glared at each other, nose to nose. Because of his considerable height, he was forced to lean over. She, in turn, stood irritatingly erect. Stubborn woman! he thought, stifling the urge to wring her pretty little neck.

How dare he think he can bully me around! Maggie fumed, her fingers itching to throw something that would wipe that mocking look off his face.

He narrowed his eyes and considered whether charm alone would work with her or whether he'd have to resort to force. He'd hate to have to lock her up to keep her from carrying out her threat. But he would if he had to. In any event, he meant to have his way. Tired from the two-day ordeal, he decided that charm would require less effort.

"Come on, Maggie," he cajoled, "have a heart. I'm tired, and I need a good night's sleep. I'll sleep on the divan and leave after breakfast."

Sensing her resistance, he tried another tactic. "I'm sure a fine, charitable woman like yourself wouldn't think of turning someone out in the middle of the night." He studied her face. There was no question in his mind that she thought she had the upper hand. Well, let her think what she wants. She'll soon learn otherwise. In fact, it was all he could do to keep from jumping up and claiming victory. But he wisely decided to wait until success was assured. Not that he had any doubt that he would stay for as long as he deemed necessary, but some inner sense told him not to take anything for granted where Maggie Turner was concerned. "One night is all I'm asking."

"Well . . ." He watched her struggle with her conscience. "All right, then. But you had better leave first thing in the morning."

"As you wish."

The tension diminished between them, and he stepped back. "I'm curious about something. How do you propose to explain my disappearance after I'm gone?"

She tossed her head back, a self-satisfied gleam in her eyes. "I'm sure that even Mrs. Pickings will find it in her heart to forgive me for throwing you out when I tell her you are a womanizing brute who made me live in constant fear for my life!" Maggie smiled a know-it-all smile that irritated him no end. "I even have a few bruises to show her."

This time she had pushed him too far. He grabbed her arm and yanked her to him. "You little wench," he hissed in her ear. "Those bruises were caused by the accident!"

"You and I are the only ones who know that," she shot back. Her voice was unwavering, her eyes bright with challenge. If it hadn't been for the traitorous pulse at her wrist that throbbed beneath his fingers, he would never have suspected the least bit of tribulation on her part. At last, a worthy adversary, he thought, releasing her.

It was serious business that brought him to Santa Barbara, but he wasn't opposed to a little diversion as long as it didn't interfere with his work or in any way encumber him. Maggie Turner was so unlike any woman he'd ever known, there was no danger of her ever becoming more than a diversion. No danger at all. So why shouldn't he permit himself a little sporting fun?

Jamie ran into the room, and Laurie-Anne straggled behind, rubbing her eyes with her little fists. The children looked like orphans, their clothes torn and dirty from their mountain ordeal, their faces smudged with dirt.

Maggie swooped both of them up in her arms and hugged them. "It's time for a bath, my little ones."

"Do we have to?" Jamie asked.

Maggie smiled and rubbed her nose lightly against his. "Yes, you have to."

She straightened up and hustled both children toward the arched doorway. She paused and tossed a look of triumph over her shoulder. "I trust we have a deal, Mr. Sanders."

"We do, indeed, Mrs. Sanders," he shot back with equal triumph.

They stared at each other in uncertainty. Part of the pleasure of winning a battle was the look of defeat on the opponent's face. But if there was defeat to be seen anywhere in that room, it was on Jamie's face, who stood by his mother's side, mulling over the indignities of being forced to bathe.

Seeing her look of distrust, Dominick feared he might have overplayed his hand. Since he realized it was in his best interest to let her think she'd won, he bowed slightly, hoping she would conclude that he was properly humbled by her generosity. "You're a fine, charitable woman," he said, keeping his voice honey-coated without sounding condescending.

His compliment was received with a self-righteous nod of her head. "I should hope so, Mr. Sanders."

Vexed by her superior demeanor, he clenched his fists to hide his irritation. "While you bathe the children, I think I'll . . . ah . . . go out and"—he rubbed his whiskered chin—"pick up a razor. I'll also make arrangements for my morning departure."

"I think that is a very good idea. One more thing—don't call me Mrs. Sanders. My name is Maggie Turner. Mrs. Maggie Turner."

Oozing warmth and charm, he bowed again. "Anything you say, Mrs. *Sanders*."

Chapter 7

The office of the *Santa Barbara Daily Press* was a square stucco building on State Street halfway between the impressive three-story Occidental Hotel and the sprawling, overstocked lumberyard.

Dominick hesitated in front of the newspaper office, his eyes on the sign several doors down that read "Sheriff."

For two years the Kissing Bandit had plagued the surrounding area. Based on a single clue found at the scene of a crime, a bass button depicting the opening of the Lobero Theater, the investigators at the Wells Fargo Detective Bureau were convinced that the bandit lived in or around Santa Barbara. They were equally sure that he was a prominent citizen who could easily get information on gold shipments.

Sheriff Eugene Badger was one of their prime suspects.

Wells Fargo had arranged for Dominick Sanders to be incarcerated in the Santa Barbara jail, where he could keep his eye on the sheriff. If it hadn't been for that unfortunate accident on the pass, he might well have had his man by now.

Dominick tightened his hand on the brass doorknob. No matter. He'd get his man; by God, nothing was going to stand in the way.

He only wished that he didn't have to depend on Maggie Turner for his cover. Damned vexing woman! Of course, he could always tell her the truth; that he was a Wells Fargo detective on special assignment.

The question was, would she believe him? He doubted it. Knowing her, she'd think he'd made the whole story up to keep her from talking to the sheriff.

But there was another reason not to tell her; once he got his man, he had no intention of turning him over to the authorities. He blamed the man known as the Kissing Bandit for the death of his family. That made it a private battle, a private war, and it wouldn't be over until he had personally avenged the death of his wife and child with his own two hands.

Maggie, with her strict moral upbringing, would be horrified to discover that she had been a willing accomplice to such a deed, however justified he thought his actions were. For the sake of her and the children, it would be better if she were forced to assist him against her will.

He regretted having to involve her, but it couldn't be helped. He was close to finding the real bandit. He could feel it in his bones, in his very blood. Tearing his eyes away from the sheriff's sign, he walked into the newspaper office.

The editor, a short, skinny man with a pencil-thin nose and a drooping mustache, glanced up from his rolltop desk and regarded Dominick with a steady gaze.

Dominick checked the name on the editor's desk and introduced himself. "McDonald, is it? Dominick Sanders at your service."

Sam McDonald greeted Dominick with a nod. "What can I do for you, Mr. Sanders?"

"I thought you might like an eyewitness account of the accident on the pass."

The editor's look sharpened; his interest was obviously piqued. "Are you referring to the stage that went over the side of the mountain?"

"So you've heard about the accident?"

"The whole town is buzzing with the news." He sat back, his hands folded across his checkered vest. "You say you witnessed the accident?"

"More than that. I was on that stage, along with my wife and children. Fortunately, my family survived with only minor injuries."

"That is indeed fortunate."

"I thought your readers would enjoy reading a story with a strong human-interest angle."

McDonald's mustache twitched in anticipation. "What do you have in mind?"

Dominick pointed to the front page of the newspaper that was spread across the editor's desk. "Look at this, nothing but crime and misfortune." He moved to the side of the desk so he could read the headlines aloud. For emphasis, he stabbed each bold-type phrase with his finger as he read: "Youths Go on Wild Spree. Thieves Steal Prize Horses. Bandits Hold Up Stage. Another Adobe House Destroyed."

He pulled his hand away, then positioned himself in a strategic place directly in front of the editor.

"Miserable news, all of it. I think your readers might like a little good news for a change. I think they would like to know how my wife and I met and fell in love. How we saved our money and moved to this lovely town, hoping to make a loving Christian home for our two"—he leaned forward and winked—"hopefully one day soon, three—children."

As Dominick spoke, the editor's eyes grew brighter. "This is wonderful." Mr. McDonald found some paper, dipped his pen into the inkwell, and began scribbling frantically to keep up. "How many children?"

"Two." Dominick waited a moment before he continued. "I'm sure your readers will empathize upon learning how our dreams were very nearly dashed when the stage went over the mountainside."

McDonald, writing fast, clucked his tongue.

". . . how we survived the long, chillingly cold night, fearful that any moment we would be attacked by grizzlies, bandits, or . . ." Dominick allowed himself a dramatic pause, "snakes."

Waiting for the editor to catch up, Dominick craned

his neck to read the scrawly handwriting. "Don't forget to mention snakes."

"Would those be rattlers?" the editor asked.

Dominick nodded. "Of the most poisonous kind." He drew back and continued to describe and embellish the details of Jamie's near-fatal fall. "My poor, fragile Maggie was almost ready to throw herself over the mountain after him," Dominick explained.

The thought of Maggie's being described in the newspaper as fragile nearly made him laugh aloud, but he wisely kept a straight face.

"Terrible thing." The editor shook his head. "Absolutely terrible."

Mustering an appropriate tone of reverence, Dominick put a hand on his chest. "It was our love and devotion to each other that helped us through that most difficult trial."

"That's good." The editor scribbled. "Our womenfolk will undoubtedly approve."

"I thought they might. Tomorrow's paper?" he asked.

"Absolutely. Special edition. I'll stay up all night if necessary. I'll arrange to have one delivered to you first thing in the morning. What did you say your wife's name was again?"

"Maggie. That's spelled with two G's. But she prefers to be addressed as Mrs. Dominick Sanders."

The children were still asleep early the following morning when Maggie tiptoed down the dimly lit hall toward the kitchen. She stopped outside the archway leading to the parlor and peered into the room. It was still too dark to see much more than the shadowy forms of the furniture. But Dominick's boots stood neatly on the floor, and his black shirt and bright-red sash were tossed carelessly across a chair, confirming his presence.

She was still annoyed at herself for letting him stay the night. But what else could she have done? He'd looked tired, and the Lord knew she was a charitable woman. Besides, if he had intended to inflict harm on her or the children, wouldn't he have done it before they were rescued? He might be a road agent, but he wasn't a murderer. The thought gave her some measure of consolation, if not complete peace of mind.

Holding her breath, she continued along the hall to the kitchen and quietly closed the door behind her.

Connie Mae's kitchen was every bit as crammed as the rest of the house, with barely enough room on the counter to set even a bowl or a spoon. It took a while for Maggie to scan the overflowing shelves of the pantry and locate the ingredients she needed to prepare breakfast.

After she found the kindling in a bucket outside the back door, she built a fire in the cast-iron stove, started the coffee, and mixed the batter for hotcakes.

No sooner had she set the table and finished squeezing the oranges when Jamie joined her. He was fully dressed and wearing Dominick's black woolen cap. The night before, Maggie had brushed the children's clothes and hung them up to air. But unless her trunk was rescued from the side of the mountain and returned intact, she would have to purchase bolts of fabric and set to work at once making them each a new wardrobe.

"Why are you wearing Mr. Sanders's hat?" she asked.

Grinning, Jamie pushed his head cover forward. "It's a beret," he proudly told her. "Aita gave it to me."

Maggie lifted a brow. "Aita?"

"That's what Dominick told me to call him. It's Back."

"You mean Basque," Maggie corrected.

Jamie gave a vigorous nod of the head. "Yes, Back. Aita said that the beret is one of man's best friends. It keeps the sun out of your eyes in the summer, and if you wear it pulled down on your forehead like this, it will keep the rain off your face."

"I can see why it's good to have a beret of your own." She picked up the bowl of batter and spooned portions onto the hot griddle, which sputtered and sizzled with each glob she added.

"Aita said you can also gather eggs in it." Jamie took an egg out of the bowl on the counter and demonstrated. "And Aita said when he was a little boy, his mother used to wrap a hot brick in his beret and put it between his feet to keep them warm in the winter."

Maggie stilled her hand at the mention of Dominick's childhood. She wanted to hear more. Not because she was interested in the man for any personal reasons, of course. It simply made good sense to know as much as possible about one's enemies.

She didn't realize that her thoughts had drifted until an acrid smell drew her attention back to the griddle. The lacy edges of the hotcakes had turned black. She scraped off the griddle and ladled on more batter, this time giving her full attention to the chore.

"Is Laurie-Anne still asleep?" she asked after a while, as she set a plate of hotcakes in front of Jamie and poured him a second glass of orange juice.

Jamie nodded, stuffed an entire hotcake in his mouth, and dashed outside, eager to explore the field across the way and, no doubt, try out his beret.

Maggie heard him cough and rushed to the door to call him back into the house, but when she saw him running with such abandon, she didn't have the heart. "Don't go too far," she called after him.

She took a minute to inhale the clear, fresh air. Accustomed to San Francisco's damp, foggy mornings, she was cheered by the lovely day that greeted her. March had never seemed so beautiful. Suddenly, all the reservations that had plagued her during the past few months evaporated. It had been a wise move, after all. And she was confident that, once she was

rid of her unwanted guest, she and the children could
make a happy life for themselves in this cozy seaside
town.

Humming to herself, she cleared away Jamie's plate
and eased it into a dishpan of soapy water. She paused
upon hearing the sound of Laurie-Anne's laughter fil-
tering through the walls.

"What in the world?" she murmured, wiping her
hands on a towel. She walked quietly through the
house to see what her daughter found so hilarious.
Laurie-Anne hadn't laughed like that since . . . well,
for a long time.

Come to think of it, none of them had laughed
much—not since Luke had died. Even before then,
there hadn't been much call for gaiety. Her husband's
health hadn't been that good for years, and he had
grown progressively weaker until even the slightest exertion brought on a fit of gasping coughs.

Once their father took to his bed permanently,
Laurie-Anne and Jamie grew to miss the rough-and-
tumble playtimes the three of them had once enjoyed.
Toward the end it had been hard for Jamie, especially,
to understand why Luke could no longer get down on
all fours and pretend he was an old mule, for example,
or one of those elephants that came to San Francisco
each spring with the Phineas T. Barnum circus.

Thinking about those long-ago days, Maggie felt a
wrench inside.

Since her father's death, Laurie-Anne had been a
sullen, fretful child. As much as Maggie understood
her daughter's insecurity, she found it extremely trying. Running a shoemaking business was difficult
enough without having a child clinging to one's skirts.

Fortunately, her San Francisco customers had felt
sorry for her and had been tolerant of her children's
presence, often waiting patiently while she tended to
their needs. But she could hardly expect the same
consideration here in Santa Barbara, where she was a
stranger. Not knowing Luke or the circumstances that

preceded her present situation, Santa Barbara residents would be less likely to accept a whining child in a place of business.

Oh, how different her life would be had her dear, sweet husband, Luke, not been burdened with weak lungs!

She chided herself for dwelling on things over which she had no control and quickened her steps. Outside the necessity room she heard Dominick's low, rumbling laughter.

"You look like a bubble man," Laurie-Anne squealed.

The door was ajar. Curious, Maggie pushed it open a crack further and peered inside the room.

Dominick stood at the mirror. Laurie-Anne, dressed in her cambric drawers and chemise, was perched on the dry sink next to him, her chubby little legs hanging over the side.

Dominick dipped his shaving brush into a small basin filled with water and swished it around until foam began to rise. He then planted a mound of bubbles on Laurie-Anne's pert little nose.

"That tickles," she said, giggling.

"Now you look like me," Dominick said. He picked her up so she could see her face in the beveled looking glass that hung on the wall between two brass sconces.

Laurie-Anne stared at herself and wiggled her nose. "I look funny."

"You look like a snowman," Dominick said, setting her down on the floor.

"What's a snowman?" Laurie-Anne asked.

"A man made out of snow, of course."

"What's snow?"

Dominick picked up a razor, unfolded it, and honed the blade along a leather strop that hung from a nail. "It's cold and white and falls out of the sky like rain."

"What's rain?"

"You know what rain is," Maggie said, meeting

Dominick's eyes in the mirror. "Remember how we got all wet in San Francisco?"

"And Jamie got all muddy." Laurie-Anne's small frame shook with fresh laughter.

The sound lifted Maggie's spirits. "He most certainly did." Reluctant to put an end to the fun, she hesitated a moment before adding, "Breakfast is ready." As she pulled her eyes away from Dominick's, she realized to her dismay that he wore nothing from the waist up. In a flash, she registered a wave of sinewy muscles rippling across a broad-shouldered back.

Flushing furiously, she turned and fled down the hall. She really wished she had her own clothes. Connie Mae's dressing gown was functional but several sizes too large, all but burying her in its voluminous folds and the sickeningly sweet smell of violets. By the time she reached the kitchen, she had managed to gain control over her senses—and her thoughts.

Glory be, what was the matter with her? Worrying about her appearance when her only concern should be getting rid of that despicable outlaw! When she stopped to roll up the annoyingly long sleeves of the dressing gown, she caught sight of her reflection in the glass door of the hoosier. The bruise on her forehead had turned a delicate blue. Her face was framed by wisps of honey-colored hair that had escaped from the braid she wore at night. Good, she thought crossly, still irked that she had allowed the outlaw to stay the night. She was not willing to admit, even to herself, that he had given her no choice in the matter, but she took comfort in the thought that her unsavory appearance would surely drive him away!

Laurie-Anne ran into the kitchen moments later, still covered in shaving cream. "My, my!" Maggie smiled as she wiped her daughter's face clean and gave her a warm, loving hug. "Now drink your juice. Then you'll be big and strong."

"Will I be big and strong like Aita?" Laurie-Anne asked.

Stifling the image of broad shoulders and rippling muscles that quickly came to mind, Maggie bit her lower lip. "Maybe."

When Dominick walked in, his presence instantly seemed to fill every nook and cranny of the kitchen like wine fills every recess of the mouth. "Good morning," he said cheerfully and poured himself a cup of coffee.

Her senses alert, she ventured a wary glance in his direction and was relieved to find that he had donned a shirt.

Still, he was too relaxed, too sure of himself, for her peace of mind, with not the slightest bit of concern evident on his dark, handsome face. It seemed to her that he had a lot to be concerned about. Not that she was an expert in such matters, of course. But wouldn't a bandit have good reason to worry?

Was he really so sure that she wouldn't turn him in? Or that the sheriff wouldn't get wind of his true identity and come looking for him?

Dominick pulled out a chair to sit on and winked at Laurie-Anne, who watched his every move with open and innocent adulation. Studying her daughter's face, Maggie stiffened. It both worried and annoyed her that Dominick had so quickly wormed his way into the children's affections. It had clearly been a mistake to agree to let him stay the night, and the sooner he left, the better it would be for everyone.

Eager to be rid of him, she quickly added more hotcakes to a plate and slammed it down on the table in front of him. He met her eyes questioningly, then reached for the clay crock of maple syrup.

"Are you angry with me?" he asked innocently.

Since she didn't want to argue with him in front of Laurie-Anne, she tempered her voice. "What on earth would make you think that?"

"Most people don't slam things down in front of me unless I'm pointing a gun at them."

Maggie nearly choked at the mention of a gun, but

managed to recover quickly for Laurie-Anne's sake. She intended to keep her temper if it killed her. "If you don't mind, Mr. Sanders, I would prefer that you not make reference to your . . . illegal activities in front of the children."

Dominick looked blank. "Pointing a gun at someone is not illegal, unless you pull the trigger. Oh, you mean robbing stages?"

"Mr. Sanders!"

He shrugged. "It's difficult not to speak about one's profession in company."

"You should have thought about that before you chose your . . . profession." She slammed an empty glass on the table in front of him, next to the pitcher of orange juice. "I expect you to leave as soon as you've eaten."

He stilled his fork. "I was thinking of renting a rig and driving up to the pass to get your baggage." He lowered his eyes and traced the slight body that was all but buried in Connie Mae's dressing gown.

Hating the familiarity of his gaze, Maggie turned back to the stove. Nevertheless, she felt his eyes on her, sensed exactly the path his gaze took. Feeling her cheeks grow warm, she scooped the last of the hotcakes off the griddle. "That won't be necessary. I'm sure Wells Fargo will make arrangements for retrieval." Thinking of the bodies of the two men that might still be lying on the side of the mountain, she shuddered.

Jamie rushed into the house. The sound of the slamming door practically shattered her already taut nerves. "Glory be, Jamie, must you slam the door?" Almost immediately she regretted her harsh words. For reasons she was at a loss to explain, Dominick managed to bring out the worst in her. Sometimes it took no more than a glance at his handsome, smug face for her to begin to boil inside.

"Mrs. Pickings is here," Jamie said breathlessly. "I saw her drive up in a horse and buggy."

Muttering to herself, Maggie hurried from the kitchen to the front door just as the woman approached. "Good morning, Mrs. Pickings. You're up and about early. Did your sister make her stage?"

"With time to spare," Mrs. Pickings said, holding up a basket. "I thought you could use some fresh eggs." She ambled past the water fountain and handed Maggie a basket filled with eggs so fresh that they still felt warm to the touch.

"Thank you. Won't you have a cup of coffee?"

"Maybe another time. I really can't stay long." Mrs. Pickings followed her into the house and down the hall to the kitchen. "I just had to tell you how very much I enjoyed reading that wonderful article about you."

Maggie practically dropped the basket of eggs. "Article?" She tried in vain to find a spot on the crammed counters for the eggs and finally set the basket on the table.

"Why, yes, you know, the one in the morning paper." Pausing for a moment to consider Maggie's astonished expression, Mrs. Pickings exclaimed loudly, "Don't tell me you haven't read it yet? Oh, dear, now I've spoiled everything. No matter. I just wanted you to know how proud I am to have made your acquaintance. It gives me great satisfaction to know that such a remarkable family is taking care of my sister's home. If there's anything I can do for you . . . Anything . . ."

She turned her attention to Dominick. "The paper said nothing about your profession, but if you need a letter of recommendation . . . by the way, what is it that you do?"

"I rob stagecoaches," Dominick said, keeping his eyes firmly on Maggie's face.

Mrs. Pickings looked flustered, and Maggie's heart literally stopped. For a horrifying moment, no one spoke.

"Don't believe anything my . . . husband says,"

Maggie stammered at last. She flashed him a look of warning, which he blithely ignored.

Mrs. Pickings burst out laughing. "I love a man with a sense of humor, don't you?"

Maggie forced a smile and in an effort to hide her mortification poured herself a cup of coffee. "Are you sure you don't want a cup?"

"Well, if you insist." Mrs. Pickings plunked her bulky body down on a chair opposite Dominick and reached for the sugar bowl. "So what do you really do, Mr. Sanders?" Mrs. Pickings fluttered her eyelashes and giggled. It was obvious to Maggie that the man had some kind of appeal that only she herself failed to see.

"Shoes," Maggie said, not giving Dominick a chance to reply this time. She set a cup of coffee in front of her guest. "We design and make shoes."

Mrs. Pickings looked from one to the other. "Both of you?"

Dominick stood and draped an arm around Maggie's shoulder. "We do everything together. Isn't that right, my love?"

"Lovely!" Mrs. Pickings exclaimed. "Just like the article in the newspaper said. Shoes, you say? Perfect. It's almost impossible to find a decent pair of shoes around here. The last time we had a traveling shoe salesman through these parts was in the fall, when we had those torrential rains. The last I saw of the man, he and his horse were floating down State Street." Mrs. Pickings chuckled and stirred a spoonful of sugar into her coffee. "I'll recommend you to all my friends."

A sudden boom shook the house, rattling the dishes and causing the windows to vibrate.

Startled, Maggie gasped. "What was that?"

Mrs. Pickings waved her hand through the air. "Don't worry. It's only the *Golden Crest* arriving in the harbor. That steamer has absolutely no schedule. It comes and goes when it darn well pleases. The only way you know it has arrived is when it shoots off its signal."

"But it must have some sort of schedule," Dominick said.

Mrs. Pickings shook her head. "None. If you're thinking about booking passage, prepare yourself to race down to the wharf at any time during the night or day, as soon as you hear the boom of the cannon. It's the only way you know it's setting sail. I once had to scramble out of bed at three in the morning and race down to the wharf. I managed to jump aboard just at the last minute."

Mrs. Pickings finished her coffee and stood up. "I'd best be getting along. Now you read that article, do you hear?"

"We wouldn't miss it for the world, would we, Maggie?" Dominick said.

Seething, Maggie walked Mrs. Pickings down the hall to the door. "Thank you for the eggs."

"I'm delighted to be of service." With a cheerful wave, Mrs. Pickings ambled along the pathway, hiked up her voluminous skirts, and climbed into her buggy.

Maggie waited until Mrs. Pickings had gathered up the reins and taken off in a cloud of dust; then she stormed back into the house to confront Dominick.

The smug look on his face stopped her in her tracks. It took her a moment to compose herself enough to notice that he was holding up a newspaper so she could read the headline: "Santa Barbara Welcomes Loving and Charitable Family!"

"The editor of the newspaper was kind enough to arrange to have one delivered to our doorstep," he explained. "It was there when I got up this morning."

Too astonished to speak, she stared transfixed at the tall bold print that took up the top half of the paper and felt suddenly sick to her stomach.

Taking a deep breath, she calmly ordered the children to their rooms. The fact that they left the kitchen without a word told her she was not as much in control as she thought. Then with a wide swing of her arm, she grabbed the paper from him and forced herself to read the article: "Mr. and Mrs. Dominick Sanders and their two children were the sole survivors of Tuesday's unfortunate stagecoach accident on the San Marcos Pass. Mr. Sanders described the ordeal as horrendous and recounted a gripping tale of fighting off grizzly bears, rattlesnakes, and robbers."

It was worse than anything she could ever have imagined. She literally began to shake and when Dominick was quoted as describing her as fragile, it was all she could do not to scream. Fragile, indeed!

She shot him visual daggers and continued to read. When she came to the part about their plans to have a third child, Maggie could no longer contain herself.

She threw the paper onto the floor. "Of all the despicable tricks!" she screamed. "How dare you put me in such a position?"

Dominick picked up the paper and folded it in half. "And what position might that be?"

"Don't play dumb with me! You know very well that we agreed to let everyone think your departure was the result of an unhappy marriage. Now, thanks to a pack of unmitigated deceptions, you have made it extremely difficult for me to come up with a plausible explanation for your departure."

"I have not made it difficult," he argued. "I've made it impossible."

Unwilling to admit that he was right, she fumed inwardly. There had to be a way to get rid of him, there just had to be. "You had no right to put me in this impossible situation! How in the world will I ever explain your sudden departure now?"

"You can't." He grinned and dark, devilish lights danced in his eyes. "That's why we have no choice but to carry on with our original plan."

"*Your* plan," she corrected. "It was never my plan." She paced back and forth, casting disbelieving

looks at the offending newspaper. "I'll tell them . . ."
More pacing. "I'll say . . ."

Finally she stopped and regarded him triumphantly.
"I'll say that you went back east to buy supplies for
our business and had an unfortunate accident." Her
eyes gleamed. "Perhaps I could say that you had an
unfortunate meeting with the Kissing Bandit."

"I'm not going anywhere."

"Then I have no choice but to turn you in to the
sheriff."

"And expose your children to gossip and disgrace?
I don't think so."

She bit her lip. He had her over a barrel and he
knew it. Still, she wasn't about to give in that easily.
There had to be a way to be rid of him. She thought
a moment. She was a reasonably sane woman who
was quite capable of taking care of herself. As long
as she maintained control—that was the key. She took
a deep breath and began again, priding herself on the
civil tone of her voice. "Just exactly what is it you
want?"

He narrowed his eyes warily. "You know what I
want. I want us to continue pretending that we're man
and wife until I have completed my business. At which
point I shall leave."

Control, she must maintain control. "If you think
for one moment that I intend to stand around idly
while you terrorize the area, you better think again."

"I have no intention of robbing anyone, if that's
what you mean. I'm looking for someone who, in fact,
robbed me. And until I find that person, I can assure
you that I'll do nothing that would likely get me in
trouble."

Not knowing whether to believe him, she pondered
her choices. She could, of course, return to San Francisco. But that would mean that Jamie would not be
able to benefit from Santa Barbara's healthier climate.
As much as she hated to admit it, Dominick was right;
going to the sheriff at this point would put her own

reputation in question. Not only would that be detrimental to the children but it might ruin her chances of making a success of her shoemaking business. There was also the matter of her finances. If she had to find suitable accommodations elsewhere, she would be required to use the money she needed to open her business. It appeared that she had no other choice but to go along with this ridiculous charade.

The feeling of being trapped and under this man's power was very offensive. Suddenly a third alternative occurred to her. If Dominick Sanders insisted upon staying, she would simply make his life so miserable that he would gladly leave of his own accord.

Lifting her chin in defiance, she eyed him boldly. For several long minutes they stared at one another, neither of them flinching or in any way backing down. An outsider would have been at a loss as to which of them had the upper hand. "All right," she said magnanimously. "I'll let you stay."

Dominick clamped his jaw shut. As if you had a bloody choice! he thought irritably.

"On one condition."

Now she was giving him conditions, for God's sake. Who did she think she was? He'd never compromised in his life, and he wasn't about to begin now. Still, he was curious. The woman had gall, and as much as he hated to admit it, she had earned his grudging admiration. "Name it!" he growled impatiently.

"I will not tolerate your outlawing ways!"

"I told you I had no intention of pursuing my profession."

"I'm fully aware of your intentions, Mr. Sanders. And I think it time that you be made aware of mine. I intend to watch you like a hawk. As long as you reside in this house, you will be a model citizen!"

Dominick threw back his head and laughed. "This I've got to see."

"Oh, you'll see it, Mr. Sanders. Make no mistake!" Head held high, she sailed out of the room. He didn't

like the sound of her threat. Nor did he take kindly
to the holier-than-thou attitude she displayed. There
was no question in his mind but that the woman was
up to something.

Chapter 8

For the next half hour or so, Maggie paced back and forth in Connie Mae's small bedroom and tried to convince herself that the situation wasn't as bad as it appeared. The man might have the upper hand for now, but she intended to do everything in her power to change that.

Feeling somewhat better, she dressed in her yellow traveling suit. Before retiring the night before, she had taken great pains to brush away as much dust and grime from the fabric as possible and had hung it near an open window to air. Even so, the skirt was wrinkled and the seam that she'd hastily repaired on the trail refused to lie flat. Nevertheless, it would have do until she had an opportunity to replace her wardrobe.

She undid her braid and brushed her hair until it shone. With nimble fingers, she then worked the long golden strands into a neat bun at the back of her head and arranged her bangs into a cluster of soft curls around her face.

Laurie-Anne and Jamie ran into her room, filled with news of their early morning explorations.

"I saw a rabbit," Laurie-Anne said.

"That's wonderful, dear."

"The kitten's gone," Jamie complained.

"Perhaps it found its way home."

"Aita said that as soon as we have our own house, we can have our own kitten."

Maggie slammed down her hairbrush. "Oh, he did, did he?" How dare he make decisions about what her children could or could not have? The man had gone too far!

Eyes ablaze, she sent the children back outside and stormed through the house looking for him, but he was nowhere to be found. She would have to wait and confront him later. Meanwhile, she set to work cleaning up the kitchen.

Normally a cheerful worker, today she muttered to herself, slammed and banged every cupboard and door within reach, and cranked the handle of the water pump with short, angry strokes. While she pumped, banged, swept, and scrubbed, she plotted ways to torment Dominick.

It wasn't her nature to be spiteful or vindictive, but she appeased her conscience by reminding herself that the man was an outlaw and as such was not entitled to normal consideration. Besides, she had no choice in the matter. It simply wouldn't do to allow this impossible situation to continue a moment longer than necessary.

A clattering sound drew her away from her thoughts. Setting the kettle on the wood stove to heat, she hurried to the parlor window to find out the source of the racket. A horse and wagon sat in front of the house, and two men were unloading pieces of lumber onto the lawn.

Fearing that the men were the radicals that Mrs. Pickings had referred to, come to tear down Connie Mae's adobe house and replace it with a more modern one, she raced to the kitchen, grabbed the long-handled broom, and dashed down the hall to the front door.

Ready to fight tooth and nail to save the house that Connie Mae had entrusted to her care, she flew outside like a farmer's wife chasing a fox away from prized chickens.

With her broom poised to strike, she charged toward the two startled men. "What is the meaning of this?"

It was then that she saw Dominick, looking over his shoulder at her as if she'd taken leave of her senses. He threw a piece of lumber onto the growing pile and turned to face her. "What are you getting yourself all in a dither about? I'm only building some crates."

Confused, she lowered the broom. The two men exchanged meaningful glances and backed away from her until they had reached the safety of the wagon.

"Crates?" she whispered, embarrassed, and feeling more than a bit foolish.

"Since I'm going to be around for a while, I decided to build some crates to store Connie Mae's numerous possessions in. I can't turn around in that damned parlor without knocking something over."

Maggie eyed the stack of lumber. "Oh, dear, I wouldn't feel right about moving Connie Mae's things."

"I'm just going to store them in that empty carriage house out back. Otherwise, I fear we'll break something."

As much as she hated to admit it, he did have a point. She would feel terrible if something got broken, and already they'd had several close calls. "If you think she won't mind."

She nodded briskly to the deliverymen. "Carry on, gentlemen." Head held high, she made a quick retreat and breathed a sigh of relief upon reaching the house.

She spent the rest of the morning hunting up pieces of fabric and newspapers to wrap around the seemingly endless assortment of fragile knickknacks, bone china dishes, and fine cut-glass vases.

Amazingly, in a few short hours she'd carefully packed each piece away and cleared off every shelf, tabletop, and windowsill. Without the clutter, the house began to take on a restful charm that lifted her spirits and made her forget, at least momentarily, her earlier resentment at Dominick for forcing her to comply with his wishes and for overstepping his authority with the children.

In no time at all, Dominick had proved himself a

capable craftsman and had constructed enough crates to hold a major portion of Connie Mae's possessions. By midafternoon, he'd carted the last of the lot to the carriage house and Maggie had finished polishing the smooth, clear surfaces of the end tables.

She was busily arranging a vase of freshly picked roses when the sheriff and his deputy arrived on her doorstep. Jamie was in the back yard helping Dominick, and Laurie-Anne was taking a nap.

Introducing himself as Sheriff Badger, the taller of the two men lifted his hat to reveal a head full of curly black hair. "Sorry to bother you, ma'am, but me and my deputy here gathered as much as we could from the mountainside. Thought you might like to come out to the wagon and claim what's yours."

Gratified at the thought of being able to dress herself and the children in fresh clothes, she thanked the sheriff and followed the men out to the wagon. "That's very kind of you, Sheriff. I had no idea I'd get my things back so quickly, if at all."

"You have Deputy Sheriff Gilroy here to thank for that, ma'am. He was up at the pass first thing this morning with as many volunteers as he could round up."

Maggie turned to the younger man. "I can't tell you how grateful I am."

The deputy yanked off his hat and grinned a lop-sided grin. His face was dotted with freckles the same rusty color as his hair. "My pleasure, ma'am."

She peered into the wagon and pointed to the black leather trunk that had once belonged to her father. "That's mine," she said.

"That's all?" the sheriff asked.

"Yes," she replied, watching the two men lift the trunk over the sides of the wagon and set it down on the lawn.

"Don't forget our carpetbag, love," Dominick's voice rang out behind her.

She turned and faced him. "Our carpetbag?"

He smiled. "The black one, remember?" He pointed to the bag that was packed between a wheel and a horsehair seat that had been salvaged from the wreckage.

Dominick held out his hand to the sheriff. "I'm Dominick Sanders. I can't tell you how obliged I am to you. Believe me, there's nothing worse than a wife with nothing to wear."

"If you've been married any length of time," the sheriff replied, "then you know it will take more than a trunk full of clothes to convince the missus that she has anything to wear."

Dominick grinned. "You're right about that, Sheriff. How does that old saying go? 'A woman with nothing to wear needs no less than three trunks to keep it in.'"

The sheriff laughed so heartily, it seemed to Maggie that it was only polite to laugh with him. But she laughed more from nerves than mirth, convinced that any moment the sheriff would suddenly realize who Dominick was and arrest her for harboring an outlaw.

"That's the way womenfolk are all right," the sheriff said, slapping his thigh. He reached over the side of the wagon for the carpetbag and handed it to Dominick.

"Thank you," Dominick said and put the bag on the lawn next to the trunk. "I can manage from here."

The sheriff nodded. "I do have some questions to ask." Maggie sucked in her breath and the sheriff glanced at her anxiously. "Nothing to worry about, ma'am. I'm required to send a report to Wells, Fargo on any incidents involving their stagecoaches that occur in my jurisdiction."

Swallowing hard, Maggie nodded. "We could talk better inside. Would you like some refreshment? I made fresh lemonade and . . ." She was talking too fast, but she couldn't seem to stop herself. "I'm sure I can find some cookies or teacakes in the pantry."

Dominick slipped an arm around her shoulders, and

although it appeared on the surface to be a loving gesture, the pressure of the hand digging into her shoulder was clearly a warning that bid her to be silent.

"My wife is still rather upset from the ordeal," Dominick explained smoothly. "Could the questions wait until she's had time to recover?"

"Yes, yes, of course," the sheriff concurred, his eyes full of sympathy. "There's no hurry. When you're ready, stop by the office."

"Thanks, Sheriff, we'll do that," Dominick said lightly, keeping his arms firmly around Maggie's shoulder. "My wife and I are eternally grateful for the return of our belongings."

"If anything is missing, just let me know."

Maggie watched the sheriff climb into the wagon and reach for the reins. There was no way she would ever be able to convince him of her innocence in Dominick's scheme after this. She had played her part to the hilt, offering refreshments like the perfect little wife and—oh, how could she?—laughing at one of Dominick's jokes!

Just wait, she swore silently. She pulled away from Dominick and stomped into the house, eager to finish plotting her revenge. She would find a way to get rid of him if it was the last thing she did!

That night after she had put the children to bed, she paced around the bedroom until the wee hours of the morning, but still could settle on no firm plan.

The problem was, every time she came up with a deliciously vindictive way to get rid of the man, she would hear her father's stern voice rising from the past to remind her of a Christian's duty toward enemies. She had never before questioned the wisdom of loving a foe, but of course this was her first experience in dealing with one.

At long last an idea occurred to her. Stopping in midstride, she sank down on the wooden chest at the foot of the bed, and a slow smile began to spread across her face. She didn't have to do anything all that terrible; just little things would do, annoying little things that might very possibly play on a person's nerves. With this thought fixed squarely in her mind, she climbed into bed and sank beneath the covers, feeling a sense of satisfaction and anticipation. It seemed that it was quite possible to accomplish her goal and still maintain her integrity. Yes, indeed it did.

In the days that followed, Maggie concentrated on those "little" things. She managed to burn their meals, serve cold coffee, and leave her darning needles positioned in such a way that Dominick never committed himself to sitting on an upholstered seat again without first searching it thoroughly. The entire time she was tormenting him, she allowed herself to be in his company as little as possible.

That was why it surprised her when he walked into the kitchen that first Sunday morning, dressed in a stylish split jacket, gray trousers, and vest, and announced his intention to join them for church.

She eyed him suspiciously. "Why?"

He looked wounded. "Why does anyone go to church?"

Being a minister's daughter, she had had it drilled into her that proper doses of religion could bring about a person's salvation—provided, of course, that the person seriously wanted to change. But she harbored no such assumptions regarding Dominick's intentions. So what was he up to?

More important, how could she turn this to her own advantage?

"Besides, I think it would look rather strange for me not to accompany my family to church, don't you agree?"

She quickly reviewed the possibilities.

It hadn't taken long to find out from the neighbors the name of the minister to avoid at all costs. It was the neighbors' consensus that more people had died from boredom from the Reverend Metcalf's sermons than had been killed during the War between the States.

Given that advice, she had decided to avoid Reverend Metcalf. But that was before she knew that Dominick would be attending church with them.

"Have you heard of Reverend Metcalf?" she asked innocently.

"Can't say that I have," he answered. "Why do you ask?"

"No reason," she said, smiling to herself. "Come along, children, it's time for church." She led the way outside, feeling virtuous and content. She was more determined than ever to make Dominick's life utterly miserable. It was her Christian duty.

The Congregational church was one of the town's most impressive churches, second only to the mission. Its Gothic buildings and handsome bell tower could be seen for miles around.

Although it was a bright, sunny day in mid-March, with not a cloud in the sky, the church was dimly lit inside and a damp, musty chill filled the air. A hushed silence stretched between flickering candles as the congregation quietly took their places on the hard wooden pews. The only sound was that of the church bells pealing out the call to worship.

Maggie resisted the urge to sit in the anxiety seats, the first row reserved for sinners especially in need of redemption, and chose instead a pew in the middle of the church, away from the drafty doorways. Without benefit of the sun, the wind off the ocean was cold.

During the unendurably long service that followed, Maggie rocked a bored and restless Laurie-Anne on her lap. She felt guilty for inflicting such torture upon her children but found some consolation in the thought that sitting through a service like this could not help but build character.

Besides, any reservations she might have had were quickly dispelled by the totally bored expression on Dominick's face. After one furtive glance at him, she smiled to herself and tried not to think about the lower portion of her body, which was becoming numb from sitting so long. Nor did she allow herself to dwell on her own boredom.

If she had to suffer a little to make him suffer a lot, she was willing to make the sacrifice. Still, it was both gratifying and worrisome to discover that the Reverend Mr. Metcalf not only lived up to his reputation but was close to exceeding it.

Jamie wiggled himself off the pew and crawled along the floor, no doubt trying to escape. Dominick caught him by the seat of the pants and lifted him back on the seat beside him.

Silently cursing, Dominick shifted his body and stifled a yawn. He frowned at the shadow of a righteous smile that hovered at the corner of Maggie's mouth. He didn't need a crystal ball to guess what was going through her mind. Damned woman! Look at her gloat! Well, it couldn't be helped. Right now he had to concentrate on getting to know as many people in town as possible. It was the only way he was going to find his man. And as soon as the reverend finished his long-winded sermon and the service was over, he intended to introduce himself around. One of the things he had learned from other detectives was the value of becoming friends with the town's busybodies and gossips. Judging by the curious stares he and Maggie were subjected to and the constant whispers that floated around them, he was willing to bet he was going to learn more about the town's inhabitants than he would ever have wanted to know.

He pulled his gold watch from his vest and checked the time registered on its ivory face. Before this day spent sandwiched between a three-year-old and a five-year-old, listening to a tedious diatribe on the evils of sin, Dominick had never fully understood the concept of hell. Now, however, he had a much more clear understanding. Both children vacillated between fear prompted by the minister's ravings and near rebellion at having to sit still for so long.

At one point Jamie lifted himself up on his knees and whispered in Dominick's ear, "What are the flags for?" He pointed to the row of American flags that hung overhead.

"To honor the men who died in service," Dominick replied, hoping he didn't have to explain the War between the States—or any other war, for that matter.

With wide eyes, Jamie looked around at the blank-faced congregation. "Do you think anyone will die at this service, Aita?"

Dominick shifted his aching backside and folded his arms across his chest. "I sincerely hope not."

At long last the reverend ran out of sins to expound upon, and his sermon ended with a collective sigh from the congregation.

Maggie was eager to leave as soon as church was over, but Dominick insisted upon staying and exchanging pleasantries with everyone. "Aren't you the one who's always so interested in being neighborly?" he teased her. He gave her no chance to respond, but introduced himself to a matronly woman dressed in black.

His easy smile and casual manner masked the real intent of his seemingly innocent questions. By the time they left the church, Dominick had learned one or two interesting things that were worth checking on. One was that Sheriff Badger's wife loved the opera. If that were the case, then it was quite possible that the sheriff had been among those in attendance at the gala opening of the Lobero Theater. It shouldn't be that difficult to find out. More difficult would be to discover whether the sheriff still had Lobero's souvenir brass button in his possession.

*　　*　　*

Early the next morning, Dominick and Maggie set out for the sheriff's office to make their report. Mrs. Pickings, wholeheartedly approving of the way the house looked in Connie Mae's absence, had generously offered to watch Laurie-Anne and Jamie for them.

"It will only upset the children to have to hear all the details of the accident again," she'd said.

"You're absolutely right," Dominick agreed.

Maggie, knowing that his main concern was what the children might say should the sheriff question them, decided to take full advantage of the morning and goad him to the limit.

"Let me do the talking," he cautioned as they walked side by side along the boardwalk of State Street.

"Don't you trust me?" she asked, adjusting the ties of her sunbonnet.

"Of course, I trust you," he said cheerfully. "But you might say something inadvertently that you would come to regret."

"I can't imagine what I could say that I would ever regret," Maggie said.

"Just in case, I'll do the talking." He opened the door of the sheriff's office and held it for Maggie.

Sheriff Badger rose from behind his desk and extended his hand. "Mr. and Mrs. Sanders. It's good of you to drop by. Sit down. Sit down."

Maggie chose the chair closest to the sheriff.

The sheriff sat down himself and shuffled through the papers on his desk. "This shouldn't take long. As I understand it, the stagecoach lost control when it was coming down the pass."

"That's true," Dominick said.

"Do you know what might have caused the driver to lose control? Did something spook the horses?"

Dominick shrugged. "It's possible."

Maggie tossed her head. "It was the driver's fault,"

she said. "And I want that in the report. He had no
regard for human lives."

"I'm surprised to hear that," Sheriff Badger said,
"Old Crabshaw had a reputation as one of Wells,
Fargo's best drivers."

"If he is the best driver, I would hate to see their
worst!"

"Yes . . . well . . ." The sheriff jotted down some
notes. "Did either of you talk to the other passenger?"

Surprised by the question, Maggie glanced at Dominick.

"The passenger slept during most of the journey,"
Dominick explained. "And was not too friendly."

"Snored all the way," Maggie added, stabbing the
desk with her finger. "And I want that in the report!"

"Snored, you say?" The sheriff wrote that down
and then tapped his pen on the edge of his desk. "It's
mighty strange if you ask me. The man had no form
of identification on him. Nothing."

"Perhaps someone went through his pockets." Maggie watched Dominick through the fringe of her eyelashes. She wondered if Dominick had made Jamie
empty the man's pockets while she was still uncon-
scious. Jamie had still been searching for the missing
key when she regained consciousness, but it had never
occurred to her that Dominick might have already
forced Jamie to empty the guard's pockets of anything
that might help to identify Dominick as the Kissing
Bandit.

The sheriff sat back in his chair and flexed his fingers. "Are you saying he might have been robbed by
a road agent?"

"That's exactly what I'm saying," Maggie said,
meeting Dominick's eyes. A battle of silent warnings
raged between them before Maggie shifted her gaze
back to the sheriff.

"It's possible, of course," the sheriff said, "but that
opens up another mystery."

"Another mystery?" Maggie asked.

"Why wasn't the driver robbed as well?"

Maggie boldly met Dominick's eyes. "I'm sure there must be a perfectly logical explanation."

Dominick's mouth twitched. "Of course there is. The thief was frightened off before he got to the driver." He turned to the sheriff. "Perhaps by the arrival of your very efficient and extremely well-organized men."

The sheriff looked pleased. "You're probably right. In fact, I'll put that in the report. It doesn't hurt to let people know we're doing our job." He picked up several sheets of paper and slipped them into a portfolio. "Unless you have anything else to add, I won't keep you any longer."

"About the passenger . . ." Dominick asked. "Have you notified the next of kin?"

"Can't," the sheriff said. "We have no idea who he was or why he was traveling to Santa Barbara. Afraid we'll have to bury him in the Strangers' Cemetery outside of town."

"You have a cemetery for strangers?" Maggie asked.

"Have to, ma'am. You'd be surprised at how many strangers ride into town and get themselves killed. One poor fellow never even made it into town. Fell off a ship right out there in the bay. He was a stowaway. No one knew who he was. Where he came from."

"Do you know who's in charge of funeral arrangements for the stranger?" Dominick asked.

"There won't be any funeral arrangements. He'll be buried tomorrow afternoon in an unmarked grave."

Dominick's eyes narrowed. "I see."

"I think that's all the questions I have," the sheriff said. "Unless, of course, you have any."

"Just one," Dominick said. "I understand you're an authority on opera."

"Not me." The sheriff grimaced. "Personally, I

can't stand it. I only make an occasional appearance to keep the wife happy. You know how that is."

"As a matter of fact, I do," Dominick said. "You said the burial was tomorrow."

The sheriff nodded. "At three o'clock sharp."

After leaving the sheriff's office, Dominick was quiet and withdrawn.

Maggie glanced at his rigid profile. "Why all the interest in the guard?" she asked. "What do you care about his funeral arrangements? The man was taking you to prison."

Dominick gave her a sideways glance. "Maggie, if I didn't know you better, I'd think that you have no respect for the dead."

"I respect the dead," she argued and then, recalling the guard's obnoxious behavior, added, "Unfortunately, it's the only way that some people *can* be respected."

"I'm glad you feel that way. Then you'll have no objections if we pay our last respects to the man tomorrow."

Maggie whirled around to face him, hands on her hips, eyes flashing. "I have no intention of going to that man's funeral!"

"Tsk, tsk," Dominick clucked. "Why, Maggie, I'm surprised. You being a fine Christian woman and all. Taking me to jail was his job. We can't judge him too harshly for that."

"I only wish he'd done what he set out to do."

"Well, in any case, I believe it's the Good Book that cautions us against hating our enemies."

His reference to the Good Book was galling. How dare him preach the gospel to her! She was so incensed she could hardly speak. "How would you know what the Bible says?"

"Don't you remember? I told you about the Basque custom of sending one son to the church. I have an uncle who is a well-respected bishop."

"Success seems to run in your family, doesn't it?" she spat out in irritation.

Dominick grinned. "Doesn't it?"

"Since you know so much about the subject, then you also know that the Bible says nothing about loving an ill-mannered boor!"

"I don't believe it's written anywhere that bad manners are a sin. If it had been, I'm sure Reverend Metcalf's sermon would have lasted at least another hour." He gave her a piercing look. "Make no mistake about it, Mrs. Sanders. You will accompany me to the funeral tomorrow." With that he stomped off, leaving Maggie to glare after him.

"Over my dead body," she called after him. "Over . . ." She stopped as an idea began to take shape in her mind. Within minutes she was strolling along State Street, smiling to herself.

Come to think of it, a fine Christian woman would go to a poor stranger's funeral. Yes, come to think of it, she would.

Chapter 9

The Strangers' Cemetery was situated on a knoll outside town. Tuesday was a beautiful, clear day, with just enough wind to stir the ocean into choppy waves topped with foamy whitecaps. A rigged Chinese junk bobbed up and down in the distance, its battened sails dipping from side to side. Nearer to shore an assortment of fishing boats, followed by a string of screeching sea gulls, searched for schools of fish.

The air was so clear that the islands of Santa Cruz and Santa Rosa no longer looked like mere shadows in the distant mist. Today it was possible to follow the outline of the rocky cliffs that rose out of the water.

Dominick brought the rented horse and carriage to a stop at the bottom of the hill in front of a weathered gate. He had been quiet all morning, barely speaking to her or the children. He solemnly jumped to the ground, tossed his unfinished cigarette away, and consulted his pocket watch, checking its time against the sun.

He walked around the carriage to Maggie's side and offered her his hand. Maggie lifted the skirt of her plain black linsey-woolsey gown and allowed him to help her down. It was the same dress she'd worn for Luke's funeral, the only dress she owned that was somber enough for such an occasion.

Neither spoke as they walked through the gate and followed the winding path up the hill to a freshly dug grave. Not wanting to look at the gaping hole, Maggie concentrated on the view.

The cemetery overlooked the crescent of yellow beach that ran from the rocky headland known as Castle Rock near the wharf to Review Hill some twenty miles away.

"I can't tell you how grateful I am that you have decided to make today as painless as possible," Dominick said. He was standing right next to her, looking intently out to sea as if he saw something that escaped her.

Maggie studied his profile, surprised by the emotion she detected in his voice. "I still don't understand why you care one way or the other about the man. I doubt very much he would have done the same for you had the tables been turned."

For a while, he remained silent. When at last he spoke, his voice was barely audible. "When I was fourteen, my father went on a business trip and never came back. It wasn't until I followed his trail that I discovered he had met with foul play. Fortunately, his death had been reported to the sheriff of the small town where his body was found. His pockets had been emptied of any identification, but the murdering thief had overlooked a gold ring on his index finger. The sheriff kept the ring. Later, I met with the farmer who found my father and saw to it that he got a proper burial."

"So that's what we're doing here," she said thoughtfully. "We're repaying your debt to the farmer."

"Some debts have to be paid by proxy." Hands in his pockets, head down, he walked away and leaned against the trunk of a windblown pine. Caught off balance by the look of sadness she had seen on his face, Maggie stood watching him. She had never expected to understand how an outlaw thought, but Dominick was beyond comprehension. The complexities of the man were downright unnerving—and no less intriguing. *He* was intriguing. If truth be known, he was the most intriguing man that Maggie had ever met.

The rumbling sound of a wagon drew her attention away from Dominick and to the dirt road below them. Two men dressed in dark suits and stovepipe hats jumped down from the front seat and hurried to the rear of the wagon to lift the pine box off. With little concern for propriety, they lugged the box up the hill and set it down without ceremony next to the pile of dirt.

Unlike the cemetery closer to town, the Strangers' Cemetery was grossly neglected. Grass and weeds all but hid the stone markers on each grave. None bore the name of the deceased, only the date of burial.

The stockiest of the two men turned to Dominick. "Would you like a moment alone?"

Dominick shook his head. "That won't be necessary."

The man shrugged and signaled to his partner to pick up his end of the coffin.

"Maybe just a moment," Maggie said.

Dominick looked at her in surprise, then shrugged his shoulders. "Very well," he said to the gravediggers. "Give us a moment."

Lowering her head, Maggie kept an eye on the road. Now that she knew Dominick's reasons for coming today, she regretted what she had planned. Listening to the sound of a horse's racing hooves on the road below, she felt sick with guilt.

The horse emerged from a grove of trees, its rider waving his hat over his head. "Wait!"

Dominick's face took on a look of sheer horror. "Damn, what is he doing here?"

Maggie took a deep breath. She had no choice but to go through with her original plan. "Do you mean Reverend Metcalf? I asked him to come." She forced her sweetest smile. "I decided you were right. It *is* our Christian duty to see that the man has a proper Christian burial."

It was late by the time Maggie and Dominick arrived at the Pickings farm to fetch Jamie and Laurie-

Anne. The sound of the mission bells rang out in the distance, announcing evening mass. Nearer to town, the lamplighter was just finishing his evening rounds.

During the drive to the farm and back, Dominick sputtered and fumed. "Two hours! The man talked for two hours straight about the glories of dying. I was sorely tempted to bestow the glory of dying on Reverend Metcalf himself!"

It seemed to Maggie sacrilegious to wish death on a minister, but Dominick had actually only stated out loud what she herself had thought during the interminably long afternoon. The ordeal left her feeling like a limp rag. She was tired, she was hungry, she had a headache, and she had only herself to blame.

Worst of all, she felt guilty. She wished he hadn't confided the story of his father's death and why he had insisted upon being present at the guard's burial. Knowing the reason for his actions, she regretted making the afternoon more difficult for him than it otherwise would have been.

What she needed to do, she decided, was to figure out a way to make Dominick leave without having to put herself through such bouts of guilt and misery. It was a problem she mulled over for the rest of the night and most of the following day.

After spending nearly three weeks under the same roof as Maggie, Dominick was beginning to think that being caught and lynched from the nearest tree might not be the worst possible fate.

Indeed, attending those weekly church services was hell, to say the least, but a necessary hell. He'd already ingratiated himself with some of the town's most scandalous gossips, which had made it possible for him to compile a list of citizens whose behavior or spending habits demanded closer examination.

Not quite as painful as the church services, but equally valuable in terms of information gathering, were the dreary teas that Maggie insisted they attend each and every weekday afternoon.

"It's good for business," Maggie insisted. "These are the people who will patronize my shoemaking business. Besides, being friendly is the neighborly thing to do."

Suspecting that the tea parties had nothing to do with business or neighborly concerns, and everything to do with Maggie's obsessive determination to make his life a living hell, he was nonetheless grateful for the opportunity to add names to his list of suspects. He'd also managed to collect the names of nearly half the people who had attended the opening night of the Lobero Theater three years earlier. Some even produced their brass souvenir buttons to prove it, unaware that this seemingly innocent gesture took them off Dominick's list of suspects.

The one persistent name on his list was that of the sheriff. But despite Dominick's discreet questions, not a soul had anything bad to say about him. Either the man was extremely ineffective in his law enforcement efforts, which would explain why the bandit had escaped every trap, or he was quite possibly the bandit himself.

In an effort to prove the sheriff's innocence or guilt, Dominick accompanied Maggie on her daily social rounds. Somehow he learned to lift the fragile bone china teacups by their ridiculous little handles. He wasn't required to say much, thank God. An occasional nod here and there was all it took to encourage the other guests to chatter on relentlessly. After nearly a dozen of these pompous little ceremonies, he even got the knack of making the tiny sandwiches last for more than two bites.

Maggie was the envy of all the other women. "You don't know how lucky you are to have such a gracious husband," one matronly woman said one afternoon. She tittered with envy. "I can't imagine Harold sitting so politely and drinking out of dainty cups."

The other women agreed. Maggie was a lucky woman.

Dominick concurred, and it irked him that Maggie didn't see it. Not only did she fail to understand why she should be the envy of every woman in town but she never gave him the slightest bit of credit for being the attentive escort.

She was too busy trying to make his every waking hour miserable. She monitored his swearing, made him sit outside in the damp night air to smoke his cigarettes, and persisted in keeping track of all his shortcomings. And then . . . then! She watered down his liquor!

Upon discovering the last offense, he rampaged through the house bellowing like an injured lion, until Jamie and Laurie-Anne scurried for cover like little mice.

"Damn it, Maggie, you've gone too far this time!"

Maggie looked up calmly from her chair where she sat mending. As always, everything about her person was immaculate, from her shiny, neat bun to the tips of her highly polished boots. "Mr. Sanders, would you mind tempering your language?"

"I have tempered my language. Would you care to hear how I would normally speak to someone who would dare to mess with my whiskey?"

She returned to her mending, stabbing a needle into the hem of one of Laurie-Anne's dresses and pulling it through the fabric with a jerky movement of her wrist. "If you don't like it around here, Mr. Sanders, I suppose you could always find other accommodations."

"I'm quite aware of your little games. You hope to make me miserable enough that I'll move out. That's what you're hoping, isn't it?"

She looked at him with large blue eyes. "Are you miserable?" she asked, all innocent-like.

He had never wanted to wring anyone's neck so much in his life. The only problem was that even as he was flexing his fingers with the thought of satisfying his desire, he was remembering how it felt to kiss her soft ruby lips. Why he kept thinking about a kiss that he had bestowed on her while they were stranded on the pass, he had no idea. The kiss had meant nothing to him. Nothing!

Yet still it haunted him.

Cursing beneath his breath, he spun on his heel, wishing he could think of a word to describe the very vexing and annoying Maggie Turner. There was no word, he decided after much thought. Not in English and certainly not in Basque.

But he needed Maggie's cooperation, and when she refused to accept any more social engagements he knew he had to take dramatic action. The sooner he found the bandit, the better.

One day he saw an ad for the opera in the newspaper and got an idea. He had proof that the bandit had attended the opera in the past. Didn't that make it likely that he would attend again?

He knew that no woman could resist a night at the opera, so he purchased two tickets and presented them to Maggie over breakfast, passing them to her over the bowls of burnt porridge.

She looked down at the tickets in her hand. "Opera tickets?"

Thinking it best not to appear too eager to attend, he feigned indifference. "Of course, if you'd rather not . . ."

"It would be a shame to waste the tickets."

"Yes," he said, "a crying shame."

He convinced himself that the opera wouldn't be that bad. Of course, he hadn't taken into consideration the torment of wearing a damned formal suit that would be more appropriate as a straitjacket.

Or was it the dress she wore that was the torment? A shimmering royal-blue gown that hugged her shapely figure and made her skin glow like a sun-kissed peach. The neckline would be considered modest by most standards, but it revealed enough of her lovely, soft curves to make a lesser man ache.

"Now that's what I call a barbed-wire dress," he mocked when she removed her wrap. "Protects the property without spoiling the view."

Maggie blushed but said nothing. Amused that he had finally discovered a way to knock her off balance, he used every opportunity to enjoy the view.

More than two hundred people were jammed into the theater, dressed in their very best evening wear. Candles flickered from behind green glass shades, casting pools of light upon the flocked red walls. Diamonds and emeralds shimmered upon the white ivory necks of the wives of Santa Barbara's finest citizens. From their place in the gallery, Dominick and Maggie overlooked the theater's four private boxes, complete with rocking chairs.

Before the curtain went up, Dominick studied the audience, rubbing the brass souvenir button between his fingers. Sheriff Badger and his wife were there, along with the Reverend and Mrs. Metcalf.

"What are you staring at?" Maggie asked.

He slipped the button into his pocket. "Nothing, my love."

The orchestra began to play and the curtain rose, followed by the most interminable singing he'd ever endured. Dominick envied the one man who was asleep, which was, in his estimation, the only way to enjoy an opera. But each time he himself tried to nod off, one of the bosomy singers would hit a high note that bounced from the large golden eagle that hung over the stage all the way up to the circular dome, then dropped down with the subtlety of a blacksmith's anvil to jar him back to consciousness.

After one such rude awakening, he ran his finger along his stiff collar and searched for a means by which to escape. Women cooled themselves with peacock fans and watched the stage with rapt attention. Their husbands looked either inebriated or perplexed.

Next to him, Maggie sniffled and wiped away a tear with a gloved hand. What was it about tortured souls in deadly conflict that women found so appealing? At the completion of one particularly long and painful aria, Maggie was sobbing, and he couldn't help but notice the charming way her lovely breasts rose and fell above the neckline of her gown.

Irritated at letting himself be taken in by her womanly charms, he brusquely thrust a clean handkerchief into her lap. Whispering her thanks, she looked up at him, teary-eyed and pink-cheeked. Under the best of circumstances, she affected him on some level that he was unwilling to divulge, but never more than when she looked so soft and vulnerable. It was all he could do to keep from taking her in his arms. He was forced to remind himself firmly that he wanted her amenable, nothing more.

"That was so sad," she sniffled later as they sat side by side in the back seat of the horse and carriage he'd hired for the occasion. The driver urged the horse forward and the carriage moved past the ill-reputed joss house, a combination Chinese gambling hall and salon that stood next door to the theater.

The glow from the newly installed gaslights flickered in the swirling mists of fog drifting in from the sea. A foghorn sounded in the distance, mingling with the clip-clop of horses' feet. A beacon of red light from the stone-towered lighthouse on the Mesa slashed through the ghostly mists like a bloodied sword.

"I certainly hope it was sad," he muttered. "I'd hate to think that damned woman was bellowing like a wounded cow because she was happy."

"Shhh. Lower your voice." She glanced at the driver's rigid back. "People will think you've no appreciation for the arts."

"It's because of my appreciation for the arts that I refuse to go to another opera," he growled. "God, what a terrible smell!"

The wind had picked up, carrying with it the oily

odor from the bay. "Those fumes are supposed to be good for you," she said. "They clean out the orifices of the body."

"Whatever gave you that idea?" he asked.

"Dr. Brinkerhoff. I read an article by him in the San Francisco paper. He explained that the sea breezes blowing across the petroleum slicks in the channel carry the fumes inland and are good for respiratory ailments."

He glanced at her incredulously. "Is that why you uprooted and moved here? Because of some quack doctor's say-so?"

"If what he says is true, then Jamie should have a long life ahead of him. And I have no reason to think otherwise. Already I've seen a vast improvement in Jamie's condition. Why, he hardly coughs anymore. Besides, Dr. Brinkerhoff struck me as a very intelligent man."

"Oh, he's that all right. By persuading everyone with a respiratory problem to move here, he has assured himself of a nice steady income for years to come. Between the opera singers trying to fool the public into believing that all that nonsense is art and a doctor who proposes suspect cures, I have to admit Santa Barbara is beginning to look like a bandit's paradise."

Nudging his arm with her elbow, she lowered her voice to a whisper. "Just because you have a criminal mind is no reason to suspect everyone else of devious motives."

"It's as good a reason as any," he whispered back. The carriage stopped in front of their house. He stepped down and held out his hand for Maggie. After paying the driver, he turned to her and crooked his arm for her convenience. "Shall we, Mrs. Sanders?"

"I've told you repeatedly, I do not want to be called by that name."

He grinned, his earlier ill temper forgotten. He was trying to get into her good graces, not alienate her more. Besides, in the softness of the night, she looked radiantly beautiful. "Do you hate it that much?"

"I loathe it."

"Perhaps you would like it better if there were more privileges that went with the name."

She lifted her head and assessed him boldly—and it was this boldness that made him decide she needed to be reminded that he held the upper hand. Without further ado, he slipped his arm around her waist, pulled her roughly toward him, and crushed his mouth against hers.

She surprised him—far more than that, shocked him—by kissing him back. She wasn't supposed to do that. That wasn't in his plan. He was the one who was supposed to do the kissing—or not, as he chose.

Releasing her like fire, he stepped back into the shadows, gasping at the soft, glowing stars in her eyes. "Is that enough reward for using my name?" he asked gruffly. He tried not to let the softness of her face affect him. But she looked so desirable, so beguiling, so tempting to him, it was all he could do not to finish the kiss he had started. Purposely striving to be hateful, he hardened his voice. "Or would you prefer something more . . . ?"

The look of confusion on her face pained him. "I would prefer that you keep your hands to yourself!" she said coldly. She picked up the hem of her skirt and turned away from him.

It wasn't enough that she distance herself. He had to purge the worrisome feelings that made him yearn to take her in his arms. To this end, he allowed his mocking, spiteful voice to follow her. "Is it only my hands that you object to, Maggie?"

She paused by the fountain. The smell of citrus fruit had replaced the sickly oil smell from the bay. "I don't think I have to spell it out for you. Goodnight." He grabbed the hateful look she gave him like a man drowning at sea. But even that wasn't enough to make him forget that for one unguarded moment he had seen something else in her eyes, something that made his heart skip a beat.

It wasn't until the wee hours of the morning that he managed to clear his head enough to go to bed. But the memory of Maggie in her lovely blue dress stayed to taunt him. And when he wasn't recalling every detail of her appearance, he was remembering the feel of his lips against hers and how, for a brief instant, she had actually kissed him back!

The next morning, Maggie rose at the first sound of roosters crowing in the distance. The early-morning hours before the children awoke permitted her the best times for thinking and planning.

This particular morning she counted out the money left over from the sale of her house and shoemaker's shop in San Francisco. Although she had purchased only the barest of necessities since her arrival in town a month ago, she had spent more than she had allowed for in her budget.

Dominick had insisted on paying for rent and other living expenses; nevertheless, food and sundries were more costly in Santa Barbara than in San Francisco. She still had enough money left to cover expenses for months to come, but she realized that the only way to ensure financial security and to repay the money she owed Dominick was to open her shoemaking business as soon as she could manage it.

She hated feeling obligated to him. The sooner she could repay the debt, the better.

But it wasn't money that worried her the most. It was what Dominick's presence was doing to her peace of mind. The little scene outside the house had weighed heavily on her conscience all night long. To think that she had kissed a bandit! Worse than that, had actually wanted him to . . . She put a clamp on her thoughts just in time. Glory be, whatever was the matter with her?

The man goaded her into the most foul of dispositions. It shocked her to think of the many times she caught herself scowling lately, even when he wasn't around. And never, *never* before had she raised her voice as she had done in recent weeks. Why, her poor father, not to mention her mother, would likely turn over in their graves if they knew she was capable of saying such dreadful, unkind things! For whatever reason, Dominick Sanders brought out the worst in her.

Even more worrisome, however, was the possibility of his bringing out the best. She had to be rid of him before she turned into some horrible sinful woman who was unfit to raise children! How much longer would she have to tolerate his presence? He had said he was looking for someone, but as far as she knew, he'd made no attempt to find the person or persons he sought. Of more concern to her was the fact that every day he remained in the house, involved with their lives, Laurie-Anne and Jamie grew more and more attached to him. They had already reached the point where they hardly left his side.

Her daughter's enchantment with Dominick was especially alarming. First thing each morning, it was Laurie-Anne's habit to bound out of bed and watch him shave, her wonderful childish laughter filling the house like music.

Laurie-Anne, who had been so fretful and solemn during the year following her father's death, had regained her normally cheerful disposition. For this, Maggie was grateful. But she couldn't help but worry about how Laurie-Anne would react upon losing Dominick.

And what about Jamie? Why, the boy actually idolized the man! Every night after supper, Jamie sat at the wooden kitchen table, forming his letters on his slate under Dominick's careful tutelage.

Maggie had enrolled Jamie in the little one-room schoolhouse that was a short walk from their home. He had a quick, sharp mind, but the lung problems

he'd suffered in San Francisco had prevented him
from attending school for nearly a year. As a result,
he had fallen far behind his classmates.

With Dominick's help, however, he had already
made great strides. Each night he recited from his
little reader with increasing confidence. He could add,
subtract, and tell time. He'd even made remarkable
progress in his spelling, although he still formed some
of his letters backward or upside down. But his printing skills had shown great improvement since Dominick had made up that ridiculous song about the perils
of wrong-way letters. Even Laurie-Anne had memo-
rized it and could often be heard singing it to herself.

Remembering how patient Dominick was with Jamie,
Maggie was quite literally torn in two. She loved
seeing her children happy, but she still wondered what
sort of influence a bandit might have on them. Was
it possible that somewhere in the harmless games and
clever rhymes he was always inventing for them, he
was in reality sending out some kind of negative
signals?

Some of his stories did give her pause. As amusing
as they were at times, bringing a smile even to her
unwilling face, she was certain she had cause for concern. Only yesterday she had walked into the kitchen
to hear Dominick in the middle of a story about a
bandit who stopped every book coming in and out of
the lending library to rob it of its vowels. "Once upon
a time," he said, "became 'nc pn tm.' "

Having been raised solely on biblical stories, she
herself certainly wouldn't have recommended such a
story. On the other hand, she had to admit that in
very short order Jamie knew his vowels and understood the importance of them. The question was,
would Dominick's tales of vowel bandits and number
thieves have an adverse effect on the children's moral
standards?

She didn't know, and wanting the very best for her
children, she could only believe that the most effective

way to ensure their safety was to inflict further misery upon Dominick so that he would take his leave. The only problem was that she had already done everything she could think of to accomplish that goal. There didn't appear to be anything left for her to do, save ask the Reverend Metcalf to move in with them. The very thought made her shudder. It seemed inconceivable that an outlaw's presence was preferable to that of a man of God, but that was the truth of the matter.

With a heavy sigh, she hid her money in one of the tin canisters in the pantry and busied herself preparing breakfast. While she worked, she mulled over the problem of how to continue making Dominick Sanders's life absolutely miserable.

Chapter 10

It was a beautiful spring morning in April, and the warm air was filled with the sounds of songbirds. Mrs. Pickings arrived after breakfast, carting fresh eggs and homemade jelly and bursting with the town's latest gossip.

How the woman managed to keep track of the endless land disputes, marriages, and births was beyond Maggie's comprehension. Even before Maggie had shown her into the kitchen, Mrs. Pickings had given an impressive rundown on the trials and tribulations of a family named Simpson.

"The house burned clear to the ground last night," Mrs. Pickings said. "Second time this year they've lost their house. Why, only this past September they had a house slip down the hill during the rains. No one was hurt, thank goodness. But can you imagine building a house on a hill? Personally, I like stability."

"Was the house that burned down last night on a hill?"

"No. They learned their lesson from the first house. They built the second house on stable ground."

"It didn't make a whole lot of difference, did it? They still lost their house."

"I suppose. But at least this time they have the satisfaction of knowing it wasn't because of poor location."

Doubting that the Simpson family would derive much satisfaction from anything at this point, Maggie poured two cups of coffee. "What do you suppose caused the fire?"

"I have my opinion." Mrs. Pickings glanced around the room as if checking for eavesdroppers. "There's a group of hooligans that has been causing trouble for quite some time now. Word is that the head of the group had a grudge against the older Simpson boy."

"That's terrible," Maggie said. "Do you know who these hooligans are?"

"I have my suspicions. You'd be shocked if you knew their names. Don't breathe a word of this to anyone."

"I wouldn't dream of it," Maggie promised.

"Very well, then, if you insist. One of the boys' names is Tubbs. His father is the president of the bank."

Maggie's eyes widened. "The Tubbs boy? Are you sure?"

"Well, you can't be sure of anything, can you?" Mrs. Pickings sniffed. "But it makes me mad every time I see Mrs. Tubbs with her nose turned up as if she were born of royal blood or something. And then there's that fancy-dancy lawyer who's always down at city hall making trouble. I wonder what he'd say if he knew how his son spends his free time?"

"Oh, no," Maggie cried out in disbelief.

"Oh, yes," Mrs. Pickings said. She then went on to name the other families whose boys she was convinced belonged to the mischief-makers.

Maggie couldn't make up her mind whether to put much stock in what Mrs. Pickings said. It was hard to believe that some of the most influential families in town had sons capable of burning down people's houses. Even Mrs. Pickings admitted that her conclusions were based on hunches rather than evidence.

"But I ask you—what is a person supposed to think when she spots a sixteen-year-old boy running down the street in the wee hours of the morning?"

"I have no idea," Maggie said, changing the subject. "Before I forget, I want to thank you for the eggs and jelly. As soon as I open my shop, I will repay your kindness by making you a pair of new shoes."

Mrs. Pickings beamed. "Why that's very kind of you. When do you plan to open your shop?"

"Just as soon as I find a suitable location. It's so difficult to look with Laurie-Anne. She's too young for school and too old to drag around town."

"Why don't you find someone to take care of her in your absence?" Mrs. Pickings paused, and after a moment her face brightened. "I believe I can help you. I know a young woman by the name of Consuela Lopez. Lovely girl, very religious. She has fifteen brothers and sisters, so she's very experienced. Rumor has it that her mother is expecting again. Would you like me to ask the girl to come by so you can meet her?"

"That would be wonderful," Maggie agreed. If the girl was as responsible as Mrs. Pickings seemed to think, at least one of her problems would be solved. "I've been meaning to ask you how your father is doing."

"Connie Mae wrote and said he has improved vastly since her arrival. He's even gained some weight."

"That's wonderful. Give her my best, will you?"

"I shall, but the reason I'm here is to tell you that Connie Mae has decided to stay with Father until sometime this fall. I thought you would like to know that there's no hurry for you and your family to move."

The additional time did relieve Maggie's mind. On the other hand, it might very well postpone the day she and Dominick would part company. "Thank you," she said. She decided to keep the news from Dominick. No sense giving him an excuse to stay longer than he already planned to. "I really would be grateful if you'd talk to Consuela about taking care of Laurie-Anne. That is, if you wouldn't mind."

"I don't mind at all," Mrs. Pickings replied. "It'll

give me an opportunity to see for myself if the rumors about her mother are true. You know how unreliable gossip can be."

Later that same afternoon, a timid knock came at the kitchen door. Maggie opened it and found herself facing a beautiful young woman with raven-black hair, clear almond skin, and gentle brown eyes. Thinking the girl was far too young for the position, no more than fifteen or sixteen at the most, Maggie politely invited her in and offered her a cup of tea. In the short time it took Maggie to put the kettle on the stove and set out a plate of freshly baked cookies, Consuela managed to make Laurie-Anne smile and coax Jamie to show off his new reading skills.

"Can you read and write English?" Maggie asked.

"Not very well, Señora." Consuela smiled at Jamie. "I look forward to Jamie teaching me. And I will teach him Spanish."

"I already know Backs," Jamie said proudly.

"He means Basque," Maggie explained.

The girl wrinkled her forehead. "What is this Basque?"

"It's a language spoken in the Pyrenees Mountains, between France and Spain."

"Arraixo!" Jamie exclaimed, eager to demonstrate.

"Arraixo," Consuela repeated. "What does it mean?"

"It's what you say when you drop something on your foot," Jamie said proudly. *"Arraixo!"*

"I'll remember," Consuela said. *"Arraixo!"*

Pleased by the girl's easy rapport with the children, Maggie made up her mind to hire her. She tousled her son's hair. "Run along now. I need to talk to Consuela alone."

While they drank tea and nibbled on cookies, Consuela told Maggie about her family. "My father makes adobe bricks, but business is poor. Last month we didn't even have enough to pay for our rent."

Maggie thought about what Mrs. Pickings had told

her about the citizens' wanting to rid the town of the
Spanish influence. "Is it because adobe buildings are
out of favor?"

Consuela nodded. "Many of them are being torn
down and replaced with wooden ones."

"It's a pity, isn't it? I think the adobes give the
town a distinct flavor." She picked up the teapot and
refilled Consuela's cup.

"My father is very saddened. He remembers when
the old walls of the presidio still stood, surrounding
the square used by soldiers. He told me that there
used to be four shiny brass cannons guarding it, one
at each corner. Outside the presidio wall, the rich
Spaniards owned large rancheros that required many
servants. As a result, everyone worked. Today, many
of my people can no longer find employment."

"It must be very difficult for your father to see so
many changes in his lifetime."

Consuela nodded. "He says the thing that is most
difficult is that so many of the Spanish people no
longer feel that Santa Barbara is their home. Without
work, many are being forced to leave the area."

"Is this why you are seeking employment? Because
your father's business is doing so poorly?"

Consuela nodded. "My older brother and I are trying to help out. The other children are too young.
Now, with the new baby coming . . ."

"I see. How old is your brother?"

"Manuel will be seventeen in November."

Maggie thought a moment. "Perhaps I could use
your brother at the shop."

Consuela's eyes shone. "Oh, Señora, he would be
so happy."

"I can't promise," Maggie cautioned. "I have to
talk with . . . with my husband." She had discussed
her shop with Dominick at great length, gratified that
he had seemed so interested. But he had cautioned
her against hiring help, using the rationale that an

employee was likely to overhear something that could cause her embarrassment.

Maggie was not fooled for a moment. Dominick's only concern was for his own neck. Well, let him be concerned. If she wanted to hire someone, she most certainly would do so!

"On second thought," Maggie added, "I'm sure there'll be no problem in hiring him—if he's responsible and interested in learning."

"He is," Consuela assured her. "Last year when my father hurt his back, Manuel took over his business and ran it almost single-handed."

"He sounds most enterprising. Now let's talk about your duties, shall we?"

The following day, Maggie and Dominick left Laurie-Anne in Consuela's care and went to town to look at available property for her business. Actually she would have preferred to look at property by herself, but Dominick insisted upon accompanying her.

After hugging Laurie-Anne, she gave Consuela a few last-minute instructions, reached for her kid gloves, and followed Dominick outside.

They walked two blocks and caught the mule-drawn streetcar that ran the length of State Street all the way to the wharf. The car was designed to carry twelve seated passengers plus however many brave souls could hold on to the shiny brass railings without falling off.

With one foot dangling in midair, Maggie grasped a railing with one gloved hand and pressed against Dominick's back. Although it took practically all her concentration to keep from flying off backward with each stop and start of the streetcar, she couldn't resist craning her neck to view the bustling business district. She'd been so busy in recent weeks that she hadn't really taken the time to explore the center of town.

The number of businesses was surprising, as were the scores of people who thronged the town, many of them tourists who had traveled to Santa Barbara to see for themselves if the "sanatorium of the Pacific" would cure their ailments and to submerge themselves in the sulphur springs at nearby Burton Mound. But not all were tourists by any means. Many were local residents who had come into town to do their weekly marketing or ranchers from surrounding areas who had ridden in on horseback or buckboards to pick up supplies.

Women dressed in calico morning gowns and carrying baskets on their arms strolled along the boardwalk, stopping to look at windows filled with goods or to examine the bins of ripe, fresh fruit displayed in front. Men dressed in blue denim pants held up by suspenders rode along the street on horseback, tipping their hats to every pretty woman they passed.

The barbershop with its red-and-white pole was sandwiched between a law office and a butcher shop. A group of women gossiped outside Grover's general store, and a tall, lean man in overalls and a red-checked shirt maneuvered a broom around them. The menfolk seemed to prefer the swing in front of Hardy's Hardware for sitting and the numerous saloons that dotted the street for socializing.

A small boy and his dog ran along the boardwalk and darted into the confectionery. The boy with his tousled blond hair reminded her of Jamie, and she thought of something.

"What does *'arraixo'* mean?" She spoke over Dominick's shoulder, raising her voice to be heard over the rumbling sound of the streetcar.

" 'Hell,' " he said, turning around to look back at her.

The conveyance jolted and she fell against the man behind her, who gave her a toothless grin and pushed her upright. Bumping her jaw against Dominick's elbow, she fought to get a better hold of the railing.

"What did you say?" she asked upon regaining her balance.

"I said *'arraixo'* means 'hell.' "

Shocked, she forgot her precarious position and let her hand slacken its hold. Without warning the mules sped up and she flew backwards, landing with an unceremonious thump in the middle of the dirt road. Her skirts awry, revealing petticoats and bared ankles, she stared like a madwoman at the back of the disappearing vehicle.

Dominick looked back over his shoulder, his face frozen in astonishment. The streetcar had gone nearly half a block before he recovered from his surprise enough to swing gracefully to the ground and hurry back to her.

With an interested assessment of her immodest display, he held out his hand. "Why didn't you tell me you wanted to get off? There is a proper procedure for notifying the driver to stop."

Refusing his hand, Maggie jumped to her feet and brushed off her skirts. Tossing her head angrily, she adjusted her hat. "How dare you teach my children your rude, barbaric language!"

He looked at her quizzically. "Why, Maggie, I do believe the fall did damage to your head."

"Nothing happened to my head!" she stormed, hands on hips. "I know what I heard, and I heard the word . . . that terrible word come out of my son's mouth."

Dominick looked startled, then threw back his head and laughed. "Ah, so that's what this is all about."

"He said that's what you say when you drop something on your foot."

"Yes, I remember now. I was chopping firewood and a log fell on my toe." He examined her disapproving face. "What do you say when you drop something on your toe?"

"I don't say anything."

He folded his arms and looked at her skeptically. "Come on, Maggie, own up. No one suffers pain without some measure of protest."

"Maybe I let out a little cry," she admitted. "But that's all, especially in front of the children." Several horses raced by, ridden by Mexican youths. Maggie waited for them to pass, then marched to the side of the street and stomped onto the boardwalk.

Dominick followed her. "What do you say when the children aren't around?"

She whirled about to face him. "I do not use foul language, Mr. Sanders, under any circumstances."

"Except for once," he said.

Her eyes widened. "I've never used bad language. Not once in my entire life!"

"I regret having to disagree with you, Maggie. But I distinctly heard you say *'arraixo.'*" He leaned over. "Remember? Back there on the streetcar? Hell?"

Maggie was so incensed she couldn't speak. Without a word, she spun around in a circle of flying skirts and strode angrily down State Street, past the remainder of the business district, her dust-covered boots beating a noisy cadence along the weathered wooden planks beneath her feet.

Laughing to himself, Dominick followed her, his eyes riveted on the charming sway of her bustle. Finally she stopped in front of the squat adobe building that housed the real estate office.

Inside, they were greeted by a short, heavy man who rose from behind a cluttered desk. "You must be Mr. and Mrs. Sanders. Come in, come in. Have a seat. I'm Jeremiah Peters."

He ran a finger along his curling mustache as he waited for them to settle down on the ladder-back chairs in front of his desk. Maggie decided that a person could play chess on Mr. Peters's plaid suit and could probably hang a hat upon the stiff handles of his mustache.

Mr. Peters's gaze swept the length of her, taking in her every curve with lingering interest. "I read the article about you in the newspaper a few weeks back," he explained. "Thought you might be paying me a visit. I'm kind of like the undertaker. Eventually everyone in town comes through those doors." He laughed at his own joke, twirled the tips of his mustache with both hands, and settled back in his cowhide chair.

"What can I do for you?" Although he was still assessing Maggie, the question was directed at Dominick.

Irritated that Mr. Peters discounted her when it came time to discuss business but not when he wanted to satisfy a lustful eye, she immediately launched into a detailed explanation as to what she had in mind, even going as far as to mention square footage. She needed a place big enough for all her tools and supplies. Then of course, a good-sized counter was essential and a spacious workbench, along with a place that would allow customers to sit and relax while she put the final polish on their shoes.

"And there must be ample windows," she added, taking a measure of satisfaction from the look of astonishment on his face. "I like to work by natural light. It's hard to see the grain of leather while working under gaslight."

Apparently not used to dealing with women in a business situation, Mr. Peters looked at Dominick as if waiting for him to concur or disagree with Maggie. When Dominick said nothing, Mr. Peters cleared his throat, his Adam's apple bobbing up and down like a rubber ball. He stood up and took a large ring of keys off a nail by the front door.

"There are two vacant buildings that fit your requirements," he said stiffly, glancing hopefully at Dominick.

"Only two?" Maggie asked.

" 'Fraid so. Of course, if it wasn't for the natural light that you need, I could put you on State Street." He led them out the door and to the corner. "The property I'm thinking of is a couple of streets over, on Santa Barbara."

Presently they came to a stone building that stood by itself on a neglected lot covered with knee-high weeds. The building itself was unremarkable, a square box with a slate roof. About the only thing of a favorable nature that could be said about it was that it did have an abundance of windows, but because of the enormous spread of a fig tree, Maggie doubted that much sun found its way inside.

"All the way from Australia," Mr. Peters explained, following her gaze. "It's said that the entire population of Santa Barbara can stand in its shade at high noon. Of course, I don't know that anyone has tested that theory."

He thrust a key into a rusty lock and the door sprang open. Cool, dank air greeted Maggie as she followed Mr. Peters inside the dimly lit building. "The tree is lovely," Maggie began tactfully, "but it does interfere with the sunlight, doesn't it?"

Mr. Peters looked around the room as if seeing it for the first time. "I suppose you could always trim it. It does seem a shame, doesn't it? A beautiful tree like that, all the way from Australia."

"The place is rather off the beaten track, don't you think?" Dominick remarked.

"It'll cost more to rent a building closer to town," Mr. Peters countered.

Maggie stopped to inspect a suspiciously shaped wooden box that filled the corner of the room. "What business did the previous owner conduct?"

"He was a coffin maker," Mr. Peters explained. "Had two unprofitable years in a row and went bankrupt."

"I've heard that dying is rather out of favor these days," Dominick said wryly.

Fighting a cold shiver, Maggie headed for the door. "I think I would prefer something closer to town." The walls seemed to be closing in on her and she was anxious to leave.

"Very well," Mr. Peters sniffed, looking offended.

"You might find the building on Cota Street more to your liking. It's just off State."

It took nearly fifteen minutes to walk the distance to Cota. The building he showed them was a two-room clapboard affair with a false front and a sagging wooden porch. "It's rather run-down," Mr. Peters conceded.

"It's perfect," Maggie exclaimed.

Dominick studied the outside of the building and cast a dubious eye toward Maggie. "The location's not bad."

"It's perfect," Maggie repeated, and her initial reaction was confirmed when she stepped inside. In no time at all, she had mentally made the necessary renovations and was more convinced than ever that she'd found the perfect place for her shop.

Dim wood floors matched the dull paneled walls and ceiling, but not even the dark oak could restrain the golden sunlight streaming through the numerous windows that graced all four walls. If she trimmed the outside bushes, she would have sun all day.

"That'll be fifty a month, plus a deposit."

Maggie winced inwardly but managed to keep her composure. She had had no idea that commercial property in Santa Barbara was so high. She quickly estimated the expense of making the building conform to her needs. Until her business was established, she would have to watch every penny. "That will be thirty-five a month, with no deposit," she replied.

Mr. Peters looked aghast. Maggie's outrageous offer apparently confirmed his opinion that women had no place in the business world. "Mrs. Sanders, surely you jest. Have you any idea how much this property is worth?"

"And have you any idea how much it's going to cost me to get this building ready to conduct business?" Maggie demanded. They stood practically nose to nose, Mr. Peters looking injured and Maggie wearing a self-righteous expression.

"May I speak with my wife in private?" Dominick asked, his eyes dancing with amusement.

Mr. Peters demurred with a sniff. "Of course."

Dominick waited for the man to step outside. "If the rent is a problem, I shall be most happy to contribute."

"I don't wish to be obligated to you any more than I already am," she said.

"Obligated?" he asked, surprised. "It's only fair that I pay part of the expenses as long as we're together."

"Which I sincerely hope won't be much longer!"

"Are you saying that you won't accept at least part of the rent from me?"

"Not only will I not accept it, but I intend to pay you back every penny I already owe you. And when that day comes, I fully expect you to leave."

"Well, then, in that case, I guess it's only fair that my sympathies go to Mr. Peters."

"You may give your sympathies to whomever you wish." She walked outside and resumed bargaining. "I'm prepared to pay you thirty-five and not one penny more."

"That's highway robbery!" Mr. Peters insisted.

"Highway robbery, indeed!" she exclaimed. "Why, I paid only twenty-five a month for the same size building in San Francisco."

Mr. Peters seemed almost ready to capitulate and might well have done so had Dominick not interjected his opinion that the location alone was worth more.

Glaring at Dominick, Maggie held her ground. In the end, she got it for forty dollars a month.

"You're a fine one!" she complained, as the two of them later walked toward the lumberyard to order shelving. "If it was up to you, I'd have paid twice as much!"

"That way you would have had to accept my generous offer, wouldn't you?" He threw her a sideways glance. "Cheer up, Maggie. You got the poor man to come down more than he intended to. The truth is, you practically robbed him."

Offended and hurt that he would side with the likes of Mr. Peters, she glowered at him. "You're a fine one to talk about robbing someone!"

"At least a bandit lets his intentions be known. That poor man was so dazzled by your beauty, he had no idea what hit him." He chuckled. "It would be interesting to know how the poor man explains that to his employer."

"Would you stop calling him 'that poor man'?" she retorted, although secretly she was pleased that Dominick thought she had beauty enough to dazzle. They stopped on the boardwalk in front of the lumberyard. "How much of my money do you expect to give away here?"

"Only as much as is fair." He held the door open for her. "I believe a person should be able to make an honest living. I only rob stages that deserve to be robbed."

"How very considerate of you." She brushed past him and proceeded to walk up and down aisles lined with stacks of lumber that practically reached the high vaulted ceiling. She stopped and rubbed her hand along a piece of smooth-finished pine. "And how do you determine whether or not a stage should be robbed?"

He slid a piece of fine oak from a wooden pallet and held it lengthwise. With one eye closed, he checked for a warped or uneven grain. "The same way I determine whether or not a woman should be kissed."

She looked at him curiously. She didn't want to ask the obvious question, but she couldn't help herself. "And how do you determine whether or not to kiss someone?"

"It has to do with the amount of profit I can expect on my investment. The greater the chance of a healthy return, the more interest I'm likely to show." He held up the oak for her inspection. "Why, Mrs. Sanders, feast your eyes on this. The perfect wood for a counter, don't you think?"

Chapter 11

Early the next morning, Consuela's brother, Manuel, arrived at Maggie's shop. Dressed in a faded blue shirt and neatly patched trousers held up by red suspenders, he greeted her with a shy smile.

Maggie had spent the better part of the hour sweeping months of dirt and grime off the floor. She invited Manuel inside and stood the long-handled broom against the wall.

The youth eyed the broom. "I'll be happy to finish sweeping, Señora," he said politely. "A lady like you should not be doing such work."

Maggie had to smile at this. "I can assure you I've done far worse. Have you ever worked with leather?"

He shook his head, his eyes round with worry. "But I can learn," he quickly assured her. "I'm a fast learner. Honest, I am."

"I'm sure you are." She was impressed with his enthusiasm and eagerness to please. A skinny lad with a nasty scar over his right eyebrow, he had his sister's same soulful eyes and endearing smile. Maggie was sure that the youth would prove worth his weight in gold, and she would have hired him on the spot had Dominick not returned from the hardware store at that particular moment and intervened.

"I think it would be better to wait a few months before we hire anyone, until we see how business is," Dominick explained to Manuel. "Why don't you check back with us? Say, by the end of the summer."

Maggie couldn't believe her ears. The audacity of

the man, making business decisions that were hers alone to make. It was enough that he had moved into her house; now he was taking over her business. It simply was not to be tolerated!

"I've already told Manuel he has a job here," she said defiantly. It was only half a lie; she might not have said so outright, but she had certainly implied her intention.

Manuel shifted uneasily, his stricken face turning first to Maggie, then to Dominick. He clearly expected Maggie's husband to have the last say.

Dominick's eyes hardened. "I see." He turned to the boy. "Please accept my apologies. We would be more than happy to pay you a month's salary for your inconvenience."

"Inconvenience!" Maggie exclaimed. "You deny this poor boy a job and call it an inconvenience?"

Clearly surprised by the vehemence in her voice, Dominick frowned and regarded her intently. She matched his stare with blazing eyes, her entire demeanor primed and ready to fight him.

Finally, he turned to Manuel and said, "Would you be kind enough to wait outside while my wife and I discuss the matter?"

Head drooping, Manuel slipped dejectedly out the door to the front porch.

Maggie fought to maintain her composure. "How dare you think you can tell me how to run my business!"

"I'm not telling you how to run your business. My sole interest is in protecting my own neck."

"Your neck?" she scorned. "How could my hiring Consuela's brother endanger your precious neck?"

"As I told you the other night, anyone spending a full day with us is likely to figure out that we're not man and wife."

"We'll have to watch what we say," she conceded.

"Now wouldn't that be a pity? Nothing gives me

greater pleasure than listening to your uncensored opinion of my worth."

"Don't worry, you'll still have it," Maggie assured him. "I'll just choose the time and location more carefully."

"You needn't concern yourself. We're not hiring Manuel."

"I've already hired him."

"Unhire him!"

"Never!"

While the battle raged inside, Manuel paced back and forth out front. On occasion, he chanced a glimpse through a window and was amazed at what he saw. Although he couldn't make out what was said, Mr. and Mrs. Sanders stood toe to toe, nose to nose, and eye to eye. Never in all his born days had he seen a woman stand up to a man like Mrs. Sanders stood up to her husband. Hearing Mrs. Sanders say something about the sheriff, Manuel frowned and resumed his pacing.

Inside, Dominick pointed a menacing finger in Maggie's face. "You wouldn't dare talk to the sheriff."

"If it comes to letting a poor boy and his family starve, I'll do whatever is necessary."

Dominick hesitated. "All right, if you feel this strongly about it, I'll let Manuel stay."

She tossed him a mocking look. "As if you have a choice."

"On one condition," he continued, ignoring her comment. "He can only work at night, when we're not here. He can sweep the floor, keep our supplies and equipment in working order, cut leather, and in general have everything ready for us by the following morning."

Thinking about the possibilities, Maggie recalled the many times she'd stayed late to clean up the shop in San Francisco after a full day of work. She winced at the memory of dragging herself home long after the

housekeeper had put the children to bed, too tired to
do more than fall exhausted on her own bed.

Nevertheless, she had reservations about restricting
Manuel to working only after normal business hours.
At the moment she couldn't for the life of her think
what those reservations were, exactly, but she had
them nonetheless. She'd won the dispute, but somehow it didn't feel like a victory. It felt like Dominick
was running her life.

"Do you want to tell Manuel the good news, or
should I?" Dominick asked.

"I'll do it," she snapped. She marched across the
room and flung open the door. Regardless of her feelings, she exercised victory to the fullest. With the
proud bearing of a triumphant general, she called to
Manuel, told him the good news, and carefully explained his schedule and duties.

His eyes wide in astonishment, Manuel mutely nodded his understanding. He cast a fearful eye in the
direction of Mr. Sanders, and his mouth dropped open
when Dominick smiled at him.

"Be here no later than five," Maggie said.

"Si, Señora, cinco. Five."

"Very well then. Go home and get some rest. You
have a full night of work ahead of you."

"Gracias, gracias." The boy turned and propelled
himself out the door like a man shot out of a cannon.

In the days that followed, Maggie and Dominick
worked side by side, bickering and snapping at each
other like two angry magpies. Nothing he said could
please her. Nothing she did earned his approval. They
argued about where to place the workbench, the
shelves, and the counter; they disagreed about what
color to paint the dreary wood walls.

At night Maggie lay in bed, staring at the ceiling
long after she'd turned out the light, fretting and fuss-
ing to herself over something Dominick had said or
done earlier.

But more and more she found herself pondering some unguarded expression she'd caught on his face that had made the blood rush through her like rivers of fire. Just remembering a certain look of his made her tremble and ache in a way that both excited and frightened her. Sensing that she was treading on dangerous ground, she held her hands to her chest to still her pounding heart and forced herself to concentrate on his more irksome characteristics until the ache subsided and her blood coursed with anger instead.

She could handle anger; what she couldn't handle was the other, more worrisome feelings that were beginning to wage their own private battle within her.

"What a despicable man!" she moaned aloud, and after assuring herself that she did, indeed, foster the appropriate contempt for him, she managed to appease her conscience. At least for the time being.

While Maggie lay in bed fuming silently and not so silently, Dominick tossed and turned on the small, inadequate divan in the parlor. Periodically he sat up, slammed his fist into the feather pillow, and tried another position. "Damned woman!" he muttered.

Never had he met such an irritating and irksome woman in his life. Even when she was positively spitting fire, she still maintained a decorum that was downright annoying. What he wanted was to see her really lose her temper.

The thought of Maggie out of control brought a smile to his face. He only hoped he lived long enough to see a hair on her head fall out of place—Lord Almighty, she was probably born with her hair tied back in a knot and her head starchily held in that holier-than-thou pose of hers. Despite the danger that was inherent in even wanting it, he longed to find a way to pry off her armor, and he regretted that he never could.

After an entire night of steaming and trying to ignore feelings that neither of them wanted to admit, the two greeted each other in the morning like a firecracker with two lit fuses. The only thing that saved them from totally blowing up was the presence of the children.

After the main renovations had been completed, the bickering increased. There were more decisions to be made, more things to argue about.

The choice of curtain fabric was preceded by a major battle that lasted for three days. Dominick was surprised to find himself arguing like a defense attorney on behalf of checkered calico. What in tarnation was he doing with an opinion on curtains? Window dressings were woman's business. When he realized that he was spending an inordinate amount of time eyeing the windows and holding up pieces of fabric to them, he began to ponder the possibility that he was being emasculated. And that put him in a worse temper than ever. Maggie was doing this on purpose, he was sure of it.

The next issue that riled him no end was the naming of the shop. Maggie had her heart set on calling it Turner Shoemaking, in honor of her late husband. Dominick hated the name Turner. It was his opinion that it sounded like some indecisive fool who couldn't make up his bloody mind. He pushed aside the possibility that there might be another reason for his unseemly dislike of the name.

Then there was the little matter of explaining the name. "I'm sure the townfolk would want to know why a family named Sanders named their business Turner," he pointed out.

"Would you rather I call it Maggie's Shoemaking?"

Dominick shook his head. "How many men, or women for that matter, would come if they thought a woman was the sole proprietor?"

"There isn't a whole lot I can do about it, since I am a woman and I am the sole proprietor."

"You can have what is known in the stage-robbing business as invisible partners."

As always, whenever Dominick made reference to his "profession" Maggie listened with grim fascination. She hated realizing that there was a part of her that wanted to know everything about him, even the part of him that she wished with all her heart didn't exist.

"Are you going to tell me what invisible partners are, or aren't you?" she spat out in irritation.

He grinned knowingly. "At times it's prudent for a lone stage robber not to let his intended victims think he's working alone. In that case, there're tricks he might play." Checking to make certain he had her undivided attention, he continued. "He might, for instance, put several hats on the surrounding bushes to give the impression that others are standing nearby, ready to open fire if the need arises."

"Is that your advice?" she asked. "To place hats in the window to make people think I have several business partners?"

"Not a bad idea. But what I really had in mind was to give the shop a name that suggests there are several owners. Something like Turner, Sanders, and Harpsquire."

She frowned. "Who's Harpsquire?"

He glanced at her in astonishment. "Don't tell me you don't know? Why he's a fine and noble thief. He once robbed a bank, a train, and a stagecoach all within twenty-four hours of each other."

Scandalized that he would suggest she should immortalize such a man, she put her hands on her hips indignantly. "For now it will be Turner and Sanders—until I figure out a way to get rid of you."

Dominick grinned and bowed from the waist. "As you wish."

Dominick made the sign himself, refusing to let her see it until it had been firmly secured onto the face of the false front that extended above the roofline.

While he worked, she busied herself arranging her tools and supplies. She set her Blake sewer on the counter designed especially for it and stood her iron lasts in a row according to size. She hung her awls neatly on the wall and stacked boxes of brass tacks, copper rivets, and steel plates on the shelf Dominick had built expressly for the purpose.

Presently the hammering and thumping overhead stopped, and Dominick called her outside to see the sign. She stepped onto the porch, shading her eyes against the bright afternoon sun, and looked up over the door. The impressive wooden sign was large enough to be read clear across the street. Big, bold letters, burned into the wood, read "Sanders and Turner: Shoemakers."

Her mouth fell open and she spun around. "You . . . you . . ." Oh, what she would give to bring herself to speak like a man! "You put your own name first. Of all the conceited, presumptuous things to do."

Dominick shoved his hands in his pocket and grinned. "Sanders and Turner sounds more natural than the other way around. And once you've had time to think about it, you will agree."

"Don't tell me what I will do!" she said haughtily. "My name should not only be first, it should be the only name."

"Your name *is* first," he said, "*Mrs.* Sanders. What we have to do is explain the name Turner. We could say it's in honor of your departed father."

"Husband," she hissed.

"Or a silent partner."

"Husband!" she almost shouted.

He shrugged. "Have it your way."

Frustration mounted inside her like a snake ready to strike. Before she realized what she was doing, she lunged forward and shoved his arm angrily.

He said something in Basque and grabbed her wrists. "Well, now, I must say, the very prim and proper lady can be a firecracker at times, can't she?"

"Kindly unhand me," she demanded, her voice firm

and unwavering, even though she felt utterly mortified. Oh, now she'd done it. Acted like one of those
common fishwives whose shrill voices she'd heard
shoot along the wharves of San Francisco. Even
worse, she had resorted to a display of physical vio-
lence, undermining her proper upbringing.

"You are hardly in a position to be giving me orders," he purred softly. "I do believe we had best
continue this discussion inside. It's not good for business for the owners not to be in accord."

Cheeks burning with humiliation, she jutted out her
chin. One way or another, she intended to maintain
her dignity. "There is nothing further I wish to discuss
with you." She pulled her arms free and stomped inside the shop, slamming the door shut in his face.

A hairpin fell to the ground in front of him. He
leaned over and picked it up. "Why, Maggie," he said
aloud, "I do believe you almost let your hair down."

Chapter 12

On a warm, sunny day in early May, Maggie's shop was ready for business. Arriving early on that opening day, she dusted and swept the already spotless floors and counters and arranged a large bouquet of flowers supplied by Connie Mae's garden. Satisfied at last that the shop was ready, she took a deep breath and turned around to find Dominick watching her with thoughtful contemplation.

"How do you think it looks?" she asked, and when his gaze lowered to take in her new blue dress, bought especially for the occasion, she blushed and hastened to clarify her question. "How do you think the shop looks?"

Dominick surveyed the premises, looking as proud as if he alone were responsible. "I think it's a mighty fine shop." He turned to her, his eyes soft. "I have to give you credit, Maggie. You have an incredible flair for decorating."

His compliment brought her pleasure, *too much pleasure*. Still, one compliment deserved another. "And you have a flair for woodcraft," she said, and she meant it.

He looked pleased. *Too pleased*. For several long moments they stood admiring the shop like two parents doting on a newborn infant.

"The curtains are perfect," he said.

After the fight he had put up over the curtains, she would have been within her rights to lord it over him. But instead she blushed prettily and pointed to the shelves he had taken such pains to construct. "I've never seen finer shelves."

There was no accounting for it; while arguments had raged between them and insults had reigned supreme, a bond had been forged, uniting them in a way that neither wanted, yet both seemed desperate at the moment to protect.

At long last Dominick turned the small wooden sign in the front window to read "Open," while Maggie straightened her dress and checked the perfectly smooth bun at the nape of her neck.

Within minutes, women dressed in stylish morning gowns and extravagant hats began streaming in the front door, their voices shrill with curiosity.

"Scouts," Dominick whispered in her ear. "They've come to look over the territory." Gracefully he spun around to greet a tall woman whose face all but disappeared beneath a hat piled high with enough feathers to hide a mule. "Mrs. Gordon. How nice to see you again."

Although Maggie was surprised that Dominick remembered each woman's name, even those he'd met only briefly at some afternoon tea, she was pleased that her shop had attracted so many potential customers. Her pleasure soon diminished, however, when it became obvious that it was neither the shop nor its lovely shoe samples that were the main attraction. It was Dominick.

Indeed, the women went to extreme lengths to get a good look at him, pushed and shoved each other in their eagerness to take their turn at the counter, and hung on his every word as if it held a divine message. Maggie thought it disgusting the way certain women— and it didn't seem to matter whether or not they were married—preened like a bunch of fine-feathered birds during mating season.

It wouldn't have been so bad if Dominick had tried to discourage their overtures. But he made no such attempt; indeed, he appeared to enjoy every sweep of

feminine lash, sashaying hip, and flattering word that
was doled out or uttered for his benefit.

Maggie could hardly get a word in edgewise.

"For you, Miss Winkerton," Dominick said smoothly,
addressing a matronly woman whose ridiculous ringlets and ruffled gown would have been better suited
to someone half her age. "May I suggest blue velvet
shoes? I do believe we can match the exact color of
your lovely blue eyes."

Maintaining her businesslike demeanor with effort,
Maggie grimaced in disapproval. The amusement on
his face when their eyes met incensed her beyond reason. Normally she would never disagree with a business associate in front of a customer, but he left her
no choice.

"Blue velvet is . . . lovely," she began tactfully.
"What did you say your name was?"

"Miss Winkerton."

"Blue velvet is lovely, Miss Winkerton, but as you
can imagine, not very practical. Perhaps I can interest
you in a high-button boot in a soft leather . . ."

"I'll take the blue velvet." Miss Winkerton's ringlets
dangled like little pendulums around her face as she
pulled out a small brocade reticule.

"Wonderful," Dominick exclaimed from behind the
counter, and the other women in line tittered in anticipation. "You don't need to pay until you pick up your
shoes. Now, if you would be kind enough to sit in
that chair and remove your boot, Mrs. Sanders will
take your measurements."

The woman giggled, yanked up her calico skirts,
and sat down with all the grace of a belly-flopping
bear. Heaving a sigh, Maggie sat herself primly on a
little wooden stool and drew her cloth tape measure
along the woman's long and somewhat pudgy foot.
Blue velvet! Of all the outlandish ideas!

Having turned Miss Winkerton over to Maggie,
Dominick directed his full attention to the next
woman in line, who promptly extended her hand and

announced that she was the wife of Sheriff Badger. "Mighty pleased to make your acquaintance," she said. "I read all about how you and your family survived that terrible ordeal. Why, you're lucky to be alive."

Dominick graciously lifted her hand to his lips. "I'm delighted to meet you at last, Mrs. Badger. And yes, we are lucky to be alive."

Watching him out of the corner of her eye, Maggie wanted to scream. Why, she thought in disgust, he acted like the only man in a bordello trying to make his decision as to which woman was worthy of his company.

Of all the egotistical . . . and to think that before opening the store that morning, she had actually regarded him with gratitude and benevolence.

"Excuse me, Mrs. Sanders."

Blinking, Maggie turned her attention back to Miss Winkerton.

"May I put my boot back on?"

"Yes, of course," Maggie said, embarrassed to be caught remiss in giving a customer her undivided attention.

For the rest of the morning and into the afternoon, Maggie did her best to ignore Dominick and failed miserably. As, one by one, the women announced their impractical and, in some instances downright unflattering, choices, Maggie grew more and more angry. It was all she could do to remain civil while she measured her customers' feet, and more than once she was tempted to point out the improprieties of certain footwear on a horse-size foot. But of course she didn't. Some things were best left unsaid, and comments about the size of a woman's foot were in that category.

According to the dictates of fashion, a woman was expected to require no larger than a size five shoe. Indeed, according to *Harper's Bazaar*, no fashionable woman would own up to as much as half a size larger.

But Maggie knew from experience that in reality the average woman wore a size six or better.

At her shop in San Francisco, Maggie had discovered that by simply marking a shoe "custom five," no matter what the size, a woman could be both comfortable and fashionable, and none the wiser. Her customers, having no clue that Maggie had given them a larger shoe and, therefore, a more properly fitting shoe, had expressed delight that Maggie's shoes were so much more comfortable than the ready-made ones sold at the general store or hawked by some traveling salesman.

Making up her mind to treat her present customers to the same face-saving method that had served her so well up north, she took careful measurements and recorded them neatly in a leather-bound notebook. As she worked, she kept an eye and an ear focused on Dominick and continued to seethe inwardly at the way the women fawned over him and made shameless advances.

It wasn't that she was jealous, of course. Glory be, what a ridiculous notion! But she did have a business to run, and it was rather unseemly to permit such open flirtation in her shop!

Maggie wondered what the women would have to say if they knew that the man who charmed them into acting like lovesick adolescents was really the notorious Kissing Bandit. The thought amused her so much that she quite forgot her aggravation and began enjoying herself. The important thing was to sell shoes, and Dominick certainly was doing that!

At the end of the day, she looked over her orders. Even with her Blake sewer, she would have to work day and night for the next month to fill them, and she still might not succeed in having the shoes ready when promised.

"I'm going to have to hire more help," she announced. The idea filled her with both tribulation and excitement. Even when Luke was alive, the shop in

San Francisco had barely made enough money to cover expenses. Never could she have afforded to pay wages. Now, in only a short time, she already had one employee and was considering the possibility of hiring more.

"Without help, I'll never get these orders done in time."

Dominick watched her lay out her supplies. "We have Manuel."

"But he knows nothing about sewing shoes together." She planned to stay late one night to show him how to cut out the leather using her patterns. But to teach him more would require hours, perhaps days of training. "We'd have to let him work days while I train him."

"As I've said before, Maggie, I don't think it's a good idea to have someone working that closely with us. A person might overhear something that could jeopardize our little ploy."

She bristled at the suggestion that they were in cahoots. "By 'jeopardize,' do you mean it might get you out of my house sooner? Well, now, I can't think of anything I'd like better."

"Let me assure you that the feeling is mutual," he replied. "But until that glorious day arrives, you're going to have to put up with my help."

"You know nothing about making shoes."

"If I can sell shoes, I can make them."

She felt her irritation rise. He was so almighty confident! "Selling shoes is not just a matter of persuading a customer to place an order," she said haughtily. "The shoes must match the customer's lifestyle and personality, and you know nothing about that." Just thinking of Miss Winkerton and the blue velvet shoes infuriated her. "Absolutely nothing!"

His eyes widened in astonishment. "How can you say such a thing? Every woman who walked into this shop got the shoe that was exactly right for her."

"If that's true, would you mind telling me what possible use Miss Winkerton has for an impractical pair of blue velvet shoes?"

He leaned so close to her that his warm breath fanned across her face like a tropical breeze. This brazen attempt to intimidate her only infuriated her more, and she stubbornly held her ground.

"She can wear them to a dance, of course."

Stretching to gain as much height advantage as possible, she boldly met his gaze. "I doubt that Miss Winkerton has ever been to a dance in her entire life!"

Dominick backed away with a careless shrug of his shoulders. "Maybe the reason she's never danced is because she's not had the proper shoes."

"I somehow doubt that," Maggie said. "A shoemaker needs repeat business to be successful. How many of our customers do you think will be satisfied with their purchases? I can tell you exactly. None!"

"Maggie, Maggie, Maggie." He purred her name like a cat being stroked by a master's hand. "Do you think that practicality is the only road to customer satisfaction? You can know everything about a person by what he or she wears. And I'm telling you that Miss Winkerton with her little bobbing curls and her little frilly bows is a woman who longs to kick up her heels. What we're doing, Maggie, is giving her the chance to do so. Who knows? Maybe the shoes will help her land a husband."

This last comment made her laugh. "So on top of being a stagecoach robber, you're also a matchmaker," she said, her good nature restored. "Your talents never fail to amaze me."

Dominick grinned. "Would you care to discuss some of my other talents?" he asked wryly.

For no good reason, her face suddenly grew hot. "I have no intention of further discussing anything," she said. "We have work to do."

"As you choose. But I'm right about Miss Winkerton. Mark my words."

Time would prove Dominick wrong. She was sure

of it. But not wanting to argue further, she bit back the retort that played on her lips and chose a medium-sized awl from the wall.

"So, tell me," he said, watching her, "what does it take to be a shoemaker besides a discerning eye?"

Since he sounded genuinely interested, she answered him. "An eye for detail. A sense of style and good taste." She flashed him a pointed look. "The qualities that you are sadly lacking."

He grinned. "You don't think the red sash that is the trademark of the Kissing Bandit reveals any of those qualities? Or the way I wear my beret?" He plucked his beret from a hook on the wall, tossed it in the air, caught it with one finger, and placed it rakishly on his head.

Not wanting to admit how devastatingly handsome he looked, she turned her attention to her work table. "If you want to learn, then I suggest you watch."

With a shrug, he pushed the beret to the back of his head and straddled a stool next to her workbench.

For the next two hours, she guided him through the first of the thirty-five steps necessary to make a shoe. She showed him how to lay out the patterns and cut the leather. Finally she demonstrated how the pieces fit together. "This is the vamp," she said, holding up the toe section. "After we sew the vamp together with the rear quarters, we'll soak it in water and nail it to a last."

He watched her carefully and asked questions—questions that were intelligent and perceptive and seemed to suggest he was interested in learning the craft. This, at least, was encouraging. Maybe he would be of help to her after all.

He insisted upon trying his hand at cutting the leather, and she was only too happy to let him take over the tiresome chore. Even with the long soaking in water to make the leather pliable, cutting and shaping it required a strong hand. During those long, lonely months following her husband's death when she ran the business by herself, the difficulty of cutting through tough sheets of cowhide had made her fingers ache and the palms of her hands grow calluses.

Working side by side, they were so engrossed in their task that they quite forgot to argue; indeed, they even managed a civil, almost friendly, tone. It suddenly occurred to Maggie how very much she had missed the companionship that comes with working in close harmony with another person, the sharing of a job well done.

Before they went home that day, Dominick had cut out several pairs of shoes with meticulous care, while Maggie sat at her little Blake sewer, stitching the uppers together. The following morning, she would teach him how to hold the shoe down with a special strap called a stirrup and attach the bottom to the uppers by stitching through a hidden channel cut into the leather sole.

It felt good to be back at work. She loved the rich smell of leather as she molded it around the lasts and enjoyed watching the finished product take shape beneath her nimble fingers.

That night she lay in bed feeling content and satisfied. Her shop was more than she could ever have hoped for, thanks mainly to Dominick and his surprising and welcome skills in carpentry. She was still galled by the sign but was willing to put her feelings aside. For now.

As long as he was willing to cooperate and work with her, she supposed it only fair that she overlook some, if not all, of his faults.

Maggie rose at the first sign of dawn, feeling more refreshed than she'd felt in months. Eager to get to the shop, she quickly finished her household chores and walked Jamie to school. He looked so grown up in his new knee-high breeches and suspenders, with

his books strapped together and dangling over his
shoulder from a leather strap. His most prized possession, however, was the black woolen beret that Dominick had given him.

The early-morning fog began to lift, and patches of
blue sky showed through the wispy clouds. Jamie and
his mother followed the dirt path that cut across a
walnut orchard and walked along a dry gully to the
little one-room schoolhouse. The entire time they
walked, Jamie talked of nothing but Dominick, calling
him by his Basque name.

"Aita said that if you're happy you must wear your
beret at the back of your head, like this." He demonstrated, turning his handsome young head so she could
see his beret to best advantage.

"How interesting," Maggie said. It had never occurred to her that a hat could be used to communi-
cate. "And what does it mean when you wear your
hat pulled to the side of your head, like this?" She
arranged Jamie's beret in a way that Dominick usually
wore his.

Jamie's eyes glinted mischievously. "Aita said that
you only wear it that way when you want a girl to
smile at you."

"What?" How dare that brazen man discuss the
subject of girls with her son!

Jamie, thinking that she'd not heard, began repeating, "Aita said . . ."

"I know what he said. Oh, never mind." Her face
softened. "You'd better hurry, young man, or you'll
be late."

Jamie gave his mother a quick hug, held on to his
beret with one hand, and cleared the final distance
with racing feet, his books banging against his back.
Without a backward glance, he ran up the wide
wooden steps and disappeared through the double
doors just before the low, grating ring of the tardy
bell pealed out its final note.

Maggie followed the same winding pathway home.

Her thoughts were troubled by Jamie's and Laurie-Anne's affection for Dominick. It was obvious by the way the children hung on his every word and followed him around the house how much they idolized the very ground he walked on.

It amazed her that Dominick never seemed bothered by their constant demands for attention. Indeed, if anything, it seemed to her that he encouraged them. Often as she labored over her chores or sat sketching shoe designs, she'd hear the three of them off in the distance somewhere, singing and laughing together, or playing Basque games that made no sense to her but seemed to require a lot of running, jumping, and shouting.

What would happen when he left? she wondered. Would Laurie-Anne once again become withdrawn and solemn like she had been following the death of her father? It was possible, and every day that Dominick remained would only make it that much more difficult for the children when the time came for him to leave.

If and when that time ever got here, she muttered to herself, surprised to find that her earlier sunny disposition had disappeared, leaving her gloomy and irritable.

Thinking that it was her failure to rid herself of him that was at the root of her ill temper, she was shocked when her heart skipped a beat at the sound of his voice drifting toward her through an open window. He was singing one of the songs he'd made up to help Laurie-Anne get dressed in the morning. "You put your arm in here, you put your arm in there . . ."

It was at that moment, while she stood there listening and absorbing every word until it echoed in her heart, that it occurred to her.

Glory be, it didn't just occur to her. It hit her like a bolt of lightning coming out of nowhere! Stunned, she stood frozen in place until Dominick finished his song.

It's not true, she told herself, fighting the rising panic inside. It can't be true. Oh, dear God, don't let it be true! But no matter how much she fought against the notion, there it was, as clear as crystal: *She no longer wanted Dominick to leave!*

Chapter 13

Maggie found Dominick in the parlor trying to teach Laurie-Anne how to fasten the papier-mâché buttons on her little high-button shoes.

Dominick looked up at Maggie and handed Laurie-Anne her other shoe. "There's a girl. Now let's see if you can put this shoe on all by yourself." To Maggie, he said, "You look like you're on the warpath."

Not on the warpath, she thought, just confused. How could a fine, upstanding woman such as herself want a man who was not her husband, never would be her husband—never could be her husband—to continue living under her very own roof? What could she be thinking of? The man was an outlaw. An outlaw!

She didn't want to think about her traitorous change of heart—so she focused on the way his beret was arranged on his head. It was worn to the side in that same rakish way she'd come to know so well. Recalling what Jamie told her, she knew now that his beret was yet another of his many ways of manipulating her.

Irritation took the place of confusion, and she accepted that as proof that what had happened outside had been nothing more than a momentary lapse of judgment. Even a fine, upstanding woman was entitled to that, wasn't she? Feeling considerably relieved and somewhat reprieved, she scowled. "For your information, I have no intention of smiling!"

He didn't appear the least bit perturbed or puzzled

by her announcement. "Don't worry," he replied cheerfully. "I'll smile enough for both of us."

"Instead of smiling, you might tell me how much longer you expect to stay." Confronting him was her way of assuring herself that she had regained her usual impeccable judgment.

"Is there a problem?" he asked innocently.

"None that can't be solved with your departure," she said, matching his demeanor. Assured that her good common sense was intact, she even managed to duplicate his light tone.

"How gratifying it must be to know one's problems can be so easily solved." He patted Laurie-Anne on the head. "There's a girl. See? You can put your shoes on all by yourself."

Laurie-Anne beamed with pride. "Mama, Mama! Look what I can do."

Maggie knelt down by her daughter and gave her a hug. "You're getting to be such a big girl." At the sound of the door knocker, Maggie released her. "I do believe that must be Consuela."

Laurie-Anne scurried down the hall to the front door to greet her. "Cowella," she shouted in her childish voice, "I can put my shoes on all by myself!"

"That's wonderful," Consuela said. "I think that deserves a celebration. We'll make some cookies later."

Watching Consuela and Laurie-Anne, Maggie nodded with approval. Already the young woman had proved herself a valuable asset. Maggie was impressed with the way she handled Laurie-Anne with warm and gentle firmness, and in some cases, good humor. For her part, Laurie-Anne seemed genuinely fond of Consuela; she waited impatiently for the girl's arrival each morning and was disappointed to see her go home at night.

It pleased Maggie that Laurie-Anne was obviously so fond of Consuela. However, it was quite another

matter when her daughter seemed more upset to see
Dominick leave than her own mother!

"You be good for Consuela, you hear?" Dominick
said. He tweaked Laurie-Anne under the chin and
winked. "And I'll take you to the sweet shop for a
treat."

"Don't I get a hug?" Maggie asked, folding her
arms around her daughter.

Laurie-Anne planted a wet kiss on her mother's
cheek and wiggled out of her arms, only to fly quickly
into Dominick's arms once again. "Can I have
bonbons?"

"Of course, you can," Dominick said, burying his
nose in the child's sweet-smelling hair and twirling her
in his arms.

Laurie-Ann responded with peals of laughter.

Hating herself for begrudging her daughter her fun,
Maggie waited. Impatiently tapping her toe, she
pulled on her gloves, picked up the basket that held
their lunch, and swallowed her annoyance, managing
somehow to wait until she and Dominick had left the
house before she spoke her mind.

"I don't appreciate your ingratiating yourself with
my children."

He slid her a sideways glance. "I would think you
would be happy that I take an interest in their
welfare."

She stopped and faced him. "You're not their
father."

"That doesn't mean I can't be a friend."

His eyes were soft, his mouth gentle, and it was
all Maggie could do not to reach up and follow the
curve of his lips with a fingertip. "And . . . and
when you leave?" she asked, her voice suddenly de-
serting her.

He looked at her hard for several long minutes.
"You're afraid they'll feel abandoned, aren't you?"

His insight surprised her. "They're very fond of
you."

"I know . . . Maggie . . .".

For some strange reason she suddenly couldn't breathe. "What is it, Dominick?"

A shadow played upon his forehead as if some silent battle raged within. "I told you I can't leave until I find what I came for."

Something in his voice, a hard edge, perhaps, made her take pause. "You've made no attempt to conduct your business."

"How can I? You can't bear to let me out of your sight."

"Can't bear . . . ?" She swallowed hard. It was true that at first she kept a close watch on him, afraid to let him out of her sight for fear he'd perpetrate one of his robberies. Now it occurred to her that there might have been a more personal reason for her vigilance, and she was almost as shocked by this sudden thought as she had been earlier at the way her heart had lifted at the sound of his voice.

"Maggie?"

"We'd better hurry or we'll be late." With that, she brushed past him and didn't dare look at him until they had reached the shop and she was safely behind her little sewing machine.

Once she started work, she tried to convince herself that what had happened earlier meant nothing. But the more she tried, the more she realized the futility of it. What had happened to her while she stood listening to Dominick sing did mean something. She was as sure of that as she was of her own name.

Her eyes sought Dominick, and she wondered about the tortured look she had seen in his eyes earlier that day when he talked about why he couldn't leave. Who was he looking for? And why did she have the feeling that it would be better for all of them if Dominick Sanders never found his man?

The last thought upset her so much, it took several moments before she could stop shaking enough to thread the machine.

During the night Manuel had set everything out in perfect order. He'd cut the sheets of leather using the patterns she'd left and followed her instructions perfectly. Each piece was laid out neatly on her workbench with the customers' names printed on scraps of parchment.

She counted each piece, then set to work teaching Dominick how to shape heels with a half-moon knife and how to buttress an insole. As usual, he caught on quickly, and soon, convinced that he could carry on alone, she settled herself back in front of her sewing machine.

Together they admired the first pair of boots they completed, their earlier awkwardness with one another forgotten. Maggie ran her fingers along the leather and, feeling the slightest hint of roughness, polished it away with a burnisher made from animal bone.

Dominick remarked on her attention to detail. "I must say, you make boots as good if not better than any man."

There it was again, the same warm rapport they'd shared on opening day. Lord Almighty, she fretted. It wasn't right to feel like this with a bandit. Not right at all.

"Is that a smile?" he asked.

"What?"

"On your face. A smile."

Maggie clamped her mouth shut. She couldn't even smile without his making her feel like she was submitting to him in some physical sense. "Rest assured that if it was, it wasn't for your benefit!"

"I can't tell you how sorry I am to hear that." He glanced at her profile and was relieved to find her glowering again. He knew how to handle her bad moods. But her smile—now that was downright disarming. Why, he'd even seen that smile in his dreams lately. Damn woman! He couldn't even dream anymore without her moving in and taking over. And earlier that morning, when she stood looking up at him . . .

Not wanting to dwell on the softness he'd seen on her face, or to acknowledge how hard it had been not to take her in his arms, he put a stop to his thoughts and worked in scowling silence for the rest of the morning.

It was Maggie who decided it was time to stop for lunch. She picked up the basket she'd brought with her and spread the bread and cheese on the counter, along with a flask of lemonade, and the plump, fresh strawberries she had picked from Connie Mae's garden while they were still covered with early-morning dew.

While she poured the juice into two tin cups, Dominick reexamined the boots they had just completed. "Do you think you could make me a pair of work boots like this?"

She eyed him thoughtfully. "Whenever I make boots for someone, I try to consider the requirements of their profession. What exactly does a bandit look for in a boot?"

"Comfort," he said without hesitation. He glanced at her wryly. "In my business comfort is of utmost importance. Sometimes it's necessary to wait for hours for a stage to arrive. The last thing a bandit wants when it's time to make a quick escape is sore feet. It probably wouldn't be a bad idea to make them bullet-proof. Don't look so horrified, Maggie. You'd be amazed at how many times a bandit is likely to be shot in the foot."

She looked down at his boots, caught herself staring, and quickly averted her eyes. "I'll see what I can do," she muttered, not at all certain she liked the idea of providing a means by which a bandit could better do his job.

After lunch, she showed him how to polish the boots, using grease instead of polish to make them waterproof. She poured the grease from an earthenware bottle onto the leather, and smoothed it out with a stick. She then demonstrated the correct way to polish the leather to a high gloss using a beef bone.

She handed him the bone, pulling her fingers quickly away upon touching his. For a fleeting moment their gazes held, then both looked away; he studied the bone in his hand, while she stared unseeingly at a list of needed supplies she had written out earlier.

As they continued to work side by side, an awkward silence stretched between them, broken only by the arrival of a customer. The silence was in such complete contrast to the constant bickering they were used to that neither knew quite how to handle it.

It had been relatively quiet throughout the morning, and they were both relieved when business picked up considerably during the afternoon so that they no longer had to contend with the strong vibrations that flowed between them.

By late afternoon, the welcome bells on the door jingled continually with the steady flow of customers. Some had stopped by just to say hello, others to place an order. Still others came to share the latest gossip. Maggie's shop was fast becoming the town's most popular place to socialize.

Mrs. Pickings arrived with George in tow. She was dressed in a deep-purple taffeta dress that made her impressive hips bulge out like the sides of a whiskey barrel. "George hasn't had a pair of new boots in ten years," she explained. "Isn't that right, George?"

George grunted and puffed on his pipe.

"If you sit down I'll measure your foot," Maggie said. "You might want to consider a heavy-soled, hobnailed work shoe this time rather than a boot."

"Ain't considering no such thing," he growled. "And furthermore, no woman is gonna touch my foot."

Surprised that the man could actually voice an opinion, Maggie pointed to the chair. "Boots it shall be then, but I still need to measure your foot."

George gruffly nodded his head toward the counter, where Dominick was pointing out the features of the new and increasingly popular lace shoe over the side-button ankle boot to an elderly woman. "Have him do it."

"I've had much experience in taking foot measurements," Maggie explained. "Isn't that right, Mrs. Pickings?"

Mrs. Pickings wasn't used to being asked her opinion. She looked momentarily flustered, but recovered quickly and nodded. "That's right, George. Women-folk are much handier at measuring than a man is. Remember how you measured the lot for the cattle fence and came up short? Three feet short, at least," she assured Maggie. "We lost six head of cattle because of the gap in the fence."

"That's no reason why I should trust my feet to a woman," George argued.

Once started on George's shortcomings, Mrs. Pickings refused to be dissuaded from continuing. "Then there was the time you decided to dig a new well. You measured our property and still managed to put the well on Doc Hathaway's property. The old doctor couldn't thank us enough," Mrs. Pickings explained. "But of course that meant we had to dig another well and . . ."

"Never mind," George growled. He plopped himself into the chair, tore off his boot, and stuck his stockinged foot in Maggie's face. "Do what you have to do and be done with it!"

At exactly five o'clock, Maggie turned the sign in the window to read "Closed." Business had been even better than the day before, but the steady stream of customers that afternoon allowed little time to fill the orders. She and Dominick decided to work for an hour or two before going home.

When Manuel arrived, Maggie and Dominick immediately began acting in a way that seemed more suited to married life. It was far removed from the stilted exchanges and strained silences that had marked their day, or the bickering of earlier days.

For Manuel's sake, he called her "Sweetheart"; for Manuel's sake, she called him "Dear." For Manuel's sake, he lay a hand on her shoulder as he reached for something; for Manuel's sake, she smiled up at him, like any loving wife would do.

In between this playacting, Dominick cut out leather and hammered soles, and Maggie sat in front of her sewing machine, enjoying the steady, gentle hum that ebbed and flowed with the pressure of her foot. While the two worked peacefully, side by side, Manuel swept the floor and wiped off the counters, and seemed completely oblivious to the harmonious scene that was played out for his benefit.

Indeed, the young man's mind seemed far away, and it wasn't until Maggie happened to notice the soft look on his face when he read the name of Lisa Tubbs on an order for shoes that she suspected her young employee might have a fancy for the girl. Recalling the young woman, Maggie could hardly blame him. Lisa had a pretty, round face, framed by long red hair and sparkling green eyes. She also had the good sense to order a practical welt button shoe.

A matchmaker at heart, Maggie couldn't resist the temptation. She finished Lisa's shoes and held them up for Manuel's inspection. "A fine pair of shoes for a fine young woman, wouldn't you say?"

Manuel nodded, his cheeks turning red. "Yes, Señora."

"She said she can't pick them up until late next week. It seems a pity, doesn't it? That she has to wait so long for her shoes?"

"Yes, Señora. A pity."

Maggie kept her eyes on her work. "Of course, if you had time to deliver them to her . . ."

"Si, si, Señora!" he exclaimed, and then, regaining his composure, he drew in a deep breath. "I mean, yes, Señora. I think I could find time to deliver her shoes. First thing tomorrow morning."

Maggie smiled at him. "Then it's settled."

Manuel returned to his broom and Maggie concentrated on the next order.

"*Arraixo!*" Dominick yelled out suddenly. Jumping to his feet, he threw down his hammer and hopped around the room shaking his hand.

Maggie quickly rushed to his side. "What's wrong, dear? What's the matter?"

"I hit my thumb with the damned hammer," he muttered, adding an irrelevant "Sweetheart" under his breath.

"Hold still," she said. Taking his hand, she examined it carefully. No skin was broken, but the thumb was slightly red and beginning to swell. "Quick," she called to Manuel, "bring me some water."

"Si, Señora." Manuel rushed to the bucket of water that they kept available for such emergencies and filled a tin cup.

"Here you are, Señor Sanders," Manuel said, setting the cup on the counter.

Dominick plunged his thumb into the water and almost at once the creases of pain in his face softened. "Thank you, Manuel."

Lifting his gaze to Maggie's, Dominick was surprised by the lines of concern that spread across her forehead. She was suddenly all softness and gentleness—traits usually evident with Jamie and Laurie-Anne but never before directed so intensely at him. Somehow he doubted that this was only an act for Manuel's benefit. Even Maggie couldn't have feigned the dark flecks of caring in her eyes and the way her lips trembled.

It occurred to him now that what he saw in her face was not just concern but something far more significant. Something that touched him on every possible level, gently drawing from him that which he had no idea he was able to give. Shouldn't be giving. Had no business giving.

But nonetheless, there he was, giving back all the same warm and tremulous feelings he was receiving. Suddenly he didn't know how to act, what to say, where to look. Nor did he know how to contain the urgent need that throbbed from within and threatened to consume the very last shred of rationality on his part.

Not knowing what else to do, he stood still, surprised by what should have been so obvious from the start, wondering how it could have happened. He'd taken such utter care to make certain that it didn't happen, that *they* didn't happen.

"How do you feel, dear?" she asked at last, her voice soft, colored by uncertainty. With a gentleness that reached beyond what was possible for a touch, she ran the tip of her finger across his skin.

"I'm fine," he said, stunned to find how very much he liked the feel of her skin next to his. His heart was beating harder than it had any right to beat. And because it came so naturally to his lips, he whispered the word "Sweetheart."

She stood gazing at him and he gazed back, and for the longest while, neither could move or speak.

And it had nothing to do with Manuel.

Indeed, Manuel's presence was quite forgotten and might have remained so indefinitely had he not knocked over the wastepaper basket with his broom.

Blinking like a person just awakened from a long sleep, Maggie put Dominick's thumb back into the water and moved swiftly away, as if suddenly reminded of some urgent business across the room that needed her immediate attention.

Dominick stared at his swollen thumb and told himself that what had transpired between them was nothing more than a moment of madness. Everyone was entitled to one such moment. It was nothing to get upset about.

But the incident had a sobering effect on him, and for the rest of the night he could think of little else. As much as he hated to admit it, Maggie was right about one thing: The sooner he found his man and moved on, the better.

Chapter 14

Three nights later, Dominick made his way out the back door with the stealth of a mountain lion tracking its prey. As his eyes adjusted to the shifting shadows of the night, he darted soundlessly through the yard toward the alley that ran the length of the property.

The black velvet sky was dotted with more stars than it was possible to count, and he thought of the many nights he'd sat tending sheep with nothing to keep him company but their constant bleats and an occasional shooting star. It was strange that during those years he'd never known any inkling of loneliness—never comprehended the full meaning of the word. Until now.

Now that he was forced to guard every expression, every word, every look, he'd become an expert on the subject. And every night that he lay on the divan and thought of Maggie in the bed down the hall, so close yet so out of reach, his knowledge of loneliness increased tenfold.

He didn't want to think of her now, or how she'd looked earlier in the evening, all soft and starry-eyed despite the way he'd ignored her these last three days. He concentrated instead on his immediate problem.

Every night for the last two months, from midnight until two a.m., he'd waited in the alleyway behind the house, where he had instructed his contact to meet him. He was beginning to think that the coded wire he'd sent shortly after arriving in Santa Barbara had not reached its destination. What he didn't want to think about was the possibility that something had happened to the person it was addressed to.

There was a lot lately he didn't want to think about. And he spent the better part of the next two hours trying his damnedest not to think at all.

He pulled out his pocket watch and saw by the light of a match that it was nearly two o'clock. He decided to smoke a cigarette before giving up his vigil. He took out a wisp of paper and, holding it in the palm of his hand, dropped a pinch of tobacco into it. Working by touch alone, he rolled the paper, tucking in the ends and licking it.

Then he sensed a presence and tensed, his hand at his waist, ready to pull out the derringer hidden beneath his vest. He dared not breathe until he heard a familiar voice. "Excuse me, sir, do you happen to have a match?"

Dominick felt a surge of relief. "Foster, you old fool. Where the hell have you been?"

A shadow loomed closer. "I was out of town on business. A big gold shipment was sent to Los Angeles. We made quite a haul on that one."

Dominick grinned. "Good for you. Wish I could have been along."

"Next time." Foster spit out his tobacco. "I was sorry to hear about Barnes. He was a good man."

"He was that," Dominick said grimly. He stuck the cigarette in his mouth and lit it.

"You said in your message he was buried in the Strangers' Cemetery?"

He inhaled and nodded. "Just outside of town."

"Poor Barnes. We couldn't even give him a proper funeral."

"Don't go fretting over that. He got himself a proper funeral, all right." Dominick grimaced at the memory. "Complete with two hours of preaching."

Foster whistled. "Two hours, eh? I doubt that he had heard that much preaching in his lifetime. How did you manage that without drawing suspicion to yourself?"

Dominick chuckled. "Let's just say I have a worthy adversary who thought that the best way to get back at me was to subject me to two hours of fire-and-brimstone preaching."

"Like I always said, there's nothing more useful on occasion than one's enemies. Got anythin' here?"

"No. But I expect to see something in the next few weeks. Word is that a big shipment is heading this way the middle of next month. Is that true?"

"It's true. June tenth, to be exact."

Dominick thought for a moment. "That's bound to create some action."

"What about the sheriff? Can we trust him?"

Dominick rubbed his chin. "As far as I can tell, he's completely above board."

Foster grunted. "What a pity. I thought we were onto something there. Are you sure? What about his deputy?"

"I'm still investigating him."

"Anyone else?"

"It's rumored that Harvey Grover, owner of the general store, has been dropping some big ones at the gaming tables."

"Maybe business is good," Foster said. "I hear the shoe business isn't all that bad either."

"As always, your information is impeccable," Dominick said, grinning.

"I also hear that your . . . ah . . . shall we say business partner is a lady of considerable charms."

Dominick stiffened. It wouldn't do for Foster to suspect anything. "The lady in question is about as charming as an alleycat. On second thought, perhaps the means by which you obtain your information could stand an overhaul."

Foster grunted. "Whatever you say. Meanwhile, I think it would be better if you lay low until that shipment is set to arrive."

"That's what I want to talk to you about." Dominick hesitated. "I'm not sure that my being here in Santa Barbara serves any real purpose. I've been here for nearly two months, and I know no more now than I did at the start. I think maybe I should return to Sacramento."

"Why so impatient suddenly? We know the man we're looking for lives in the area. With fewer than three thousand people in Santa Barbara, there's a good chance you even know him. Maybe even sold him a pair of shoes. It's only a matter of time until he'll give himself away. They all do sooner or later. If you dropped out of sight now, it could cause speculation, and we can't afford anyone to go probing into your affairs at this point. Just keep your eyes and ears open."

"All right, Foster, but after I find my man, I'm leaving here."

"*Our* man, Sanders. It's our man, and don't you go forgetting it. We can't have you acting out a personal vendetta."

Dominick's eyes hardened. For three long years, he'd lived for the day that he found the man responsible for his family's death. He had a personal vendetta, all right. Had the right to one, and there wasn't anyone who was going to convince him otherwise. *Not even Maggie.*

Not sure where the last thought had come from, he dropped the butt of his cigarette on the ground and crushed it with his shoe. "Just get me out of here. The sooner, the better."

"Don't tell me the alleycat is more than you can handle." Foster chuckled. "I know several of us who would gladly take your place."

"Believe me, you'd have a better time in front of a lynching mob."

"That bad, eh? Well, cheer up. You only have a few more weeks left. I'll send last-minute instructions through the usual channels." Foster squeezed Dominick's arm. "We're going to get him. Take my word for it." With that, Foster disappeared as quietly as he'd come.

Dominick stood listening until he was certain Foster was gone, then retraced his steps through the garden to the house.

He closed the back door softly so as not to wake anyone and tiptoed through the dark kitchen to the parlor. He was about to undress when Laurie-Anne cried out. Fearing that she might wake Jamie or Maggie, he hurriedly felt his way to her room and pushed open her door.

"Aita?" she called, her voice muffled.

"What is it, little one? Why are you crying?"

"I had a scary dream," she sobbed.

He sat on the side of her bed and gathered her in his arms. "There, there, little one. There's nothing to be afraid of."

"Would you stay with me, Aita?"

"I'll stay with you, but you must lie down and let me cover you before you catch a cold."

Laurie-Anne lay her head on the soft feather pillow and Dominick drew the warm woolen blanket over her shoulders. "Now you can pretend that you're a sheep and I'm a shepherd watching over you. How's that?"

Laurie-Anne giggled. "Sheep don't sleep in beds."

"You're right, little one. Sheep sleep out under the stars. At night they look like puffy clouds that have fallen to the ground. A shepherd has to make sure that none of the clouds drifts away."

"Mama told me that an angel came down and told the sheep about a baby being borned," Laurie-Anne said. "Do you think the sheep were scared of the angel, Aita?"

"It's hard to know. But I do know this: A star shone in the east when that baby was born. And on every Christmas Eve since that long ago night, sheep always face east when they sleep."

"Do you think the sheep are looking for the baby?"

"It's possible."

He heard a soft sound like a sigh from the other side of the room, and thinking it had come from Jamie's bed, he fell silent, not wanting to disturb him further. He picked up Laurie-Anne's warm little hand and squeezed it, then stroked her back until her even breathing told him she had fallen asleep.

Watching her in the shadows of the night, he was surprised to find himself reluctant to leave her side. All those years he'd watched over sheep, he had never imagined how much more satisfying it would be to watch over a child.

Maggie was right, he thought. It was dangerous for him to stay longer. He must finish his business and leave before it became impossible for him to do so.

Pulling himself away at last, he stopped to check on Jamie, then left the room quietly, his footsteps muffled by the handmade braided rug. The door sighed on its leather hinges as he slipped past it.

In the parlor he lit a stub of a candle and, too unsettled to sleep, searched through the cupboards of the sideboard until he found a bottle of red wine. After uncorking it, he located the wine glasses.

He sensed rather than heard Maggie approach. Turning, he could just make out her lovely feminine form through the archway, in the shadows of the hall.

"What are you doing up?" he asked, forcing a coldness into his voice in a desperate attempt to keep her at a distance.

"I . . . I thought I heard something. I was just checking on the children." She held the small opening at the neck of her nightgown closed with one hand and stepped back further into the shadows where it was even more difficult for him to see her. "Good . . . good night."

She retreated, and he could just barely make out the misty film of her nightgown floating around her as she fled.

"Wait!" he whispered harshly. He grabbed the wine bottle by the neck and, picking up two glasses, strode down the long hall after her.

She stopped at the end of the hall in front of her room. She was no longer hidden by the night. The soft light of the moon streamed in through the narrow window over her head and captured her in its silver-blue aura. Her hair streamed down her back in a single braid and on some level it irked him that she still maintained such rigid control, even at night.

But that thought was followed by the realization that she was not wearing her usual bustle. Her nightgown followed the natural curves of her body, giving her a vulnerability that nearly pulled his heart from its moorings. His breath left him in an involuntary gasp.

"What is it, Dominick?" she asked, her voice alarmed.

"Nothing." *Everything.* He walked toward her, thinking how beautiful she looked. "I . . . I don't feel much like sleeping." He felt helpless suddenly, unable to think straight. Nothing, not even the nights he'd lain in the darkness thinking of her, had prepared him for this overwhelming feeling of longing at the sight of her standing in her nightgown.

"Are you hungry?" she asked, turning so that she fully faced him. "There's roast beef . . ."

"I'm not hungry, I . . . Would you have a glass of wine with me?"

She hesitated a moment, and he suspected that she was worrying about the propriety of sharing a drink with a man while attired in her nightclothes. "I would like that," she said, surprising him.

She sounded demure, almost shy, so unlike herself. But what the hell, he wasn't feeling much like himself either. Reckless, that's how he felt—the one way he couldn't afford to feel. Not if he meant to find his man.

Maybe it was the full moon. It always seemed to

rile up the sheep, why wouldn't it affect humans the same way?

She sat down on the wooden sea chest beneath the window, out of the light of the moon.

Regretting that he could no longer see her face—and yet grateful that he couldn't—he poured her a glass of wine and handed it to her before pouring one for himself. He settled himself on the floor and leaned back against the wall.

"Laurie-Anne had a nightmare earlier," he said.

"I know," she replied. "I went to her room, but you were already there."

"I . . . uh . . . told her a story," he explained, wondering if she resented his intrusion.

"Is it true?" she asked. "Do sheep really face east on Christmas Eve?"

So she'd been listening. He wondered if the sound he had thought was Jamie had been Maggie instead. "Absolutely." He fell silent a moment before adding, "It's also true that they face east every other night of the year as well."

She laughed, and her laughter only reminded him of the dangerous ground he was treading on. Quickly he took a sip of wine. Maybe he should have been honest with Foster. Told him the real reason he had to leave Santa Barbara. The truth . . . .

"Thank you," she said at last, "for staying with Laurie-Anne until she fell asleep again. She's suffered from nightmares off and on ever since her father died."

"It must be hard to lose a parent so young." He'd been nearly a grown man when he'd lost his father, all of fourteen, and even that was too young.

"It's been hard for both of them. They idolized their father."

"Tell me about him. Your husband. What was he like?"

The question caught Maggie off guard. She didn't

think she could talk about Luke to anyone, let alone
an outlaw.

But tonight he didn't seem like an outlaw. Tonight
he was none of the things she knew him to be. She
took a sip of wine, just a drop—enough, she hoped,
to clear her thoughts. It wouldn't do to forget who he
was and what he was capable of.

"He was a very kind and patient man," she began
and found that she was able to tell him about her
deceased husband without the usual sorrow or pain.
"I knew when I married him that his lungs were weak,
but I was convinced that it was because he didn't take
care of himself. I was determined to remedy that situation. It's frightening to think that no matter what you
do, you can't always protect a loved one."

"I know," he said hoarsely. "I felt the same way
about my wife, Louise."

She gasped in surprise. "I . . . I didn't know you'd
been married." A domestic outlaw? She wondered if
his wife knew that he was an outlaw and, if so, how
she lived with it.

"We were only married for a year. She died during
childbirth."

"I'm so sorry." This last piece of information was
unexpected. More than that, it was alarming to know
something so personal about him, something that elic-
ited a more sympathetic response than she was prepared to give or even wanted to give.

Shaking suddenly, she took another sip of wine, and
was almost relieved when he changed the subject and
began talking about his childhood.

"Tell me about your father's country," she coaxed,
after a while.

He picked up the bottle of wine and held it out
toward her. She lifted her glass. In the light of the
moon, the wine looked purple, almost black.

"Basque is a very old country." He set the bottle
on the floor between them and resumed his earlier
position. "So old that some people think that Basque

was the language of Adam and Eve." She saw his shoulders lift in the darkness. "Who can say for sure? Most of our history has been lost in time." He laughed softly. "Basque is like a virtuous woman; it has no past."

She laughed too, and their warm, musical laughter blended together. Longing took hold, deepened, and grew into yearning until the carefully constructed barriers of the past no longer existed.

He told her about the little village his father grew up in, built by his ancestors' own hands, and then he described the small schoolhouse where his mother had once taught.

"When they came to this country, my mother held classes for the neighbors' children at our kitchen table. I used to make up stories for her to use with the children."

"Like the missing vowel stories?" Maggie asked.

"Among others."

"Have you been to Basque?"

He shook his head. "No. But we lived in a small village of Basque people in the Sacramento Valley, so I grew up with the customs. My father spoke mostly English to us. He said it was a mistake to burden us with a language that would be of no use to us and would only serve to isolate us. My mother, however, spoke Basque as well as English. She wanted us to know both."

"You once told me that your father met with foul play."

"Yes." His voice hardened. "According to the farmer who found him, he was left to die in the dirt like an animal."

The sharp edge in his voice made her shiver. "It . . . it must have been very difficult for you."

"It was. My mother was never the same. She died two years later."

"How sad."

"Yes, it was."

She gave him time to reflect in silence before telling him about her own childhood. "My father was a Protestant preacher," she explained. "Luke was the organ pumper for my father's church. On Sunday mornings I used to sneak behind the organ to talk to him, and he'd forget to pump. I'm afraid that raised a few eyebrows in the congregation."

"Why, Maggie, I can't believe it. You would do something so shocking as that?"

She giggled and hiccupped. "Glory be, I do believe that the wine has gone to my head."

Dominick searched for her glass in the dark and refilled it. "Where all good wine should go. Do continue, Maggie. What other dastardly deeds are you guilty of?"

"I have never . . . hic . . . done a dastardly deed in my . . . hic . . . life."

"It can't be true!" he exclaimed. "Not one?"

Maggie giggled. "Well, maybe just an itsy . . . hic . . . bitsy one."

"I knew it! Are you going to tell me what it was?"

"Certainly not," she replied.

"Ah, Maggie. Come on, you can trust me."

"I may be tip-tipsy," she said, struggling to keep her tongue from stumbling over her words, "but I'm not stupid."

Dominick grinned wickedly and reached for the wine bottle. He poured the last few drops in her glass and kept badgering her until at last she admitted her dastardly deed.

"Once, my sister and I . . . went swim-hic-swim-hic . . . swimming dressed only in Nature's garb."

"No!" he said, seeing a vision of her lovely, slim body dripping wet beneath the warm glow of the morning sun, her soft, silky hair streaming down her back. A stirring in his loins took away his breath, and he quickly pushed the image out of his mind. He sensed, somehow, that to give in to such feelings would only make it that much harder to walk away from Maggie and the children when the time came. He couldn't chance it—didn't dare. He'd worked too hard and too long to risk it all now. There was simply too much at stake. "I . . . I don't believe it."

An hour passed, two, but neither noticed as they talked in the dark hallway, the moon dancing at their feet. Their whispers and soft laughter created a magical and intimate circle in the quiet of night.

He watched in fascination as a narrow beam of moonlight played along the white hem of her nightgown. As the night progressed, the light worked its way up her body like the lover he longed to be, until even the soft outline of her breasts was touched by the intimate fingers of silvery light.

He saw her shiver, felt his own body course with hot, liquid fire. Much to his horror, he felt his resolve begin to waver.

"You're cold," he said at last. "I'm sorry. I should never have kept you up in that damp night air."

"It's all right. I don't mind. In fact, I rather enjoyed out little . . . hic . . . oops." She laughed softly. "Talk."

"It was nice, wasn't it?" His voice was hoarse, his heart heavy. Standing, he knew by the stiffness in his legs how long they must have been sitting there. "I think I can sleep now."

"If not, you could count sheep."

This brought a laugh from him. "As a former shepherd, I'm afraid that counting sheep would seem too much like work. I'd never get to sleep for fear one was missing."

She stood up and laughed with him, then swayed. He reached out to steady her, taking her by the arm.

A sudden tension filled the air. "I . . . I never thought of counting sheep as work," Maggie whispered.

For a moment neither moved. He thought of the times he'd grabbed her and kissed her, telling himself that those times meant nothing. He only did it to get her off balance so he could keep the upper hand. Not exactly noble behavior on his part, but with Maggie, a man needed to use every tactic at his disposal.

But tonight . . . tonight. Now that was another matter. He wanted to kiss those wonderfully warm, wonderfully tempting lips, but not for his usual reasons. Far from kissing her to keep her in place, he longed to kiss her and to be kissed by her for the pure pleasure of it. And it was this undeniable fact that kept him from doing what would normally have come so natural to him.

Feeling somewhat unbalanced and more than a little foolish, he released her and watched helplessly as she slipped away.

"Good night," she whispered. With that, she closed the door between them.

"Good night," he mumbled, and cursed himself for letting the moment pass. He stood silently staring at the closed door. He could knock, but then what? What would he say? "I want to kiss you?" That wouldn't work. A kiss was not something announced in advance, at least not verbally. Besides, he had no intention of taking advantage of Maggie's wine-induced state of vulnerability.

Lord Almighty, what was he doing? When had he ever been at a loss as to how to kiss a woman? And when had he ever thought about it, for that matter? He either kissed a woman or he didn't, and never wasted energy thinking about it. The fact that he was thinking about it now worried him.

It worried him a lot.

Maggie sensed his presence outside her door, although there was really no way of knowing for certain if he was still standing where she left him, looking handsome and desirable and utterly irresistible.

An adobe house was built to last forever, and very little sound penetrated the thick walls and heavy wood doors. But something told her he was still outside her door; she would have bet on it. What she didn't know was why.

There was so much lately about him that she didn't understand. The way he drew her toward him, then pushed her away. Looked at her, didn't look at her. Spoke words that seemed to convey a message contrary to the one contained in his eyes. Ignored her, provoked her. Smiled at her, growled at her—sometimes in the same instant. It was enough to drive a person to distraction.

Shivering in the cold night air, she backed her way across the room and climbed trembling into bed, where she buried herself beneath the warm down covers. In the confused fog of her mind, she imagined herself sinking into his warm, strong arms, his hands pressing into her back.

Locked in this imaginary embrace, she recalled every word they'd exchanged that night. If that had been all she remembered, she would have drifted off to sleep content. But it wasn't all. Far from it. The wine was playing rather fanciful tricks with her memory, and her thoughts flashed back and forth in time. She could recall with chilling clarity his kissing her during their ordeal on the pass, outside the house . . .

Not for one moment had she misunderstood the reasons behind his kisses. He'd meant to manifest his power over her, to degrade and humiliate her, nothing more. But even knowing this, she still couldn't deny that his kisses held an underlying sensuality that would forever be engraved in her memory.

But he hadn't kissed her tonight. She hated to admit it, but she'd given him every possible opportunity, standing at the door long after it was proper to take her leave.

Waiting.

Looking up at him in a way she knew was a brazen invitation.

Waiting.

Moistening her lips as he'd stood watching, the hunger so evident in his smoldering eyes.

And still she'd waited.

But he hadn't kissed her, and the only way she could quell the disappointment was to imagine what it would feel like if he ever got around to kissing her for all the right reasons.

Chapter 15

The following day, Maggie left Dominick in charge of the shop and walked the short distance down State Street to Grover's general store. Inside, a fan circled lazily overhead, stirring the air and blending the delicious odors of rich coffee, spicy sausages, and tangy cinnamon together in such a way that one hardly noticed the less appealing smells of kerosene and leather wafting in from the back of the store.

The manager, Mr. Grover, greeted her with a friendly nod. He stood behind one of two counters that ran the length of the store. A tall, lean man with stooped shoulders, he had a long, narrow face and a broken front tooth that caused him to whistle when he spoke.

"Good morning, Mrs. S-S-S-Sanders," he wheezed out politely. "What can I do for you today?"

"Good morning." Maggie handed him her neatly written list, careful not to disturb the jars of hard candies and pickles that were displayed on the counter.

Mr. Grover adjusted his wire-rimmed spectacles and read her list. He shuffled back and forth behind the counter filling the order, stopping occasionally to question her about quantities and point out any new products that might interest her.

"S-s-see this here," he said, holding up a thin-necked bottle filled with a red substance. "It's called Heinz Tomato Catsup. It's a brand-new product. They're billing it as blessed relief for the women of the household."

"Ready-made catsup?" Maggie shook her head in disbelief. "What will they think of next? Better add a bottle of that blessed relief to my list."

While she waited, she made her way around the endless barrels and bins that held everything from sugar to nails and ducked beneath a hanging harness to examine the bolts of fabric that were stacked on a wooden table. A lovely blue calico caught her eye, and she decided it would make a perfect dress for Laurie-Anne.

The door swung open and Maggie recognized the woman who swept in as Mrs. Tubbs, the wife of the bank president and the mother of Harvey Tubbs, the boy Mrs. Pickings insisted was behind much of the mischief in the town. She had a body shaped like a hot-air balloon, and a round face to match. It seemed only fitting that she greeted Maggie with rounded eyes and mouth.

"Why, Mrs. Sanders, how nice to see you. You don't know me, but my daughter, Lisa, bought a pair of shoes from you and they are simply perfect!"

Pleased by the compliment, Maggie nodded. "I remember Lisa. A lovely young woman with excellent taste."

"And she was most impressed with you. How very thoughtful of you to arrange to have her shoes delivered."

"We only deliver to our most . . . valued customers," Maggie explained hastily. She had neither the time nor the inclination to run a delivery service, and she couldn't afford for her customers to think otherwise.

"Your most valued customers? How very thoughtful." It was apparent that Mrs. Tubbs assumed she would naturally fall into this category. "I've been telling everyone to order shoes from you. In fact, I intend to order a pair for myself."

Maggie smiled. "I appreciate your recommendations, Mrs. Tubbs. Come into the shop anytime and I'll take your measurements."

Mr. Grover greeted the banker's wife from atop a ladder. He reached for a box of mother-of-pearl buttons on the uppermost shelf and then climbed down. "Any news on those bank robbers?"

Maggie dropped the edge of fabric she was examining. "Glory be! Don't tell me the bank was robbed!"

"You mean you haven't heard?" Mrs. Tubbs exclaimed, clasping her small, pudgy hands to her ample chest. It was obvious that she was delighted to find someone with whom to share her knowledge. "Everyone is talking about it. My husband discovered the vault open first thing this morning. He worked until nearly eleven last night, so obviously the robbery occurred sometime after that. I can't tell you how many times I've begged him not to work so late. He works every night, and even on the Sabbath! Why he hardly sees his own children and . . ."

She stopped suddenly, as if she feared she was boring Maggie with her personal problems. With an apologetic smile, she continued, "As I was saying, had the robbers showed up while he was still in his office, heaven only knows what might have happened."

"I'm so glad to hear he's all right," Maggie said.

Mrs. Tubbs shuddered. "He's lucky to still be alive, that's what I think. And I told him, he better show his gratitude to the Lord by upping his tithes. Maybe now, he'll listen to me and spend more time with his family . . ."

Mrs. Tubbs continued, but Maggie was no longer listening. She was too engrossed in her own thoughts. Not for a moment had she stopped thinking of the early-morning hours spent with Dominick. Had, in fact, relived practically every magical moment they'd spent talking in the dark, sipping wine and laughing together. Gazing at one another.

As much as it mortified her sense of propriety to admit it, she even recalled how she had waited for him to act upon the desire so evident in his eyes. She'd almost convinced herself that he had, that the kiss that seemingly hovered between them had been more than her imagination.

But now she wasn't thinking about such things; she was thinking about clothes, Dominick's clothes, and cold fear gripped her heart. Dominick had been fully dressed when she saw him. She remembered that distinctly, but at the time she'd not thought much about it. She had assumed he'd stayed up late reading, as was often his habit. But what if there were another reason? What if he had progressed from robbing stages to robbing banks?

Troubled by the possibility, she kept her thoughts to herself, as Mrs. Tubbs rambled on uninterrupted.

"Don't you worry, my dear." The woman patted Maggie's arm, obviously mistaking her silence for apprehension. "The sheriff is using every available man to track the robber or robbers down."

"That's a relief," Maggie said, fighting to keep her voice normal. She paid for her purchases and left the store, her heart so heavy it felt like lead in her chest.

Taking the longer route down State Street on the way back to the shop, she hastened toward the crowd that was milling feverishly about in front of the bank. The residents of Santa Barbara were never satisfied with rumor alone. Every whisper, every hint of scandal, every bit of scuttlebutt had to be verified in person. Whether this was the town's strength or weakness she didn't know, but at the moment she was grateful for the opportunity to hear for herself the most current reports.

Straining to hear all of the excited chatter, Maggie quickened her steps. She caught a glimpse of Mrs. Pickings, who, believing it her civic duty to get to the bottom of things, fired questions to the crowd with the zeal of an overambitious journalist. Everyone talked at once, and soon Mrs. Pickings, looking thoroughly disgusted, threw up her hands and swept into the bank, muttering something about getting the story straight from the horse's mouth. The crowd stared after her uncertainly, no doubt wondering if they should follow, but then they resumed talking among themselves.

"And the sheriff said . . ."

"The safe door was blown right off the wall."

"There ought to be a law."

"My good man, there is a law . . ."

Nodding to the people she recognized, Maggie hurried past, burdened by her growing suspicions. It couldn't have been Dominick who robbed the bank.

Dear God, don't let it be Dominick.

Maggie returned to the shop, hardly able to think.

Dominick sat at the workbench hammering nails into the heavy-duty heels he'd been working on all morning. His hand stilled when the bells on the door announced her arrival and he spun around on his stool to greet her, his face split in two by a wide grin. When he saw the expression on her face, his smile faded and he watched her with dark, troubled eyes.

"Thought it was a customer," he called out, as if to apologize for the smile—or maybe it was something else he was apologizing for. She had no way of knowing.

"It's been quiet this morning," he added.

She closed the door firmly behind her. "There was some trouble at the bank." She chose her words carefully, watching his face, hoping beyond hope that she would not see signs of guilt.

"Oh?" His face revealed nothing. "What kind of trouble?"

"A robbery."

He put the hammer down on the bench and stood up. "Is that so?"

She set her package on the counter between them. "Happened last night sometime."

"I guess I have myself some competition in town," he said lightly.

She inhaled deeply, regretting what she had to do now.

The hours spent in the hallway had changed the way they acted toward one another. Their usual clash during breakfast had been replaced by a heightened awareness of each other that manifested itself in lingering gazes and a more gentle exchange. Disagreements had been met with compromise, smiles replaced insults. Upon their arrival at the shop, every touch, whether accidental or otherwise, had brought an instant apology from one and a look of confusion to the other.

Reluctant to do or say anything that would spoil the growing bond between them, Maggie dreaded the question she was now forced to ask. Dreaded even more the possible answer the question might bring.

"Dominick, you didn't . . ."

The sudden jingle of bells announced a customer. Maggie recognized her as Mrs. Wassail, a friend of Mrs. Pickings, whom she'd met at one of the teas she and Dominick had attended. The woman was accompanied by her plain and rather dour daughter, whom she introduced as Eloise.

Maggie watched as Dominick turned his attention to Eloise. In no time at all he managed to bring a smile to the young woman's face, and this only added to Maggie's misery. Dominick brought out the best in everyone but her!

Before long, the shop was filled with customers whose voices were shrill with excitement. Every last rumor heard outside the bank was repeated and exclaimed over. Bits and pieces of information were expanded upon until new rumors were created and repeated with increasing conviction to everyone who entered the shop.

Miss Winkerton stopped by to pick up her velvet shoes. She tried the shoes on, tiptoeing around the shop like a child just learning to walk. Growing braver, she held up the hem of her gray woolen dress primly and twisted herself around so she could better view her shoes from every possible angle.

"They're perfect." Dominick grinned. "What did I tell you? The perfect shoe for the perfect lady."

Miss Winkerton looked at Dominick with adoring eyes. "You are brilliant. These are the most beautiful shoes I have ever owned. I should never have doubted you for a moment."

"Oh, yes, you should have," Maggie mumbled under her breath, confused and somewhat embarrassed by her ambivalent feelings for Dominick. A short time ago, she had been ready to forget his past, forget everything but the promise she'd read in his eyes.

Had he played her for a fool? Robbed a bank and made her unwittingly drink to his deed? The thought of keeping company with a bank robber was unbearable, and she watched Dominick with growing suspicion.

No longer blinded by feelings of warmth, she concentrated on his dark side and told herself that the smile that had earlier filled her with longing was nothing more than a ruse by which to manipulate feminine hearts.

Her irritation expanded to include her customers. Look at them, she thought, lapping up his charm like kittens lap up milk. It galled her how they seemed to think Dominick was some sort of godlike creature who could do no wrong. He didn't even have the decency to give credit where credit was due. He accepted compliments with the grace of an actor in a one-man play. Maggie was the one who designed the shoes and taught him everything he knew. But did anyone give her credit? Absolutely not!

Waiting to see Miss Winkerton make a fool of herself, Maggie was amazed at the transformation that took place once the shoes were on her feet. The unbecoming pallor of her skin disappeared behind a rose-colored flush. The heightened color emphasized the rusty tones in her hair and complemented her large brown eyes.

Maggie sucked in her breath. Why, Miss Winkerton looked mighty attractive and, smiling like she was now, she even looked downright pretty, and younger than her thirty-some years.

Dominick bowed from the waist. "Would you do me the honor of granting me this dance?"

Miss Winkerton giggled and coyly batted her lashes. "Why, Mr. Sanders, I can't dance."

"Of course you can," he insisted. He slipped one hand around her ample waist and pulled her toward him. "The only thing you have to remember is that dancing is like robbing a stage. It takes split-second timing."

His outrageous statement brought an appreciative laugh from Miss Winkerton. "You are such a tease," she cooed.

Peering over Miss Winkerton's head, he watched Maggie's response to his absurd behavior with a momentary loss of composure. Eyes round in disapproval, she stared at him with a mouth wide enough to corral a horse in. But he saw none of these things. For he was remembering how the moonlight had played upon her loveliness and how the soft lights of desire had danced in her eyes. All at once, his own longing was that much more difficult to bear.

Gripping Miss Winkerton's hand tighter, he hummed the bandit song he knew would distance Maggie and led the shyly blushing spinster in an easy-to-follow folk dance. Today, more than any other, it seemed imperative to keep Maggie at bay. Better yet, to make her hate him. If he couldn't stay away from her, he'd have to make sure she hated him enough to stay away from him. To do anything less would put his plan to avenge his family's death in jeopardy. And that he could never do.

Simplicity gave the dance a courtly air, and they

finished to the enthusiastic applause of the other customers, who stood around the couple in a circle.

"I simply must have a pair of those velvet shoes,"
a matronly woman insisted, pushing her way to the
counter.

"Me, too," parroted a younger woman, shifting a
chubby baby from one hip to the other.

"You wait your turn!" another customer cried out,
ramming through the crowd with her elbows held out
in front of her like a bull's horns, ready to jab anyone
who got in her way. "I was here first!"

Sighing, Maggie took their orders, knowing that
after witnessing the coming out of Miss Winkerton
nothing she could possibly say would convince them
to pick out something more practical.

After Miss Winkerton literally danced out of the
shop, the remaining customers waited patiently for
Maggie to take their foot measurements. The discussion shifted back and forth between the bank robbery
and the advantage of straight military heels over the
newer concave design.

With each mention of the robbery, Maggie monitored the slightest change of expression on Dominick's
face. It was hard to discern anything of consequence.
For the most part, he seemed his usual self, managing
to mix charm with arrogance and coming up with a
combination that practically had the customers eating
out of his hand.

As the day wore on, it struck her that maybe his
laugh was beginning to sound a bit forced. And was
it only her imagination that he was more restrained
than usual in dishing out compliments to their female
customers? Then there was the way his eyes kept seeking her out, only to turn elsewhere when, unable to
ignore his troubled gaze, she looked back at him, her
unasked question trembling on her lips.

Maybe he was tired, she thought. They had stayed
up talking until nearly four-thirty this morning. Even

she was beginning to feel her energy level drop with every passing hour.

Besides, if he had robbed the bank, why would he spend the day working so hard to sell shoes? Wouldn't it be more likely that he'd take the money and leave town?

He didn't rob the bank!

He might have.

Couldn't have.

Did!

Oh, the unbelievable torture of not being able to make up her mind one way or the other.

Her father had trained her from earliest childhood to sift through the facts until she had formed a fair and logical conclusion. But with Dominick it was so difficult to separate truth from fiction.

Still, she was reluctant to believe the worst about him.

And so the torturous question remained: Did he or didn't he? She simply had to know.

Chapter 16

That night, after the four of them had shared a simple supper of cold ham and boiled potatoes, Maggie sat on the edge of the Spanish-tiled fountain in front of the house, watching Dominick run around the yard in long, easy strides.

Despite the hectic day at the shop, his energy seemed boundless as he wove in and out of the hedges with Jamie and Laurie-Anne in hot pursuit.

Maggie pulled a knitted shawl around her shoulders to ward off the cool ocean breeze. The sun had disappeared into a bank of rising fog, leaving behind a sky streaked with shades of bright red and orange.

Hushed voices replaced boisterous shouts as the vigorous game of tag turned into the more subdued game of hide-and-seek.

Jamie called out. "Over here!"

Laurie-Anne giggled, her little legs running as fast as possible, her feet seeming to head in no particular direction.

Dominick jumped out from behind a tree. "I found you!" This was followed by peals of laughter.

Listening to the three of them, Maggie felt the ache in her heart grow until it was almost unbearable. It was easy to believe that the Dominick Sanders who took such pleasure in humiliating her was, indeed, a bank robber. It was at moments like this that she had her doubts.

How was it possible for a man to be so filled with contradictions? With an ease that amazed her, he had coaxed Laurie-Anne out of her sadness, had patiently tutored Jamie in his reading and numbers, had made a spinster feel pretty, had talked about his simple upbringing in the dark of night. These were the things she wanted to think about—not what he might have done.

The first star of the night appeared in a gap in the patchy cloud cover. But it was the appearance of the stoop-shouldered lamplighter, whistling cheerfully as he made his rounds, that signaled the end of another day.

Reluctant to put a damper on the children's fun, Maggie waited until the lamplighter had worked his way to the end of the block before calling to them. "Jamie, Laurie-Anne. Time for bed."

Jamie's voice answered her from the darkness. "Do we have to?"

"Yes, indeed. You have school tomorrow." Maggie stood.

Dominick lifted Laurie-Anne onto his shoulders and carried her to the edge of the courtyard where Maggie waited. "Watch your head," he cautioned, and Laurie-Anne, holding on for dear life, ducked her head to keep from hitting it on the overhang of the porch.

Not wanting to meet his eyes, Maggie stared out into the shadows of the yard and called Jamie once again. She felt Dominick's gaze burning into her, sensed some sort of indecision on his part as he stomped past her into the house with Laurie-Anne still riding high on his shoulders.

She waited for Jamie to drag himself reluctantly across the courtyard. Taking his hand in hers, she followed Dominick into the house.

Moments later, she stood in the necessity room and scrubbed Laurie-Anne's hands and face, then stood over Jamie while he splashed playfully in the basin of warm water she set out for him.

After their prayers, she told them a story and sang them a song until they were both sound asleep. Blowing out the candles, she quickly slipped down the hall and retired to her own room. The last thing she wanted to do was confront Dominick with her troubling thoughts. Not tonight, not while memories of him laughing and playing with her children were so vivid. Not while she could still remember so clearly the warm feelings they had shared in the hallway the night before.

What little sleep she managed was filled with strange and troubling dreams.

She awoke with a start, expecting to see him standing by her bed as he had in her dream. But there was no one in the room. Still, it was hard to shake off the sense that he'd been in her room, standing next to her as she slept. The feeling was so strong, she swore that she could smell the warm masculine odor she knew to be his.

The red tinge of dawn bled through the window, making her wonder how it was possible to feel so much pain and not be physically wounded.

She wanted so much to think he'd turned over a new leaf. He'd told her as much, hadn't he? She wanted to believe him for Jamie's sake, for Laurie-Anne's. But more than anything she wanted to believe him for her own sake.

Two nights later, he was waiting for her outside the children's room.

Standing in the dimly lit hallway, legs apart, arms folded across his chest, he made an imposing figure. There was no question in her mind that he had purposely positioned himself in such a way as to prevent her from avoiding his company for yet another night.

"I think it's time we talk," he said.

Surprised to find herself suddenly trembling, she shook her head. "I'm tired, Dominick. I've had a hard day."

"Then I suggest we get this over with as quickly as possible."

"Can't this wait until tomorrow?"

"It's waited long enough," he said tersely. "I mean it, Maggie, neither one of us is going to get any sleep tonight unless we talk."

Maggie's mouth went dry. "Very well."

He nodded approval and stepped aside, allowing her to brush past him without comment. He followed her to the parlor and sat in an overstuffed chair. "Please have a seat," he said politely, with none of his usual mocking tone.

She didn't want to sit on the divan that served as his bed, so she sat on the edge of the piano stool, feet planted firmly in front of her, hands on her lap, and fervently hoped that he couldn't hear the wild beating of her heart.

"You've been avoiding me," he said.

She met his eyes. "Given our living conditions and the fact that we work together, it would seem that avoiding you would be an impossible task."

"It would seem so. But, nonetheless, you've managed to do exactly that. My concern is that the children can sense this strain between us. Last night Laurie-Anne awoke several times during the night, and I wonder if perhaps it didn't have something to do with the tension in this house during the last two days."

She closed her eyes, feeling totally defeated. It was true what he said about Laurie-Anne. He was also probably right as to the reason for her daughter's anxiety.

When she failed to reply, he continued, "Would it be correct for me to assume that your behavior is related in some way to the robbery at the bank?"

Clasping her hands together, she forced herself to sit taller. "Since you brought the matter up, I must admit the robbery has caused me some . . . distress."

He considered this for a moment. "Because you think I'm involved?"

"Are you?"

"Would you believe me if I said no?"

"Is that your answer?"

"Not necessarily."

She shot to her feet. "I'm not playing games."

"Nor am I." He stood lazily, but there was nothing languid in the way he looked at her.

"Then give me a straight answer."

"Fair enough." He rubbed his chin. "No, I did not rob the bank."

She walked back and forth in front of him. Should she believe him? Could she believe him? *Dare* she believe him? "Then why were you still dressed that night when we talked in the hallway?"

"I had not yet retired."

"It was after two o'clock in the morning."

He hesitated, and she sensed that he was coming to some sort of decision. "You know that I am trying to find someone."

She stopped her pacing and faced him. "So you say. But to my knowledge, you have not taken measures to locate this . . . person."

"I met with someone that night who is helping me in my search. This person had vital information that I needed. I met him at two and we finished our business around two-thirty. That's when I returned to the house and heard Laurie-Anne cry."

She eyed him with suspicion. "What is the name of the man you supposedly met?"

"I didn't *supposedly* meet anyone," he said curtly. "I did meet him. As for his name, I am obliged to keep his identity secret."

"How can you expect me to believe a man who . . . who . . ."

"Is admittedly the Kissing Bandit?"

She glared at him. "A man who has forced himself upon me and my family."

"I have never forced myself upon you," he said.

"You've forced yourself!" she shot back. "What do you call living here against my wishes?"

"Necessary," he replied, his dark eyes piercing her.

Ignoring his answer, she continued to list his offenses. "And what about telling everyone that you're my husband?"

"I did that to protect you."

"And then you have the audacity—the audacity!—to pretend that you know how to sell shoes."

"I do know how to sell shoes."

"And if that's not bad enough," she scolded, refusing to be interrupted, "you force yourself into my children's affections and . . ."

"I repeat, I've never forced myself into anyone's affections."

"Oh, yes, you have. You act so smug and so damned sure of yourself!"

He started to say something but exploded in laughter instead. "Why, Mrs. Sanders, I do believe you used a swear word!"

She colored furiously, mortified at the slip of her tongue. "Now look what you've done," she charged. "I don't even know what I'm saying anymore."

Looking exceedingly pleased with himself, he gave her a consoling pat on the arm. "Don't worry. Slips of the tongue are most becoming. A few more slips, and I daresay things will get rather interesting around here."

She pulled away from him indignantly. "There won't be any more slips!"

"I'm truly aggrieved to hear you say that. As for the other, if you're so sure I robbed the bank, why don't you turn me in?"

"You know why I don't turn me in," she stormed. "You know what it would do to Jamie and Laurie-Anne if you were hauled off to jail."

"And you, Maggie?" He moved closer and stroked her cheek with his finger, his face suddenly serious. "What would it do to you?" His words were a caress, eliciting more of a physical response than a verbal one. "And what would it do to you . . ." His gaze dipped down to her trembling lips. ". . . if I should suddenly lean over and . . ."

His lips reached hers before he finished his sentence. His hand around her waist drew her body fully into his arms. He angled his mouth against hers until the stubborn set of her lips softened, yielded. She responded with a muted, throaty sigh and opened her mouth in full surrender.

Gently moving his tongue inside her willing mouth, he gathered the warm, velvety moisture like a bee gathers honey, and withdrew. To his delight, her tongue followed his like a dance partner, taking from him, giving to him.

But it wasn't enough—could never be enough—and knowing that, he pulled away. Had it not been for the children, he would never have tried to convince Maggie of his innocence. As long as she believed him to be guilty, he was safe. They were safe. But once the suspicion left her face, he had been unable to resist her. He should have known that even the slightest truce between them was dangerous. Still, he couldn't seem to help himself. "Maggie . . . I'm sorry."

She stared at him, uncomprehending, her lips still swollen from his kiss.

He saw the look in her eyes and ached inside. Never had he felt like such a heel. She deserved so much more than he could ever give her. But knowing her as he did, he realized she would never be able to forgive him his past, no matter how much he might regret it himself. Nor would she be able to forgive what he must do in the future. He knew that, knew that as certainly as he knew his name. Still, he had to test her.

"Maggie," he said, his voice low, "if someone you loved was hurt by another person, what would you do?"

A look of uncertainty crossed her face. "I don't know."

"Would you seek justice?"

"Yes, of course, I suppose. It depends on the circumstances."

"What kind of justice, Maggie?"

"I don't know." Her eyes darkened with worry. "You're frightening me, Dominick. I don't know what you're talking about."

"I'm talking about murder, Maggie. What kind of justice would you seek for murder?"

Her expression changed to one of horror as understanding dawned. "It's up to the courts to seek justice."

"Under any circumstance?"

"It's the law, Dominick. And the Bible . . ."

"The Bible says an eye for an eye."

"It says thou shalt not kill."

It was the reply he had expected—dreaded—the one answer that defied dispute. As difficult as it would be, he had no choice but to hurt her now to keep from hurting her more down the road.

"I'm sorry," he repeated, but this time he spoke in a flip, almost mocking tone. It was his way of distancing himself from her. And the farther away he could drive her, the better for both of them. With this thought in mind, he spoke more harshly. "I'm sorely tempted to continue kissing you, but I know how you hate having men force themselves on you."

So stunned was she by his sudden stinging words that she could hardly speak. "Damn you!" she sputtered at last, shocked at how easy it was to swear once she'd started—and how satisfying. "I would like nothing better than to see you behind bars where you belong!"

"Oh, dear. Another slip of the tongue."

Though she was seething inside, she could think of nothing more to say. What she wanted to do was slap that smug look off his face. What she wanted to do was to tear out her own traitorous heart and stomp on it. What she wanted to do was to forget forever the day she'd met him.

Instead, she whirled about in a circle of skirts and stormed out of the room, followed all the way down the hall to her room by his soft, low chuckle.

She was far too humiliated to notice that his laughter was flat and hollow—not really laughter at all but rather the sound of a heart filled with remorse.

Chapter 17

In a bewildering state of semi-sleep, Maggie fought her way through a tangle of blankets, aware on some level that her heart was racing. She was lucid enough to know she'd been dreaming but felt far too languid to fight off the effects.

Her heart pounded as she recalled the still-vivid details of her dream: the runaway stagecoach, the dark bandit who saved her, the unmasking that gave the bandit a name. This was followed by a collage of lingering kisses and perplexing questions about murder and justice. Then the dream faded at the sound of a drum that filled the air with a rapid beat.

It was the repetitious banging that brought her to full consciousness. Rolling out of bed, she grimaced when her feet touched the cold wooden floor. She didn't bother to light a candle but quickly reached for her robe and tore open her door.

Muffled voices could be heard somewhere in the distance. She couldn't understand what was being said, but the urgency in the words was clear. She flew down the hall calling Dominick's name. "What is it? What's happening?"

"It's me, Señora. Manuel."

"Manuel? What is it? What's wrong?"

Behind her a scraping sound of flint preceded a flare of light. In the flickering flame of the oil lamp, Manuel looked disheveled and grim.

"I'm mighty sorry to have to bring such bad news, Señora Sanders, but I thought you'd want to know."

In confusion, she glanced at Dominick, who was half dressed. His unbuttoned shirt hung outside his pants, revealing the gleaming skin of his chest.

"What bad news?" she demanded sharply.

"Your shop . . . it's on fire, Señora."

"Oh, dear God, no!" Instinctively she turned to Dominick, her earlier humiliation forgotten. "What shall we do?"

"I doubt that there's much we can do. I'll go and see." His low voice had a calming effect on her, and for a brief moment she dared to hope that her memory had only been another dream.

"Wait. I'll go with you."

"Stay here, Maggie." Dominick reached for his belt. "You can't leave Jamie and Laurie-Anne by themselves."

She thought quickly, then said to Manuel, who stood watching them both anxiously, "Manuel, go get your sister. Tell her I need her to watch the children. Hurry!"

He was gone in an instant, the sound of his feet quickly fading in the distance.

Maggie started toward her bedroom but stopped in the hallway at the sound of her name.

"You don't have to go," Dominick said. "I'll take care of whatever needs to be done."

She turned to face him, suddenly aware of her disheveled appearance. She had been so upset the previous night that she'd not taken the time to braid her hair. Now it fell to her shoulders in a jumble of tangled curls.

"I know you will," she whispered, wondering where the conviction that she could trust him had come from. But at that moment she sensed his sincerity and knew that no matter how much he had disappointed her in the past, and was likely to in the future, he would be there for her tonight. "I need to be there, too."

She expected an argument, but after searching her

pale, earnest face, he simply shrugged and reached for his boots.

Although it seemed like an eternity, it was actually only minutes later that Consuela arrived, dressed in a robe and brandishing an ivory rosary. "I'll pray for you, Señor, Señora. I'll pray that your shop can be saved."

Maggie gave the girl a quick hug. "Thank you, Consuela."

Maggie followed Dominick outside. Taking her hand, he led her down the narrow, dark street, past the shadows of cottages and businesses. Occasionally a horse neighed or a dog barked, but otherwise the street remained eerily deserted.

Maggie prayed that Manuel had been mistaken about the seriousness of the fire, but the bright glow above the row of wooden buildings in the distance confirmed that his every word was true.

Rounding the corner, Maggie stopped dead in her tracks. She surveyed the scene with disbelief and horror, stunned by the devastation before her. Nothing had prepared her for the brightly blazing inferno that had once been her shoemaking shop.

The building was engulfed in flames. Like a hungry monster, the fire roared and crackled, its hot tongues licking and devouring everything in its path. The sign that had caused her such tribulation pulled free from its moorings and fell to the ground, shooting sparks high into the air.

Volunteer firemen, dressed in red shirts, black pants, and leather helmets, adjusted the stream of water that shot from Santa Barbara's recently purchased horse-drawn steamer. With a hiss and a vibrating swoosh, an arc of water reached the fiery roof. Smoke belched from cracking windowpanes followed by the popping sound of exploding glass.

Dominick pulled Maggie away, shielding her body with his own until the immediate danger had passed.

The foreman bellowed instructions through the fire horn, sending three men scurrying to the hand pumper.

Past Dominick's shoulder, Maggie caught a glimpse of Manuel, his young face contorted with a dark, murderous rage completely unlike anything she could imagine him capable of. Despite the inferno before her, her smoke-filled gaze remained riveted on the boy's hate-filled face. Thinking she had mistaken what she saw, she called to him, but her voice was lost in the sound of crackling flames, and he soon disappeared into the gathering crowd.

Maggie suddenly realized that the firemen had shifted their attention to the surrounding area, watering the roofs of nearby buildings and clearing away brush and tall, dry grass to minimize the danger to other structures. There was nothing more they could do for her shop but let it burn itself out.

With a cry, she started toward the burning building, intent upon saving her beloved Blake sewer. Instantly Dominick grabbed her by the shoulder and pulled her away from the intense heat and flying embers.

Too much in shock to fight him, she collapsed in his arms sobbing, and buried her head in the comforting security of his powerful chest.

By the time the sun rose, only the charred black ruins and a few smoldering embers were left, surrounded by weary firemen covered from head to toe in ashes and soot.

The foreman ambled over to Maggie, politely removed his smudged fire hat, and introduced himself as Hank Mason. "Sorry, ma'am. We did everything we could. One good thing about the Spanish adobes, they're not a fire hazard. But these wooden buildings . . ." He shook his head. "They ain't nothing more than tinderboxes."

"I know," Maggie replied stoically. "I do appreciate everything you and the other men did. How . . . how do you suppose the fire started?"

"Hard to say, ma'am. There'll have to be an investigation. That's the sheriff's department. But from our initial observations, I'd say it was kerosene. That would make it arson."

The thought that someone would purposely destroy something of hers sent a sickening jolt through Maggie. She looked over at Dominick and noticed that a muscle in his jaw tightened as if he, too, was shocked by the foreman's news.

She turned back to the fire foreman. "But who . . . why would anyone want to destroy my business?"

"I doubt that you had anything to do with it. It was the building. There's those in town who resent the tearing down of buildings built under Spanish rule. A very fine adobe once stood on the property. There was a lot of controversy when it was torn down to make room for a wooden building."

"But that was my business," Maggie protested. "What possible right does someone have to destroy my property?"

"No right, ma'am. No right at all."

After Maggie finished her conversation with the foreman, Dominick insisted on taking her home. Worried that she was too much in shock to walk the distance, he sent Manuel to the livery stable to rent a two-man shay and then drove her home himself.

Consuela greeted them at the door, her rosary still clutched in her hands. She listened grimly as Dominick described the devastating scene they had left moments earlier.

"Burned to the ground. Nothing could be saved."

"How terrible," Consuela gasped, her face pale with horror. "Holy Mary, Mother of God," she prayed aloud, lifting her eyes toward the ceiling.

"Thank you, Consuela. Is Jamie at school?"

"Yes, and Laurie-Anne is playing with her dolls in her room."

Holding Maggie by the arm, Dominick walked her to the parlor. "I think Mrs. Sanders could use a cup of tea." He helped her to a chair and knelt to unbutton her boots.

Consuela hurried to the kitchen, and soon the rattle of dishes added a sense of domestic harmony that made all the events of the last several hours seem like a bad dream.

"I think you should go to bed," Dominick urged.

Maggie stared listlessly into space. "What am I going to do?" she whispered. "All the money I had was in that shop. Everything that Luke and I worked for."

He pulled off both her boots and then took her hands in his. "You need rest. There'll be time enough later to think about everything else."

She lifted her eyes to meet his. "But . . ."

"No buts, my love. Come on. You're going to bed." Rising to his feet, he easily picked her up in his arms. He carried her to her room and laid her gently on the bed. Then he took a heavy quilt from the cedar chest at the foot of the bed and covered her still trembling body.

A timid knock at the door was followed by Consuela's soundless entry into the room. She set the tray that she carried next to Maggie's bed and looked questioningly at Dominick for further instruction.

"Thank you, Consuela. I'll take care of it from here." He dismissed the young woman and poured Maggie a cup of tea. "Here, drink this."

He handed the cup to her and helped her hold it to her lips. "My mother used to say that tea was the substance of the soul. That's a girl. Drink up." As soon as she finished the first cup, he poured more.

After she finished the tea, he wiped the soot off her face with a damp cloth.

Maggie lay back against the pillow, thinking how gentle his touch was, how comforting. In the soft morning light, the sharp angles and hard planes of his face were softened by shadows. His mouth, usually lifted in derision, curved upward now with a sensitivity that made something inside her ache.

He rubbed a spot off her forehead and held her in a steady, caressing gaze that was as gentle as spring rain. She felt at once like a babe in arms and a lover about to be claimed.

He dabbed her face carefully with a clean towel and drew the covers up over her shoulders until they reached her chin. Then he leaned over and kissed her gently on the forehead.

Keeping his face in view until the last possible moment, she finally succumbed to sleep.

She awoke with a start and stared in confusion at the shadows dancing across the ceiling. A sound nearby told her she was not alone. Turning her head toward it, she waited until her eyes focused in the soft light of the single gaslight and a tall, dark form next to her took shape.

"I brought you some warm milk," Dominick said. "Fresh from the Pickingses' farm."

Though she felt groggy, she struggled to sit up, wondering why her limbs felt stiff, almost wooden. Once she had gotten upright, she waited for him to fluff the pillow and arrange it behind her back, against the brass headboard. After he had made certain that she was comfortable, he gave her a glass that was warm to the touch.

"Thank you," she said in a hoarse voice. Her throat felt parched, and her nose was still filled with the strong, acrid smell of smoke. "Is Mrs. Pickings still here?"

He shook his head. "No, she only stayed long enough to gather all the facts of the fire. I do believe that woman has missed her calling. She's got more of a nose for news than our very own newspaper editor. Her questions were even more astute than the sheriff's."

"The sheriff was here?"

He nodded. "Took a full report."

Maggie raised the glass to her lips and sipped slowly, savoring the warmth that filled her mouth and soothed her dry, burning throat. Suddenly she was struck by the unnatural quiet of the house, and she lowered the glass in alarm. "Where are the children?"

"In bed," he replied.

Her eyes widened. A dozen horrible thoughts crossed her mind. "Are they all right? They're not sick, are they? I heard Jamie cough last night and . . ." She set the glass on the end table and pushed the blankets away.

Chuckling softly, he sat on the edge of the bed and laid a finger on her lips to quiet her. "Everyone is in fine health. They are simply doing what it is natural for them to be doing at ten o'clock at night. They are sleeping."

Not sure she'd heard him right, she looked past his broad shoulder toward the windows. The fringed shades were half drawn against a dark sky. Her eyes widened in astonishment. "I slept all day?"

"I daresay you were in shock." He gently pushed her back and tucked the quilt around her.

She leaned her head against her pillows. Memories of the fire came back in awful detail. It was true, then. When she awoke her first thought had been that she'd had the worst possible nightmare. "My whole business is gone. How am I going to support the children?"

He wished he could think of a way to offer her more than consolation. Never had he felt so helpless, so completely at a loss for words. "Don't think about this now. There will be time enough later. We'll find a way to rebuild your shop. Trust me, Maggie. Right now I want you to concentrate on taking care of yourself. You haven't eaten all day. What would you like?"

She shook her head. "Nothing, thank you."

"Perhaps later," he said. "For now, finish your milk."

She sat silent for a moment, then seemed to draw

from some inner source of strength. "You're right." She had regained her normal voice, and the expression of despair that moments earlier had shadowed her face had changed to a look of resolve and determination. "We will rebuild!"

Surprised by her exuberance, he watched her warily, wondering if the sudden transformation was a delayed reaction to shock.

Her hair tumbling to her shoulders as it did made her seem young and vulnerable. She was still wearing the torn shirtwaist, the soft blue fabric falling from her smooth, ivory-white shoulder. But there was nothing in her demeanor to suggest that she was anything but her usual proper self. She sat with her back rigid against the pillow, her eyes narrowed in concentration. She didn't appear to be in shock.

It amused him that she could look so prim under the circumstances. At the same time, he felt a sense of disappointment. For a short while Maggie had abandoned all pretense and let down her guard. He had seen her cry, shared her pain. But now, apparently, it was back to business as usual.

Oh, Maggie, Maggie, he thought. What would it take to make you permanently abandon your armor? Who would it take?

He wanted it to be him. He wanted to be the one who freed the fiery passion that he sensed waited for release inside her. Wanted that more than life itself. But he couldn't take the chance. He'd never thought that he would be tempted to abandon his search for the man responsible for his wife's death.

Maggie not only tempted him, she unknowingly demanded that he forget everything that had ever happened before he met her—and he could never do that.

His only hope was that if Maggie ever did let down her guard completely, it would be after he was gone.

He waited for her to finish the milk, then took the empty glass from her and placed it on the bedstand.

To his surprise, she threw back the coverlet and

shot out of bed. Before he could stop her, she had bolted across the room and flung open the mirrored doors of her wardrobe.

Momentarily speechless, he watched shoes and clothing come flying out of the closet. He ducked to avoid a slipper that zoomed over his head and knocked over a vase. "Maggie, what the hell are you doing?"

She held up her Sunday best, a taffeta silk shirtwaist and an oxford shirt with a percaline dust ruffle, and then reached for her very best high-button shoes. "I'm getting ready to rebuild."

Dominick took in the various articles of clothing strewn about the room and wondered if Maggie hadn't lost more in the fire than her business. Perhaps he should fetch a doctor, he thought, watching her with narrowed eyes.

"If you would be kind enough to leave," she said, "I wish to change."

"You what?" he sputtered. "At this time of night? Have you taken leave of your senses?"

She regarded him calmly, clearly surprised by his tone. "I have a business to rebuild. You said so yourself."

"It's shock," he said. "That's why you're acting like this."

"I assure you, my faculties have never been better," she announced with conviction. "I intend to speak with the banker, Mr. Tubbs, about a loan."

He looked at her incredulously. "Tonight? If you drag him out of bed at this hour, he's more likely to shoot you than to grant you a loan."

"Don't be ridiculous," she said. "Mr. Tubbs might very well still be at the bank. Mrs. Tubbs told me herself that her husband often works late. Now if you would be kind enough to stay here and watch the children . . ."

"You're not leaving this house!"

Her eyes widened. Their gazes met across the bed

and collided. "How dare you tell me what I can and cannot do!"

"Someone had better!" he stormed. "Do you know how dangerous it is for a woman to be out in the middle of the night, alone and unprotected? You'd be a target for every outlaw in the town."

"As you well know, I have considerable experience in dealing with outlaws!"

His lips compressed into a thin line. "But you do not have the first notion how to handle yourself in the presence of a rapist!"

"I wouldn't be so certain of that, Mr. Sanders!"

"Is that so?" he challenged. With that, he put his booted foot on the bed and lunged toward her.

Chapter 18

With a startled cry, she jumped back and ducked away from him. Like wild animals meeting by surprise, they eyed each other warily. Dominick was bent over at the waist, arms curved in front of him menacingly.

Much to his chagrin, she didn't look the least bit alarmed or intimidated. Damned woman! She didn't even have the decency to let him see her cringe.

If anything, she was her usual straight-arrow self, watching him with a boldness that would have turned back a charging bull. Damned fool, that's what she was. Well, he intended to show her just how very vulnerable she was!

With the determination of a general about to lead an army into battle, he darted around the foot of the bed. Matching his speed, she picked up her skirt and leaped up on the mattress. He hopped up on the bed after her, letting out a loud whooping sound. She jumped to the floor and raced for the door.

"Aha!" he cried triumphantly. With a flying leap he managed to block her way. He had her! By George, he had her! But it wasn't enough; he wanted more. In the deep recesses of his mind he honestly believed that if he could control her, he could also control the way he felt about her.

With this in mind, he kept badgering her, watching her face for a sign that she recognized his victory. Hating the part of him that was struck by the illogical need to see her admit defeat, he forced a lecherous leer and felt a sense of remorse when a look of uncertainty crossed her face.

Unable to stop himself—afraid of what would happen if he did—he lunged forward, letting out a blood-curdling howl designed to push her away, even as he meant to make her stay.

She fled to the other side of the room and beseeched him with fearful eyes. "Don't, Dominick," she pleaded.

"Don't what?" he taunted, advancing.

"You made your point."

Her words were music to his ears. Now maybe he could stop this madness. "Are you willing to own up to the possibility that I might be right and you wrong?"

She hesitated. "On some things."

"Not good enough!" he thundered. He had the upper hand with her for once, and he intended to make the most of it. Yes, indeed, he meant to make her pay for every sleepless night he'd spent thinking of her. *Intended to make her regret his falling in love with her when it was against his best interests to do so.*

Oh, yes, she deserved everything she had coming to her.

She lifted her chin and he felt the advantage slipping away. "Say it!" he ordered. "Say that I'm right. A woman has no business being on the streets at this hour."

"You're right," she said, sounding more like she was choking on her food than capitulating.

He straightened. Her safety was assured, but everything else remained the same, including the urge to take her in his arms. "Either you get back to bed or I will put you there myself."

"I'm quite capable of putting myself to bed!" she retorted.

"Very well." He stepped aside and motioned with his arm for her to pass.

Head held high, she brushed past him, but as soon

as she had managed to put a safe distance between them, she made a dash for the door.

Cursing under his breath, he knocked over an end table in his haste to stop her. In one mighty movement, he grabbed her by the arm and flung her to the floor.

"You little cheat!" he growled, straddling her.

"Let me go, you brute!" Kicking and screaming, she beat on his chest with her fists.

"A regular wildcat, aren't we?" he rasped, warding off her blows. He grabbed her wrists and forced her arms over her head. He was completely on top of her now, the weight of his body containing, if not altogether controlling, hers.

"So," he growled, "you think you can handle a rapist, do you? And what . . ." he asked, his voice suddenly hoarse, "would you do if he held you down like this and . . ." Lowering his head, he brushed her lips with his own and then pulled back to laud his advantage over her.

It was at that moment that he realized it was she who held the advantage. Her soft, curving hips molded beneath him, her lovely, firm breasts pressed against his chest. The warmth of her body mixed with his own warmth until his blood ran like liquid fire through his veins. His limbs were ablaze, his loins ached. He needed to feel strong, but instead he felt weak and completely at her mercy.

Strangely enough, she grew still beneath him, no longer fighting him. For a moment—or maybe an hour—they looked into each other's eyes. Finally, her soft red lips parted in what could only be read as an invitation to do what he'd wanted for so long to do— tried not to do, dared not do, even now.

Stunned by the feelings that suddenly overcame him, he released her arms and rolled off her. "Do us both a favor and put yourself to bed," he said. Without as much as a glance at her, he stood, ran his fingers through his disheveled hair, and left the room.

*   *   *

The grandfather clock chimed the hour of two o'clock, and still he couldn't sleep. He was too riled to sleep, his body taut, his loins filled with an aching throb that begged for release.

The sound was so soft that at first he thought he'd imagined it. And when he heard it again, he thought it was one of the children and stood up, prepared to investigate. Then she came into view, looking more beautiful than it seemed possible for any woman to look.

She met his eyes briefly and then quickly looked away. "I couldn't sleep.'"

He drew a breath through his lips. "I couldn't either."

She raised her eyes to his shyly. "I apologize for my behavior earlier. You were right. I had no business leaving the house at such a late hour."

He would have welcomed her apology earlier, but not now. Now he had no desire to discuss right and wrong. "I'm the one who should apologize," he said. "I had no right to use physical force to hold you against your will."

If she was surprised by his apology, she kept it well concealed. "I guess the fire made us both loony," she said.

"A fire can do that, I suppose," he agreed.

She nodded. "I'd best let you get some sleep." She stood in place looking at him, her eyes soft, her lips parted in a way that could be an invitation, but he wasn't sure. Whether it was or not, it was enough to shoot to hell the last bit of resistance on his part.

"Maggie." Her name fell from his lips in one last, gallant attempt to resist the temptation she offered, but realizing that she was not going to heed his warning to leave, he conceded defeat. Like a man possessed, he moved toward her and pulled her into his arms.

Lowering his head he pressed his mouth against

hers. Afraid that if he unleashed the full force of his passion he would awaken from his dream, he made himself hold back.

But no dream could be this sweet, this receptive, this responsive, this demanding.

Whispering his name, she opened her mouth to him, allowing his tongue freedom to explore the lovely sweetness within. Her own tongue met his in a private dance for two that was both familiar and new.

She slipped her arms around his neck and moaned softly as his hands worked down the length of her body.

"Maggie," he whispered, "I need you." He pulled back momentarily and she cried out in protest. He chuckled and lifted her in his arms. Pressing her body to his, he carried her down the hall to the bedroom.

He laid her down gently amid the tangled bed-clothes and kissed her with rising passion that threatened to explode. Gasping, he pulled away, tore off his shirt and trousers, then joined her on the bed and took her in his arms.

"Are you sure you want this, Maggie?" he asked.

She looked at him with eyes burning with desire. "I . . . I think so."

He kissed her smooth forehead. "What do I have to do to make you know for sure?" He watched her and waited.

"Tell me the truth," she whispered. "Did you rob the bank?"

He considered how to answer. So much was at stake. His future, her future, and the future of a murderer hung on the words he was about to utter. All he had to do was to admit to the robbery and it would end right there. She would turn against him and he would be free to do what he'd come to Santa Barbara to do. He would be safe. She would be safe. All he had to do was to tell one stinking lie, and they would both be safe. But, Lord help him, he couldn't bring himself to lie to her, no matter how necessary it was.

He held her face in his hands and searched it lovingly. "I give you my word, Maggie. I was nowhere near that bank."

"In that case, Mr. Sanders . . . Dominick . . . I am very sure that I want this." In little more than a whisper, she added, "Want you."

Damning himself for failing to do what a better man would have done, he crushed her to him, kissed her fully on the lips, and plunged his tongue deep into her waiting mouth. From that moment on, nothing else existed.

With quaking heart, he unfastened the hooks of her nightgown, working the soft fabric down her shoulders as he held her gaze locked in his.

When the full extent of her beauty was revealed, he inhaled deeply. A soft gasp escaped him as he touched her lovely round breasts and felt her ripe pink nipples bud beneath his quivering hands. "Oh, Maggie," he moaned. "You are so beautiful."

With ultimate care, he finished undressing her, fighting the pulsing need to move quickly. Inch by inch, he let himself explore, admire, and adore each glorious and womanly curve. His lips and fingers blazed first one path, then another across her hot, velvety body until every part of her knew his touch.

And when he was finished, she returned the favor, letting her fingers and her lips trail delicious sensations across his chest and arms and shoulders until he could no longer contain himself.

A smile played on her lips as she reached down and wrapped her fingers around the throbbing pulse of his manhood. He moaned with pleasure and rolled on top of her, taking care not to hurt her. "Oh, Maggie, my dear precious Maggie."

At the precise moment when need was a sharp, exquisite pain demanding release, he entered her, or rather was drawn inside her by some invisible force that neither could control. Like the awakening of nature in springtime, he felt her open up and, once he was firmly in place, close around him, embracing all that he had to offer and pulling more from him than he thought it possible to give.

Sometime during the night, she cried out. Awakening instantly, he drew her into his arms and cradled her until the sobs subsided. "It's all right," he whispered, "I'm here to take care of you."

"My Blake sewer . . ." Another sob escaped her, sounding like it had been torn from some deeply hidden place at her core. Lifting his fingers to catch the last remnants of pain and despair on her trembling lips, he felt a teardrop.

"Don't cry," he whispered. "Please don't cry."

Her lips came together, and he traced them with the tip of a finger, then cupped her face in his hands. "You mustn't worry," he said soothingly. He kissed her again, tasting salt and sweetness, happiness and sadness, but more than anything feeling the warmth of her response.

He ran his hands down her bare back. Then worked his fingers down her shoulders until he could cup the gentle rise of both her breasts. He felt a thrill when her hand pressed his more firmly next to her skin, then slipped down the length of him to do to him the very things it had been his intention to do to her. Soon he was the one gasping.

"Oh, Maggie!"

They made love with the same desperate need and passion as before, but their earlier intimacy had helped them define a deftness of touch that brought an added sweetness to their pleasure. No longer did he have to guess what would bring a moan of delight from her. He knew. Just as she knew how he wanted to be touched in return.

Sometime later, sated and exhausted, emotions and bodies spent, they clung to each other, and at the first sign of recovery, made love again. The third time was more thoughtful, more gentle, but no less erotic—in some ways maybe even more so. Later they lay locked in each other's arms in sweet bliss, reflecting on the many changes a single night had brought.

"Mama, Mama."

Maggie had no sooner walked into the kitchen than Laurie-Anne threw her arms around her mother's legs. Running her hand through her daughter's sleep-tousled hair, Maggie met Dominick's eyes, unsure how to act. She decided to act as normal as possible, but soon realized the futility of it.

"Normal" for them was to exchange insults and barbs, and Maggie couldn't for the life of her think of an unkind thing to say to him.

So she stood looking at him.

And he looked back, thinking of how she had been when he stole away from her bed earlier to light the fire. Asleep, her head tucked in the crook of her arm, her lovely golden hair fanning across her pillow and part of his, she had looked incredibly vulnerable and soft. But she didn't look vulnerable now. Nor, for that matter, did she look particularly soft. He was surprised—more than that, disappointed—to see her looking her usual staunch, disciplined self.

He hadn't known what to expect from her this morning, but it certainly wasn't this. Never had she looked so prim and proper, dressed as she was in a plain gray skirt, a high-necked pleated waist (rather than ruffled), her hair pulled back tightly into its usual bun. Or did he only seem more staunch today because he had finally seen the other side of her? Knew what deep, burning passion she was capable of? Knew what lay beneath her prim clothing and proper facade?

She blushed prettily and averted her gaze to the dirty dishes on the table. "You fed the children?"

Surprised and even gratified to see her blush, he nodded. "I thought you could use the extra sleep. Want some coffee?" He reached for one of the large ceramic cups he preferred.

"Thank you," she said, taking a dainty teacup out of the cupboard. She raised her voice to be heard above Laurie-Anne, who was giving her brother a piece of her three-year-old mind. Jamie was unimpressed, and Laurie-Ann promptly kicked him in the shins.

"Ow!" Jamie yelled, holding his leg and hopping around the kitchen on one foot.

Maggie shook her head in rebuke. "Laurie-Anne, you mustn't kick your brother!" Laurie-Anne hung her head sheepishly, and her mother turned her attention to Jamie. "And you, young man, are to stop teasing your sister."

"She won't leave my beret alone," Jamie grumbled.

"I want a bar-ray," Laurie-Anne said, pouting.

Dominick ruffled Laurie-Anne's hair. "If you wait until after I've made your mother's breakfast, I will give you your very own beret."

"You said berets were worn by men," Jamie protested. He folded his arms in front of him and made a face at his sister.

"What do you say we make an exception this one time?" Dominick cajoled. He gave Jamie a wink and was rewarded with a reluctant nod. "That's a good sport. Now run along and get your schoolbooks or you'll be late for school."

"Oh, dear, is it that late already?" Maggie exclaimed. She took a hasty sip of her coffee. "Let me get my shawl."

"I can walk to school by myself," Jamie said.

Maggie frowned in uncertainty. "Are you sure?"

"Consuela let me walk by myself yesterday."

"When I was Jamie's age I had to travel three times as far," Dominick added.

Jamie had clearly heard the story before. "Uphill both ways. Isn't that right, Aita?"

"Absolutely."

"My goodness," Maggie mocked gently. "Both ways, you say? Wherever it was you lived, it must have been a geographical wonder." To Jamie she said, "Since you only have to go uphill one way, I suppose it's all right, then."

Jamie, sure that freedom to walk to school by himself was the first step toward manhood, hugged his mother without the usual prompting and dashed out the back door.

"He's growing up so fast," Maggie said wistfully.

Dominick set a plate of warm blueberry muffins on the table. "You'd better eat."

A silence stretched between them as they sat across from one another eating muffins and drinking coffee as if these two simple acts required their complete concentration. It seemed rather odd to him that she seemed shy in his presence after the night spent in his arms, but knowing Maggie as he did, he supposed she was feeling guilty about what had happened.

Watching her, there was no question in his mind that their relationship had changed dramatically. He had denied his feelings, fought against them, but in the end he'd realized how he'd failed on both accounts. The biggest test still lay ahead, though. He had yet to find the man responsible for the deaths of his wife and child. And no one, not even Maggie, must be allowed to keep him from his quest. For him, there could be no more failures like last night.

"I can see by the way you're dressed that you've got business on your mind," he said, his voice stilted by the feelings he held back.

"Just as soon as the bank opens, I'm going to talk to Mr. Tubbs about a loan."

He lowered his mug. "Maggie, I've been thinking. I'll . . . uh . . . give you the money."

"I can't let you do that, Dominick. I already owe you money. Besides, it'll take a lot of money to start another business. I'll have to replace all my tools. And my sewing machine. Do you know how much that cost me? Not to mention the fabric. Velvet's not cheap, and since it has suddenly become the rage, I'm going to need several bolts. Then there's leather. You know I refuse to use anything but the finest grade."

He waited until she fell silent, then pulled a wad of bills from his shirt pocket and threw it on the table in front of her.

Paling, she stared at the money, her eyes round with disbelief. She looked up from the bank notes into his eyes. He flinched inwardly at the accusations he read on her face. "Where . . . where did you get that money?"

"What does it matter?"

"The bank," she whispered. "You lied to me."

"I didn't lie, Maggie. I swear to you."

"You lied," she cried. "Everything you said was a lie. Last night was a lie. All those things you whispered in my ear . . ."

"Dammit, Maggie! It was not a lie!"

She closed her eyes as if she could no longer look at him. "Where did you get the money?"

"Can't it suffice to say it's mine?" Her eyes flew open, and he could see all too clearly the distrust in her face. Something hardened inside him, and his voice, when he spoke again, was cold and distant. "Is it so hard for you to believe I might have come by the money honestly?"

"Since you have no gainful employment, I find it extremely difficult to believe."

"I guess there's no point in arguing about it. The money's yours if you want it. Take it or leave it."

"I could not in good conscience accept money with such a questionable background."

His face darkened. Had she thrust a knife in him, she couldn't have hurt him more. The pain was so deep that for one terrible moment, he wanted nothing more than to hurt her back. "Lucky for me that you don't use the same standards for going to bed with a man."

A look of shocked disbelief crossed her face, followed by a willful rise of her chin. "I can assure you that last night will not be repeated."

"You're damned right about that!" Grabbing the money from the table, he rushed out of the house. The slamming of the door ripped through the peaceful morning stillness like the sound of gunshots.

Chapter 19

Maggie sat in the hardback chair in front of the bank president's desk and presented her need for a loan in a clear, businesslike manner.

Mr. Tubbs puffed on his cigar and listened politely, interrupting once or twice to ask a relevant question, then making a careful notation on a piece of paper. He was a short, pudgy man with long, graying sideburns and a protruding stomach.

When she had finished her story, she handed him a list of tools and supplies she'd lost in the fire, with the Blake sewer topping the list.

The banker waved the blue curling smoke away with his hand and read over the list. Presently, he glanced up at her and cleared his throat. "Your loss seems quite extensive. Do you really need so many lasts and awls?"

"I need different sizes," she explained. "I make footwear for men, women, *and* children, including infants."

"I see." He sat back in his chair and fingered the chain of the gold watch that looped from his pocket to his belt. "I would like to help you out, Mrs. Sanders . . . eh . . . by the way, where is your husband? Maybe it would be better if I discussed the business aspects with him."

"My husband was unable to accompany me," she said, trying to hide her annoyance.

"Perhaps it would be best to postpone this meeting to a later date? One more convenient for your husband." Mr. Tubbs gave her a condescending wink and reached for his cigar. "You're far to pretty to worry your little head over money matters." He stuck the cigar in his mouth and rose, clearly calling the meeting to an end.

Maggie stubbornly remained in her seat. Feet planted squarely in front of her, she sat erect, her body rigid with determination. "I'm afraid that's not possible. I need the money now," she said firmly. She had no intention of being so easily discounted or dismissed. "Now if you would be kind enough to give me my loan, I will not take up any more of your time."

The banker's bushy brows rose in surprise. "I'm afraid it's not quite that simple. As you must have noticed, Santa Barbara has undergone enormous growth in recent months. Buildings are going up faster than lightning. New hotels, a new school and churches, you name it. The bank's resources have been pushed to the limit. I'm sure you can understand . . ."

"Are you turning me down?" she asked, stunned. She had known it wasn't going to be easy to obtain a loan, but it never once occurred to her that she would be flatly denied.

"I would like to help you, really I would. Perhaps if I spoke to your husband . . ."

She rose abruptly. "That won't be necessary." Head held high, she sailed out of his office and through the lobby of the bank without a backward glance.

Much to her dismay, Dominick stood waiting for her outside the bank. He leaned against a post, with his arms folded and his legs crossed at the ankles. His beret perched on the side of his head, giving him a rakish look that was hard to resist.

Had he not lied to her, she would have welcomed his company at that moment. Welcomed it? Glory be, she would have been in his arms so fast he wouldn't know what had hit him. As it was, his presence only added to her depression.

If only he had looked the least bit remorseful for what he'd done. Instead, he looked positively smug. One glimpse of his face and she felt her heart crumble in a dozen different places. The man she had seen in her bedroom last night, had held in her arms, no longer existed. She wondered if he ever had.

She didn't trust herself to speak, and so she marched past him. Her dainty boots pounded out a warning on the splintered planks of the sidewalk, but he chose to ignore it.

"The offer still stands," he said, falling in step beside her.

"So does my answer," she snapped, hastening her steps.

They walked down State Street without speaking, at least not verbally. But they spoke nevertheless. Every movement of the arm or leg conveyed her renewed vow that what had happened between them would never happen again.

At the corner of Figueroa, they waited for a carriage to pass before crossing the street, careful to walk as close as it was possible to walk without touching. It wouldn't do to stir up the town's tongue-waggers.

He stopped in the middle of the boardwalk, but she kept going. "All right, let's say I give you the money and we pretend it's a bank loan," he called after her. "If it makes you feel any better, I'll even draw up a contract. We'll keep it all nice and legal."

Spinning around to face him, she glared accusingly. "You're a fine one to be talking legalities!"

"Which only goes to show that I'm willing to do anything to make my offer more acceptable to you."

"So you did rob the bank."

"What do I have to do to prove to you that I'm telling the truth?"

"I'm not sure there's anything you can do," she said.

"I see." A couple strolled by, and he lifted his beret

and nodded grimly. As soon as they were out of ear-shot, he continued. "Since you're so stubborn, let's say I did rob the bank. Then the money would, by law, belong to Wells, Fargo. You wanted a bank loan and I'm offering you one. The only difference is that you won't need Mr. Tubbs's approval. What do you say?"

"I say that you are the most despicable man I've ever met."

Her insult was met with a look of approval. "You don't have to flatter me. I told you I'd give you the money."

"When are you going to understand? I don't want your money. The sooner you get out of my life, the better for all of us."

"That, Maggie, is one area where I can assure you we totally agree." He readjusted his beret, pushing it to the back of his head.

Feeling a traitorous twist of her heart, she whirled about and stomped the rest of the way across the dirt-packed street.

"Where are you going?" he called.

"As far away from you as I can get!" she shot back.

She marched into the hardware store for no other reason but to escape him. As soon as she stepped through the door she found herself encircled by three women whom she recognized as having ordered shoes from her.

"You poor thing," Mrs. Quitter crooned, her three chins wobbling as she spoke. "I was just telling Mrs. Meyers here that we must find a way to help your lovely family."

"Terrible thing," Mrs. Meyers agreed, peering at Maggie through her eyepiece. "First a bank robbery, then a fire. What on earth will be next?"

"And don't forget," added Mrs. Hopkins, leaning on her wooden cane, "this poor dear was almost killed when the stagecoach ran off the side of the mountain."

Mrs. Meyers dropped her eyepiece, and it bounced back into place upon her hefty bosom. "It's all too terrible. But as I was telling Mrs. Quitter here, us women must stick together. You must tell us how we can be of assistance."

"Well . . ." Maggie began, weighing the woman's sincerity.

"Come along, child," Mrs. Meyers urged. "Don't be shy."

"I've just been to the bank to see about a loan. Without my shoemaking shop, I . . . we have no way of supporting the children."

"Of course you don't!" Mrs. Meyers exclaimed, nodding her head assertively.

"You're such a wise woman, Mrs. Meyers," Maggie said. "As I was saying, I went to the bank and Mr. Tubbs turned me down."

"No!" all three women exclaimed in disbelief.

"Indeed," Maggie assured them. Through the wavy glass window she could see a tall figure across the street. Damn the man. Was he going to shadow her all day? Turning back to the three openmouthed women, she added, "I simply don't know what I'll do."

"Don't you worry," Mrs. Meyers said. She turned to her two friends. "We'll help her, won't we?"

"I don't know how you can help," Maggie said.

"Of course we can help," Mrs. Meyers assured her. "Mrs. Hopkins here is the head of the Woman's Christian Temperance Movement."

Mrs. Hopkins nodded vehemently. "I am indeed. And last year we actually got the town to vote for becoming dry."

"Really?" Maggie asked, surprised. She could think of at least twenty saloons, or grog shops, as they were called locally, that operated on State Street alone.

"Indeed! And for two blessed months we put old John Barleycorn out of business," Mrs. Hopkins said, her eyes gleaming with the memory. "But, alas! The state supreme court ruled that local option was unconstitutional." She jabbed the tip of her cane onto the floor for emphasis. "Unconstitutional, my bustle. No man who voted was thinking about the constitution. What they were thinking of was their own favorite grog house!"

"Hear, hear," Mrs. Quitter exclaimed.

Mrs. Meyers, too overcome with emotion to speak, pulled a lace handkerchief from her sleeve and dabbed at an eye. "To make such gains and have it taken away by legalities. I just can't bear to think about it."

"I'm so sorry," Maggie said, looking from one woman to another. "This is all very interesting, but I really don't see what any of this has to do with rebuilding my business."

"Well, of course it does, dear." Mrs. Meyers sniffled into the handkerchief and looked to the other two women for confirmation. "Doesn't it?"

"Yes, yes, yes," Mrs. Quitter agreed. "I wouldn't be surprised if the person or persons who set your building fire weren't under the influence."

Mrs. Meyers nodded in approval. "That's excellent. And if this person was under the influence, why that means that this matter can be taken up officially by the Woman's Christian Temperance Movement!"

"What did I tell you?" Mrs. Quitter said, looking pleased.

"How do I contact this organization?" Maggie asked, confused.

"You already have," Mrs. Hopkins explained. "*We* are the organization. And we are going to help you get back on your feet."

Without another word, the three women hustled Maggie out of the store and across town, stopping to explain Maggie's plight to everyone along the way who would listen.

Much to Maggie's surprise, offers of assistance began pouring in. The blacksmith offered to make her a set of awls in exchange for a pair of work boots. Mr. Williams, who owned the tannery, donated several pieces of choice calfskin, along with a piece of fine oak tan leather large enough to sole several pairs of shoes. For good measure, he even threw in some waterproofed pieces of pebbled box calf stock. "This should make a perfect pair of storm boots," he said.

Agreeing wholeheartedly, Maggie thanked him and was already thinking up designs when the members of the Woman's Christian Temperance Movement whisked her out of the store and marched her to the next targeted business.

Mr. Grover, the owner of the general store, listened to what had now become a practiced presentation from Maggie's self-proclaimed guardian angels and immediately agreed to supply her with brass tacks on credit, and as much catsup as she could use.

"Just in case you need some blessed relief," he explained, whistling through his broken tooth. "Come to think of it," he added, as he recorded her purchases on a piece of paper and tacked it to the wall, "I do have an empty building over there on Sycamore that I'll let you have if you like. I won't even charge you rent until you show a profit."

Maggie was so touched by the generous offer, she almost burst into tears. "That's wonderful. I can't tell you how much I appreciate your help."

Mr. Grover blushed. "Don't mention it. The building . . . eh . . requires some fixing up."

"That's no problem," Maggie said, assuredly. "I'm an old hand at fixing up buildings. Just you wait and see."

Maggie felt less confident after she had given her thanks, said good-bye to the members of the Woman's

Christian Temperance Movement, stopped by the house to pick up her measuring tape and notebook, and walked alone to the address Mr. Grover had written down for her.

Trying to be discreet, she searched for Dominick, who was nowhere to be seen. But instead of feeling relief that he no longer followed her, she only felt more miserable. She had believed a bandit's lies.

Oh, Lord, if only that was the half of it. All through the night, while she lay in his arms dressed only in desire and need, it had never once occurred to her to feel guilty. But she felt guilty now. Guilty because she felt no remorse for sharing his bed. And nothing, not his betrayal of her or the clamoring shame spiraling from her rigid upbringing and strong moral beliefs was ever going to rob her of the one glorious night they had spent together.

This, of course, made no sense. She hated the man. Hated everything he stood for. How, then, was it possible for his kisses to hold such power over her, even now, as she stood alone on a deserted street?

She peered through her tears at the address on the paper, thinking she'd misread it. She hadn't.

She stared openmouthed at the two-story architectural monstrosity, sure that Mr. Grover had given her the wrong address. Never in her life had she seen such a ghastly pink building! The person who painted it must have been color-blind, she decided, or at the very least completely lacking in taste.

Any hope that there was some sort of mistake was dispelled when one of the keys Mr. Grover had entrusted to her slid easily into the ornate lock of the bright-pink front door. It took only a slight turn of her wrist for the door to spring open, with a snakelike hiss of hinges.

A stale, musty smell greeted her from within. Obviously the building had not been properly aired for quite some time. Once inside, she gaped in disbelief at the surroundings. The parlor was even more garish than the outside. A bright-scarlet rug lay in the middle of the dull wood floor. The walls were covered in flocked paper a shade lighter than the rug. Velvet rose-colored sofas and matching overstuffed chairs faced a pink marble fireplace. In the center of the room, directly opposite the staircase, a life-size statue of a naked woman was enthroned on a dingy white pedestal.

Maggie had never in her life seen such utter disregard for good taste. How could a nice, quiet, respectable man like Mr. Grover own such an eyesore? she wondered.

Although Mr. Grover had agreed to let her use only the first floor, she walked up the stairs, curious to see if the second floor fared as badly. Incredibly, it did.

The upper level was divided into a series of tiny rooms, each decorated in much the same style as the downstairs. Thick velvet drapes at the windows blocked out most of the light. Mirrors were placed in the most surprising places. One room was decorated entirely in mirrors, including the ceiling!

Shaking her head in puzzlement, she went back downstairs, wondering how she would ever manage to make the garish parlor into a proper place of business.

A banging at the door startled her. Thinking it could be Mr. Grover, she hurried to answer it, only to find Dominick standing on the porch. He whipped off his beret and bowed.

"I just thought you might like to know that my offer still stands," he said.

"Would you like to know what you can do with your offer?" she spit out.

He raised an eyebrow. "Is this going to be another one of your slips of the tongue?" he inquired.

"Certainly not! How did you know where to find me?" she asked suspiciously. So he was following her.

She hated to admit it, but the thought gave her some satisfaction.

"I ran into three of our customers who were all too happy to tell me where my wife was," he said. "Members of the Woman's Christian Temperance Movement, I believe. Are you going to let me in or aren't you?"

She turned and he followed her inside. Spinning on her heel to face him, she was surprised to see a look of utter disbelief on his face.

"Mr. Grover said I could use this old house for my shop," she explained, feeling suddenly defensive. "As soon as I fix it up, it'll be perfect."

He pulled his eyes away from the naked statue and stared at her. "Your shop?" He scanned the room, then threw back his head and laughed aloud, his hearty guffaws bouncing off the walls like a rubber ball.

Staring at him in consternation, she wondered what he found so amusing.

"I can't believe it!" he sputtered, before surrendering to another bout of laughter. "The prim and proper Maggie Turner."

Hands on her hips, she eyed him with curiosity. "Would you mind telling me what's so funny?"

He was laughing so hard that he slid down the wall until he was sitting on the floor. He laughed until tears ran down his cheeks. "Maggie, Maggie, you have no idea, do you?" he sputtered. "This is a bordello. A house of ill repute."

Thunderstruck, Maggie looked around the room with a shock of realization. Of course! How could she not have guessed? Dominick must think her an ignorant fool. Not that it mattered what he thought, of course . . .

"It *was* a house of ill repute," she corrected him, maintaining a businesslike demeanor. "It will soon be my new shoemaker shop."

Much to her chagrin, this declaration brought another outburst of merriment.

Though she stared at him, she suddenly realized she was in a quandary. Common decency required her to turn down Mr. Grover's offer. It simply wasn't appropriate for a businesswoman such as herself, a mother of two, to be anywhere near such a scandalous place.

But she didn't have many options left. Indeed, she had none. Taking the money from Dominick was out of the question. And she would die rather than throw herself on Mr. Tubbs's mercy or ask Dominick to intervene on her behalf.

Now she chose to ignore him and pulled out her notebook and measuring tape. Muttering to herself, she began taking measurements of the windows. "I think if I put a counter here, and my workbench between those two windows there and . . ."

Dominick watched her, still shaking his head in disbelief. "What are your plans for the naked lady?"

"You can put her upstairs if you like," she said crisply.

He shrugged and wrapped his arms around the statue's middle. Battling his way up the stairs with it, he huffed and puffed, stopping at the halfway point to rest. Maggie interrupted her measuring long enough to glance up at him.

"I don't think I've ever had such a difficult time carrying a lady to the bedroom," he moaned, mopping his brow with a handkerchief.

Ignoring the unexpected flush that washed over her at the memory of his carrying her to bed, she forced her voice to be steady. "Perhaps some of us would do well to take a lesson from your friend."

"Maybe so," Dominick called back. Much to her relief, he showed no sign that he'd noticed the sudden blush in her cheeks.

"At least this lady knows not to deck herself out with corsets and other unnecessary clothing," he

added, before disappearing down the hall and into one
of the tiny rooms.

Seconds later, she heard a thud overhead, followed
by an explosion of laughter. "My God, Maggie!
Would you look at all the mirrors!"

Chapter 20

It was the latter part of May, and a balmy desert wind blew through the open windows of the old bordello. Inside, Maggie worked feverishly. Already she had stripped the flocked paper off the walls, torn down the faded draperies, and hidden the suggestive pictures of naked ladies in an upstairs bedroom.

She decided not to take the chance that the previous business might have left behind some undesirable essence that permeated the wood. Getting down on hands and knees, she attacked every square inch of the floor with strong lye soap and a hard-bristled brush, not satisfied until she'd managed to scrub clear down to the natural wood.

She had just begun to work on the baseboards when a knock came at the door. Drying her hands on her apron, Maggie opened the door and was delighted to see Manuel standing on her porch.

"Manuel! Do come in! Come in!" She hustled him inside, apologizing for the wet floor, the smell of disinfectant, and for not having any refreshments to offer him on such a warm day.

After showing him around, she invited him to sit down on one of the velvet-covered chairs she'd brought down from an upstairs room. Of all the furniture in the place, this chair was the least objectionable. "So what do you think?"

Manuel nodded politely. "I think it's fine shop, Señora Sanders."

Maggie was pleased. "So do I." She contemplated

Manuel thoughtfully, puzzled by the way he seemed to avoid looking directly at her. "I haven't seen you since the night of the fire."

At mention of the fire, Manuel hung his head and concentrated his attention on his lap.

Thinking that he blamed himself for the fire, she tried to relieve his mind. "I don't blame you for anything that happened that night, Manuel. And of course Mr. Sanders and I want you to come back to work for us. You can start today if you like. I'm sure Mr. Sanders would be delighted to have you help outside, and if not, you can begin work cutting out patterns."

"I can't work for you anymore," Manuel said.

"Oh?" When Manuel offered no further explanation, Maggie remembered something. "Manuel, the night of the fire . . . the look on your face . . . Is there something about the fire that you need to tell me? Is that why you've been avoiding us?" When the youth made no effort to answer her, she lowered her voice to little more than a whisper. "Manuel?"

This time he stirred slightly but still refused to meet her eyes. "I know who burned down your shop."

She stared at him in surprise. "The sheriff said it was a bunch of radicals from Spanishtown."

The boy's face was dark with anguish. "I tried to stop them, Señora Sanders. You must believe me."

"I believe you, Manuel. But I don't understand. Why haven't you told the sheriff their names?"

"I can't," he whispered. "Please don't make me."

"But . . . why?"

"The radicals had nothing to do with the fire. It was someone else."

Maggie frowned. "None of this makes sense. Why would anyone want to hurt me like that?"

"It wasn't you they wanted to hurt. It . . . it was me."

"You?" She stared at him in disbelief. It was difficult to imagine that anyone as likable as Manuel had enemies. "But why? Why would anyone want to harm you? Manuel, you must tell me everything you know."

"I can't," Manuel said.

"You must!" Maggie insisted.

"Maggie!"

Surprised by the sharpness in Dominick's voice, Maggie looked up to see him standing at the front door. "Whatever it is, Dominick, it will have to wait. I'm busy right now."

"I'm afraid it can't wait." To Manuel he nodded and said, "I need to discuss something of prime importance with my wife. Would you please wait outside? It should only take a few minutes."

Relieved to have an excuse to escape Maggie's grilling, Manuel slipped past Dominick and shot outside without a backward glance.

No sooner had he left than Maggie inquired angrily of Dominick, "Would you mind telling me what was so almighty important that it couldn't wait until I had finished talking to Manuel?"

"You can't force the boy to divulge information that could put him in harm's way. There's no telling what these hoodlums are capable of doing."

Maggie paled. "You don't think they would do bodily injury to Manuel, do you?"

"It's my guess that anyone capable of such destruction of property is probably capable of anything. I do know for sure that it would be a mistake to force Manuel to identify them."

"But I have the right to know," Maggie protested. "They burned down my building." Suddenly something occurred to her, and she narrowed her eyes in suspicion. "And why do I get the feeling that you know something you're not telling me?"

"I wish that were true, but I'm afraid it's not. I have made it my business to keep in close contact with the sheriff. He has his suspicions but unfortunately is unable to prove anything."

At the thought of Dominick working with the sheriff, Maggie laughed. "Your boldness never fails to amaze me. I wonder what Sheriff Badger would say if he knew who you really are?"

"Don't worry, Maggie. One day, with a little luck, you might find out. Meanwhile, don't push Manuel. There's a very strict code among the criminal element. Rule number one requires swift retaliation to anyone who names names." Maggie let out a gasp and his eyes softened. "I know you hate this, Maggie."

She took a deep breath. What she hated was that Dominick knew so well the rules by which criminals played their deadly games.

"Let me handle this." His eyes softened. "Please."

What he was really doing was asking her to trust him, and that was the very thing he'd made it so difficult to do. "I don't want anything to happen to Manuel."

"It won't," he promised.

"Or to my business."

"The only way I can guarantee that your business will be safe is if you don't hire him back."

She thought about this a moment and felt anger building within her. Since moving to Santa Barbara she had been forced—blackmailed was more like it—to do many things against her will. Just thinking about it infuriated her. The way Dominick forced her to compromise her moral beliefs. Making her lie and pretend they were married. Forcing her to break God only knows how many laws. Making her love him, making her hate him. Well, enough was enough!

"I won't let a bunch of hoodlums dictate what I can and cannot do," she exclaimed indignantly.

Warm lights of approval flickered in the depths of Dominick's eyes. "That's a girl, Maggie. I knew I could count on you."

Her mouth dropped open in confusion. It was her decision to rehire Manuel and her decision alone. So why was Dominick looking so damned pleased with himself?

* * *

For the next few days, she continued to scrub and sterilize the inside from wall to wall. Meanwhile, Dominick and Manuel painted the outside a sparkling bright white with blue trim and matching blue shutters. Dominick taught Manuel some Basque folk songs, and Manuel returned the favor by teaching him a few Spanish ones, and their cheery voices rang out as they worked. On occasion, she heard their laughter and felt a surge of envy for the rapport that had sprung up between them.

How she longed to join in! What she wanted to do was to laugh with Dominick as freely as he laughed with Manuel. That, of course, would be a mistake. As grateful as she was for the way he was helping her get her shop in order, she didn't dare permit herself the luxury of relaxing in his company. Not after what had happened between them that one glorious, never-to-be-forgotten night.

Every lowering of the guard allowed for a lingering gaze or a tender word to pass between them. And with each and every such occurrence, it became all that much harder to resist the urge to run into his arms and forget the rest.

So she scrubbed and cleaned vigorously and organized her brand-new tools. Most of all, she concentrated on avoiding Dominick as much as she possibly could, wondering all the while if she wasn't just postponing the inevitable.

When at last the house had been painted and scrubbed, Dominick made another sign, which simply read "Sanders Shoemakers." But he was careful to wait until Manuel had left for the day before hanging it from the roof.

No sooner had he started hammering than Maggie came racing outside to see what he was doing.

One glance at the sign, and she was ready to explode. She was not going to have a bank robber's

name on her shop! "You're not putting that sign up!"
she stormed, shaking the ladder beneath him.

Cursing her, he scrambled onto the roof just as the
ladder crashed to the ground.

"Damn it, Maggie, you could have killed me."

She glared at him furiously, with her eyes blazing
and her hands on her hips. Oh, how she loved seeing
him stranded on the roof, dependent on her to rescue
him. "That was my intention. But since I failed, I will
settle for your taking that sign down immediately. I
don't want your name on it!"

"I think we both know that I was the one who drew
in the most customers."

"But I'm the one with business expertise. What
good are customers if you can't provide them with
goods?"

"And what good are goods without customers?" he
asked reasonably.

She backed away. "Have it your way."

"Where are you going?"

She turned and waved. "Home."

"Maggie, damn it! Come back here! You heard me.
Just wait until I get my hands on that pretty little neck
of yours. Just you wait, Maggie!"

Chapter 21

It was evening by the time someone walked by and heard Dominick's call for help. Dominick thanked his rescuer, a seventeen-year-old Chinese youth who spoke little English, and stalked angrily along the dark, lonely streets all the way home.

His rage at Maggie had not diminished in the least during the hours he'd spent on the roof. If anything, the closer he got to the house, the more furious he became. He stomped onto the porch, his footsteps echoing through the very foundation, and then he paused.

The house was dark and silent. He pulled off his boots at the front door so as not to wake the children and then felt his way down the hall to Maggie's bedroom.

The door squeaked on its hinges when he pushed it open. A soft gasp rose from the bed, and an evil smile curved his lips.

"Aha!" he bellowed, lunging across the room. Sprawling onto the bed, he caught her before she had a chance to escape.

She screamed and he covered her mouth with his hand. "Hush or you'll wake Jamie and Laurie-Anne."

"Let me go!" she cried against his palm.

"I thought you might like to know how it feels to be stranded," he rasped in her ear, "with no one to help you escape."

He moved his hand from her mouth and when she didn't scream, he relaxed and immediately realized his mistake. The urge to strangle her was overshadowed by the need to kiss her.

He lowered his head and captured her lips. Her mouth softened beneath his, but only for a moment. The next thing he knew she was pushing him away.

Grabbing her by the arms, he held her down. "Damn it, Maggie. Hold still."

"Get out and leave me alone!"

"You don't mean that and you know it. Admit it." He pressed his fingers into her flesh. "We're good together. What happened the other night . . . we can have that again."

"Don't you dare!" she sputtered.

"Why not, Maggie? You want me, I know you do. Just like you did the other night."

"That was before I knew you'd robbed the bank!"

"Damn it! I told you I wasn't responsible for that."

"I don't believe you!"

"Maggie, Maggie," he cried. "I can't tell you how it wounds me to hear you say that." In a softer voice, he added, "You're right about one thing. Your virtue is intact as long as you believe me guilty of such a transgression." He nuzzled her ear. "I could never make love to a woman who thinks I'm a fiend."

"Don't, Dominick . . ."

"Don't what, Maggie? Don't kiss you? Don't touch you here and . . . here?" He smiled to himself as he felt her resistance melt away. He ran his hands down the length of her lovely, warm body in a slow, tantalizing circle that was intended to torment. His pleasure increased when she began to writhe beneath him. Pleasure became ecstasy when her soft, velvety cry for more filled his ears. "Please . . ."

"Please what?" he asked.

"Don't tease . . ."

His fingers circled her breast. "I wouldn't want to compromise you. I know how you feel about going to bed with a bank robber."

"Dominick . . . please don't do this to me!"

He moved his hands down to her thighs. "I'm only doing it for your own good," he replied. "I respect a woman's right to say no."

"Damn you!" she spit out.

His hands touched the wet softness between her legs. "Oh, dear," he gasped. "Another slip . . ." He pulled his hand away, knowing that if he didn't get the hell out of there, he would be hopelessly caught in his own trap.

He pulled away from her. "See you at breakfast."

"I hate you, Dominick Sanders! Just wait. I'll get even with you!"

His hoarse voice floated to her from the doorway. "I look forward to it."

After he left, Maggie paced her bedroom floor in agitated circles, calling him every hideous name she could think of. But no amount of name-calling could cool down her torrid flesh. She felt like her whole body was on fire. How was it possible to desire a man whom she absolutely detested? A man who not only robbed stages but banks—and the Lord only knew what other transgressions he was guilty of.

He had robbed the bank, she was sure of it. but then again, she wasn't sure of anything where Dominick was concerned. Glory be, she wasn't even sure of her own feelings!

What if he was telling the truth? What if she was putting herself through this torture for nothing? He did seem sincere. Still, the doubts lingered, and it was these doubts that kept her from following her heart and going to him.

She'd made that mistake once. She would not make the same mistake twice!

The grand opening of Sanders Shoemakers in the old bordello was the main topic of conversation wherever two or more people gathered. The doors had been open barely an hour when the old receiving parlor was filled with potential customers, mainly women curious to see the inside of a building that had previously been off-limits to them.

As might be expected, a few men came for old times' sake. Some even had the poor judgment to bring their wives, who quickly became suspicious if their husbands showed the least sign of familiarity with the place.

"How come you keep looking at the stairs?" one woman demanded, poking her husband in the chest with her parasol.

"No reason, my dear."

A Maurice Dooley heaved his bulky body into the shop, slumped over the counter, and breathed his sour whiskey breath right into Maggie's face.

"Brings back old memories," he said, his bloodshot eyes lingering on the spot where the naked statue once stood. "My favorite was Ginger. Boy, you never saw such a build. Why, one time, she . . ."

"Would you like a pair of boots?" Maggie asked.

Dooley looked momentarily surprised. "How did you know about the boots?" He ogled her, his attention riveted by the rise of her breasts. "Did she train you to use boots, too? If so, I pay you double."

Aghast, Maggie drew back.

The man reached into his pocket, pulled out a large bill, and slapped it onto the counter. "I want the room with the mirrors."

Dominick took the man roughly by the arm. "If you come with me," he said lightly, "I will personally escort you to the mirror room."

"Well, now, isn't that downright thoughtful of you?" Dooley gave Maggie a leering wink that made her shudder. "I'll be waiting. Don't forget the boots."

"We aim to please," Dominick said. The man, unsteady on his feet, practically had to be dragged up the stairs. Watching Dominick's struggle, Maggie couldn't help but laugh. She was reminded of the day Dominick had battled the naked statue all the way up.

Relieved that Dominick had handled the man, Maggie turned back to her customers. A woman who introduced herself as Mrs. Jenkins ordered a pair of riding boots. "I can't believe the difference! Why, it hardly seems to be the same place. I hated that awful wallpaper. Why do you suppose they always decorate bordellos in scarlet? Do you suppose it's some sort of aphrodisiac?"

Trying to keep her composure, Maggie measured the woman's foot. "How do you know how this looked when it was used as a . . . uh . . . back then?"

"I worked here, of course."

Shocked, Maggie nearly dropped the tape measure. "You did?"

"Absolutely. Every night but Wednesdays. The men always had something else to do on Wednesdays. You know, lodge meetings, that kind of thing."

Maggie couldn't believe her ears. "You were a . . ." She blushed.

"They called us white doves." The woman's laugh was as raucous as a bluejay's call, with no heed to decorum. "Don't ask me why. Now I'm respectable." She thrust her painted face close to Maggie's and whispered, "The only difference between being respectable and being a white dove is the pay. Now I give it out for free." She backed off and looked around. "To tell you the truth, I kinda miss the old place."

Not knowing how to respond, Maggie jotted down the woman's measurements. "Your shoes will be ready by the end of the week, Mrs. Jenkins."

"Call me Flossie. And don't you worry about a thing. Don't let those hoity-toity women who are too good to step into this 'sinful' place bother you. I'll get all the girls together and tell them to come and buy their footwear from you. I daresay they'd like to see the old place again. Maybe we can have a reunion."

"That sounds like an interesting idea," Maggie said, not wanting to offend her. Despite the woman's bawdy talk, she was open and friendly and Maggie rather liked her.

She walked back behind the counter just as Dominick returned, looking thoroughly pleased with himself. "Mr. Dooley wanted mirrors. I locked him in so he can spend the day looking at mirrors to his heart's content."

Maggie didn't like the idea of a strange man being locked upstairs, but she was too busy to argue about it.

At exactly five o'clock, Dominick turned the sign over in the window and declared the shop closed. After a sigh of relief, Maggie cleared off the counter and checked her supplies against her orders.

"We only did half the business we did at the other store," she lamented. "Some people refuse to come here because of this house's history. I think it's absolutely ridiculous to let the past color the future."

"Why, Maggie, you never fail to surprise me."

Seeing the mocking look he gave her, she clamped her lips together. No matter what she said, it always touched on the basic issue between them.

He leaned against the counter and folded his arms. "You let my past color your thinking about us."

"Why did you do this, Dominick?" she said softly. "Talk about something that's out of the question?"

"If I weren't the Kissing Bandit, would you feel differently?" He was looking at her so intently, it was hard for her to breathe, impossible for her to think.

"Since you are the Kissing Bandit, it makes no sense to suppose otherwise."

"Maggie, I . . ." He stopped.

"What is it, Dominick? What were you about to say?"

"Nothing. It wasn't important."

She studied his face and thought of the many times since that night they'd made love that he'd started to say something—yet hadn't. "Don't tell me then!" she snapped.

Her voice was harsh with anger, but in reality she was hurt. Every night she lay in bed thinking about the one never-to-be-repeated night she had spent in his arms. It was so easy during the long, lonely hours of night to forget who he was, to forget the crimes he was guilty of. It was only during the harsh light of day that she remembered.

"Don't be angry with me, Maggie." He grabbed her by the wrist and pulled her toward him. Gazing into her eyes, he cupped her face with his hands. "Oh, Maggie," he whispered. "I never meant for this to happen. I was going to do my business and leave Santa Barbara." His voice grew hoarse. "Leave you . . ."

"But you must leave," she whispered. "If you don't, I'm afraid that your past is going to catch up with you. I can't bear to think of you being hauled off to jail and . . ." She bit her lower lip, unable to voice her greatest fear.

"Knowing you, you wouldn't even visit me."

Because she felt her heart was about to break, she drew back and he released her hand. She turned away from him, and gripped the edge of the counter for support. Pretend, that's what she had to do. Pretend it didn't matter, he didn't matter. Nothing that happened between them mattered. "Of course I would come and visit you," she squeaked out.

"Why, Maggie? To taunt me?"

Not able to pretend a moment longer, she whirled around to face him. She wanted to tell him everything she was feeling, openly and honestly. She was tired of pretending that what they had shared that night was nothing more than lust, tired of holding back, tired of waking each morning and wondering if this would be the day the sheriff would come for him.

But she never got the chance to tell him any of it. For at that moment a sudden yelping sound erupted from the direction of the staircase.

Maurice Dooley stood on the top landing, stark

naked. "Where are they?" he bellowed. "Where are those boots?"

Dominick glanced at Maggie, who stood gaping at the man in undisguised horror. Eyes bright with amusement, he leaned over and whispered in her ear, "Do you want to measure him, or should I?"

Chapter 22

The following Saturday, Maggie was awakened by the sound of Jamie's and Laurie-Anne's laughter, and the low-timbred sound of Dominick's voice mingling with the children's.

Smiling at the peaceful, happy sounds, she reached for her robe and followed the aromatic smell of fresh coffee all the way to the kitchen.

As usual, the children were hanging on to Dominick's every word as he made a production out of pouring batter on the hot griddle in all sorts of strange and wondrous shapes.

"Look!" Jamie shouted. "It looks like a big bear."

"Let me see," Laurie-Anne said, standing on tiptoe by the cast-iron stove.

Dominick set the bowl down and lifted Laurie-Anne in his arms to see the bear-shaped griddle cake for herself. Laurie-Anne giggled. "I want to eat the bear."

"And so you shall," Dominick said, setting her back on the floor. "Let's see, we need raisins for the eyes and . . ." He turned to get a bowl and noticed Maggie. "Good morning," he said cheerfully. "Jamie, why don't you pour your mother a cup of coffee?"

Laurie-Anne ran over and tugged on her mother's robe. "Aita is going to take us to the seashore. Are you coming, Mama?"

Maggie thought of the work that waited for her at the shop. Orders were stacked up. There were uppers to be sewn together, soles to be stitched, heels to be cut. "I'm afraid not. Mama has work to do."

"Aita said we can't work today," Jamie said, handing her a cup of coffee.

"Thank you, Jamie." She took a sip of the delicious hot brew. "And why can't we work today?"

"It's June first," Jamie explained. "That means it's Aita's birthday."

"His. . ." Maggie glanced at Dominick, who shrugged.

"Don't look so surprised, Maggie. Even outlaws have birthdays."

"Please, Mama, say you'll come," Jamie pleaded. "Aita said we can watch the horses race along the sand and we can swim and take a picnic lunch and . . ."

Maggie couldn't help but laugh. "Slow down, son. You're talking so fast you're making my head spin. Of course I'll come. We can't let a birthday pass without celebrating, now can we?"

She looked at Dominick and wondered about the closed look on his face. Something was not quite right, though she couldn't for the life of her think what it could be. His laughter seemed forced to her, the look he gave her too penetrating. Despite the bright sunlight that streamed through the windows and flooded the kitchen with its golden warmth, a cold chill crept up her spine.

The sun was high in the sky by the time they joined the long line of carriages and carts along Bath Street, or Banos Street, as it was still called by locals—so named because it was the only street that led to the bathing beach. Dominick had rented a low phaeton for the occasion, complete with a docile gray horse that needed constant prodding, which Dominick provided with verve and good humor.

Jamie and Laurie-Anne sat in the back seat waving to the people on foot and laughing at Dominick's silly song about a horse. *"There was a horse named Cas-*

tor!" he sang out. He winked at Maggie and continued, *"Who couldn't go any faster . . ."* The song got sillier, the children laughed louder, and Maggie relaxed, her earlier misgivings about neglecting her work forgotten.

The sparkling blue Pacific Ocean lived up to its name; not a single whitecap marred the dazzling, mirrorlike surface. No sooner had Dominick hitched the horse to a weathered post than the children raced down to the tiny creek that ran beneath a rickety bridge. Velvety brown cattails grew along the water's edge around clumps of crisp watercress.

"Come along, children," Maggie called, carting a picnic basket and a sun parasol. She walked daintily across an alarmingly flimsy bridge, hoping the weathered slats would hold her weight.

Dominick and the children chose the wiser course across the creek, along a path of half-submerged rocks. Reaching the beach before she did, Jamie and Laurie-Anne had their shoes off instantly and were already racing across the golden sand toward the water.

"Wait for me!" Dominick quickly pulled off his own boots and woolen socks and rolled up the cuffs of his trousers.

Watching the three of them romp in the gently rolling surf, Maggie smiled and waved. She picked out a shaded spot near one of the bathhouses and unfolded a plaid woolen blanket.

She sank down onto the blanket, knees first, then breathed a contented sigh. She was glad that she'd let the children talk her into taking the day off. In the bright glare of the sun, it was hard to give much credence to the sense of foreboding that had haunted her all morning.

Bathers dressed in their long-legged bathing suits dotted the beach. Children laughed and played. A group of Chinese youths sat in the shade of the awning, their long black hair braided in single queues that hung down their backs. Snatches of their singsong voices reached Maggie, as did the sound of a distant gunshot, signaling the start of the Arlington Jockey Club race on East Beach.

The races were too far away for Maggie to see much, but she could hear the gunshot signal the start of each contest and the roar of the crowd cheering the horses on.

A lumber schooner skirted the bay, blasting its horn and startling the sea gulls that circled overhead seeming to imitate Laurie-Anne's childish voice calling Dominick.

"Aita, Aita."

After a while, the children grew chilled and Maggie and Dominick dried them off with the fluffy Turkish towels they had brought. Jamie built a fine castle similar to the one in his storybook at home, while Laurie-Anne made Dominick a birthday cake in the sand, complete with pretend candles made from little twigs and seashells that she'd gathered from the beach.

"It's beautiful," Dominick said, his voice hoarse with undefined emotion. "The best birthday cake I ever had."

Pleased by Dominick's response, Laurie-Anne asked Dominick to help her spell his name. Taking a stick in hand, Dominick scratched the letters A-I-T-A on the little sand cake.

"Aita," Maggie read aloud. "Does that actually mean Dominick in Basque?"

His back was toward her, and she wondered if she only imagined that he stiffened. "Not exactly."

Something in the way he kept his eyes averted alerted her. "What exactly does it mean?"

"It's not important."

"If you don't mind, I'll make that decision. This concerns my children."

He turned to look at her. "All right, Maggie, if you

insist. But don't go getting yourself all in a dither over this."

"I have never been in a dither in my life!"

He laughed at this. "I can recall a few times . . ." Suddenly his expression grew serious. "It means 'Papa.' "

Maggie nearly choked. "How dare you presume to have my children refer to you as such!"

"See? I told you. You're all in a dither."

"I am not in a dither!"

"All right, what would you have them call me? Mr. Sanders? Don't you think our friends and neighbors would think it rather strange that the children refer so formally to the man who is supposedly their father?"

"You could have asked my permission!"

"I never ask for anything unless I know in advance that the answer is yes."

"Aita, Aita, come here!" Laurie-Anne called, having discovered a sand crab.

Dominick waved. "I'll be there in just a minute." He turned back to Maggie. "I couldn't care for Laurie-Anne and Jamie more if they were my own flesh and blood."

He reached toward her and touched his hand gently to her cheek. She closed her eyes and pressed against his palm.

His voice softened. "Maggie, I can't forget the night we shared."

"Don't," Maggie pleaded. She opened her eyes and looked up at him.

"Don't what, Maggie? Don't tell you how I feel?" His voice broke. "Maggie, all these weeks I tried so hard not to . . . let my feelings get in the way. Not to let myself become involved. I think we both know how much I failed."

She took in a deep breath and, thinking of her own failure, moved away from his touch.

Looking as if she'd struck him, he stood. "I think

you have the right to know that I expect my business in Santa Barbara to be completed the week after next. I'll be gone soon after.''

"I see," she whispered.

A sigh escaped him, like the last breath of a dying man. "Somehow, I expected more of a response. It wasn't so long ago that you would have given the world for me to leave. Remember? All the torture you put me through?''

"Don't say any more," she said. "I think it's better if you just leave.''

He stared at her in uncertainty, not sure what he had expected from her. He'd known from the start that what they shared was only temporary. He had no right to expect more and, given his obsession to take another man's life, had no right to share even these few precious moments with her.

She was so good, so moral, always striving her best to do what was right and chastising herself because it was never enough. It was ironic that the very virtues he most admired about her were the ones that made it impossible for them to be together. If only she were less virtuous and less upright in her beliefs, maybe then she could find it in her heart not to judge him too harshly. But that wasn't going to happen, and it was time he accepted that. Reluctantly, he allowed the barriers that should never have been lifted in the first place to drop firmly back in place between them, separating them on every possible level but one—the one having to do with the heart.

"Maggie, I hope . . . that no matter what happens or whatever you hear about me in the future, you always remember how very much I care for you and the children." After a moment he whispered, "How very much I love you.''

"Don't say that!" she cried, angry at him for making her face the very thing she feared most. "Don't call what we shared love. Call it lust, call it craziness, but don't call it love." In all honesty, it wasn't his fault.

In retrospect it was obvious from the start that despite who and what he was, she loved him with all her heart and soul. There were so many reasons to love him; she could list every one of them, dozens of them, hundreds. And there was only one reason why such a love was not possible. He was a bandit. Only one reason, but she had Jamie and Laurie-Anne to consider and it was reason enough.

Frowning, he stepped back. "Why not, Maggie? Why not say what's true? It would help if I knew for sure how you felt about me. You've never told me. Not even that night when we made love."

She closed her eyes. To look at him only confused matters. "You know how I care for you," she whispered, knowing full well that wasn't what he wanted to hear.

"Is that all?"

Unable to speak, she nodded.

"At least you're honest," he said softly.

He turned and called to the children. "Come on, I'll race you to Castle Rock."

Maggie watched the three figures race over the sand dunes toward the rocky headland until she could no longer see them through her tear-filled eyes.

School was adjourned that following Wednesday for the summer, and by Thursday morning Jamie was already restless and bored. He begged Maggie to let him go to the shop with her and she finally gave in when he promised to stay away from the second floor of the building.

She needn't have worried, for Jamie was more interested in the huge, sprawling cottonwood tree on the property next door than he was in the off-limits areas of the house; he spent the entire morning building a fort with scraps of wood he found stacked in the back alley.

Business was rather slow that morning, for which Maggie was grateful. Without her sewing machine, it took longer to fill her orders. Neither she nor Dominick spoke as they worked. Dominick prepared the leather and Maggie began putting the pieces together, and both tried not to think about the other.

Since the day at the seashore, things had been strained between them. Maggie tried so hard to forget the soft words he had spoken in declaring his love. But the words kept repeating themselves in her head until they echoed in her heart. The urge to be as honest with him as he had been with her was so strong, she was almost afraid to speak for fear of giving too much away. For the same reason, she was careful not to touch him, although her hand literally ached with the need to do so. She even arranged her work area so that she couldn't see him at the counter, only to find herself on occasion watching his reflection in the window.

Unable to deny her love for him, she could only hope that if she did not openly admit it, refused to acknowledge it, called it by some other name, the feelings would go away. Hiding beneath a cover of indifference was the most difficult thing Maggie had ever had to do. It was also the most necessary.

By noon, most of the cutting and sewing had been completed, mainly because Dominick had become expert in cutting the leather for her.

"I've decided to make you a pair of boots," she announced. "It doesn't look right for a shoemaker not to have decent footwear."

"A shoemaker, eh? Coming from you, I consider that quite a compliment. Will you have time to make them before I leave?"

Swallowing hard, she turned away, unable to bear the thought of his leaving. "I'll start on them today."

She reached for her tape measure. She wondered how she would find the heart to make them when all she could think about was that he would be gone. "They'll . . . be my going-away gift to you."

He sat on a chair and took off his boot. "That's mighty considerate of you." Watching her with dark, intense eyes, he stretched out his right leg.

She sucked in her breath and plunked herself down on her little wooden stool. She worked the tape measure along the considerable length of his foot, refusing to meet his eyes.

"There." She stood and quickly moved to the counter to write down his measurements in her notebook. "I'll make you a pair of custom boots that will be the envy of the town." She made a quick sketch of a man's boot. "I'll need some more leather."

"You will make the boots comfortable now, won't you?" he asked. "Knowing how my profession requires it."

"My boots are always comfortable!"

"And bulletproof?"

She whirled around to face him, only to see the teasing lights in his eyes. "Perhaps you'd do better to have the blacksmith make your boots."

Dominick laughed good-naturedly. "I don't think he has your style." Their gazes met and held. The smile on his face faded, replaced by a look of longing that matched the need that trembled on her lips.

"Eh . . ." he began at last, backing toward the door. "Since it's quiet, I'll go and purchase the leather for you now."

"That would be best," she whispered.

"I'll take Jamie with me. I promised him a trip to the sweet shop."

Nodding, Maggie pulled herself out of her inertia and quickly checked her supply of shoelaces. "Make sure Mr. Williams gives you his very best leather," she called, keeping her back toward him for fear he'd see the tears that had suddenly sprung to her eyes. "Make sure it's the leather that comes from the hips." Sometimes Mr. Williams tried to give her the thinner flank leather, but it was the hip leather that was strongest and that best kept its shape.

"Maggie . . ."

Her heart nearly stopped. *Dear God, don't let him say anything that would make it harder to see him go than it already is.* "What is it, Dominick?"

"Eh . . . Nothing." And with that he was gone, the door slamming shut behind him and between them.

After he left, Maggie marched back and forth along the length of her shop. Forcing a deep breath, she swallowed back the lump in her throat. Normally she would have relished the opportunity to work alone in her shop. Today she had no desire to work.

Still, because she didn't know what else to do, she sat on the chair in front of the workbench and solemnly began to push an awl through a piece of leather and thought about the heaviness in her heart.

Dominick would soon be gone permanently, and her problems would be over. It's what she wanted. Of course it was what she wanted.

She threw down the awl. Oh, Maggie, Maggie, who are you fooling? Not yourself and probably not Dominick.

Dominick. Just thinking his name made her ache with longing. How was she ever going to come to this shop without him by her side? How would she ever get through the days? The nights? The rest of her life?

Her thoughts were interrupted by a salesman dressed in a checkered suit who brandished a valise filled with samples. "Feel this," he said, pulling out a square piece of leather and spreading it across the counter.

Maggie fingered the leather, impressed by its softness.

"That there is genuine kangaroo leather," he drawled. "Yes, siree. All the way from Australia. Believe me, a person with tender feet can't go wrong with a pair of shoes made of kangaroo leather."

"It does feel soft," Maggie agreed. "But will it hold up under normal use?"

"That, my little lady, is an excellent question. Let me assure you that not only is kangaroo twice as soft and flexible as most tanned leather but it's twice as durable." The salesman twisted the sample as if he were squeezing out an old rag, then flattened it out on the counter. "As you can see, it's virtually indestructible."

"That's remarkable," Maggie said, impressed.

"Ah, but the best is yet to come. Just wait till you feast your eyes on my best beaver felt." He reached into his valise for another sample. Shaking it out first, he then spread it on the counter in front of her. "You haven't lived until you've sunk your feet into a pair of slippers made from beaver felt."

Maggie ordered both the felt and the kangaroo leather and, after sending the satisfied salesman on his way, returned to her work.

A short time later, the door opened and a tall, blond man walked in. The man, who was dressed impeccably, looked familiar and Maggie tried to remember where they might have met. He sauntered to the counter and swept off his fashionable derby. "Mrs. Turner, isn't it? What a pleasant surprise."

Maggie studied his face, trying to recall where she had seen him. "And you're Mr. . . ."

"W. K. Stevens. Don't you remember? We met on the stage outside of Ballard."

"Of course." She smiled prettily. "You gave my little boy chocolate bonbons."

"So I did. I'm glad to see you looking so . . . healthy."

Recalling her motion illness, she blushed with embarrassment.

He glanced past her shoulders to the shelves on the back wall. "I need a pair of boots like that." He pointed to one of the samples sitting on the shelf. It was the same boot she planned to make for Dominick.

"Do I place my order with you or do I wait for the owner?"

"I am the owner."

Mr. Stevens looked amazed. "I would never have guessed it. Forgive me. But the name outside said . . ."

"Sanders," she said. "That's . . . ah . . . my married name."

"Oh, you've remarried? Why is it that I'm not surprised? Albeit disappointed. But as Shakespeare so aptly put it, a rose by any other name would still be beautiful. A woman as lovely as yourself is bound not to find herself single for very long."

Maggie cleared her throat. It suddenly occurred to her that should Dominick walk in, Mr. Stevens would recognize him as the same man who had been held prisoner that day in the stage. Thinking it best to make sure that the two never met, Maggie hurriedly reached for her measuring tape. The quicker she took his order, the quicker she could be rid of him.

Rushing around the counter, she kept one eye on the door and another firmly fixed on her customer. It horrified her to think that she had been put in the awkward, not to mention illegal, position of having to protect an outlaw. Not that she had much choice in the matter. If the truth were to come out, it would mean . . . oh, Lord, she couldn't even think what it would mean. All she knew was that she had to protect Dominick at all costs.

She settled herself on her stool and asked him to remove his boot. "What brings you to town, Mr. Stevens?"

"I believe I told you that first day we met that I was thinking about purchasing some property on the other side of the pass. Well, I bought several hundred acres outside of Ojai Valley. I'm in town to stock up on supplies."

"I see." She smiled politely and cast another furtive glance out the window. So far no sign of Dominick.

"I come into town every two or three weeks. Would it be possible to have my boots ready the next time I come?"

"Of course." She drew back and rapidly wrote his measurements down, her mind racing. Two or three weeks. Dominick would be gone by then, so there would be no more chance that they might run into each other.

Mr. Stevens replaced his boot, then, tipping his hat politely, he bowed. "It was a pleasure to see you again."

"It was nice seeing you, too."

As soon as Mr. Stevens left her shop, Maggie raced to the front window to scan the street in search of Dominick. To her relief, he was nowhere in sight. But of course there was still the possibility that the two men would see each other in town. She shuddered to think what would happen if Mr. Stevens recognized him. Of all the days for Dominick to have Jamie with him.

In an effort to calm her nerves, she tried to concentrate on work. She cut out the sole for Dominick's boots and expertly engraved her trademark word "Custom" into the leather. Holding the sole up to check her work, she realized to her dismay that she had misspelled the word "custom," spelling it with an "a" instead of an "o." Custam.

Heaving a sigh, she pushed her work aside and paced from window to window, wringing her hands. She was convinced that her worst fears had come to pass, and that Dominick was, at that very moment, locked behind bars, or—just to think about it made her gasp—hanging from a tree.

She stepped outside on the porch and looked up and down the street in both directions. A horse and buggy passed by, kicking up a cloud of dust, followed by a mule-drawn wagon and a lone horseback rider.

Where was he? she worried. What was taking him

so long? She could imagine Mr. Stevens's spotting him, turning him in to the sheriff. Could envision the look of confusion and horror on Jamie's face when the man he'd come to revere was handcuffed and hauled away. Could feel the pain in her own heart at the thought of never seeing him again. Glory be, where was he?

Chapter 23

When at last Dominick and Jamie returned having taken what seemed to her was their own sweet time, she was so relieved to see them both that she promptly burst into tears.

"What's wrong, Mama?" Jamie asked, his eyes wide with worry.

"Nothing." She avoided Dominick's probing gaze. "I'm just glad to see you, that's all. You have no idea how quiet and lonely it was around here without you." She gave Jamie a big hug.

Satisfied with his mother's explanation, Jamie held up a small paper sack for her inspection. "Look what Aita bought me, Mama. Bonbons."

She glanced inside the sack and sniffed appreciatively. "That's wonderful, Jamie. I hope you don't spoil your appetite. Now be a good boy and run along outside and play. I need to talk to Dominick."

Jamie needed no further prodding. Hugging his sack of bonbons to him, he ran outside and slammed the door, eager to return to his building.

She turned to Dominick, who was watching her with keen interest, his brow puzzled. "I can't tell you how gratifying it is to know how much I was missed."

"Oh, Dominick, I was worried about . . ." She hesitated, feeling suddenly foolish beneath his steady gaze. "Jamie," she finished with a wavering voice.

His face darkened. "Don't you trust me with Jamie?"

Strange as it seemed, she did trust him. She trusted

him completely with her children, and that was the crazy part. She had never met a man she trusted more—nor had she ever met a man who gave her more reason not to trust him. It was a paradox, to be sure. He was a paradox. He pulled her apart, ripped her in two. She was so confused she didn't know what to think.

She swallowed hard. "Mr. Stevens is in town."

It was obvious by his expression that he had no idea who Mr. Stevens was. "The bonbon man," she added. "Shakespeare." When he still looked perplexed, she sighed in exasperation. "The passenger who rode in the stagecoach with us."

His eyes hardened. "Oh, that Mr. Stevens." He glanced around the room as if expecting the man to emerge from a corner. "Where is he?"

"I don't know. He ordered a pair of boots and said he was going to purchase supplies. Oh, Dominick, what if he sees you?"

He raised an eyebrow, his eyes gleaming with a mischievous twinkle. "What is this I hear? Concern?"

She shot him visual daggers. This was not the time to play games, nor to pretend that he was invincible. "Why wouldn't I be concerned?" And because she didn't dare to say what was in her heart, she fell back on her old refrain. "Once the truth is known, my reputation will be ruined."

"Don't worry, my love. There are those in town who already consider your reputation suspect." He stood back and regarded her with an amused look. "Don't look so surprised. There aren't many women who would set themselves up in business in a deserted bordello." He chuckled to himself and inspected the leather soles that Maggie had worked on while he had been gone.

"I don't find it the least bit amusing."

Checking the undersides, he glanced at Maggie. "Are these for my boots?"

She nodded.

He peered at the sole in his hand. " 'Custam'?"

"I made a mistake," she explained and, because he was looking at her with an odd expression on his face, added, "Haven't you ever made a mistake?"

Dominick set the soles back on the counter. He'd never before known Maggie to make such an error. Everything she did at the shop was precise and accurate. He would never have guessed that concern for him would interfere with the quality of her work. The misspelled word told him a lot about Maggie; it told him the very thing he most wanted to know.

She loved him. He let the thought sink in until it had filled every fiber of his being. But instead of feeling elated he was filled with remorse and guilt. He felt so undeserving of her love. So humbled by it. Perhaps it was time he leveled with her. Surely he owed her that much. Still, he dreaded the thought, dreaded seeing what he now knew was love die before his very eyes.

The door to the shop flew open, startling them both. Maggie, thinking it was Mr. Stevens returning, practically jumped out of her skin. At Maggie's cry of alarm, Dominick spun around.

Flossie stuck her head in the open door. "I brought the girls," she called out cheerfully. "And they all want a pair of your fanciest shoes."

Before either Maggie or Dominick could say a word, the shop was filled with more silk and feathers than she had ever seen. The sickly sweet fragrance of lilacs, honeysuckle, and violets filled the air. Lively chatter was punctuated with robust laughter. The women gaped at the surroundings, clapped their hands, and expressed surprise at how different the old place looked. Much to Maggie's horror and Dominick's amusement, the discussion soon centered on the likes and dislikes of the bordello's former clients.

"Who would have ever thought this place could look respectable?" one woman asked during a lull in the conversation. Her eyelids weighted down with blue powder, the woman fluttered her long, sweeping lashes at Dominick and gave his shirt a suggestive tug.

One of the "girls," as Flossie called them, introduced herself to Maggie as Taffy. "Do you think you can make me something in purple?"

Another woman dressed in magenta taffeta, planted herself in front of Dominick, lifted her skirt up to her thigh, and revealed long, shapely legs ringed in black-and-red garters. "What do you think about something in pink, big boy?"

Dominick grinned. "Why not?"

Maggie tried to cover the pang of jealousy she felt by glaring at him. "Why don't you get behind the counter and take orders . . . big boy?"

He leaned over and whispered in her ear, "Shame on you, Maggie! I never thought you were the kind of woman who would kiss and tell."

Mortified, she turned on him, then remembered her customers. Not wanting him to guess that she felt the least bit jealous, she tempered her voice. "I was only repeating what Miss *Garter* called you."

"With a slight difference," he said softly, "She's only guessing."

"She sounded mighty certain of herself," Maggie whispered back, appalled to find herself discussing something so intimate with him. Why, she had never even talked of such things to her husband!

Feeling her cheeks aflame, she turned to the nearest customer. "Would you like something in velvet?" She pulled out bolts of crushed velvet and spread them across the counter.

The woman puckered her painted face and shook her head. "I don't know. Maybe I should try something in gold, instead. What do you think?" She wiggled her hips and laughed. "They used to call me Goldie."

"I see." Maggie flinched inwardly. What ever had happened to good taste and decorum? she wondered.

But, eager to please her customers, she took down their orders without comment.

By the time Flossie and her girls were finished, Maggie had enough orders to cover expenses for the next three months. She glanced down at her pad. "Glory be!" she declared. "Gold boots and pink shoes. What is the world coming to?" But secretly she was pleased.

The next day, Maggie hurried to the shop ahead of Dominick, excited to get started on her orders. A large wooden crate was sitting on the front porch.

She unlocked the door and dragged the crate inside. Reaching for an iron bar, she pried off the top planks of wood and pawed through the straw packing material inside. Her fingers touched hard metal.

She quickly pulled out the rest of the straw and gasped at the wondrous sight before her. It was a Blake sewing machine, just like the one she'd lost in the fire! Afraid to believe her eyes, she lifted the bright, shiny machine out of the crate and set it carefully on the counter. She touched it, stepped back to get a better overall look, rubbed her hands over it again, and blinked her eyes. She didn't know whether to laugh or cry.

It was a miracle, that's what it was. A miracle!

The door flew open and Dominick strolled in, filling the room with a presence that made her momentarily lift her eyes from the machine.

He gave the sewing machine a cursory nod. "I see it arrived."

Her mouth dropped open in astonishment. "You're responsible for this?"

"Ordered it the very next day after the fire. A friend of mine was going to Los Angeles, and I asked him to check around for one. Obviously, he . . ."

He stopped talking as she flew into his arms and wrapped her arms around his neck. "Oh, Dominick! You couldn't have done anything nicer!"

He smiled and drew his arms around her tiny waist. It felt so good to have her pressed against him, her every womanly curve molded in perfect accord with his own body. His mouth felt dry with desire. For two bits, he would have swept her up in his arms and made good use of one of the upstairs bedrooms.

Closing his eyes, he let a kiss escape from between his lips and settle in the silky strands of her hair. Knowing he would never degrade her by taking her like some cheap prostitute only confirmed what he wished was not true: Despite his best efforts to the contrary, his love for this woman kept growing stronger each day.

He had never meant this to happen, never meant to let her into his heart. Indeed, he had guarded his heart so intently, he'd not been aware of the many ways Maggie had won him over. She'd touched him on so many levels; the heart was the least of it. Knowing all this didn't make it any easier for him. And knowing that she loved him in return only added to the torture.

Somehow he must find the strength to tell her the truth, tell her that if everything went according to plan, he would soon have the pleasure of killing the man who had robbed him of his family.

Oh, Maggie, he moaned silently. *What you think me guilty of in the past is nothing compared with what you will know I'm guilty of in the future.*

Maggie would never understand. Not with the strong moral upbringing so thoroughly ingrained in her. No, she would not understand, nor would she forgive him. More than that, he was certain that once the truth came out she would hate him and never want to see him again.

It was with this last thought in mind that he roughly pushed her away. "Does this mean you don't care where my money came from?"

As he hoped, her sense of right and wrong came into play.

She looked at him in confusion, unsure, no doubt, whether he was finally confessing the truth or making a joke of her earlier suspicions. "It means nothing of the sort. You . . . you didn't . . ." She cleared her throat. "I don't believe you robbed the bank, Dominick." She gazed at him with clear blue eyes, baring her soul and more of her heart than he had the right to claim.

He frowned. If she had the slightest inkling of what she did to him when she looked so damned trusting, he'd be a doomed man. "Are you sure? I'd hate to think of your conscience bothering you every time you sit down to sew." He glanced up at the ceiling. "You being a minister's daughter and all."

"It . . . won't," she said, her face shadowed with uncertainty as she glanced at the machine.

"I'm glad to hear that." Resisting the urge to set her mind at ease for fear she'd come flying into his arms again, he pulled his watch out and checked the time. "I'd better go. I have an appointment."

She looked surprised. It wasn't like him to disappear during their busy morning hours. "Where are you going?"

"Am I required to give you a full accounting of how I spend my every waking hour?"

She looked hurt. "Of course not. But we have work to do."

"Why do you suppose I bought you the sewing machine?" He plucked his beret off the hat rack and left before she could question him further.

It was late afternoon by the time he returned, a grim look on his face. His eyes were darker than usual, his mouth set in a straight hard line. He hardly glanced at her and made no mention of the impressive number of shoes she had sewn together in his absence.

Although she was curious as to what had put him in such a black mood, she went about her business without inquiring.

She was so intent upon her work that she failed to hear the bells jingle on the front door.

When Dominick spoke, she jumped. His eyes sharpened as he repeated the question. "I asked if Mrs. Meyers's shoes were ready."

Maggie lifted her foot off the pedal of the sewer. "Yes, indeed." Nodding a greeting to the woman, she reached for a shiny pair of black leather shoes. It was the first time Maggie had seen Mrs. Meyers without the other two members of the Woman's Christian Temperance Movement in tow.

"My, my!" Mrs. Meyers exclaimed. She lifted her eyepiece and examined the softly rounded tongue and evenly spaced button loops. Nodding her head in appreciation, she ran her finger along the row of shiny black buttons and turned both shoes over to check out the medium concave heels. "Beautiful!"

Maggie was pleased. Nothing brought her more gratification than for someone to recognize her careful craftsmanship. "The shoe was stitched with our strongest flax thread," Maggie explained, "and the soles were cut from the finest oak sole leather."

"May I try them on?"

"Please do."

Mrs. Meyers slipped her stockinged feet into the shoes and, using the silver button hook Maggie handed her, pulled each tiny button through the loops. Then she took careful little steps around the shop.

"I've never worn a pair of shoes so comfortable." Mrs. Meyers glanced at Maggie suspiciously. "Are you sure these are my size?"

"Absolutely," Maggie assured her. "A custom size five. Measured to match your feet perfectly."

"Well, if you're sure . . ." Mrs. Meyers still didn't look convinced. "My others shoes always pinch my feet."

Dominick slid a conspiratorial look at Maggie. "That's because you never found yourself a shoemaker who knew the business like my wife and I do."

He put his arms around Maggie's shoulders and squeezed, bringing a blush to her cheeks.

"Well, that explains it," Mrs. Meyers said. "Wrap up my old shoes. I intend to wear these home. Maybe they'll improve my spirits." With a gasp, she pressed her fingers to her lips and glanced anxiously at Maggie. "You do know I'm talking about nonalcoholic spirits?"

Maggie smiled. "I never doubted it for a moment."

Mrs. Meyers breathed a sigh of relief and fanned her flushed face with her hand. "It's been a terrible day. One thing after another . . ."

"I'm sorry to hear that." Maggie stepped away from Dominick and scooped up Mrs. Meyers's old shoes from the floor.

While Maggie wrapped the shoes, the woman proceeded to fill them in on the details of her day, throwing in enough opinion to confuse matters thoroughly. "I was on my way to the bank . . . I don't know what this town is coming to. It used to be such a fine old town. I never got to the bank. I'm telling you there simply isn't a decent place anymore to raise a family, that's all there is to it. Ever since the corkscrews and bungstarters have reopened, things have gotten progressively worse."

"Don't tell me there was another fire?" Maggie asked.

Mrs. Meyers looked surprised. "Oh, my goodness, I thought you would have heard by now." Hand on her chest, she looked helplessly at Dominick. "I hate to be the bearer of bad news, but you'll find out soon enough." She leaned over the counter and spoke in a hushed voice. "The stagecoach was robbed at the pass."

Maggie felt an icy chill. "Really? When?"

"Why, today. At noon. The driver was shot right through the heart."

Maggie gripped the edge of the counter. "Is . . . is he dead?"

"My goodness, of course he's dead. How many hearts do you think can tolerate a bullet? Dreadful thing. Is that my package?"

Maggie stared unseeing at the package on the counter in front of her.

"Oh, yes. Yes, it is." Maggie handed it to her.

"How much do I owe you?"

"You don't owe me a thing, Mrs. Meyers. If it weren't for you and the Woman's Christian Temperance Movement, I don't know what I would have done."

Mrs. Meyers reached across the counter and patted Maggie's hand. "We were delighted to help. You've done wonders to this old building. Who would ever have thought it could look so respectable?" She picked up her package and ambled to the door. "Wonderful!" she exclaimed, doing a little jig. "And who would have thought that feet don't have to hurt? What on earth will they come up with next?"

Holding herself perfectly still, Maggie waited until Mrs. Meyers had danced her way out of the shop before turning to face Dominick.

But he was nowhere to be seen.

That's when she knew without a doubt that her suspicions were true.

Tears sprang to her eyes. "How could you?" she cried. "Oh, Dominick, how could you?"

Chapter 24

Afraid that any variation from her regular activities might arouse suspicion, Maggie closed the store at the usual time and walked home, following her normal route.

She was careful to be friendly and polite to anyone she met along the way, which meant that she had no choice but to stop and chat with the members of the Woman's Christian Temperance Movement who stood across from Grew's Brewery and Saloon, clucking their tongues and shaking their heads.

"It's a sad day," Mrs. Hopkins said, staring down her rather long and pointed nose at the inert body of a man lying face down in the street.

"My goodness!" Maggie exclaimed. "Is he all right?"

Mrs. Hopkins poked him with the tip of her cane. The man snorted and rolled over, the undeniable smell of stale alcohol emanating from his dusty clothes. "Other than being inebriated, there's nothing wrong with him."

They were joined by a short man with a balding head and sweeping mustache. Tipping his felt bowler hat, he nodded politely. "Good evening, ladies."

Mrs. Quitter raised her head haughtily. "Good evening, Mr. Grew."

"And what is the Woman's Christian Temperance Movement doing in front of my place of business? Not trying to close it down again, are we?"

Mrs. Meyers lifted her eyepiece. "We wouldn't

dream of it, Mr. Grew, being that you have a wife and infant to support now. How *is* your lovely family?"

"They're just dandy," Mr. Grew said. "Why little Harry Junior has already decided upon his profession."

"How can that be?" Mrs. Quitter asked. "He's only six months old."

"Search me. I guess younguns grow up faster these days. All I know is that I asked him where he wants to work when he grows up and he said, "Goo, goo!" He let out a roar. "Get it? Grew Brewery. Goo, goo." Still laughing, he stepped over the still form of his customer and headed across the street toward the saloon, whistling.

"That man makes me so mad!" Mrs. Hopkins said, pounding the tip of her cane on the boardwalk.

"Calm down," Mrs. Quitter cautioned. "It can't be good for you to get yourself all worked up."

"I'm sure Mrs. Quitter is right," Maggie said. "Perhaps you ladies had best hurry home. It will soon be dark."

"Oh, my, where did the time go?" Mrs. Meyers fluttered her hands. "It's the shoes. I usually tell the time by how sore my feet are." She lifted the hem of her skirts so the others could admire her shoes.

"Beautiful!" Mrs. Quitter declared.

"Most stylish," Mrs. Hopkins agreed.

"My feet feel so good, I would swear it was no later than ten o'clock in the morning." To Maggie she added, "You are truly a genius."

"Not exactly," Maggie said modestly. She bid the women good night, anxious to continue on her way.

Her mind was in turmoil, and she was relieved that she was not required to make any more stops.

Worried sick, she hastened her stride. What would she find upon her arrival? The sheriff waiting for her? It stood to reason that if Dominick were caught, she would be charged with harboring a criminal.

Damn him! Why in heaven's name had she ever let this happen? Why hadn't she gone directly to the sheriff upon first arriving in Santa Barbara? Before Dominick had had a chance to work his way into her heart.

Where was he now? He wouldn't have gone home, certainly. Or would he? The thought of a murderer being with her children filled her with horror even as she stubbornly refused to believe that Dominick could take another life. Dominick a murderer? Not possible! Oh, please, don't let it be true.

She quickened her steps, and by the time she reached her street, she was practically running. Skirts aflutter, she rushed through the courtyard and into the house.

Laurie-Anne's voice drifted out from the kitchen where Consuela was fixing the evening meal. Jamie's laughter was followed by the clanging sound of pots and pans. The sounds from the kitchen were so normal that her racing heart slowed to a more steady beat.

She collapsed on the divan in relief. She still didn't want to believe that Dominick could actually kill someone. It was true that he angered her at times. Lord, his actions sometimes even put the thought of murder in her own heart. But there were times when he made her laugh. Times when he was so kind to the children, he took away her breath. Times when he had only to look at her and she felt all warm and shivery inside. Times when . . .

Proof, that's what she needed! Proof that he was incapable of murder. She glanced around the parlor. There had to be something. Thinking of the necessity room, where he kept his personal belongings, she tiptoed past the kitchen down the hall.

His razor and strop hung neatly from a hook. A tray atop a bureau held his personal effects. She touched his tortoiseshell comb and ran a finger across the cool hardness of a small collection of coins. A lump formed in her throat. She picked up a metal picture button and studied the design. It surprised her that a tiny picture of the Lobero Theater was stamped into the brass. It was the same button she'd seen Dominick rub between his fingers on occasion. She replaced the button and felt the room swim before her very eyes.

Unable to breathe, she rushed from the room and bumped into Jamie.

"Mama!" he exclaimed. "I didn't know you were home!"

He wrapped his arms around her waist and buried his face in her skirts. After a moment he looked up. "Is something wrong?"

Struggling for composure, she forced a smile. "Mama has a lot to think about, that's all." She stroked his head and pushed a wayward strand back into place. "Don't you worry. Have you seen Aita?"

He shook his head.

Slipping her arm around his shoulders, she walked with him into the kitchen. Consuela stood at the stove stirring the contents of a large stockpot. The air was filled with a spicy fragrance. "Good evening, Sēnora."

"Good evening, Consuela."

"Mama, Mama!" Laurie-Anne shouted, flinging herself against her mother.

Smiling down at her daughter, Maggie hugged her affectionately.

"I helped Conwello set the table," Laurie-Anne said proudly.

"What a big girl you are." Maggie gave both children another hug before setting them free.

To Consuela, she said, "I have some urgent business to take care of in town. Would you be able to stay the night? You can sleep on the spare cot in the children's room."

"Si, si," Consuela said. "I would be happy to spend the night." The girl eyed her curiously. "Is everything all right?"

Not wanting to alarm her, Maggie forced a smile. "Everything's fine. You didn't by chance see Mr. Sanders, did you?"

"No, Sēnora Sanders. Not since this morning."

"I see. If you do see him, please tell him I need to talk to him." She glanced at the table. "Please feed the children without me."

"As you wish."

Maggie left the children in the kitchen with Consuela and hastened to her bedroom to freshen up. She was shocked at her pale reflection in the beveled mirror. Pinching her cheeks, she busied herself with her toilet. If she was going to her own execution, she had every intention of doing so in style.

Undoing her bun, she drew her hairbrush through her long tresses. But her memory of the look on Dominick's face each time he saw her hair tumble around her shoulders only brought tears to her eyes. Her vision blurred so she could no longer see, and she tossed the hairbrush aside and threw herself across the bed. But the bed only reminded her of Dominick and the one magical night they had shared there.

"Damn him!" she cried, pounding the pillow with her fists. "I hate him!" She sobbed, and her tears soaked the pillow until she had cried herself into a state of exhaustion.

That was when she felt it; a burning fire in her chest that threatened to consume her but instead left a raw wound inside that was far more painful than anything she had ever imagined.

A liar, a thief. Oh, she could have forgiven him that.

But a murderer? Never!

Hearing a twig snap, Dominick ducked behind the bushes. When he peered through a small gap, he recognized the familiar tall form as belonging to Foster.

"There you are!"

Foster spun around and drew his gun, but his face relaxed when he saw it was Dominick. "Don't sneak up on me like that!"

Dominick stepped into the clearing. "I remember

when I wouldn't have been able to sneak up on you. Could it be that time has dulled your senses?"

Foster slipped the gun back into its holster. He then drew out a leather pouch from inside his shirt and pinched a spot of tobacco between his fingers. "Time hasn't dulled anything!" he growled.

"Oh, no? Then what happened on the pass?" Dominick demanded. "There wasn't supposed to be any trouble."

"There wouldn't have been if you'd listened to me. You were so damned cockeyed sure we could trust the sheriff." He cursed under his breath and dropped the tobacco on the tip of his tongue.

"You think the sheriff tipped off the driver?"

"Someone did. I know that driver. He wouldn't have been so aggressive unless he'd known the sheriff's men were nearby. Damned fool! Saw himself the opportunity to play hero and he took it."

Dominick frowned. He still wasn't convinced that the sheriff was responsible. He'd gotten to know Sheriff Badger fairly well during the last few weeks. Thanks in part to Mrs. Pickings, who knew pretty much everything that went on in the town, he had managed to keep track of the sheriff's comings and goings. If her information was correct—and as far as he knew it always was—then he was right about the sheriff. "Suppose you tell me what happened to the money?"

"That might be a real interesting question to ask the sheriff," Foster said. He spit out a stream of brown tobacco juice. "The way I figure it, the sheriff told his men to wait for him below the pass. He then met the stage, grabbed the money, and no one was the wiser. All he'd have to say was that the Kissing Bandit got away."

Dominick's eyes narrowed in thought. He had to admit that Foster's theory did make sense. "You could be right."

"Coming from the Kissing Bandit himself, I'd say that was a compliment."

Dominick looked grim. "Don't call me that."

Foster looked surprised. "Why not? It's true enough. Just because someone beat you to the punch . . ."

"I can assure you, it won't happen again," Dominick vowed. The possibility that the sheriff might have gotten the best of him was no small matter. Had he become so enamored of Maggie that he'd been blinded to everything else around him? With Maggie life seemed so bright and cheerful. She'd almost made him forget that the world had a dark side. That people had a dark side. She'd almost made him forget a lot of things. But no more would he allow her to keep him from doing what must be done.

Sucking in his breath, he stared unseeing past Foster's shoulder. "We have a week until a shipment of gold is sent to San Francisco. Then we'll see who beats whom to the punch!"

It wasn't until the following morning that Maggie managed to gather the courage necessary to complete her mission. Dressed in her Sunday best, she left the house and walked the three blocks to the sheriff's office.

Sheriff Badger greeted her warmly and offered her a cup of coffee. She shook her head politely. The sheriff had a reputation for making coffee that could burn through cast iron. It was difficult enough to be there without subjecting herself to further discomfort.

"What brings you here so bright and early?" He slid his hip onto the corner of his desk and folded his arms across his chest.

She glanced around, noticing that the deputy sheriff was away from his desk. "Do you mind if I sit down?"

"Not at all." He jumped up and moved a pile of Wanted posters off a ladder-back chair. "Excuse my bad manners, ma'am. It's not often that a lady such as yourself pays me a visit.

Maggie sat down gingerly. Her heart beat so rapidly she was afraid it would jump right out of her chest. She would have given anything—anything at all—not to be there. "I heard there was another stagecoach robbery."

The sheriff looked grim. "If I ever get my hands on the man responsible, I'll . . . well, he'll rue the day. Take my word."

"Do . . . do you have any idea who he might be?"

He looked surprised at the question. "Why the Kissing Bandit, of course. One of the other passengers managed to escape." He checked a piece of paper on his desk. "A Miss Carol Caudill. Traveled all the way from Boston to teach at the school. She said that scoundrel kissed her, and when the driver tried to save her, he was shot."

Maggie closed her eyes.

"Are you all right, ma'am? You look a bit faint. Let me get you some water." He poured a glass of water from a pitcher and brought it to her.

"Thank you," Maggie said, taking a sip.

"Did you have any special interest in the robbery?" he asked.

Maggie set the glass down on his desk. "I'm afraid so. I know . . ." She cleared her throat. "I know the identity of the . . . the Kissing Bandit."

Her announcement was greeted by astonishment. "Good God! A lady such as yourself? This is extraordinary. Is it someone in town?"

She nodded.

"I was afraid of that. Well, don't keep me in suspense. Speak up, Mrs. Sanders. Tell me the scoundrel's name!"

"Dominick." She said his name so softly that Sheriff Badger almost lost his balance trying to catch it.

"Who?"

"Dominick."

He stared at her in shock. "Your husband?"

"He's not my husband," she explained. "He . . . he forced himself upon me."

"My word! Forced himself?"

"Not in the way you think," she hastened to explain. She meant to keep some semblance of dignity if it was at all possible.

"In what way did he force himself then?"

Starting from the beginning, she told him of first meeting Dominick when he was a prisoner on the stage.

"Strange," Badger said, rubbing his cheek. "No one told me to expect a prisoner. Go on. What happened next?"

As accurately as she could, she related everything about the accident, explaining in more detail than was necessary how Dominick had saved Jamie.

"He's wonderful with the children," she said, sniffling into her handkerchief. "He was more of a father to the children than Luke."

The sheriff looked confused. "Who's this Luke fellow? Is he involved with the holdups?"

"Certainly not!" Maggie gasped. "He was . . . my husband, of course." She explained that Luke had died over a year earlier. "It's not that he didn't try to be a good father. It was his health, you understand."

"Ah, yes. Now, getting back to your . . . ah, present husband."

"He's not my husband."

"So you said. Do you know where Dominick Sanders is at the present time?"

She shook her head. "I have no idea. He didn't come home last night."

"Do you think he left town?"

"I don't know. It's possible." She blew her nose. "What's going to happen to him? If you find him, I mean?"

"He'll have a trial and he'll probably hang."

She let out a sob, bringing the sheriff to her side.

"Now don't you worry your pretty little head about a thing." He patted her on the arm. "He will never bother you again."

"If only I'd come to you sooner, none of this would have happened and . . ."

"The important thing is that you came to me now." He heaved his bulk into a chair and drummed his fingers on his desk. "Anything missing from the house? His clothes, personal effects?"

"No, nothing."

"Well, then. Maybe he'll be back. What do you say I come back to the house with you and have a look around? Maybe there's something among his things that will give me a clue as to his whereabouts."

"If you think that's best."

"It never hurts. You'd be amazed at the clues that criminals leave behind. Sometimes I think they want to get caught. We had a case here about two years ago that you wouldn't believe. The man held up the bank, leaving behind a letter addressed to himself."

Maggie suspected that the sheriff was trying to relieve her anxiety, but nothing he said seemed to make sense. All she wanted was to get this over with as soon as possible.

As if reading her mind, he stood and reached for his hat. "Ready, ma'am?"

Dominick sat in the parlor waiting for her, his face drawn and pale from lack of sleep, his long legs sprawled out in front of him. The black stubble of a beard shadowed his unshaven chin. *Where was she?*

He'd been waiting for over an hour. She wasn't at the shop and he couldn't think where else she might have gone. Dammit, why hadn't she told Consuela where she was going?

No matter. He would wait however long it took her to return. And when she did, he would tell her everything. She would hate him, but it was better that way. Making her hate him would be his final gift to her.

He tensed at the sound of her footstep on the porch. His heart leaped when seconds later, she walked into the room. He was so relieved to see her, it took a moment or two before the sheriff's presence sank in.

He glanced at the sheriff, then swung his gaze back to her. "Maggie?"

With a backward glance at the sheriff, she moved closer to him, her face devoid of all color. "He knows. I told him everything."

Stunned by this admission, he sat so still he could have been a statue. He felt betrayed. It never occurred to him that she would actually turn him in. Not after what the two of them had shared. If she had plunged a knife in his heart, she couldn't have hurt him more.

"Did you hear what I said?"

"I heard. Why, Maggie? After everything we've been through. Why didn't you come to me first?"

"I wanted to. I didn't know where you were." In a softer voice, she pleaded with him, "Don't make this any more difficult for me."

"Difficult for you!" He laughed, but there was no mirth in his laughter. "I'm the one whose neck is on the line."

"Do you think I'm happy about any of this? How could I keep quiet? The bank was one thing . . ."

"What about the bank?" Sheriff Badger demanded.

Ignoring the sheriff, Dominick stood. "I told you I had nothing to do with the bank."

"I know very well what you told me!" She lowered her voice and looked at him beseechingly. "I wanted to believe you. I really did, Dominick. Even after I saw you with all that money, there was still a part of me that wanted to believe. But robbing a bank is one thing. Killing another human being is quite another."

"You have no proof that I was anywhere near the pass during that holdup."

"We don't need proof." Sheriff Badger stepped forward and snapped a pair of handcuffs around Dominick's wrists. "The folks around here take their banks seriously. Mighty seriously. If we can't hang you for the murder, we'll just have to hang you for the bank robbery." He clucked his tongue. "What a pity you can only hang a man once."

Dominick kept his eyes riveted on Maggie's face. "I wouldn't be so sure about that, Sheriff." Without another word he walked out of the room, followed by the sheriff.

Following a long, sleepless night, Maggie prepared breakfast for Laurie-Anne and Jamie. Not wanting to upset the children needlessly, she tried to act as normal as possible, but she knew by their worried faces that they sensed something was wrong.

"What do you say I ask Consuela to take you on a picnic? Wouldn't that be fun?"

"Can Aita come too?" Laurie-Anne asked.

Maggie reached across the table to brush a strand of blond hair away from her daughter's face, wondering how to answer her.

"I'm afraid not, dear heart. He's gone away."

"When's he coming back?" Jamie asked. "He promised to take me horseback riding on the beach."

She closed her eyes. "I don't know when he's coming back."

"But he promised he'd take me on Saturday."

"I told you, Aita is gone. Now I don't want to hear another word about it!" She regretted her sharp words even before she saw her son's shocked expression. "I'm sorry, Jamie. I didn't mean to raise my voice. Mama has a dreadful headache. Listen, I'll tell you what. I'll take you horseback riding on Saturday. What do you say to that?"

She reached out to Jamie, but he pulled away. "I want Aita!"

"I know," she whispered. "I want him too."

Chapter 25

Consuela arrived at her usual time the following morning, looking pale and uncomfortable. She refused to meet Maggie's eyes and seemed reluctant to begin her duties.

"Is there something wrong, Consuela?" Maggie asked.

"I don't know how to say this, Sēnora Sanders."

Feeling a tightness in her stomach, Maggie gave Laurie-Anne a gentle shove toward her brother. "Jamie, be a good boy and help your sister finish dressing."

She waited for the children to leave the room and then stood. "What is it you want to say to me, Consuela?"

"There are rumors that Sēnor Sanders is in jail."

"That's true."

"And that you were . . ."

"Living in sin?" Maggie finished for her.

The girl blushed and lowered her eyes. "I like working here. You and the señor were always very kind to me." She burst into tears. "But Papa forbids Manuel and me to work for you anymore."

Maggie reached into the cuff of her sleeve and pulled out a clean white handkerchief. "It's all right, Consuela. I understand. Here, take this."

Consuela took the handkerchief and wiped her eyes. "I don't believe that Sēnor Sanders did the terrible things they said he did." She pulled an ivory rosary out of the deep pocket of her skirt and fingered the beads. "Sometimes he paid me extra money and when I pointed out his mistake, he said that I was the one in error."

Fighting back her own tears, Maggie slipped an arm around Consuela's shoulders. "Mr. Sanders is a very kind man."

The young woman beseeched Maggie, "How could someone so kind do the things they said he did?"

"I don't know," Maggie said. It was a question she had asked herself all through the long and sleepless night. "I just don't know."

As soon as Consuela had taken her leave, Flossie arrived on Maggie's doorstep, dressed in a garish purple dress trimmed with feathers to match.

"Oh, you poor, poor child," Flossie cried, pushing her way past Maggie and leaving a trail of feathers behind. A strong, almost sickening smell of perfume wafted after her as she marched into the parlor. "I rushed over as soon as I heard the news."

Maggie's heart sank. Obviously, the news was all over town. "You heard everything?"

"How could I possibly know if I heard everything until I know what everything is?" Adjusting her bustle, she settled on the divan and peeled off her purple lace gloves. "But from what I did hear, I understand the man is barbaric. Imagine him forcing his attentions on you. It just proves what I've said all along—it's the respectable-looking ones you have to watch out for."

"He didn't force his attentions on me."

Flossie's powdered blue eyelids flew open. "You mean he paid you?" She sat back, hand on bosom, with a self-satisfied nod. "What a relief! I admire a criminal with integrity, don't you?" She shook a glove at Maggie. "I hope you made him pay you what you're worth."

"Flossie, I appreciate your kindness, but you don't understand . . ."

"If it has to do with a man, I understand." She folded her gloves across her lap and scowled like a scolding aunt. "You can be perfectly frank with me. Believe you me, there's nothing you can tell me that I haven't heard before. Wives always complain that their husbands don't talk. Well, it's just not true. Most of the wives in this town would be shocked if they knew just how much their husbands say when they're in the right company."

She winked. "Of course, I would never think of divulging anything of a personal nature. I'm a professional. Or at least I was until Mr. Grover inherited the old place and decided to close it down. Can you believe that? Been in his family for years. Why his dear, departed mother would turn over in her grave if she knew that her very own son had turned his back on a fine family tradition."

"His mother owned the place?" Maggie asked in surprise.

Flossie stopped and fanned herself with her gloves. "Don't tell me you never heard of Lillian Grover! A fine lady she was. Treated her girls with respect. Anyway, as I was saying, if there's something you have on your mind, feel free to say it and it will never leave this room."

Maggie's resistance began to weaken; the need to talk to someone about her feelings could no longer be denied. "I guess it doesn't make any difference. You're going to hear the whole story soon enough, if you haven't already."

"I'm not so sure about that. I'll hear the sordid details, no doubt. What I won't hear is how much you love him. And that's what I think we ought to talk about."

Maggie gaped at her. "He's a criminal!"

"He's a man." Flossie shrugged and straightened the feathers around her neckline, rearranging them so that her décolletage was set off to full advantage. "It's quite possible to love the man and loathe his profession."

"Flossie, really! The idea is utterly preposterous."

How could Flossie possibly know what she herself had refused to admit, even to Dominick?

"I wouldn't be so sure of that. I saw how you two looked at each other."

"What?"

"In the shop. He could hardly take his eyes off you and you . . . well, I know what I saw."

"He's a criminal," Maggie said helplessly.

"Makes no difference. You remember Goldie, don't you? Rumor has it that she was once in love with Jesse James."

"Jesse James? The train robber?"

"The very same. Of course, she hasn't seen him in over a year, since coming here from San Francisco, but she still talks about him. I don't understand it myself. I met Mr. James once, and he has something wrong with his eyes. He blinks constantly. If you ask me, it's terribly distracting."

She blinked her eyes to demonstrate. "Do you see what I mean? But, knowing Goldie, she probably thinks his blinking is charming. There's no accounting for taste, is there?"

"I guess not, but . . ."

"Now don't you go apologizing. It happens to the best of us. Why, I once took a fancy to a man who later turned out to be a horse thief. Boy, talk about staying power!"

Maggie's face flamed scarlet. "My word, Flossie!"

Flossie squeezed her hand apologetically. "I'm sorry. I forget that some subjects are considered taboo in polite company." Her face softened. "What I mean to say is just because you love someone doesn't mean you have to like everything about them. Look at my Harold. Do you think he likes it that I know how half the men in town want it served up in bed?" She shrugged. "So he's not crazy over that part of me. So what? Don't stop him loving me none."

"I never thought of it quite that way," Maggie said slowly. She closed her eyes and thought of how she'd fought to control her feelings for Dominick. Failing miserably, she'd switched to denying them, with almost as little success. Now she no longer had the strength or the inclination for pretense, and she eagerly leaped at Flossie's invitation to honesty. "Oh, Flossie, you're right. I do love him. I tried so hard not to. Glory be, if my father were alive it would kill him to know that his very own daughter was in love with an outlaw."

"It's a shame, that's what it is, that your father taught you that loving someone is wrong. Most people have some strange notions about love. It's not something you can control. Love just happens, that's all. But, like I said, I was a professional. I know about these things. So what are you going to do?"

"What can I do? I can't stay here. I can't even send the children outside to play because of all the talk. To make matters worse, the young woman who took care of the children turned in her resignation, which means I can't even work at the shop. Not that I blame her, mind you."

"So where will you go?"

"Back to San Francisco. I have a friend I can stay with for a while until I decide what to do."

"I don't see why you don't just stay right here in Santa Barbara."

"I couldn't do that. To live in Santa Barbara without Dominick would be worse than death." She burst into tears and, embarrassed at showing such raw emotion, looked away. "Besides, my reputation is ruined."

Flossie dismissed the gravity of Maggie's concern with a wave of her hand. "Don't let that bother you none. There're advantages to having a bad reputation, believe me. For one, you're not expected to go to church. And you never have to attend one of those dreadful charity teas. Having a sterling reputation can be a terrible burden. I thank my lucky stars every day that I don't have one."

Despite her depression, Maggie laughed. Flossie had a way of turning the most negative aspects of anything into something positive. The idea of not having to live one's life to please others was contrary to the principles taught her by her preacher father. It surprised Maggie that she was tempted to abandon those rigid beliefs and embrace instead Flossie's unorthodox thinking. "If it weren't for the children . . ."

"Ah, yes, the children. I suppose you have to protect them. Well, I hate to see you go. The girls and I were looking forward to getting to know you better."

Maggie squeezed Flossie's hand warmly. She had never had a friend so open and giving of herself, and so unjudgmental. She honestly felt she could tell Flossie anything.

"Does Dominick know how you feel about him?"

Startled by the question, Maggie shook her head. "I turned him in, remember?"

Flossie shrugged. "You didn't have much of a choice. If he's got any sense at all, he'll know that. But if I were you, I'd tell him how I feel before it's too late."

"But what could I possibly tell him?" Maggie asked. And why, oh, why, hadn't she told him her feelings before now? Lord knows, he'd given her ample opportunity. Was it fear? Fear that loving a bandit made her less of a person, somehow, and less deserving of Jamie and Laurie-Anne? But in wanting the best for her children, hadn't she denied them the part of her that was the best? The part that could love openly and unconditionally? "What possible difference would anything I say make to him?" she whispered, fighting back fresh tears.

"Listen, the way this town feels about the Kissing Bandit, the man's going to hang from a tree before you know it. Knowing that you care for him won't exactly make the occasion a joyous one, but it might take the edge off a bit."

The thought of Dominick hanging from a tree was shattering. "Maybe you're right," she stammered.

"Of course I'm right. I once had a man die in my arms during . . . you know . . . and after that, I always insisted they pay me ahead of time. Anyway, he's the one who told me about the dying part. Last words he said were 'Flossie, I die a happy man knowing you care.' "

"So you think I should tell him how I really feel?" *I love you, Dominick* . . . Could she really say those words? Would he let her? Or was it too late?

Flossie took Maggie's hand and squeezed it gently. "The way I see it is that we're only in this world a short time. If we can help some guy die a happy death, what could it possibly hurt?"

Chapter 26

Flossie volunteered to return later that night to stay with Jamie and Laurie-Anne while Maggie visited the jailhouse. Still not sure that she was ready to face Dominick—or even if she should, Maggie reluctantly accepted her offer.

As the day grew long, she became even more certain that she was making a mistake. What if he didn't want to see her? What if he didn't want to hear what it was she had to say? Who would blame him?

Still the words "I love you" ached in her breast until she thought she would explode. They trembled on her lips, begging for release. Her very footsteps seemed to beat out the three-syllable phrase: *I love you, I love you, I love you.* Convinced at last that it wasn't wrong to love him, she made no more effort to fight it.

Later that afternoon Mrs. Pickings arrived. "It can't be true," she exclaimed, sitting on the divan and fanning herself frantically.

"I'm afraid it is," Maggie said, politely answering the questions that followed.

"Not married, you say!" Mrs. Pickings exclaimed at one point. "My word! And me such an impeccable judge of character."

Maggie suspected that Mrs. Pickings was more scandalized at her own failure to guess what was going on under her very own nose than at anything she and Dominick were guilty of.

At long last the woman left, and Maggie decided

not to receive any more visitors. Besides, she had her hands full with Jamie and Laurie-Anne.

Jamie clearly sensed that something was wrong, and he refused to accept his mother's explanation that Dominick was away and wouldn't be back. The boy kept running outside to look for him, where he was subjected to the curious stares of neighbors.

After dragging him in for the umpteenth time, Maggie angrily forbade him to leave his room.

"Aita promised to take me horseback riding, and he always keeps his promises!" he insisted.

"Sometimes things happen that prevent us from keeping our promises," she explained gently, trying not to notice the tears he clearly didn't want her to see. She also saw that he was beginning to wheeze. His breathing difficulties had all but disappeared since their arrival in Santa Barbara.

The fact that he was starting to wheeze now puzzled her. Although it was June, a month that locals said was normally cloudy and drizzly in Santa Barbara, the weather had been warm and sunny, with very little wind. Maybe Santa Barbara's mild climate had less to do with Jamie's being so healthy and robust in recent months than she'd thought. Maybe there were other factors, like suffering a loss, that caused the lungs not to function properly. That theory would account for his serious setback following his father's death. It would also explain the sudden improvement in his health in recent months.

Perhaps Dominick had provided the magical combination of love and security that Jamie needed. It was a thought still very much on her mind after she had put the children to bed that night and returned to the parlor to wait for Flossie.

Less than five minutes after she'd left the children's room, Laurie-Anne, dressed in a white linen nightgown, padded barefoot into the parlor looking lost and confused, her rag doll clutched in her arms.

"I want my Aita to come home."

Sighing, Maggie took Laurie-Anne onto her lap, and although she had explained his absence at least a hundred different times already that day, she patiently explained it again. "Remember I told you that Aita won't be coming home?"

Laurie-Anne burst into tears for the third time since supper. "Why not?"

"Don't cry, dear heart," Maggie murmured into her young daughter's hair, but even as she was saying it, her own tears came. Never had she felt so inadequate as a mother. Never had she felt so inadequate as a woman.

Exhausted, Laurie-Anne quickly fell asleep in Maggie's arms, the tears still shimmering on her flushed little cheeks. Maggie carried her to bed, covered her with a warm quilt, and tiptoed across the room to check on Jamie.

Jamie's breathing had grown progressively worse in the past few hours. Concerned, Maggie stood watching him, monitoring each rasping breath. It terrified her to think that his lungs might give out like his father's had. How much worse might his condition become if he found out that his beloved Aita was in jail and might possibly be hanged? She shuddered at the thought of either of her children finding out that she was the one responsible for Dominick's arrest.

The sound of carriage wheels out front announced Flossie's arrival. Tiptoeing from the children's room, Maggie closed the door softly behind her, then rushed to greet her new friend and show her into the parlor.

"I can't tell you how much I appreciate you coming over tonight. I hope they'll be all right." She was worried that Jamie or Laurie-Anne might wake up in her absence. As sweet as Flossie was, her dark-blue eye makeup, brightly painted lips, and flaring-red cheeks could very easily frighten a sleepy child.

"Don't you worry about a thing," Flossie said, making herself at home. "Taking care of a child can't be any harder than taking care of a man. Men are just little boys at heart, you know."

Maggie reached for her cloak and draped it around her shoulders. "I suppose you're right. I won't be long." Maggie glanced down the hallway toward the children's room and stifled the urge to check on them one more time before she left. "Jamie is having breathing difficulties . . ."

"Now don't you go worrying about a thing. I've had some experiences with hard breathing."

Maggie couldn't help but laugh at this. "I'm sure you have, Flossie."

Realizing her gaffe, Flossie laughed with her. "What I meant is that my sister had consumption as a child. Hot baths, that's the secret. If Jamie wakes up, I'll put him in a hot bath." Flossie waved her hand. "Now be off with you."

Maggie hesitated, her heart squeezed tight against the horrifying thought that refused to go away. "What if Dominick doesn't want to see me?"

"Well, now, it seems to me that a person in jail doesn't have a lot of choice. It's not like he can run off and hide."

"I guess you're right."

" 'Course I'm right. I learned that if you're lucky enough to get a man cornered, you'd best take advantage. He'll listen to you. There ain't much else he can do."

With an uncertain nod, Maggie put her hood over her head and slipped out into the dark night.

The outskirts of the business district were deserted, the way lit only by the light of a million stars and an occasional gaslight. But as she approached the center of town, puddles of light poured out from the windows and swinging doors of the various hotels and saloons that lined State Street. Raucous laughter and loud music competed with the sounds of flapping signs and banging shutters.

The outer edge of a tropical storm at sea had

reached shore, blowing sand inland. Coarse grit whirled along State Street, pelting Maggie's face until her flesh stung and her eyes teared.

With her head lowered against the wind, she crossed the street to avoid passing the Grew Brewery. She dreaded having to face anyone she knew now that her terrible secret was out all over town. Still, the sound of fiddles and stomping feet was comforting, and she was reluctant to leave it behind.

The narrow alleyway that ran behind the red-brick jailhouse was dark but offered a welcome respite from the wind. It also offered protection of another sort. She didn't want to have to explain her visit to the sheriff. Nor could she bring herself to face Dominick directly. She was too afraid of what she would see in his face, in his eyes, as he looked at her. *Lord, don't make him hate me . . .*

A small rectangular hole was cut into the brick wall. The flickering light of a candle shone from behind vertical bars, casting a small patch of banded light onto the ground.

Heart pounding, she stood in the square of light. Even on tiptoe she was unable to reach the window. "Dominick," she whispered, and when there was no response, she repeated his name, this time in a voice edged with panic. Oh, dear God, surely they haven't hung him yet!

"Maggie?"

She was so relieved at the sound of his voice that for a moment she was speechless. "I . . . I have to talk to you," she managed at last.

"Why?" he asked curtly. "Why did you come here? To make sure I hadn't escaped?"

His voice was hard, angry, making it that much more difficult to say what she had come to say. Making it that much more necessary. Shivering against the cold chill that gripped her suddenly, she drew her cloak tighter and pressed herself against the rough brick wall.

"I want to tell you that I'm sorry. I really do care for you." There it was again, that awful word "care." What was wrong with her? Why couldn't she just say what she wanted so much to say? "For . . . for part of you."

There was a moment's silence and even the wind-blown trees on the other side of the fence seemed to be caught in the suspended hush that stretched from the alleyway to the cell. Then his voice floated from the window. "What part of me is that, Maggie? The part that you care so much about?"

His voice wasn't harsh now. It was soft with some undefined emotion. Soft on her ear, but even softer on her heart.

She closed her eyes and visualized him. "The part that is kind and good." *And loving and caring and . . .*

"So you do acknowledge that I'm not all bad."

Her eyes flew open. "I never thought you were."

He surprised her with a laugh. "It's a fine time for you to be having second thoughts."

"I'm not having second thoughts," she replied. "I did what I thought was right." *Oh, please, Dominick, you must understand that.*

More silence. And then, "Any regrets, Maggie?"

She knew what he was asking her; she had asked herself the very same question. Regrets? Lord, she'd be here all night if she had to name them. "None," she said, taking the easy way out. The less painful way. "Have . . . have you any regrets?"

"Maybe one," he said.

She swallowed. "What is that?"

"If I told you, you would think me wicked through and through."

Oh, Dominick, she thought. Don't tease me now. Not when there's so little time left. "The children keep asking for you. I don't know what to tell them."

"Tell them . . . tell them to be good."

Tears burned her eyes. "They . . . they've grown very fond of you." Her voice choked, she fell silent, and for several moments neither spoke. Maggie's quiet sobs blended with the soft sounds of the night. Suddenly, she realized that the wind had died down, with only an occasional gust blowing down the alleyway.

"Maggie, when they hang me, will . . . will you come?"

She squeezed her eyelids shut to hold back the fresh tears that sprang to her eyes. "No," she whispered.

"I didn't think you would."

"I will if you want me to." It would kill her. Lord, it would kill her. But if he really wanted her to . . .

"I'd rather you didn't. I'd hate to die seeing you looking so self-righteous."

Bristling, she stiffened her back. "I'm never self-righteous," she said self-righteously.

"Oh, Maggie, Maggie." He chuckled. "Is there anything else you want to tell me before it's too late?"

"No," she said tremulously.

"Nothing?" he persisted. "You know that my days on earth are numbered. I don't want you to spend the rest of your life feeling guilty."

"Well, maybe there is something . . . Flossie said that sometimes you can't help how you feel about someone. She said it's possible to have certain feelings for someone even if he's an outlaw. She has a friend who has certain feelings for Jesse James."

"Some men have all the luck."

"What I'm trying to say is that maybe we can't help how we feel about another person. My father always said that we can control our feelings, but I don't think that's true, do you?"

"Dammit, Maggie, I'm about to stretch rope, and you're talking philosophy. Get to the point!"

"You don't have to yell," she said, miffed.

"I wasn't yelling." When she failed to respond, he apologized. "All right, I was yelling. I'm sorry."

"Apology accepted," she said. The wind had picked up again, and dark shadows shifted uneasily around her. She huddled closer to the wall. "I have certain feelings for you."

Silence.

She glanced up at the window and wondered if she imagined that the light from the candle had suddenly grown brighter. "Did you hear what I said?" she called.

"I heard, Maggie. I'm just trying to figure out what kind of feelings you're talking about."

Maggie bit her lip, fearing his rejection. "The good kind."

Silence.

She held her breath. *Say* something. At that moment even rejection would be better than nothing. "Dominick, did you hear what I said?"

"I heard."

"Well, say something!"

"All right, I want to make sure I understand this, Maggie. By the good kind, do you mean the sort of feelings that make you all warm and cozy inside or do you mean . . . ?

"I love you!"

"Why, Maggie . . . Was that a slip? Don't answer that."

"I . . . I have to go."

"I'm glad you came. I really mean that."

"Would it have made a difference?" she asked. "Would knowing how I felt have prevented you from . . ." "Killing a man" was what she tried to say, but the words caught in her throat.

It was several moments before he answered her. "You aren't to blame for any of this," he said finally.

Although his answer absolved her of any guilt, it devastated her to know how little influence she had on him. "Dominick . . ."

"Maggie?"

"It . . . wasn't a slip." She didn't wait for his reply; she turned and fled down the long, dark alleyway.

Inside the cell Dominick listened to the sound of her

retreating footsteps until they faded in the distance. Closing his eyes and seeing a vision of her, he whispered her name and cursed the day he'd met her.

It was so dark at the end of the alley that Maggie didn't see the man until she ran blindly into his large, bulky body. Startled, she screamed and fought against the rough hands that grabbed her. She kneed him below his waist and heard him groan under his breath. He loosened his hold and she quickly pulled free.

Without a moment's hesitation, she raced across State Street straight for the building with the brightest lights and found herself in front of a hotel. She glanced back over her shoulder and caught sight of a man silhouetted in the shadows at the end of the block.

Gasping with fear and exertion, she ran past the startled, velvet-suited doorman and into the lobby of the hotel. It wasn't until she'd taken a moment to catch her breath that she realized a fancy dress ball was in progress. Feeling conspicuous next to the elegantly dressed women and their formally attired escorts, Maggie hid behind a potted palm tree where she could watch the front door of the hotel to see if anyone followed her inside.

She was shaking so hard that her teeth chattered. It was difficult to know if it was from fear or cold or the strain of the last two days. She gradually let the lilting sound of violins playing a Viennese waltz wash over her, and finally she began to relax. Wistfully, she directed her gaze to the grand ballroom, her feet keeping time to the music as she watched the graceful couples whirl around the dance floor like leaves in the wind.

Someone was approaching. Maggie pulled her hood down over her brow and kept her head lowered. A familiar voice prompted her to peer cautiously through the palm leaves. She recognized Mr. Grover, who was whistling his words more than usual. Curious as to whom he was talking to, Maggie strained to get a better view of his companion.

To Maggie's surprise he was with Miss Winkerton, who blushed prettily and fluttered her eyelashes until the poor man looked thoroughly flustered. And if that weren't enough, Miss Winkerton shamelessly took every opportunity to pull up the hem of her ball gown and reveal her blue velvet shoes.

"I can't dance," Mr. Grover said, the word "dance" hissing like a steaming teakettle.

Miss Winkerton tilted her head coyly and tickled his chin with the tip of her blue silk fan. "Why, there's nothing to dancing. It's like robbing a stage. All it takes is split-second timing."

Mr. Grover laughed at this and seemed to relax. "Why, Miss Winkerton, I do believe you are the most amusing woman I've ever met."

Without another word, Miss Winkerton led the bashful Mr. Grover through the archway leading to the ballroom.

Maggie stood watching the first seeds of love being sowed between the unlikely couple and blinked back tears.

Dominick had been right about the velvet shoes. Maggie had always thought comfort and practicality the most important considerations in designing shoes. Never had it occurred to her that shoes could do more than protect the feet or make a fashion statement. Why, the right pair could help open up a heart to love!

Unable to bring herself to watch the couple any longer, she slipped out of the hotel and scanned the street for signs of her pursuer. Seeing nothing that looked suspicious, she asked the doorman to hire her a shay to take her home.

The town clock struck eleven as the shay barreled down a dark, deserted street on the way to her house. The wind had stopped and the night seemed almost eerily quiet. Only the steady clip-clopping of the horses's hooves and an occasional "Giddy-up" from the gravel-mouthed driver broke the silence.

Suddenly a rough male voice called out, then another. Tensing, Maggie narrowed her eyes to make out the shadows along the side of the road. Undefined forms moved stealthily toward an open field. Glancing back over her shoulder, she caught a glimpse of a familiar face beneath the gaslight.

"Stop!" she ordered the driver.

The driver pulled on the reins. "What's the matter, ma'am?"

"Back there. Did you see?"

"Just a gang of hooligans," the driver informed her. "Nothing to worry your pretty little head over."

"Turn around!" Maggie ordered. "At once!"

"I don't think that's a good idea, ma'am."

"I said go back."

The driver muttered under his breath, but he picked up the reins and turned the horses around.

Maggie waited until the shay was parallel to the circle of dark bodies. The sickening sound of flesh pounding flesh, followed by grunts and groans, filled her with alarm. She had to do something—and fast. But what?

If only she could see, know who it was that she was dealing with. They had to be from families she knew, probably were even customers of hers. Of course, Mrs. Pickings had expressed her own opinion enough times about who was behind the town's troublemakers. Another dull thud followed by an anguished cry convinced Maggie that is was time to test some of Mrs. Pickings's theories.

She stood up in the shay. "Why, Harvey Tubbs, is that you? Just wait till I tell your father." It would give her great pleasure, in fact, to tell his tightfisted banker father a thing or two about his trouble-making son—if indeed, the troublemaker was the Tubbs boy.

Her threat was met by a chillingly tense silence, and she didn't know whether to be encouraged or fearful.

She fought against the latter and steadied her voice. "And Timothy Parker! Shame on you!"

One by one, she named all the families that Mrs. Pickings had voiced her suspicions about in the past. And one by one, the shadowy figures began to back away and disappear into the night until only a lone male figure remained.

"Manuel?" Maggie called in a tremulous voice. "Are you all right?"

Manuel limped toward her until he stood in the glow of the gaslight. It was then that she could see his bloodied lip and swollen eye.

"How . . . how did you know their names?" he asked.

Something in his voice gave Maggie pause. Without meaning to, he had confirmed a growing suspicion of hers. Maggie was willing to bet that these boys were the same ones who had been responsible for the burning down of her shop.

She swallowed the sudden rage that threatened her good sense. There would be time enough later to handle the others. Now her main concern was for Manuel.

"I have my ways," she announced matter-of-factly.

He limped to the side of the shay, holding his stomach. "Are you going to turn them in?"

"In good time."

"If you hadn't come . . . I mean . . ." He looked away and quickly wiped a sleeve across his eyes.

She pretended not to notice so as not to embarrass him further. "If I hadn't arrived at that moment, I daresay you would have seen to it that the population of this town suddenly dropped by seven. Would you like a ride home?"

"Thank you, Señora Sanders. I would indeed."

He told the driver the directions to his house and settled on the horsehair seat next to her. "You could have been hurt back there," he said. A note of awe crept into his voice.

"Yes. Well, a woman must do what she must." She

eyed him thoughtfully. "Now, are you going to tell me why that group of hooligans is bothering you?"

Manuel glanced at her sideways. "Harvey Tubbs's sister . . ."

Suddenly understanding dawned. Maggie tried to see his face in the dark. "So that's it. Lisa's brother is against your seeing her." She didn't need to hear any more. The Tubbs family was prominent in the town, and she supposed it wasn't too surprising that it wouldn't want a family member to become romantically involved with a Mexican youth. Like other multiracial towns, Santa Barbara split its loyalties three ways, among the Chinese, the Mexicans, and the whites. Only when the barriers between the groups were crossed did trouble brew. Manuel and Lisa had made the mistake of crossing a forbidden line.

The driver pulled up in front of a run-down shanty in the heart of Spanishtown. The air was foul with the smell of farm animals. Somewhere in the shadows came the braying sound of a mule. A baby cried in the distance.

"You must make certain that someone looks at those injuries, do you hear?"

He nodded vigorously. At that moment he would have done anything Maggie told him to do.

"And don't worry about the Tubbs boy. If I have anything to say about it, he won't be bothering you anymore."

"Señora Sanders . . . gracias."

Chapter 27

It was close to midnight by the time she arrived home. She thanked Flossie, promised to write as soon as she was settled in San Francisco, and wrapped her arms around the feathers and ruffles to give her a hug. After Flossie left, she quickly readied herself for bed. But she couldn't sleep. All she could think about was Dominick and how empty the house was without him.

At the first glimmer of dawn, she packed the children's clothes, along with her own. After breakfast she took the children to the wharf to book passage on the very next liner to San Francisco.

Laurie-Anne ran along the wharf, chasing sea gulls and watching passengers disembark from a steamer, but Jamie stayed by his mother's side, coughing and wheezing, his difficult breathing making him anxious and fretful.

Colonel Hollister, the tall, rail-thin owner of the luxurious Arlington Hotel, stood at the bottom of the gangplank, steering the obviously wealthy passengers to the Arlington's horse-drawn trolley and the second-class passengers and traveling salesmen—or drummers, as they were called—to the omnibus that would take them to the more modest Ellwood.

Maggie read the schedule that was posted above the ticket counter. "I don't understand," she said to the red-faced man who sat inside a wooden cage, smoking a pipe. "It doesn't say what time the *Golden Crest* leaves."

The man spit out the stem of his pipe and shrugged.

"Your guess is as good as mine. Could be tonight. Could be tomorrow night. Could be next week sometime."

"How is a person supposed to make plans for departure when the ship has no schedule?" Maggie asked crossly.

"The ship shoots off its cannon when it's getting ready to leave. You can hear it all over town."

"I'm quite aware of that," Maggie said. The loud booms had practically thrown her out of bed on more than one occasion. "But that means I would have to drag two young children out of bed at a ungodly hour and race to the dock to try to catch it before it leaves."

"You could wait to book passage on one of the other steamers," the clerk suggested. "Unfortunately, it could take a while. It's now the main tourist season, you know. I could add your name to the waiting list. Of course, you can always take the stagecoach. Now that the Kissing Bandit is behind bars, I daresay it's much safer."

Just the mention of Dominick was enough nearly to shatter her. She forced herself to hold her head high, reached for the coins in her reticule, and booked passage for three.

After purchasing the tickets, she called Jamie and Laurie-Anne to her side. "Come along now. We've got work to do."

The hardest part was returning to her little shoe shop for the last time. She stood in front of the building, holding Jamie and Laurie-Anne by the hand, and gazed teary-eyed at the sign Dominick had hung over the door. How they had argued over that sign!

But it wasn't the arguments she remembered. It was the other times, the times they didn't argue, the night they made love.

Next to her the children grew restless. "Can I go and play in the tree?" Jamie asked.

"I want to go too," Laurie-Anne said.

"Not now," Maggie said. "I need you to help me. Come along."

She hustled the children inside and was surprised to find Manuel hard at work behind the counter. He grinned sheepishly at the sight of her.

He had polished the shoes and boots that were waiting to be picked up to a lustrous shine.

"I thought I'd finish up your orders," he explained. "I let myself in with the spare key."

"You did a beautiful job. But . . ." His eye was black and swollen shut. "I thought your father said you could no longer work for me."

Head down, he scraped one foot along the floor. "I decided it's time I made my own decisions." He looked up at her, his face grave. "I guess a man must do what he must."

Understanding the tribute he was paying her, Maggie nodded. "I guess he does at that."

"Anything else I can do for you?"

Maggie thought a moment. "I would be most grateful if you would run down to the livery stable and rent a horse and wagon so that we can take my things down to the wharf."

"I'm sorry, Señora Sanders, that you are leaving."

"Thank you, Manuel. So am I. I'm sure you'll be able to find another job. If you like, I will write a letter of recommendation."

"That's kind of you, Señora. But I don't think too many gringos will hire me, and they're the ones who own most of the businesses in town."

"What a pity. They'll never know what a hard worker they've missed."

"If you like, Señora, I will be happy to deliver these shoes for you."

"That would be a great help," she said.

"If you give me your address, I shall send you the money I collect from the customers."

"That won't be necessary," she said. "I want you to use the money to help your family."

"Gracious, Señora. You are very kind."

After Manuel left, Maggie set right to work, grateful that she had something to do to keep her mind occupied.

"Bring Mama her tools," she instructed. "Be careful, now. Jamie, don't let Laurie-Anne touch the awls." She dragged out the crates that were stored in the cupboard beneath the staircase and began filling them.

By the time she had finished packing, Manuel had returned with the wagon. Together they loaded the crates onto the back.

While Manuel drove the load to the wharf, she and the children walked the short distance to the general store to return the keys to Mr. Grover. She wasn't aware of how much she dreaded facing him and the other townspeople until she caught sight of herself reflected in one of the windows that she passed on the way. Her head held high, her back as stiff as a board, she hardly recognized the determined face and flashing eyes as her own.

She could almost hear Dominick now, making some comment about her looking like a Prussian soldier about to march to war. He would probably accuse her of looking self-righteous. Well, if that's what it was going to take to get through the next few hours, she would look as self-righteous as she darn well chose!

She walked through the door of the general store and was immediately aware that everyone inside had suddenly stopped talking. Cold, accusing eyes followed her progress to the counter. Unspoken words of condemnation seemed to replace the very air, making it difficult to breathe.

Passing one of her neighbors, she nodded. "Good day."

She greeted Miss Winkerton with a smile. "Your blue velvet shoes look lovely."

Miss Winkerton glanced anxiously at Mr. Grover and murmured a demure thank-you.

Maggie dropped Jamie's and Laurie-Anne's hands and fumbled in the little coin purse wrapped around her wrist. "I'm returning the keys, Mr. Grover. I no longer have use for your building."

Mr. Grover looked flustered. "Sorry to hear you're leaving town, ma'am."

He sounded so genuinely sorry to see her go that for a moment Maggie was caught off balance. She had expected the townspeople to scorn her after the news of Dominick's arrest and word of her own scandalous behavior became public knowledge. What she was unprepared for was any show of kindness.

"Thank you, Mr. Grover."

"Here," he stammered, pushing a bottle of catsup into her hand. "You might be needing some blessed relief."

Maggie fought to hold back tears. "I might at that."

"Take care now, you hear?"

She managed a smile. "You too." And because she was afraid of making a fool of herself, she grabbed the bottle of catsup, groped blindly for Laurie-Anne's hand, and quickly left the store, stopping only to make sure that Jamie was following close behind.

She had one more stop to make.

Walking briskly down State Street, she entered the bank. She put Jamie in charge of the catsup bottle and instructed both children to wait in the lobby for her. She then headed straight for Mr. Tubbs's office. In passing, she ripped a Help Wanted sign off the front of a teller's window, and marched into the president's office without knocking.

"Good day, Mr. Tubbs."

The banker looked up from his desk. "Why . . . ah . . . Mrs. . . . ."

"I answer to both 'Mrs. Sanders' and 'Mrs. Turner,' " Maggie said, enjoying the look on his face at her boldness.

He coughed. "Won't you sit down?"

"I don't intend to stay that long. I just came to tell

you that I know that your son is one of the boys responsible for burning down my business."

Mr. Tubbs paled. "I have no idea what you're talking about."

She arched her eyebrows. "You remember, don't you? How the building I rented was burned to the ground, forcing me to come in here to ask for a loan so that I could get my business started again. You must remember, Mr. Tubbs? The loan you refused to give me?"

"I think there must be some mistake. Harvey is a good boy."

"How could you possibly know that? According to your wife, you spend every waking moment here, at the bank. I've heard tell that you work until eleven o'clock at night and even on the Sabbath." She clucked her tongue. "Shame on you, Mr. Tubbs. The Sabbath." She turned and started for the door. "I'm sure the sheriff would be most interested to know how your son spends his time in your absence."

"Wait . . . Mrs. . . . Ah . . . About that loan . . ."

She whipped around to face him. "Thank you, Mr. Tubbs. That's really most generous of you. But I have no need for a loan at the present time. However . . ." She tossed the Help Wanted sign onto his desk. "Perhaps we could strike a bargain of a different nature."

Little beads of sweat broke out on his forehead. "A bargain? I'm not sure I understand."

She nodded toward the sign. "I happened to notice that your bank is advertising for a teller."

Mr. Tubbs rubbed his chin. "Ah . . . it would be difficult to hire you. Nothing personal. But a bank has to be concerned about its reputation and since your husband . . ." He stopped. "Ah . . . Mr. Sanders has been arrested . . ."

"I see your point," Maggie conceded. "I had no intention of applying for the job. But I do have someone else in mind. I believe you know him. His name is Manuel Lopez."

Mr. Tubbs looked sick. "Ah . . . yes."

"Then I'm sure you'll agree that he's a fine young man and a hard worker. He would be an exemplary employee. Why, with someone as responsible as Manuel working for you, I'm just willing to bet you'll be able to spend more time with your family. I would venture to say that would solve a lot of problems in this town. Don't you agree?"

Mr. Tubbs stammered his words out in a string of unintelligible sounds. "I . . . uh . . . well, now."

"That's all right, Mr. Tubbs, you needn't thank me. Just tell me what time you want Manuel to start work in the morning and I'll be on my way."

"Ah, time . . . what . . . I don't . . . I . . . mean . . ."

"Would nine o'clock be all right?"

"Now just a minute," Mr. Tubbs bellowed. His eyes bulged in outrage as he finally found his voice. "This sort of thing is simply not done in business!"

"Of course it is, Mr. Tubbs. Lots of businessmen give employment to their future sons-in-law." She gave him a coy smile. "Actually it's a brilliant business decision. By hiring Manuel, not only are you ensuring your daughter's future, you're keeping your very own son out of jail."

Mr. Tubbs sputtered and fumed, but in the end he relented. She offered him no other choice.

At four o'clock the next morning the loud cannon boom shook the house, signaling the near departure of the steamer that would take her away. Dragging herself out of bed, she dressed in the light-blue traveling suit she had laid out the night before and hurried to the children's room.

Laurie-Anne refused to cooperate. "I want Aita," she cried, burying her face in her pillow.

"I know, dear heart," Maggie said, and it was all she could do to keep her own tears from coming. "Come on, now, help Mama. We have to hurry. Jamie, wake up."

It seemed to take forever to get the children dressed, but in reality it took less than fifteen minutes. Outside, the air was damp and foggy.

Coughing and breathing heavily, Jamie climbed into the shay that Maggie had rented and settled next to his sister. Maggie wrapped a blanket around both children, then took the driver's seat and picked up the reins. "Git-up," she called.

The silver thread of dawn outlined the top of the mountains behind them as they arrived at the pier. A few people stood along the edge waving to the ship, which had already set sail.

Watching the *Golden Crest* skirt the shadowy forms of the Santa Barbara Islands in the distance, Maggie used a word that Dominick would surely approve, then picked up the reins and went home.

Later that day she and the children arrived at the hotel on the corner of State and Anapamu streets to inquire about the stagecoach.

The clerk was a gray-haired man with a protruding stomach and a nervous twitch. "Don't you worry about a thing, ma'am. With that rascal behind bars where he belongs, the pass is safe for travel again."

"What about other road agents? Won't they be tempted to replace Dom . . . the Kissing Bandit?"

The clerk shook his head. "What bandit would be foolish enough to come anywhere near a town that just captured the most notorious bandit this side of Jesse James?"

It seemed to Maggie that the man had a valid point. Without further ado, she purchased three tickets for the stage that was scheduled to leave for San Francisco the following morning.

The sun shone bright when she and the children, along with a middle-aged couple and a traveling salesman, boarded the stage in front of the hotel.

The drummer tipped his hat, introduced himself as Harold Whittaker, the finest salesman this side of the Mississippi, and upon taking his seat inside the stage, promptly proceeded to entertain the children with a little fabric doll that fit over his hand.

Nearly three hours after the stage had begun its journey, it came to an abrupt stop just before the summit of the San Marcos Pass. Thinking that the driver wanted them to walk, Maggie reached over to tie Laurie-Anne's sunbonnet. "Hold still, Laurie-Anne."

The door flew open, followed by an abrupt command. "Out. All of you."

Maggie caught a glimpse of a man wearing a burlap sack over his head. The sunlight caught the shiny barrel of his gun. Her throat dry with fear, she hugged her children close to her.

The older couple stepped outside first, followed by the drummer. When it was her turn, Maggie told the children to wait for her inside the stage. She lifted the hem of her skirt and stepped out.

The bandit signaled toward the door with his gun.

"Please," she begged. "They're only children."

He turned to her, and she felt faint. Holes had been cut into the sack to allow for his mouth and eyes. But it was his clothes that caught her attention. He was dressed in black pants and shirt, a bright-red sash tied around his waist. Sickened, she turned her head, unable to look at him.

The bandit pointed his gun toward the strongbox next to the driver. "Throw it down."

The driver did as he was told, then immediately held his hands up over his head again.

"I'll take the ring," he said, his voice a rumble in his throat. He nodded toward the older woman's hand. "Now."

Her face pale with fear, the woman twisted the gold ring off her finger and threw it on the ground.

Signaling Maggie to stay, the bandit ordered the other passengers inside the stage and slammed the door. Without a word, he stepped close to Maggie and grabbed her around the waist.

"Don't, Dominick," she cried out, his name slipping out before she thought. "Please don't . . ."

"Don't what?" the bandit asked hoarsely. Leaning toward her, he inched the mask up. She closed her eyes so she wouldn't have to look him in the face. Lord—this was the man to whom she had given her heart and soul. How could he?

She kept her mouth clamped firmly shut as he kissed her and rubbed her lips quickly with her hand when he released her, not wanting any essence of him to remain.

With her eyes blinded by tears, she turned and stumbled toward the stage, anxious to get away from him. How she hated him, hated the day she had ever set eyes on him!

Shouts sounded behind her and she turned back. Relief washed over her when the sheriff stepped out from behind a boulder. He was pointing both his guns at the outlaw. But it was the man behind the sheriff that held her attention.

Thinking she was seeing double, she blinked her eyes. But there was no mistake; Dominick stood behind the sheriff, watching the bandit with dark, narrowed eyes.

She couldn't speak, she couldn't move. All she could do was stare at him in bewilderment. Reluctantly, she pulled her eyes away from Dominick and studied the outlaw. If he wasn't Dominick, then who was he? And why had he seemed so familiar to her?

She again met Dominick's gaze, and for a moment she forgot where she was, forgot about the bandit, forgot about everything around her. But reality took hold with a vengeance when she suddenly found herself crushed to the outlaw's chest, his iron arms around her waist.

"Don't come any closer!" he bellowed, holding his gun to Maggie's temple. He was holding her so close that she could feel the hard muscles of his chest pressed against her shoulders.

He backed into the bushes, dragging Maggie with him. Once he was out of sight of the others, he spoke in a low, threatening voice. "Tell Dominick Sanders the next time I see him, he's a dead man." With those chilling words, he shoved Maggie to the ground and disappeared into the thick brush.

The next thing she knew, she was in Dominick's arms. "Are you all right?" he asked. His face was so filled with alarm and concern, she could only gaze up at him in speechless wonder.

It wasn't until he pressed her further for a health report that she managed to find her voice. "Glory be!" she sputtered. "Dominick Sanders, would you stop playing doctor and just . . ." Her voice faltered. "Hold me."

Chapter 28

What happened next was all a blur—a wonderful, heavenly blur. She was vaguely aware of Dominick's insistence that the stage return to Santa Barbara rather than continue on to Ballard, which was closer. He sat on the seat beside her and she shamelessly clung to him, not caring that the other passengers might think her behavior brazen or otherwise improper.

Laurie-Anne sat next to Dominick, watching him as if she would never let him out of her sight again. Jamie, playing guard, hung out the window, giving periodic reports.

"Don't worry, Mama," he cried solemnly. "If that bandit comes back, I'll save you."

Maggie smiled at her son's earnestness. "Thank you, Jamie." Somewhere in her consciousness, it registered that he was no longer wheezing or coughing. He had, in fact, stopped the moment he was reunited with Dominick.

The stagecoach arrived back in town behind the sheriff and his men, who had already spread the word that there had been trouble on the pass. No sooner had the stage drawn up in front of the hotel then it was surrounded by a noisy crowd, all eager to know everything that had happened.

Mrs. Pickings, considering it her civic duty to learn firsthand just which of the rumors were true, lifted her strident voice above the noisy crowd, demanding the facts and quickly silencing anyone who wasn't in a position to give them to her.

The editor of the newspaper, Mr. McDonald, took a much more tactful approach and therefore wasted valuable time listening to unnecessary and inaccurate suppositions. He did manage to question the driver, and he tried to talk to Maggie, but Dominick quickly whisked her and the children into the hotel and out a back door leading to an alley. In no time, he hired a horse and wagon and drove them back to the house.

Despite Maggie's protests, he carried her inside and laid her on the divan in the parlor. "Jamie, go and get your mother a quilt and a pillow."

He took one of Maggie's feet and started unbuttoning the tiny buttons on her boot.

"I'm perfectly all right," she insisted, although secretly she loved all the attention.

"You are not all right," Dominick said. "You were accosted by a stranger."

"I was not accosted. I was kissed."

He glowered. "Must you be so stoic about it? You could at least show a little indignation. You've shown plenty in the past when I kissed you."

She thought about this for a moment. "Did I?"

"You know you did." He started on her second boot.

"Would you mind telling me what's going on? Do you know what you've put me through these last couple of days?" She was confused, she was angry, but more than anything she was hurt. "If you weren't the Kissing Bandit, why didn't you tell me?"

"Dammit, Maggie! Settle down. When I said I wanted you to show indignation, I meant toward the scoundrel who kissed you, not me."

Jamie returned, dragging a quilt behind him. "Ah, here we are," Dominick said, standing up. He shook out the quilt and tucked it around her, then arranged a pillow behind her head.

"Are you going to answer me or not?" she asked.

Laying a finger on her bottom lip, he hushed her.

"Later. Now I want you to humor me and get some rest."

"Please, Dominick, I have to know."

He looked at her for several moments before he spoke. "I know you do, Maggie. And I'm going to explain everything to you later. Trust me."

She opened her mouth in protest, but something in his face made her bite back her words. Something told her that this postponement was more than just a convenient out, that it was necessary for both their sakes. But why?

After she was settled, he led the children to the kitchen, which was soon filled with the noise of banging pots and pans, punctuated by sudden bursts of laughter.

Listening to the happy sounds, Maggie told herself that she'd only imagined the look on Dominick's face. He was going to explain everything and it would all make perfectly good sense. Because she wanted so much for that to be true, she forced a deep breath. Much to her relief, the turmoil she'd felt since Dominick's arrest began to fade, and she relaxed as a sweet, lulling serenity took its place, pushing her worrisome thoughts away.

In short order Dominick returned carrying a tray with tea and toast. "I thought you could use some nourishment." He set the tray on a table and picked up a warm brick wrapped in a beret. "An old Basque custom," he said, tucking the brick between her feet.

The warmth traveled up her legs and Maggie sighed, "That feels wonderful."

Sipping her tea, she watched him light the wick in the oil lamp. It would soon be dark. What an unbelievable day! There was so much she wanted to ask him. So much she wanted to say.

"Dominick . . . I thought . . ."

"I know what you thought." He looked at her through eyes filled with tenderness. "I'll explain everything. But now I want you to think only of getting some rest."

"But he said . . ."

Dominick's face grew still. "What did he say?"

She shuddered at the memory. "The next time he sees you, you're a dead man."

"Now that's good news if ever I heard it."

"Dominick, please don't make light of this. He sounded serious."

"I daresay he was serious. That's why it's good news. If he's threatening to kill me, I must be closer to catching him than I thought."

His face grew dark, its lines deepened. But the sudden look of hatred in his eyes was what made her shudder. It was then that she knew her ordeal was far from over.

Later that night, after Dominick had prepared a light supper of smoked ham and cheese, Maggie bathed the children and got them ready for bed.

After Jamie and Laurie-Anne had been properly tucked in, Dominick sat by their sides and told them a story of a thief who stole the good manners from a town and the awful things that happened when its citizens no longer knew how to say please and thank you.

By the time the thief had been captured and good manners restored, Laurie-Anne was already asleep and Jamie was fighting a losing, but no less gallant, battle to stay awake.

Dominick kissed both children on the forehead, then tiptoed from the room, leaving Maggie to check the bed coverings and blow out the candles.

He was waiting in the parlor for her, a glass of brandy in his hand. "Would you like some?" he asked.

Shaking her head no, she sat in one of the two chairs next to the cast-iron wood stove and watched his face.

"You're not the Kissing Bandit." What a blessed

relief it was to say those words. She wanted to say them again, to shout them. But there was something in the way Dominick stood so silent and still that alarmed her.

She closed her eyes, suddenly not wanting to hear what he had to say, for she knew—sensed—it was not what she wanted to hear.

"Look at me," he said softly. He set his glass down and knelt in front of her. Taking her icy-cold hands in his, he rubbed them tenderly. "Maggie?"

Only when she looked at him did he drop her hands and stand. "I *am* the Kissing Bandit."

Sickened, she stared at him, hoping she'd misunderstood. "I don't understand. The man who robbed the stage . . . Why did the sheriff free you? I don't understand any of this. Dominick, please tell me everything. I have to know!"

He walked around the room, then gripped the back of his chair as if he needed support. For several moments he said nothing, but stood with his head lowered. When at last he spoke, his voice was so low that she had to lean forward to hear.

"Several years ago I took a job on a ranch owned by a man named George Hansen. The property was located outside of Santa Maria. For five years I worked for Hansen, and we became very close. I came to think of him as a second father, and he considered me the son he had never had." He stopped and finished his brandy.

Thus braced, he continued. This time his voice was stronger. "I knew how to care for sheep. One doesn't grow up in a Basque family without learning about sheep. But it was Hansen who taught me the business end. I got so good I could predict wool prices in advance, and it was on my advice that he mortgaged his ranch to the hilt. He then sank every last penny into the purchase of more sheep."

He paused, and for a moment she thought he was not going to continue. "Go on," she whispered.

His hands clenched into tight fists, he inhaled deeply. "Had everything gone according to plan, he would have been a very wealthy man. But an earthquake shook the area, causing the sheep to panic. Before I could calm them, they stampeded over a cliff to their deaths. Lord, I'll never forget that day as long as I live." He rubbed his forehead as if he wished he could erase the memory. "Cattle bellow when they stampede, but sheep run in eerie silence. It was the sound of their hooves that alerted me. There was nothing I could do but watch helplessly as they dropped silently over the edge into the canyon." He paused for a moment before continuing. "Hansen's entire investment was wiped out in a flash. I blamed myself for his misfortune."

"But it wasn't your fault," Maggie said.

"I was taught the way of the Basque, who believe that a sheepherder is responsible for any misfortune to the flock left in his care and must do whatever is necessary to make amends if something happens to them. When the bank refused Hansen a loan to replace his sheep, he stood to lose everything, including his ranch."

"Remembering her own loss because of the fire and how the bank had turned down her request for a loan, she felt her blood boil. "That's terrible!"

"I learned that the bank was transporting a gold shipment by stage. Once I verified that the shipment belonged to the same bank that was threatening to take away Hansen's ranch, I donned a disguise and robbed the stage. Since the bank would get the money back immediately, I managed to convince myself that all I was doing was borrowing the money for a few short hours."

Maggie listened to this confession with a heart filled with pain. Nevertheless, she couldn't bring herself to condemn him. "You did it to save Hansen's ranch." Put in those unselfish terms, it somehow seemed less of a crime—at least that's what she wanted to believe.

He nodded. "My gun wasn't even loaded. One of the women passengers was so frightened that she started hyperventilating. I didn't know what to do, so I kissed her, hoping to calm her nerves."

She wanted to laugh at the thought of Dominick's thinking his kiss would calm anyone's nerves.

"Instead of calming down, she passed out. I swear to you, Maggie, that was the end of it. I gave Hansen the money. He promptly paid the bank. I married his daughter, and we eventually bought a ranch of our own."

"I don't understand. You said that was the end of it. What about the other stage robberies?" She searched his face with beseeching eyes. "Don't tell me they were all for honorable reasons as well."

"All I can tell you is that after that one time, I lived a respectable life. But I was haunted by what I'd done. Before I knew it, the legend of the Kissing Bandit had become a favorite topic in every saloon in the area. Everywhere I went, there was reference to it. My only hope was that in time the jokes and tales would die down. Believe me, no one was more surprised than I when the bandit struck again!"

Maggie's eyes widened. "You mean someone else pretended to be you?"

"That's exactly what I mean! What I didn't know was that George Hansen had suspected me of being the Kissing Bandit from the very beginning. He considered it too convenient that I came up with the money at that particular moment. Obviously, he didn't believe me when I said I had suddenly come into an inheritance. Contrary to what you think, Maggie, I'm not a very good liar."

"So what happened next?" Maggie prodded.

Dominick took a deep breath and continued. "Wanting to prove his suspicions wrong, Hansen took to riding the stage up and down the pass, hoping to come face-to-face with the bandit himself. I think he had some idea that if he confronted me I would give up my life of crime. Sure enough, on one such occasion, the bandit showed up. Hansen tried to unmask the man, thinking it was me, and was shot in the heart."

"Oh, no!" Maggie cried out.

"It gets worse," Dominick said grimly. He poured himself more brandy before he continued. "Upon learning of her father's death, my wife went into labor prematurely. Three days later she and the baby were dead."

"Oh, Dominick," Maggie cried softly. She wanted to take him in her arms and hold him, but something in his face stopped her. In the soft shadows of the room he looked like a stranger. "I'm so sorry," she whispered.

Dominick stared at the amber liquid swirling in his glass. "For months after the tragedy I rode the countryside like a madman, not knowing what to do. All I knew was that someone, somewhere, was going to pay for what had been done to my family."

The lust for revenge darkened his face. But it was the hatred in his voice that made her blood run cold. Shivering, she crossed her arms.

"For three years I tried to do just that. But I lacked vital information. He was always one step ahead of me. I decided to get myself hired as a Wells Fargo detective."

Maggie stared at him in astonishment. "You're a Wells Fargo detective?"

He nodded. "The day that we met on the stagecoach was all a ploy. The man who was supposedly guarding me was actually working with me."

"Working with you?" she gasped. "Is that why you insisted on giving him a proper funeral?"

The harsh lines on Dominick's face softened with the memory. "Thanks to you, we gave him one, didn't we? I'm sure Barnes would have been impressed."

"But I really believed . . . I mean . . . he was so . . ."

"Obnoxious?" Dominick nodded sadly. "Barnes

loved playing that part. The idea was to have me incarcerated in the Santa Barbara jail so that I could work undercover. At the time, we suspected Sheriff Badger was our man. It would explain how the bandit knew which stages carried shipments across the San Marcos Pass and how he always managed to escape our traps."

"Is that why you pretended to be a prisoner? So that you could watch the sheriff?"

"Something like that. Actually, we thought if the sheriff were involved, my being arrested would complicate matters for him. We were convinced that he'd arrange for my escape so he could continue robbing stages. As long as I was on the loose, everyone would assume I was responsible. The last thing the real bandit would want would be for me to be captured."

"Obviously you were wrong about the sheriff. But how did you convince him to set you free?"

"Once I was certain that the sheriff was not involved, my partner, Foster, presented him with my credentials."

"Your partner?"

Dominick grinned. "I believe you two have met. Remember, in the alley behind the jailhouse? He vividly recalls meeting you."

"Oh, no!" Maggie cried, blushing. "You mean the man I ran into in the alley was your partner?"

"Don't worry. He's none the worse for wear. Except for the fact that he speaks an octave higher."

He laughed at the horrified look on her face and took her hands in his.

"Oh, Maggie, I admit I should never have stolen that money," he said solemnly. "At the time I was young and idealistic and thought anything was right as long as justice prevailed. I hope you can find it in your heart not to judge me too harshly."

"I have no right to judge you, Dominick. But the thing I can't understand is why you didn't tell me any of this before? Why didn't you tell me you were a Wells Fargo agent?"

"I wanted to. Believe me, Maggie, I wanted to tell you a hundred different times. But I was working undercover and was obliged to keep my identity hidden."

"But you could have told me," she protested, biting back the hurt and anger that were clouding her judgment. "It would have made such a difference knowing that you weren't the bandit."

His eyes filled with sadness. "I didn't tell you, Maggie, because to tell you that would have meant telling you the rest also."

Her heart nearly stood still. "There's more?"

"I'm afraid so. As I already explained, I mean to find the man responsible for the loss of my family."

"I know, Dominick. But how could you think I would judge you in an unfavorable light for wanting to bring a man to justice for what he did to your family?" She saw his face darken with something that was more lethal than hatred, and she was reminded of a reference he'd made in the past about justice and murder. "That . . . that is what you plan to do, isn't it? He is entitled to a fair trial."

"He's entitled to no more than my father-in-law got, and that's a bullet in the chest."

"Don't!" she cried out. "Oh, Dominick, please don't say it. The robbery I can forgive. But what you're talking about is . . ."

"Justice!" he said grimly.

"No, Dominick. For once, let's not have any lies between us. It's murder you're contemplating, and I can't sanction that, nor will I ever forgive it."

He drew back, his face as dark as a storm cloud. "I knew you would never understand. That's why I kept my plans secret."

"I'm trying, Dominick. I want to. But . . ."

He grabbed her by the shoulders. "Maggie, what if

it had been someone you loved? Would you feel any different then?"

"It's still murder, no matter how you try to justify it."

An invisible barrier dropped between them and she felt his withdrawal, saw it in his eyes, but more than anything, felt it in her heart.

He released her and turned his back. It was as if a door had slammed in her face. Even his voice sounded farther away. "I don't have any right to ask this of you, knowing how you feel, but I want you stay here in Santa Barbara. It's not fair to deny Jamie the climate he needs because of something I've done."

She stared at his rigid back, his firm, straight shoulders, the determined way he held his head, and she searched for something less perverse in his bearing. She wanted so much for him to give up the chase and let the sheriff bring the Kissing Bandit to justice. But all she saw was proof that he was totally committed to avenging his family's deaths and had no intention of stopping until he had accomplished the grisly deed. She swallowed her horror and hurt and choked back the tears.

"I would love to stay. For Jamie's sake. But how can I subject my children to all the malicious talk? I fear that my reputation is ruined beyond repair."

He turned and gave her an anguished look. "I'm afraid you might be right." He leaned over and brushed her forehead with his lips. "You look exhausted. I think you ought to get some sleep. It's been a difficult time for all of us."

She grabbed his hand and held it to her chest. "Please, Dominick. I beg of you. Don't do this."

"Maggie, I have to. Please understand."

But she didn't understand. She understood none of it. She loved him and wanted him. Loved him with heart and soul, mind and body—with everything she had. Why, then, was his hatred for a murderous stranger so much greater than her love for him?

He took her face in his hands and gazed lovingly at her. Finally his eyes lingered hungrily on her lips.

She fought to turn her head away. "I will not kiss a cold-blooded murderer."

"I'm not a murderer," he said softly. He turned her face toward him until it was inches from his own. "Not yet."

Chapter 29

The following morning, Maggie woke up with a headache that grew increasingly worse all through breakfast. Adding to her distress, Jamie and Laurie-Anne argued over everything from the color of the orange juice to who had the most blueberries in their hotcakes. After one such heated disagreement, Jamie knocked his orange juice over. Whether by design or accident, the juice ran onto Laurie-Anne's lap.

Laurie-Anne screamed and Maggie in desperation sent Jamie to his room and hauled Laurie-Anne into the necessity room, where she was promptly stripped and washed.

"I want . . . my Aita," Laurie-Anne sobbed.

Maggie's frown softened. She knew that both children felt Dominick's absence, which accounted, no doubt, for their behavior that morning.

"I know," Maggie said. "I want him too." Bracing herself against the sharp pain that pierced her heart, she finished dressing Laurie-Anne and brushed her hair.

"When's Aita coming home?" Laurie-Anne asked.

"I don't know," Maggie said, working her daughter's long blond hair into a braid. "Glory be, Laurie-Anne, you're as wiggly as a kitten."

"I want Aita," Laurie-Anne persisted.

"Keep still!" Maggie scolded. Her harsh words brought tears to Laurie-Anne's eyes and, feeling guilty, she dropped the braid and threw her arms around the little girl. "There, there, don't cry. Would you like a pretty blue bow in your hair?"

Laurie-Anne shook her head. "I want my ba-ray."

"Your beret? Of course. Bring it to me and I'll pin it on for you."

Laurie-Anne hesitated at the door. "Is Aita coming back?"

"I don't know, dear heart. I wish I did."

While Laurie-Anne searched for her beret, Maggie returned to the kitchen and cleared away the breakfast dishes.

Hearing the sound of wagon wheels out front, she dried her hands on her apron and rushed to the window in time to see Mrs. Pickings coming up the walkway, looking very self-important and righteous.

With a sinking heart, Maggie remembered the times Dominick had accused her of looking much the same way. Had she really looked that bad? Sure that the woman had come to ply her with more questions, Maggie opened the door and braced herself.

"You poor child," Mrs. Pickings said, handing her a basket full of fresh eggs and brushing past her.

Dumbfounded, Maggie closed the door and followed Mrs. Pickings into the parlor, not knowing what to make of the change in the woman's demeanor since the last time they had spoken.

Mrs. Pickings glanced around the tiny room with an approving look. "I don't know how you do it," she exclaimed. "How do you manage to maintain such an orderly house, care for the children, run a shoemaking business, *and* be a Wells Fargo detective?"

Maggie stared at her, thinking she hadn't heard right. "What did you say?"

"Oh, dear. I know it's supposed to be a secret. Believe me, I won't breathe a word to anyone."

"What makes you think I'm a . . ." Maggie set the basket of eggs on a table and lowered herself onto the divan.

Mrs. Pickings sat down next to her and patted her

on the knee. "Mr. Sanders told me." She thrust out
her bosom and sniffed proudly. "Said he knew a trust-
worthy woman when he saw one. Knew I could be
trusted to keep your secret. Mercy me." She clapped
her hands together. "Imagine sacrificing your reputation just to make this town safer for the rest of us!
Like I said to George, there aren't many women who
would compromise their morals for the benefit of
others."

"It was . . . nothing," Maggie choked.

"Nothing? What modesty! Nothing is more valuable
than a woman's virtue. But don't you worry. Anyone
who dares to judge you in an unfavorable light will
have me to deal with."

"Thank you, Mrs. Pickings. I can't tell you how
much I appreciate your support."

"It's the least I can do. It's not every day that a
person gets to assist a Wells Fargo detective. Mercy
me. Just being in the same room with you makes me
feel safer."

Maggie smiled graciously, but inside she was thinking that if she ever got her hands on Dominick Sanders again, she would . . .

"Do you, uh . . . have a gun?"

Maggie drew back in horror. "I beg your pardon?"

"A gun. Don't detectives have to know how to handle a gun?"

"Oh, yes, of course. Well, I suppose I do. I mean
. . . I do."

"Where is it?"

Maggie leaned forward. "I'm not at liberty to say.,"

Mrs. Pickings's gaze traveled down the length of
Maggie's skirt, all the way to the ruffle at her hem.
A knowing smile played at the corners of her mouth.
It was obvious that she thought Maggie had a revolver
hidden somewhere in the folds of her clothing. "Don't
you worry about a thing. I won't breathe a word to a
soul."

"I can't tell you how very relieved I am to hear that."

Jamie ran into the room, and Mrs. Pickings stood up. "My, my, young man, you're getting to be so tall." She headed toward the door. "I would love to talk to you more about this, but I promised to chair this year's church bazaar and I'm already late for a meeting. Besides, I have to investigate a rumor."

She winked. "It has to do with Miss Winkerton and Mr. Grover. Rumor has it that wedding bells are likely to ring by next spring."

"Really?" Maggie exclaimed.

"I haven't verified it yet," Mrs. Pickings cautioned. "But I have it on very good authority that Mr. Grover didn't take Miss Winkerton home from the charity ball last Friday night until after two o'clock in the morning! Why, the only other time Mr. Grover stays up that late is when he's winning at poker. If the man would give up his gambling habits, I daresay he would be quite rich."

"Why, that's wonderful, isn't it? I mean, about him and Miss Winkerton."

"I guess it is, at that. There's nothing like a woman to turn a man around. But who would ever have thought it? Personally, I always thought Miss Winkerton was . . . well . . . too timid to land herself a husband. It just shows that anything is possible." Reaching the front door, she stopped. "Don't you worry about a thing. No one will hear a word from me about you being a Wells Fargo detective." Her gaze dropped down to encompass Maggie's skirt. "Not a word!"

No sooner had Mrs. Pickings left then three members of the Woman's Christian Temperance Movement arrived.

"We know we're not supposed to say a thing," Mrs. Hopkins began. "We promised Dom . . . Mr. Sanders, didn't we, girls?" Mrs. Quitter and Mrs. Meyers nodded in agreement.

Mrs. Hopkins continued. "But we just wanted to

tell you that we don't hold anything you did against you. I mean, a Wells Fargo detective has to put public welfare above virtue."

"You know . . . ?" Maggie gasped in surprise. She looked from one to the other. "All of you . . . ?"

"Don't worry about a thing." Mrs. Hopkins sniffed and held herself rigid. "Mum's the word."

The other two women not only concurred but tried to think of a way to turn the situation into one of their projects.

Mrs. Meyers insisted that she had heard it from a reliable source that a woman who claimed to have been kissed by the bandit during one of his many robberies thought she smelled alcohol on his breath. "Of course, she said she had never tasted alcohol in her life, being a Mormon and all, but she was almost positive that something was on his breath. Now I ask you, what else could it have been if it wasn't alcohol?"

"Had to be alcohol," Mrs. Hopkins insisted.

"Most definitely," Mrs. Quitter agreed.

On this basis, the three members of the Woman's Christian Temperance Movement voted to offer their services as Maggie's assistants.

"Well . . . I . . ." Maggie tried to think of a way to turn down their generous offer without offending them.

"It seems to me a Wells Fargo agent can't have enough assistants," Mrs. Meyers said, with a girlish giggle.

"I'm sure you're right," Maggie said. "If I can think of a way you can help, I'll be sure to let you know." She showed them to the door just as a fine horse and carriage pulled up and stopped directly in front.

"My word!" Mrs. Meyers exclaimed. "What is the mayor's wife doing here?"

"I can't imagine," Maggie said, although she had a very good idea exactly what the mayor's wife was doing there.

For the remainder of the day, a constant stream of

visitors filed through Maggie's front door. The "secret" was out all over town.

By the time Maggie wearily showed her last visitor out, the lamplighter was already making his rounds and she was exhausted.

She fed and bathed the children and put them to bed earlier than usual. After she changed into her dressing gown, she lit the gaslight in the parlor and settled down to read, but the book she'd selected from Connie Mae's extensive collection of popular novels lay unopened on her lap.

A knock at the front door startled her, and the book went flying across the floor. Reluctant to talk to yet another person about her "secret," she called through the door, hoping that whoever it was could be sent away.

"Who else would you be expecting this late at night?"

"Dominick?" In quick order, she unbolted the door, her heart pounding wildly as he brushed past her, filling the house and warming her heart with his presence.

His eyes glittered from the soft shadows of the entry room. "I'm glad to see you're still in town." He turned and walked down the hall to the parlor.

After she closed and bolted the door, she joined him. He sat on a chair, his beret on his knee. She was so relieved to see him. After he had left the house the night before, she had wondered whether he would ever return. But he was back, and that could only mean that he had changed his mind about taking the law into his own hands.

Sensing the restless energy that surged through him, she sat gingerly on a chair opposite his, waiting for him to say the words she so needed to hear. "Considering I was bombarded with visitors, I don't know how I could have managed to pack up and leave."

He grinned. "What do you think, Detective Maggie? Brilliant, huh?"

She frowned. "I think there's no end to your shameless ways."

He shrugged. "I was only thinking of your reputation. It turns out folks will forgive anything if the motivation is sound. That should be of great comfort to you."

"There is only one thing that would bring me comfort," she said. She held his gaze for a moment before he turned away. Swallowing hard, she changed the subject. "I think the least you could do is tell me where you've been all day. What am I supposed to tell Jamie and Laurie-Anne?"

"Tell them I'm staying at the Regal Hotel." He studied her face. "Don't look so devastated, Maggie. I can hardly justify staying here now that our secret it out. Even I can't think of an honorable excuse for living in a state of unholy matrimony."

"So what are you doing here?" she asked. *Please say it. Say that you're not going to kill.* "How do you plan to justify a late-night visit to an unmarried woman?"

"Business. I need to ask you some questions."

"About what?"

"About the holdup. You got the closest look at the bandit. Is there anything that struck you as odd?"

"Every time a man holds me at gunpoint, it strikes me as odd," she said irritably. She'd hoped he had come to see her for more personal reasons, to tell her that he had no intention of killing anyone. But it was apparent that nothing was more important to him than finding his man.

"You know what I mean. Anything about his manner or voice that would help us identify him."

Maggie studied his face. "Us?"

"Wells Fargo."

Maggie felt a flood of relief wash over her. His mentioning Wells Fargo could only mean that he'd given up the idea of acting alone. Encouraged, she thought back to the holdup. "As a matter of fact, he did seem familiar to me. That's why I was so sure at first that it was you."

Dominick stroked his chin thoughtfully. "Is that why you so willingly let him kiss you?"

"The reason I let him kiss me was that he was holding me at gunpoint."

"That's what I admire about you, Maggie. You're always so damned practical. Now, you said he seemed familiar?"

"He did." She thought for a moment. "I don't know . . . something about his kiss . . ."

He narrowed his eyes and sat forward. "His kiss was familiar and you don't know why? Good God, Maggie, how many men have you kissed in Santa Barbara?"

"You don't have to be so nasty!" she retorted. "You're the only man I've kissed. In Santa Barbara, that is."

"Thank you for clarifying that," he growled. "But if that's true, how is it that this man's kiss seemed familiar? Is it possible you knew the man in San Francisco?"

Maggie thought for a moment. "I don't think so."

"Come on, Maggie, think!"

"I *am* thinking. It all happened so fast!"

"All right." Dominick ran his hands through his thick hair. "Let's start from the beginning. Repeat everything he said, exactly as he said it."

"Oh, Dominick, please don't make me repeat his threat against you."

"Everything!"

She took a deep breath and began again, retelling everything exactly as she remembered it. "The door to the stage flew open."

"Go on."

Dominick listened intently to her every word, stopping her occasionally to ask a question or to clarify a point.

"He was dressed exactly like you were dressed when

we first met," she said. "And he's about your height."
She thought a moment. "Come to think of it, he's
probably an inch or two taller." She then recited everything that followed. "After making that threat, he
threw me on the ground and disappeared."

"Anything else?"

She frowned in concentration. "Not that I can think
of."

Dominick stood and began pacing back and forth in
front of her. "All right. Let's start from the beginning."

"I told you everything I know."

"You may have forgotten something. The voice . . .
tell me about that."

"It was deep, rather gruff, like he was trying to
disguise it."

"There's only one reason I can think of for a robber
to disguise his voice. He obviously thought you might
recognize him. Dammit! The man is right under our
very noses. Why can't I catch him?" He raked his
fingers through his hair in frustration. "Tell me again
about his kiss."

"There's nothing to tell."

"What do you mean there's nothing to tell? He
must have removed his mask when he kissed you.
What did he look like?"

She blushed. "He only lifted his mask a little. At
least, I think so. I wasn't exactly looking. I . . . uh
. . . had my eyes closed."

He looked at her in astonishment. "You what?"

"I . . . thought it was you."

His face softened. "And you wanted me to kiss you,
right?"

She bristled. "Certainly not! I thought you were a
murderer and I didn't want to look you in the face!"

He frowned in concentration. "You must have noticed something. Did he have a mustache? Thick lips,
thin lips? Was he a good kisser or a bad one?"

She gave her head a careless toss. "I wouldn't
know."

"Oh, wouldn't you, now? Could that be because you lack experience?" He grabbed her by the shoulders and pulled her to her feet. Slipping his hands down her arms to her waist, he drew her closer. "Was it a soft and gentle kiss, like this?"

He demonstrated, gently nipping her lower lip before brushing it with feathery kisses. As he pulled away, his breath hissed out against the soft smoothness of her skin. "Or one filled with passion, like this?" His mouth angled onto hers.

When at long last he released her, she swooned against him. "The first one," she whispered.

Dominick drew back in confusion. "What?"

"His kiss was more like the first one."

She sounded so earnest, he threw back his head and laughed aloud. "Oh, Maggie, you're one in a million, do you know that?" His face grew serious again. Abruptly, he released her and turned. "What are your plans?"

"I'm thinking of giving up my job as a Wells Fargo detective and staying here in Santa Barbara," she said.

A smile played at the corners of his mouth. "That's probably for the best, Mrs. Sanders."

Suddenly something occurred to her. "Oh, no!" she wailed. "I just remembered! I shipped all my tools to San Francisco."

"You needn't worry," Dominick said. "I had your crates returned to the shop."

She stared at him in disbelief. "You what?"

"Do you think I could stand by and let you leave? Jamie needs to live in this climate, and I couldn't bear to let him suffer on my account. The problem is, I underestimated you. It never occurred to me that you would chance the stagecoach after our last disastrous trip."

She looked at him suspiciously. "How did you know I would miss the boat?"

"I paid the captain not to sound the cannon until he'd already set sail."

"You what? Why, you . . ." She shot across the room and launched herself at him, intent upon wiping the smug smile off his face. But he was too fast for her. He grabbed her by the wrists and pulled her down onto the divan with him.

"Ah, Maggie," he moaned, breathing in the sweet smell of her hair. He captured her lips with his own and kissed her soundly. "Do you know how wonderful you made me feel when you came to the jail and told me how much you cared for me?"

"I believe I told you I loved you," she whispered as she ran a trail of kisses up his cheek. For Maggie it was a very important distinction, and when she saw his face soften at her words, she realized that if anything was to save him, it was her love for him. The knowledge gave her hope and courage. Shamelessly, she pressed against him, watching the lights in his eyes flame with desire. Savoring the power she wielded, she was determined to make the most of it.

"I remember," he breathed heavily.

"Do you remember asking me if I had any regrets?" She wrapped her arms around his neck and flicked his ear with her tongue.

He moaned softly. "I believe you said you had none."

"That wasn't exactly true," she admitted. "I regret not having told you my feelings sooner. Maybe if I'd been more honest with you, you might have been more honest with me."

His hand moved down to trace her neckline. "Do you remember I told you that I did regret one thing?"

She nodded. "You refused to tell me because you said I would think you thoroughly wicked. Not that I don't already."

He laughed softly. "Then I guess it makes no difference. What I regretted was all the times I wanted to make love to you and didn't." He let his hand drop lower until it covered one lovely, firm breast. "So has your opinion of me changed now that you know?"

"Not one bit," she said softly. She wiggled back against the divan, pulling him down on top of her. "Would it surprise you to know that I regret much the same thing?"

Taking his mouth away from the sensitive spot he had found beneath her ear, he looked deep into her eyes. "Oh, Maggie, don't tell me," he moaned. "You mean you wanted me every bit as much as I wanted you?"

She nodded. "And after tonight . . ." Before she could finish, he stiffened and stood up. Watching him walk away from her, she felt as though her whole world was about to collapse. "Dominick?"

He lay one hand on the wall and hung his head. "You know my job's not done. The bandit is still out there somewhere."

When he wouldn't look at her, she sat up, warding off the cold shiver that had quickly erased the heated wake of his touch. She'd practically thrown herself at him, thinking that the love they shared was far more important than his sick need for revenge. Knowing now how little she meant to him, she felt cheap and degraded. If he really and truly loved her as much as he said, he could never do anything that went against everything she believed in.

"There are other detectives. Surely you aren't the only one who can bring him to justice."

"This is my fight, Maggie. I have to see it through to the end." He turned and studied her for a moment. "Don't look at me like that, damn it!"

"How do you want me to look at you?"

His voice softened. "Like you looked at me a few minutes ago when I kissed you. Like you looked at me when I told you how many times I wanted to make love to you. Like you looked at me that one night when we made love."

Maggie stared at him in confusion. What kind of man could talk so easily of hate one moment and love the next?

"Please, Maggie. I have no choice. I must take responsibility for the deaths of my father-in-law, my wife, and my child. And, more recently, that of the stagecoach driver. I have to find a way to stop the man before he takes more lives. After the fiasco on the pass, there's a strong possibility that he'll drop out of sight for a while. That's usually what he does after a near capture. That means I must return to Sacramento for instructions from my superiors and work on a way to force him out of hiding."

"That could . . . take years," she protested.

He nodded grimly. "It already has taken years."

She caught her breath. "If you refuse to give up the search, will you promise me one thing? Promise me that you won't take matters into your own hands. The man is entitled to a fair trial."

Harsh lines cut into his face. "Don't ask me to make a promise I can't keep."

Her eyes filled with tears. "Don't you see what's happening?" she cried. "You're letting him rob you of another family!"

The muscle at his jaw hardened. "If I fail to see that justice is served, than I don't deserve another family."

"Justice!" She spit the word out. "You're not interested in justice. If you were, you'd let the law take its course."

"You think you have all the answers, don't you, Maggie? Suppose you tell me where the law was when my father was murdered?"

"Your fa . . ." Her eyes widened. "This obsession you have with the Kissing Bandit isn't about your wife or baby, is it? It's about your father!"

He looked at her in astonishment. "What are you talking about? My father was shot down by the side of the road by an unknown assailant years before the Kissing Bandit existed." He tightened his fist and slammed it into the palm of his hand. "When I get finished with him, he'll . . ."

"He'll what?" Maggie demanded. "Be lying on the side of the road too?"

"This has nothing to do with my father!"

"You don't know that, Dominick. Anger that's been buried often shows up in unexpected ways. You can bring the man responsible for your wife's death to justice by simply turning him in. But you can never bring the man who killed your father to justice, and that's where the anger lies."

"You're wrong, Maggie. This is not about my father."

"All right," she said, too tired to argue further. Besides, she wasn't even sure she was right. Maybe in her effort to make sense of all this, she was grasping at straws. Tears of defeat filled her eyes. "Don't do this to us," she pleaded. "To the children. I beg of you."

"Maggie, dammit, ask me to be faithful to you. Ask me to cherish you to my dying day. But don't ask me to give up searching for the man who robbed me of my family!"

When she refused to rescind her request, he stormed past her and out into the cold, dark night.

Chapter 30

The next day, she picked up the keys from Mr. Grover and returned to her shop, finding the crates waiting on the porch for her as Dominick had promised. While the children occupied themselves, she unpacked her tools, hung each one neatly in place, and tried not to think of the empty feeling inside. Dominick was gone. It was over. All that remained was the pain.

In an effort not to give in to the despair that threatened to overcome her, she threw herself into her work. In no time at all, her shop was ready for business.

During the next few days, her life fell into a regular routine. Her reputation as a detective fired the imagination of the townspeople, and she was regarded as a celebrity. People traveled from as far away as Ventura and Ojai to purchase a pair of shoes from the woman who had once been a Wells Fargo agent.

Even Señor Perez relented and allowed Consuela to return to her duties, but only after Manuel had explained Maggie's role in procuring his job as a bank teller.

On Friday morning, Flossie and her girls stopped by. Goldie proudly displayed her shiny gold shoes and ordered two more pairs.

Although it was the end of July, Maggie's customers, in anticipation of the winter rains ahead, began ordering waterproof boots. The boots required more cutting and stitching than shoes did, and without Dominick's help she was soon overburdened with orders. Fortunately, Manuel agreed to help out during weekends and evenings, and she arrived in the morning to find the leather pieces all cut and ready to be stitched.

She worked long hours but took little pleasure in sitting in front of her Blake sewer. She no longer enjoyed the smell of leather or felt satisfaction at running her finger across its smooth grain. Things she had once loved to do had no meaning for her anymore.

Even the children sensed it.

"What's the matter, Mama?" Jamie asked one morning as she prepared breakfast.

"Nothing, son."

"You miss Aita, don't you?"

"I guess I can't fool you, can I?" She smiled and ruffled his hair.

"I miss him too," Jamie said. "Can we go to Sacameano to visit him?"

"That's 'Sacramento,' Jamie. Maybe. We'll see."

Jamie thought about this a minute. "Do you want a bonbon?" He held out a paper sack.

"Glory be, Jamie! Bonbons before breakfast," she exclaimed, but when she saw the disappointment on his face she quickly changed her mind. "Maybe one."

She jammed her hand into the sack and drew out a chocolate candy. "Mmmm, it looks good." She popped it into her mouth and let the rich chocolate and the smooth caramel coat the inside of her mouth. She tried to guess the name of the ingredient that gave the bonbons their unique flavor and lingered on the lips and tongue long after the chocolate had dissolved. A flavor that had lingered in her memory even longer. Something about it . . .

Of course! Suddenly she remembered why the bandit's kiss had seemed familiar to her. His lips had tasted like bonbons!

Funny how she had forgotten that little detail until now. She wasn't even certain whether or not it was important. So the bandit liked bonbons. So what?

Still, she felt that the sheriff should be told. She brightened as an idea began to form. If she could help the sheriff find the bandit before Dominick found him, maybe she could prevent Dominick from doing something she was certain he would regret.

Glory be, why hadn't she thought of it sooner? She waited impatiently for Consuela's arrival, then hurried to the sheriff's office.

Sheriff Badger greeted her warmly. "I still can't believe that Dominick Sanders was a Wells Fargo agent. I always thought I could pick out those agents a mile away." He chuckled. "Have you heard from him since he left for Sacramento?"

She shook her head. "He's probably busy."

"I suppose so."

"The reason I'm here is that I remembered something about the holdup. I don't know whether it's important or not."

"Why don't you let me be the judge of that, ma'am?"

Maggie hesitated, embarrassed to be discussing something as intimate as a kiss, and the fact that it was a kiss that she'd been forced to endure did not diminish her discomfort. "I remembered that the bandit's kiss tasted like bonbons."

"Bonbons?"

"Yes. You know, those chocolate confections that come from France?"

"Can't say that I do."

"They're quite good. My children love them."

"I'll be sure to put that in the report," he said. "About his kiss tasting like bonbons."

Her face positively stinging, she stood. "I have to go. It's almost time to open the shop."

She left, feeling somewhat foolish. Obviously the sheriff hadn't been impressed with the bonbon information. She wished now she hadn't bothered to tell him. A fine detective she made!

She reached her shop and let herself in the front

door. Putting the visit to the sheriff's office out of her mind, she threw herself into her work, willing the pain inside to go away. But the pain wouldn't relinquish its claim on her, nor could she keep herself from periodically interrupting her work to rub her fingers along the tools that Dominick had last held in his hands.

Many had been the time that she'd sought relief from the pain by sitting in the chair behind his workbench or by singing aloud the same songs he sang. Sometimes she felt his presence so strongly that she turned, expecting to find him there behind her. On other occasions, she swore she heard his voice calling her, and it was all she could do not to answer him.

But none of these feelings were as strong as they had been that morning following her trip to the sheriff.

Just before the church bells chimed out the noon hour, Mr. W. K. Stevens came strolling into the shop, looking dapper in a plaid suit and a fine straw hat.

Looking up from her workbench, Maggie greeted him with a friendly smile.

He took off his hat and leaned over the counter. "Good day, Mrs. Sanders. I must say you're as pretty as a picture sitting there."

"Why, thank you, Mr. Stevens."

"I'm in town to purchase supplies," he explained smoothly. "You said you'd have my boots ready."

"They are ready," she said. "Let me just give them another quick polish."

"Take your time." He took something out of a paper sack and slipped it into his mouth.

Watching him, Maggie had a frightening realization. Bonbons!

"Is something wrong?" he asked.

"I . . . beg your pardon?"

"You looked at me rather strangely." He waited expectantly.

Willing her heart to stop pounding, she forced a

smile. "I just remembered I promised my children to stop by the confectionery to buy them some bonbons."

"Well, here," he offered, sliding the bag across the counter. "Give them mine. That'll save you the trip."

"That's very kind of you. They love them so much. My children, I mean. Sometimes I do believe they would eat nothing else if it were left up to them. Why, just this very morning, my son was eating them before breakfast!" She was talking too much, but she couldn't seem to stop herself. "They do have a unique taste, don't they?"

"It's rum," he said.

She stared at him in horror. "Rum? They put rum in candy?" Glory be, the members of the Women's Christian Temperance Movement were right. There *had* been alcohol on the bandit's lips!

He laughed at her expression. "It's only rum flavoring. I can assure you there's not one drop of alcohol in bonbons."

"Even so, I wonder if it's wise for children so young to acquire a taste for rum."

"I doubt that you have cause for concern. Bonbons have as little chance of giving your young ones a taste for rum as ginger beer soda has of making them like ale."

"I do hope you're right," she said. Her legs threatened to buckle beneath her as she reached for Mr. Stevens's boots, which stood on the shelf next to Dominick's. Glancing back at the man, she quickly pulled a boot off the shelf and rubbed it with a soft piece of deerskin.

Careful not to be caught staring, she assessed him as she worked, taking careful note of his height and build. It had to be him! The Kissing Bandit. It was quite possible that she would make a pretty good detective after all!

But the satisfaction that came from solving the mystery that had stumped Dominick and his men was soon replaced with rage. This man had ruined the lives of people that she cared about.

Not only that. He'd kissed her and pushed her around like she was nothing more than a sack of flour. How dare he! She was tempted to tell him a thing or two, but thought better of it. He was a murderer, and heaven only knew what he would do if he suspected that she knew something.

"Looks like a mighty fine boot," he said, watching her.

Forcing a smile, she held it up for him to see.

"Yes, indeed, mighty fine."

She gave both boots a quick polish and wrapped them in paper. She was shaking so much that she could hardly tie the twine around the package. He watched her every move, and she was certain he would hear her heart pounding and the rush of blood coursing through her veins.

"That will be three-fifty," she said.

He gave her four dollars. "Keep the change. It was a pleasure doing business with you, Mrs. Sanders."

She smiled. "The pleasure was all mine."

She waited until he had left before she allowed herself to take a deep breath. "It's him," she mumbled, checking outside the windows to make sure he was gone. "It's got to be him."

But who should she tell? Not the sheriff. She doubted that he'd be too enthusiastic about arresting a man on the basis of a bonbon candy.

"Oh, damn!" she said aloud. "Dominick, where the hell are you?"

"Why, Maggie, I do believe that counts as *two* slips."

She spun on her heel, her hand clutching her chest. She was so relieved to see him, she thought she would faint. "Oh, Dominick!" she gasped. "Where in the world have you been?"

"Is this the proper greeting for someone you claim

to love?" He was standing at the top of the stairs, looking down on her with dark, questioning eyes.

Overcome by myriad feelings, she lashed out at him. "You're a fine one to talk about love. You leave without a word. Never write to tell me where you are. Never . . ." Suddenly she thought of something. "Have you been staying up there? On the second floor?"

He lifted a hand. "Where else could I find a room with mirrors on the ceiling and be entertained by the voice of an angel? This morning I heard you singing our song."

"I was not singing," she said, embarrassed. "I never sing."

"Well, you sang this morning," he insisted. "And yesterday. And the day before that. While you were sewing away on your sewing machine. *'The bandit grins like it's a joke'* . . . Remember?"

Come to think of it, she did remember, but she wasn't willing to own up to it. Not when he was looking so gosh-darn smug and pleased with himself. To think that all the time she was pining away he had been spying on her! "When you have finished serenading me, you might be interested in knowing that I know the identity of that horrid Kissing Bandit."

"What?"

"I said . . ."

"I know what you said, dammit!" He ran down the stairs and was at her side in a flash. "This is no time to play games, Maggie. The name!"

She plunked herself down in front of her sewing machine, unable to resist taunting him as he had so often taunted her. "Why should I tell you?"

"Because I insist."

"This is your fight, remember?"

"Is that bitterness I detect in your voice?"

She whirled around to face him. "And why shouldn't I be bitter. This is my fight too!"

He was clearly surprised. "Your fight? How do you figure that?"

"You're not the only one who's eager to see this man brought to justice. The only difference between us is that I believe justice means putting him behind bars where he belongs and you believe justice is the same as murder! If you remember, he put me through the indignity of holding me at gunpoint and putting his mouth where it wasn't wanted!"

"I'm sorry."

"And furthermore, he made me think you were the one guilty of those heinous crimes . . ."

"I'm sorry . . ."

"And . . ." On and on she raged, weeks of frustration spewing out of her like hot ashes from a volcano. "But do I have a concern in this matter? No . . ."

"I'm sorry . . ."

"You think the only one who has any interest is you . . ."

"I'm sorry."

She looked at him in disbelief. "What did you say?"

"For the hundredth time, I said I'm sorry."

"But it was the only time you sounded sincere."

"Maggie, I *am* sorry."

"Oh, Dominick!" She burst into tears. "I hate it when you sound sincere."

He knelt by her side and folded her in his arms. "In that case, I'll try my best not to sound sincere too often," he promised. He gave her time to pull herself together before questioning her further. "Now would you stop torturing me and tell me the name of the Kissing Bandit?"

"All right," she conceded. "It's Mr. Stevens."

When he showed no sign of comprehending the name, she threw up her hands in frustration. "I don't believe you! You meet a woman once, and you remember everything about her. I do believe you know the name of every woman in this town. But a man . . ."

She folded her arms across her chest. "Mr. W. K. Stephens. Shakespeare. Bonbons."

His expression changed. "He's the bandit?" The disbelief on his face was replaced by an expression of contemplation. He paced back and forth in front of her, then faced her squarely. "Are you sure?"

"If you like, I could ask him to kiss me again so I could verify it."

"I can't believe this. Yet in some strange way it all makes sense." He banged his fist on the counter. "Damn! What a fool I am!"

Worried about what he might do, Maggie touched his arm. "Of course, there's always the possibility that I'm mistaken."

He covered her hand with his own. "No, you're right. It all makes sense. Mr. Stevens boarded the stage at Lompoc to get a look at the passengers and determine if the stage had a shipment of any worth. No one ever thought to look for the bandit among the passengers. That's how he always knew which stages to rob!"

"How could he know what the stage was carrying?"

"A driver who's entrusted with a valuable shipment can be downright edgy. If I recall, there was nothing edgy about our particular driver."

"So you think Mr. Stevens boarded our stage to see if it was worth robbing?"

"It would certainly explain why we weren't held up. I couldn't understand it. We'd put the word out that Wells Fargo was sending a secret shipment by stage that day to its Santa Barbara branch."

"Maybe he was waiting for us. Maybe if we hadn't gone over the cliff, he would have held us up."

Dominick shook his head. "He would never have held up the stage once it had picked up speed going downhill. No, the time to do it was before we got to the summit."

"Do you think he knew you weren't a prisoner?"

"How could he? It's more likely he has a soft spot for pretty widows."

"I doubt the man has a soft spot for anyone or anything," she said, thinking about the murders he'd committed.

"You're right about that." He brushed past her.

"Where are you going?" she called after him.

He turned, his face harsh and unrelenting. "To give Mr. Stevens exactly what he deserves!"

Chapter 31

Dominick's cramped legs ached. He'd been crouched behind a large boulder overlooking the San Marcos Pass road since before dawn. Now the sun was almost directly overhead, and its harsh rays beat down on his back as he watched the dusty road below.

A movement caught his eye, followed by a flash of white. Foster was giving the all-clear sign.

Shifting his weight, Dominick checked his pocket watch. The stage was due at any moment, and he'd seen no sign of an ambush. He went over the details of the carefully laid plans, searching for something he might have overlooked. There was simply no way for Stevens to know that the shipment of gold was a trap.

A rumbling sound in the distance signaled the approach of the stagecoach, followed by a flock of starlings that abandoned the safety of the surrounding trees and took to the sky. The stage was approaching the long, difficult uphill haul. He checked the gun in the holster on his hip and peered through a clump of bushes to the dirt road below.

The sound of a gunshot made him jump to his feet. "Let's go!" he shouted to Foster. Damn, he thought, racing down the hillside to meet his partner on the road below. Stevens had not waited for the stage to begin the tedious climb toward the summit. Rather, he'd stopped the stage far earlier than expected.

With a flying leap, Dominick hopped into his saddle, pressed his heels against the horse's flanks, and tore ahead of Foster. The hooves of his horse thundered along the road toward the stagecoach, kicking up dirt and sending rocks flying down the side of the mountain. By the time he reached the scene of the holdup, the sheriff and some of his men were already interrogating the shaken passengers and driver.

Dominick jumped off his horse. "Did anyone see where he went?"

The sheriff pointed toward the thick brush. "He headed in that direction."

"Was he on foot?"

"Yeah, but we'll never find him." The sheriff pushed back his hat and surveyed the overgrown terrain. "A man could hide forever in there."

Cursing, Dominick followed the sheriff's gaze. Years of tracking down sheep had taught him the fine art of hunting. Lost sheep always headed downhill. Was the same true of a hunted man?

"I'm going in after him."

Sheriff Badger shook his head. "It's too dangerous. He could be two feet in front of you and you'd never see him. You wouldn't even know where to begin looking for him."

The sheriff was right. But hatred took precedence over wisdom. The need for revenge was more pressing than any thought for his own safety. Dominick quickly scanned the area, his eyes hard with lethal purpose. He'd sacrificed too much to stop now. "I'm going in."

Foster rode up, reined in his horse, and dismounted. Dominick filled him in on the situation. "I want you to circle around and move in from the rear."

Foster nodded, climbed on his horse, and rode off.

Knowing he would never get his horse through the thick brush, Dominick started out on foot. A short distance from the road, he found the empty Wells Fargo box. He froze in place and listened. Not as much as a bird could be heard singing.

He tried to decide if he should follow the overgrown trail to the river or circle around. Then something caught his eye. A footprint.

Crouching down, he studied the detailed imprint. A wide grin crept across his face. Why, Maggie Turner, he thought approvingly. You're my kind of woman!

Head low, he crept through the underbrush. For once, luck was on his side. The ground was moist because of an underground spring and it was easy to pick out the bandit's footprints. Nevertheless, the trail was difficult to follow. Scrambling under bushes and over fallen logs, he was almost sure he'd lost it. It was then that he spotted another footprint.

A movement caught his eye. Hunched down on the ground, he waited for a moment before lifting himself up on his elbows. He strained to pick out any unnatural sounds, but the sound of water tumbling over rocks and winding its way down the mountainside made it impossible to hear anything else. Sitting up, he moved a branch aside, and his mouth went dry. Stevens was sitting by the creek, soaking his bare feet!

Dominick sucked in his breath. The moment had been long in coming and he didn't want anything to go wrong. He pulled out his gun and stepped into the clearing.

A twig snapped beneath his feet and Stevens reached for his gun.

"Drop it," Dominick ordered, and when his opponent hesitated he thumbed back the hammer of his gun.

The click made the proper impression, and Stevens tossed his gun onto the ground.

"Wise decision," Dominick said, moving closer. He kicked Stevens's weapon away with his foot. "Now stand up."

Stevens stood, his hands raised shoulder high. He was dressed in a black shirt and pants, with a red sash tied around his waist. Except for his blond hair, he could have passed as Dominick's brother.

Stevens greeted him with a curt nod. "So *you're* Dominick Sanders. I should have known who you were the day I saw you on the stage with that Wells Fargo agent."

"You *knew* Barnes?" Dominick asked in astonishment.

"He arrested me a few years back on what he insisted was fraud. It was most considerate of him not to recognize me that day on the stage."

It all began to make sense. "That explains why we weren't held up."

"I make it a policy never to hold up a stage carrying Wells Fargo agents." Stevens grinned. "It's my way of showing respect."

"That's mighty thoughtful of you."

"It would seem that I underestimated you. I didn't think anyone was foolhardy enough to try to track a man down in such thick growth."

"It would appear that I've done my share of underestimating you," Dominick said.

Stevens's lips curled. "I guess that makes us even."

"Not quite. I think you'll agree that since I have the gun, I have the advantage."

"Perhaps, a slight one," Stevens agreed. "So tell me, what have I ever done to you that made you so determined to capture me?"

"As you are aware, I'm a Wells Fargo detective. It's my duty."

Stevens shook his head. "There's a difference between duty and a vendetta. I know a vendetta when I see one."

"Very well. Do you remember shooting an old man about three years ago? I believe he tried to pull your hood off?"

Stevens nodded. "I had no choice. The old man attacked me."

"The man you shot was my father-in-law."

Stevens accepted this piece of news nonchalantly. "If only he'd done as I told him, I daresay he would still be alive today."

"He thought you were me."

Stevens seemed surprised by this. "Why would he think that?"

"Because I was the original Kissing Bandit."

Stevens laughed. "Is that so? Well, I'll be. I thought all the stories I had heard about the Kissing Bandit were untrue. I decided it was a perfect setup. People love legends. I've been accused of holding up every stagecoach in the country. Everyone wanted to be held up by the Kissing Bandit. Since I supposedly operated in every state and territory in the country, I figured no one would ever be able to track me down." Stevens regarded Dominick with a look of respect. "How did you know where to find me?"

Dominick reached into his pocket and drew out a metal button. He tossed it onto the ground next to Stevens. "I found that next to my father-in-law's body. One of the passengers said it fell out of the bandit's pants pocket during the scuffle. The button depicts the Lobero Theater, which was dedicated on Washington's birthday three month's before my father-in-law's death. Those buttons were given out on opening night. Since there are generally no tourists in Santa Barbara in February, I had to assume that anyone in attendance that night lived in the area."

Stevens shook his head in disbelief. "You based that conclusion on a mere button?"

"It was the only thing I had to go on."

Dominick reached into his coat pocket and took out a small leather case, which he tossed into the rapids. "Those were my Wells Fargo credentials. I won't be needing them any longer. From now on, I'm a free agent."

At long last, Stevens had the good grace to look worried. "What does that mean?"

"It means you're a dead man."

Stevens turned to run, but tripped over his boots and went flying face down into the dirt.

Dominick sprang to Stevens's side and jabbed the barrel of the gun against his head. "That was not one of your better moves."

It gave him great satisfaction that the man should die face down in the dirt. Just like his father . . .

That thought, coupled with what Maggie had said, came as a shocking blow. Dominick held Stevens responsible for the death of his wife, their baby, and his father-in-law. Wasn't that enough reason to shoot him? So why in the world was he thinking about his father?

As he pondered this question, he glanced at the black leather boot that lay on its side. They weren't Stevens's boots, they were his. Maggie must have given Stevens the wrong boots by mistake. Even as he thought it, he corrected himself. Maggie didn't make careless mistakes. Every shoe, every tool, every piece of material in the shop was methodically labeled. So what was Stevens doing with the wrong boots? And why did that damn mispelled word seem to shout out at him?

Custam, custam, custam!

Keeping the gun pointed straight at Stevens, he bent over, picked up the nearest boot, and tossed it to him. "Put it on," he said. "I don't believe a man should die with his boots off."

Stevens rolled over and threw the boot aside. "Shoot me if you must. But there isn't any way that I'm putting those damned boots back on. They practically crushed the bones in my feet. That's the last time I ever trust a woman to do a man's job."

Dominick surprised them both by exploding into laughter.

Stevens rubbed his chin. "Do you mind telling me what's so damned funny?"

Sputtering his words between fresh peals of laughter, Dominick couldn't begin to tell him. "If it weren't for a woman doing a man's job, neither one of us would be sitting here," he said at last.

The laughter left his face, and he felt a sudden tug in his chest. It was the same tug he had felt the night he stood in a jail cell and Maggie told him she loved him. The same tug that nearly tore his heart out when he first discovered she'd mispelled the word "custom."

The same tug that practically rendered him helpless every time he looked into her eyes and saw her love for him shining in their glorious depths. Suddenly it dawned on him what a fool he had been. He stared at the pitiful man at his feet and felt drained of all the hate.

"You robbed me of my family, Stevens, and you're going to be punished. I'll see to that. But the one thing you're not going to do is rob me of another family."

It was a cool, crisp autumn night. The light of a full moon shone through the branches of a nearby tree. But Maggie wasn't thinking of the moon. Her heart was aching, that's what it was doing. Aching with worry for Dominick. Aching with unbelievable longing and need. Just plain aching . . .

Where was he? she wondered. It had been weeks since she'd last seen him. She didn't even know if he was dead or alive.

News of the stagecoach robbery that day had traveled fast. Closing up her shop, Maggie had raced to the corner of State and Anapamu to meet the beleaguered stage. Nearly the entire town had turned out. Fighting her way through the crowd, she managed to ask Sheriff Badger if he'd seen Dominick.

That's when he told her that Dominick had disappeared on foot on the trail of the bandit. The sheriff and his men had followed Dominick but lost him in the heavy brush.

She hadn't been able to think straight since. She was so intent upon her thoughts that she failed to see the tall figure approach her porch.

A pair of boots shot out of the dark, dropping at her feet with a thud. Recognizing them as the ones she'd given Mr. Stevens, she cried out in alarm.

Dominick was by her side in a flash. "Good heavens, Maggie! Do you want to wake up the whole town?"

"Dominick!" she gasped. "Is it really you?"

He pulled her into his arms and held her tight. "Who else would you be expecting at this hour?"

With a cry of relief she flung her arms around his neck and buried her face against his strong, massive chest. "I was so worried. I was so sure you were dead."

"Why, Maggie, I do believe you love me."

"You know I do," she sniffled through her tears. "How many times do I have to tell you that?"

"Oh, Maggie, no matter how many times you tell me, it could never be enough." He held her at arm's length, his gaze dropping down to take in the lovely, soft rise of her breasts. "Why, Maggie, I do believe you wearing one of your barbed wire dressing gowns. The one that protects the property without impeding the view."

Watching her cheeks grow pink, he lifted an eyebrow and let his gaze settle on her trembling lips. "Tell me something: if you love me so much, why did you give my boots to that no-good scoundrel?"

Looking up at him and willing her heart to stay put, she touched his cheek with her fingertips. "Do you remember you told me once how important it is for a bandit to have comfortable boots?"

"I remember."

"Well, I thought I would make the man a mite uncomfortable. His feet are a half size larger than yours."

"A half size, eh?" He grinned and his white teeth flashed in the dark. "That explains it. He was so damned uncomfortable by the time I found him, he could barely walk. He was actually soaking his sore feet in the stream. I held him at gunpoint and, gentleman that I am, told him to put his boots back on."

Maggie swallowed hard. "And . . . and did he?"

"He absolutely refused. He told me that he would never again trust a woman to make his boots!"

"How did you know I gave him your boots?"

"Don't you remember? You misspelled 'custom,' and that word made the best imprint in the ground you could ever imagine." He chuckled softly. "Led me right to him."

She felt a tightening in the pit of her stomach. "You didn't . . ."

"Kill him?" His jaw tightened. "I wanted to. God, how I wanted to. I stood there pointing my gun at him, my finger on the trigger, thinking about what he'd done to my family. But I knew that if you . . . that if I . . . Will you listen to me? I sound like a bumbling schoolboy." He gave her a sheepish grin and raked his fingers through his hair.

"I guess what I'm trying to say is that I will always be grateful you found it in your heart to forgive me after you knew I was the original Kissing Bandit. But knowing that you would never forgive me for killing a man, I couldn't bring myself to pull the trigger. I tried . . . but all I could think about was you and the children. And I realized I wouldn't be killing Stevens. I'd be killing myself."

Afraid to believe what she was hearing, she stared at him in confusion. "Does that mean that . . . you didn't kill him?"

Dominick nodded his head ever so slightly. "I loved you too much to risk losing you. I guess I always knew that you would be the one person who could keep me from doing what I'd set out to do. That's why I fought my feelings for you from the start. I tried, how I tried, not to love you . . ."

Maggie nodded and smiled. "I know, Dominick, I tried too. Only for different reasons."

He caressed her face and smiled as he recalled the battles they'd waged, neither of them suspecting at the time what it was they were really fighting—or how futile that fight would be. "I didn't think I could live with myself if I failed to do what I'd set out to do."

"And can you?" she whispered.

He leaned his forehead against hers. "Oh, God, yes, Maggie. To think I was so close to losing this."

"So what *did* you do?"

"When Foster showed up, I let him take the scoundrel to the sheriff. But not before I forced a full confession out of him. I didn't want you to have any lingering doubts about me. It took some doing, but he finally admitted to robbing the bank."

She stared at him in astonishment. "Mr. Stevens robbed the bank?"

Dominick nodded. "Said he was thinking about switching to robbing banks permanently, to throw us off his trail. But he missed the excitement of stage robbing and decided against it. I just wanted you to know that I wasn't responsible for the bank robbery."

"Oh, Dominick. I always knew that. Deep down inside."

His eyes softened. "What you didn't know is how much you and Stevens had in common."

"What?"

"It turns out that Stevens was staying at Mrs. French's boardinghouse and when it burned down, he decided to purchase property outside of town."

Maggie shook her head in disbelief. "You mean if it hadn't burned down, I would have been living under the same roof as the Kissing Bandit?"

He laughed. "Imagine that."

She laughed too. "It appears that I was doomed from the start." Suddenly she thought of something. "Mr. Stevens wouldn't happen to know Mrs. French's forwarding address, would he? She still owes me three months' rent."

"That's nothing compared to what she owes him. Mrs. French found out about his double life and helped herself to the gold from one of his heists. One night she set fire to the property and disappeared." He shook his head. "And to think, Mrs. French ran the most respectable boardinghouse in town. I wonder what Mrs. Pickings would say."

Maggie giggled. "I can only imagine."

Dominick's face grew serious. "As for the rest, well . . . I'm here to stay if you want me."

His words were such music to her ears, she could only stare at him in speechless wonder.

"Am I right, Maggie?" he asked. "Can you find it in your heart to forgive me that one misguided moment when I robbed that stage?"

"Oh, Dominick," she whispered without a moment's hesitation, "I forgive you."

"Would you also forgive me should I get it into my head to redo the sign over the shoemaker's shop?"

This she had to think about. "It depends what you intend it to say."

"I think it should say 'Sanders and Sanders: Makers of Fine Shoes.' "

She looked up at him with eyes that shone with love. " 'Makers of Fine *Custom* Shoes,' " she corrected.

" 'Custom' it shall be. Spelled with an 'a.' "

"Certainly not!"

"Please, Maggie. It was the 'a' that first told me that you loved me. It was that same 'a' leading me to Stevens that reminded me of your love when I was so close to throwing it away on some vengeful foolishness."

Melting beneath his warm, loving gaze, Maggie could hardly deny his request. Her need for perfection was overcome by the need to please him. "Then an 'a' it shall be," she whispered.

He grinned. Picking her up, he whirled her all around the water fountain. Overhead, the stars shone bright and the moon grew fuller. "You, Mrs. Sanders, are my kind of woman."

For once Maggie didn't object. Instead she nuzzled the warm skin at his neck and whispered into his ear. "And you, Mr. Sanders, are my kind of man."